ONE MORE MOVE:
A CADE TAYLOR NOVEL

MICHAEL HEARNS

This book is a work of fiction. Names, characters, and incidents are products of the author's imagination or are used fictitiously. Any resemblance to actual events or locales or persons living, or dead is entirely coincidental.

ISBN: 978-1-7344075-6-3 Paperback
ISBN: 978-1-7344075-8-7 Electronic Book Text
ISBN: 978-1-7344075-7-0 Hardback

Library of Congress Cataloging-in-Publication Data
Name: Hearns, Michael, author
Title: One More Move: A Cade Taylor Novel/Michael Hearns
Description: First edition. Miami: Beati Bellicosi (2022)
Identifiers: LCCN ISBN

First Edition: July 2022

Editor: Julie Hutchings
Cover Design by Dillon Hearns
Author Photo by Dillon Hearns

For additional information and speaking engagements visit Michael Hearns on the worldwide web: http://www.MichaelHearns.com

Beati Bellicosi Publishing a division of Beati Bellicosi multimedia

Printed in the U.S.A

Also by author Michael Hearns:

"Trust No One" 2020 Beati Bellicosi

"Grasping Smoke: A Cade Taylor Novel" 2021 Beati Bellicosi

Acknowledgments

It has been a series of unlikely events in my life that have brought me to this point of my life where often reflection is larger than projection. We all know many people some even very dear to us who weren't able to live to this junction in their lives. For that I am grateful for the life I have and for the life I have had. I hope you feel the same way.

I would like to give an abundant thank you to my editor Julie Hutchings. "One More Move : A Cade Taylor Novel" is the third installment in the Cade Taylor series of books and Julie has been onboard for all three Cade Taylor novels. She is in my opinion, the best editor in the publishing world. Her love and affection for Cade Taylor shows through every praise and yes every criticism. With each novel she signs on to take the journey with Cade Taylor through the abject rawness and into the gleaming polish. I am incredibly grateful and appreciative of her and her editing.

I would also like to thank my family and the extenuation of family that I have been blessed with in my lifetime. In this life I have learned that family extends beyond birthing suites, and umbilical cords. It is the amalgamation of children, friends, and those we hold dear.

"Blood makes you related. Love makes you a family."

I would like to thank my son Dillon Hearns for everything he has brought to my life. We have constants in life, and Dillon has been a constant source of love and joy for me. I love you Dillon tremendously.

It is paramount that I thank my wife Ricki Witt Braswell. She has been a continual source of inspiration, love, and support. She is a person who lives her life as authentic and true as any one person can possibly be. We have choices in life, and she chose me. The makes me the luckiest man on earth. I love you Ricki with a passion and fire that would engulf continents.

I would like to quietly thank Dr. Padraic G. O'Malley, Dr. Lewis Earnest, Dr Jayan Nair, and Stephanie Witt for all they have done for myself and Ricki.

As I said, we have choices in life. If you are reading this then you have more than likely chosen to let me be your author of choice. I thank you the reader for providing that privilege to me. I also thank the growing legion of Cade Taylor fans who have embraced the books and Cade Taylor into their lives. I am humbled, and most thankful. Within the context of choices, in a world where you can be anything, choose to be kind. It's an infectious concept. Thank you all.

To Ricki and Dillon. I love you both.

Chapter One

I DIDN'T EVEN TURN my head.

We were parked in front of 251 West 20th street in Hialeah, Florida. From the car's passenger window I could see factories, small businesses, Florida East Coast railroad tracks, the elevated Metrorail tracks, wooden fences, wrought iron fences, chain link fences, creosote wooden telephone poles, concrete telephone poles, duplexes, and single-family homes whose homeowners had intentionally removed the grass from the front yards and, in its place, poured concrete that was justifiably painted green.

Like I said. I didn't even turn my head.

Hialeah is one of the most densely populated cities in Florida. There are 260,000 people crammed into this municipality in Miami Dade County. It's the 6th largest city in Florida and 96% of the residents speak Spanish at home. The zoning in Hialeah is nonexistent. I'd been an undercover detective in the Coral Gables Police Department's Vice Intelligence and Narcotics (VIN) Unit for nearly nine years. Detached to the Drug Enforcement Agency (DEA) for the past seven years, I'd been engaged in large cocaine and high-volume money laundering cases for what seems like a never-ending and ongoing continuous existence.

That's how I came to be there, sitting in DEA Agent Scott Lew's 1999 BMW X5 E53. It was obviously right off the car carrier from Greer, South Carolina. German engineering by way of South Carolina. It was November of 1998, and the new 1999 models were rolling out in waves every week. Although normally working with DEA Group Six, today I was assisting DEA Group Four. That was Scott Lew's group. I didn't know much about him except that he'd told me he was originally from Chicago. By his University of Michigan keychain, I deduced he was a Wolverine alumnus. Now I was in his car, not saying much and staring out at this fractured landscape in the "The City of Progress," Hialeah.

"*La Ciudad de Progressia.*"

This was the most wacked progressive scenery I had ever seen. It was early autumn and although it was a very sunny day there was a slight chill in the air. My car was parked two blocks east of where we were, on Bright Drive at the Hialeah Masonic Lodge. The instructions were clear in the standard operation plan: I would park at 11am at the Hialeah Masonic Lodge and DEA Agent Lew would pick me up and drive me to meet with someone the DEA only knew as "the Ecuadorian."

The plan was straightforward. I was to meet the Ecuadorian inside a nearby restaurant. A team of DEA agents would be covertly parked outside the restaurant, waiting. The Ecuadorian was to have twenty kilograms of high-grade Colombian cocaine. For the privilege of owning that cocaine I was to hand him $400,000. I'd be carrying a phony cellphone that was actually a monitoring device we call a kel. Upon completion of the deal, I was to give the takedown signal and say loudly, "Business as usual." Monitoring the kel, Agent Lew and his DEA team would storm into the restaurant and arrest the Ecuadorian. Like I said, it was a standard operation plan.

Standard.

It was a bargain basement price of $20,000 per kilogram. This caused my suspicions to perk up. The price seemed to be too low for a first-time transaction. I couldn't tell if it was my jaded demeanor or my experience that jangled my suspicions. The VIN lifestyle was seeping into my psyche with each and every drug deal. I often wondered if I was part of the solution or if I was part of the problem.

I'd checked the $400,000 out of the Coral Gables Police property room safe earlier that morning. The currency was part of a cash seizure from a different drug deal or money laundering operation, and was now crammed into a brown leather satchel innocuously resting on the back seat right behind me in Lew's BMW.

The cocaine was useless if it couldn't be sold. Yet here I was with confiscated money from a different drug deal perpetuating the cycle again.

The cycle here in South Florida never changed. An endless supply of buyers and sellers, users, and losers. It was the Miami I knew. The Miami that plays on the local news as you vacuum your rug or flip through the channels. The stories get lost in the minutiae of life. The backdrop soundtrack of life in Miami. Another shootout on a Miami street, another body discovered in the trunk of a torched car behind a South Dade warehouse, another Coast Guard seizure of multi tons of cocaine at Government Cut. The drugs, the money, the murder all became a slight hum in our ears as it played out daily. The energy of Miami pops with vibrancy in the equilateral sunshine and has an equally robust mysterious darkness when the sun sets. The vibe of Miami has an energy, and we are all part of that energy. It's a carousel city. When you're riding the splendidly painted spinning carousel and look out from your perched seat, you can see everything whirling by. You don't realize that you're the one who's actually whirling. Because your painted pony of a life languidly lulls you along, you're detached from the reality that exists just beyond the painted kaleidoscopic facade.

Whereas someone like me, who's tasked equally with dealing with both the swirl and the stationary becomes just like the aimless carny with the greasy T-shirt and dangling cigarette. The one who watches the carousel for disruptions while simultaneously scanning the crowd to see who will get on the painted pony and beguiled mirror ride next. Whether I knew it or not, I'd signed on for a front row seat to the great human parade. Ringmaster and shit shoveler behind the elephants all rolled into one.

Looking out at the convergent and simultaneously divergent

urban landscape made me think of what's commonly referred to as the definition of Hialeah:

"*It's corruption, it's dysfunction, and it's nonstop construction.*"

My reverie was broken by Agent Lew's voice.

"How you feel about all this? It's a pretty standard plan, should be an in-and-out."

There was that word again. *Standard*. There is never anything standard about cocaine and money and what happens when the two intersect. The volitivity and unperceivable, unpredictable machinations of the drug trade are fraught with *standard* mishaps.

I turned my attention from the window and looked at Agent Lew.

"I'm okay. What are we waiting on?"

"We still need to get a few guys in place, but our source texted me and said the Ecuadorian is running a little late."

"Who's the source on this one?" I asked him.

"I'm keeping that close to the vest. He's reputable and comes from a family of reliable information. But you know, for discovery purposes I need to keep that to myself," Agent Lew said, as if conducting a civics lesson to a Cub Scout pack.

"You know, that's one thing I never really understand. You feds need a local guy like me to do your deal, but you're all hung up on what might happen in court six months from now, whereas I'm more concerned about the next six minutes." I turned my attention back to the blighted panorama outside the BMW's window.

I'm sure the instrumentation of the BMW was probably still very new to him. None of the radio stations had any presets and there was a light illuminated on one of the oval gauges. If my South Carolina German was as good as I thought it was, it meant the gas cap needed to be tightened.

Agent Lew looked straight ahead through the windshield. He was in his early forties, with a neatly trimmed mustache and goatee. His hairline was receding from his forehead in a uniformed retreat, exposing a rather large forehead that seemed to continue up to his cut short hairline. There was a slight creased impression across the bridge of his nose from where he often either wore sunglasses or regular eyeglasses. I liked Agent Lew, but I bristled sometimes with the way "the alphabet" agencies made decisions and did things. Agent Lew's cell phone rang.

"Give it to me" he said into the phone by way of answering it. He held the phone to his ear, looked straight ahead and listened. He didn't say much as the murmured voice talked to him. The conversation was one-sided for about forty seconds. Then Agent Lew spoke.

"Okay. Yeah, it's pretty standard."

There was that word again: *standard.*

"Okay. I got Cade Taylor here with me from the Gables VIN unit. We got the 400 here with us too. I'm going to drop him off on 29th behind the Sunoco gas station. Yeah, that one, the one right off Palm Avenue. He's going to walk under the gas station overhang by the pumps into the restaurant. Get it out on Tac 5. Cade Taylor from the Gables is a friendly.'

Agent Lew then looked behind him at the money and then directly at me. He was still holding the phone to his ear.

"He'll be carrying the 400 in a brown leather bag, almost like a pilot's bag. Taylor's wearing black jeans, black Bass shoes with gray heels, and an olive-colored shirt under a black, well-worn, cashmere, mid-thigh jacket. Make sure that the units know who Cade Taylor is and what he looks like. We don't need any mistakes today."

The last comment was one of those moments where I just looked away for the briefest of seconds and thought about all the smooth as glass deals I'd done—as well as the absolute fiascos I'd been involved in. They popped in and out of my mind in millisecond vignettes. The moments of reflection were part of the mosaic of my life in the past year. The calendar edged closer each day to the anniversary date of when my marriage to my now ex-wife, Gina, fell into a heaving, staggering, gasping collapse. In less than a year I found myself divorced, displaced from my marital home, and living in a condo. I spent the last eleven months wondering where my life had gone and where it was heading. The certainties of past promises and filled dreams were pondered by me many a late night through the bottom of an empty glass. I'd learned how to raise a silent toast thinking about the past and to not wanting to go back. I was slowly learning that wondering too much about where my life had gone was not going to help me get to where my life was going. I looked at Agent Lew as he hung up the cell phone.

"Surveillance units say they think the Ecuadorian arrived at the restaurant. A guy in a dark suit just got out of a yellow cab and went inside."

"A yellow cab? Did they get the taxi number or stop the cab so we can know where they came from?"

"Shit," Agent Lew said as he quickly dialed his cell phone. After a few seconds, the other guy picked up. "Hey! You guys get the number of the cab or stop the cab and get some information?"

There was a sickening pause. Inwardly, I began to curse the day.

"Okay, you and Marroquín break off and find that cab. We can cover this with what we got, but you two *go find that cab*."

Scott Lew hung up and then casually tossed his cell phone into the center console cup holder. The ease of his demeanor was an attempt at hiding his very recent disappointment in his team members. He looked straight ahead. It was obvious he was angry with himself and his team for not getting the taxi information. Knowing where the Ecuadorian had come from could lead us to more cocaine or money if we knew where he'd been picked up by the taxi. This was an investigation gaffe. The fact that we were now down two from our team also had not been discussed in the *standard* operations plan. I could see Lew mulling the scenarios in his mind.

"I'm sending two of my guys, Matias Marroquín and Vincent Walker, to go find the taxi. We still got enough to cover this meet." said Lew.

"We can delay," I suggested.

"Well, we don't know if it was him for sure. For all I know the Ecuadorian might already be there."

"I thought you said this source of yours was, 'reputable and comes from a family of reliable information,'" I shot back at him.

Agent Lew ignored my dig and just calmly said, "Let's stay the course and head over there." With that comment he put the BMW into drive and eased away from the swale area of the street. He picked up the portable radio nestled between his legs, glancing down at the LED screen making sure he was on the correct frequency he began to speak into the radio.

"Units on TAC 5, myself and the package will be arriving in a few minutes, everyone be ready and be set."

There was a little bit of redundancy in his transmission, but I knew what he meant and I'm sure whatever was left of the team also knew what he meant. Lew drove west and I watched the landscape change marginally. Moving away from the Florida East Coast railway tracks was momentary. The tracks went a few blocks north and then curved west across Red Road. With the route he was taking we'd just be crossing those spine-jittering tracks a few blocks away. True to form he turned north on Red Road, and we did indeed cross the tracks just north of 74th Avenue. Hialeah has its own numbering system for streets and although the sign in Hialeah says West 21st Street, to the rest of Miami Dade County it's 74th Avenue. Nearly every person who isn't a Hialeah resident invariably not only gets lost in Hialeah, but incredibly frustrated by the street signage, lack of street signage, or the absolute douche wagons who drive its streets in the most haphazard way. If you can think it, you can do it in Hialeah. We passed auto parts stores, paint suppliers, used car lots, and the occasional combination of a Santeria Botanica and pet shop, which in and of itself is oddly disturbing. The Nachon Lumber Supply House, with its immense sign depicting a caricature of a construction worker holding a piece of lumber in a very anatomically strategic position, went by in a blur. The next big landmark was the expansive Gilda Cuban Cracker Company. The building encompassed two or three city blocks and its white and blue paint scheme meshed nicely with the manicured hedges along the sidewalk.

I knew we were getting close to making our turn. My instincts were verified when Lew picked up the radio and spoke.

"Units on Tac 5, we are making the eastbound turn now. Stand by."

We turned on West 29th Street right by the Taco Bell whose sign was upstaged by the McDonald's sign just a strip mall parking lot away. In the distance before us I could see the thick stand of Australian pine trees that lined the western side of the famed Hialeah horse racing track. We passed one loading dock and small business after another on both sides of the street. The racetrack trees became even taller as we drew closer. The Hialeah Racetrack was an institution in the horse racing world. It was built in 1922, the grounds were grand and there were paddocks, stables, riding rings, training centers, and groomsmen and jockey quarters all on the property. The stately Australian pines rimmed the entire forty block equestrian oasis. The center track was an oval that encircled a lush lagoon where an estimated 300 pink flamingoes roosted. Sometimes when the horses galloped down the back stretch of the course the flamingoes would take flight, creating a colorful juxtaposition of fluttering pink and thundering browns and blacks. The racetrack was directly in front of us. We were now approaching the west side of the Sunoco gas station.

"Units on Tac 5, we are pulling up. The package will be exiting. Stand by."

Lew swung the car into the narrow alley running north and south behind the Sunoco and the restaurant, coming to a halt somewhere between a greasy puddle and a cratered pothole. I rolled down my window.

"All right Cade, we got this covered. We got it all covered," he said as I opened the car door.

He seemed to speak in a redundant manner in life and on the radio. I opened the back door, pulled the leather satchel across the seat towards me, and closed the door again.

"Just toot your horn if you can hear me on the kel," I told Lew through the open window.

"Right. Don't forget—we got this. We're the good guys. Remember? Even in the shit, I let Jesus take the wheel," he said as started to drive slowly south down the alley.

I spoke out loud in the direction of the kel cell phone in my hand. "Dominoes car three, come in for a large peperoni pick up."

I heard the faint horn of the BMW as he crept down the alley. I stood there for a moment and took in the sights and smells of where I was. The Sunoco was moderately busy with two of the six gas pumps being used by customers. There were three different cars backed in at the rear of the station. Each car was facing the gas station. I stepped around the low hedge line and around one of the two concrete telephone poles onto the gas station property. Low down by my thigh, I held the satchel by the handles. As I walked in front of the three parked cars, I deftly put my palm on the hood of each car with my free hand. If any of these cars were related to the Ecuadorian, I wanted to leave a forensic handprint behind to help identify that indeed this was the car at the drug meet. The dark blue and sunscreaming yellow colors of the Sunoco station gleamed in the midday November sun. I could see the edge of the restaurant's roof line from the gas station property. It ran the entire length from the sidewalk on Palm Avenue all the way to the back of the very same alley that Lew had just driven through. The roofline of the restaurant was flat. The entire building was one large rectangle with a four-foot roof façade around the length in red Spanish barrel tile. There was one large window to the rear of the north wall, and a smaller window right next to it. Judging by the plumbing stack jutting above it on the roof line, the smaller window was obviously the bathroom window. Both windows were covered in iron anti-burglar bars. Although curved and decorative, the bars intended real use could not be denied. I made a mental note that neither I nor any Ecuadorian this day would be leaving the restaurant via the bathroom window.

Rounding the gas station overhang and humming ice machine, I saw that there was an automatic car wash set at an odd angle, almost encroaching upon the restaurant's property line. The traffic on Palm Avenue was steady and very heavy. Palm Avenue was one of the major thoroughfares in Hialeah and the two lanes each way were traditionally packed with vehicles. As I neared the sidewalk the enormity of the Hialeah racetrack loomed over Palm Avenue. It appeared that the restaurant had built an extension right up to the sidewalk. It was flat-roofed and not nearly as tall as the original restaurant. The rippled and crude masonry line where the two structures joined together were concealed barely under layers upon layers of white paint. Three windows faced Palm Avenue, all three uniformly adorned with the same white curved ornate anti-burglar bars. Between each window was a porchlight. The low overhang, the protruding bars, the porchlights, and the narrow sidewalk all made for treacherous walking with Palm Avenue traffic whizzing inches away. Once again, I thought to myself, *The zoning in Hialeah is nonexistent.*

There was darkly tinted glass double front doors. Nothing says security incompetence like anti-burglar bars on each and every window and having a very exposed double glass door in the front. The parking lot was nearly empty. There was another single hung door just down from the main doors, also sans anti-burglar bars. The front door was under an aluminum roof that sheltered the outdoor tables from the blazing South Florida sun. The most distinguishing feature about the place was the neon sign poised above the roof, attached to a thick pole. The name of the restaurant was written in a regal font that curved around a Spanish coat of arms.

El Segundo Viajante.

The Second Traveler.

With an air of cool detachment, I approached the dark-tinted double glass doors of *El Segundo Viajante,* but I was acutely aware of anything that may be a threat. Although cumbersome, I opened the door with the same hand I was using to carry the bag of cash. I wanted to keep my right hand free in case I needed to pull my 40. caliber Glock tucked deep behind the belt line of my pants against my lower back.

The interior of the restaurant was slightly cooler than outside. I stood just inside the door, somewhat hidden by a partition, I tried to gather as much as I could about the restaurant before venturing any further, where patrons and most notably the Ecuadorian could see me. The parquet tile floor was accented by the deep mahogany wood of the walls. Rustic wine racks hung above doorways and various coats of Spanish arms were on the walls. The tables all had rose-colored table clothes held in place by square panes of clear glass. It was easier to wipe the tabletop glass clean than to change the tablecloths. No booths, only tables. Each table had black lacquered curved high back chairs. The tables were set with white restaurant-grade china.

As I started to move from the partition the first person I saw was a lone diner with combed-back blond hair. He was wearing a dark suit. I surmised he was the one from the taxi. Engrossed in the menu, he didn't even seem to notice me as I came in. This guy was definitely not from the southern hemisphere and most definitely not Ecuadorian.

Great.

I lost two back-up team members chasing a phantom taxi because the one guy in the place who was more North American than me doesn't own a car. As I stepped further, I saw the only other occupied table. The problem was it wasn't just occupied by who I gathered was the Ecuadorian. There was a second patron at the table. This was unexpected. Two potential adversaries.

The Second Traveler.

Chapter Two

THE MAN THAT the DEA called "the Ecuadorian" immediately spied me as I stepped into full view. He was seated at the center of the table, facing me. Seeing the satchel in my hand, he broke into a big open smile. He had a medium complexion, and his dark black hair was thick and radiant due to its lack of highlights. He had a thick mustache that spread across his face with his smile. He was wearing a blue iridescent shirt.

His companion was sizably bigger and was wearing a brown blazer with a mustard-colored shirt underneath. He wasn't entirely bald, nor was he routinely shaving his head. He had a sparse growth of stubbly hair. He was clean-shaven and appeared to be clearly a trusted or perhaps even a hired protector for the Ecuadorian. He sat on the Ecuadorian's left at the end of the table. The table was festooned with water glasses, wine glasses, an open bottle of red wine and an already dug into breadbasket. Parcels of the crumbly Cuban bread were on side plates. The Ecuadorian motioned me to the table with an eagerness and jovial expression similar to that of a child who sees a firetruck drive by. I guess seeing $400,000 walk into a restaurant will do that to people. With excited urgency he said:

"*Bienvenido, bienvenido, por favor siéntate. Los camarones al ajillo aquí es increíble, tienes que probarlo!*"

[Welcome, welcome, please sit down. The garlic shrimp here is amazing, you have to try it!]

I pulled out the lacquered high back chair and sat across from him. I put the bag down by my left foot, ensuring it was out of the reach of the imposing unexpected guest to my right. I mustered the best Spanish I could:

"*Soy tremendo gringo, pasemos nuestro tiempo en Ingles por favor.*"

[I am a tremendous gringo, lets conduct our time in English please.]

Both men broke into their own unique version of a hearty laugh. Independently of each other through their smiles as if to each other as well as if to themselves they said, "Tremendo Gringo." The Ecuadorian ran his hand across the glass tabletop as if he was smoothing the rose colored cloth underneath the glass.

"Very well. Welcome and like I said, do try the garlic shrimp, it is very good."

"You're a good host, but I don't intend to be here long. Two things: Do you have the twenty and who is this?" I said, staring at the large guy to my right.

"You Americans. Always in a rush. You rule the world with disease and gunpowder and then expect the rest of us to march lock step in line with you. Do I have the twenty? Yes, I have the twenty. I have even more than the twenty should we continue to do business," he said.

The large fellow slid a side plate to me. It had a thin line of cocaine on it.

"A sample. So, you will know the quality of your twenty," said the Ecuadorian.

"You think I touch this? You think the owner of the Hyundai dealership drives a Hyundai? This is business. Plain and simple. You want me to reach in the bag here and pull you out a hundred-dollar bill so you can hold it up to the light? This ain't some HBO movie, *caballero*. I got my 400 right here. Where is your twenty?" I said as I turned the side plate over dumping the cocaine on the table.

"Right now, I am a little put off by your manners my American friend." he said, the smile long gone from his face.

"We aren't friends, we aren't pals, we aren't amigos, we aren't even associates. You want to talk about manners? You brought this human eclipse with you without notifying me we'd have company at the table," I said with indignation.

"You don't have to buy my twenty. There are plenty of people in Miami who will buy my twenty," he snapped.

"Good luck with that. I'm here and now—as in the present."

Looking directly at the huge man to my right, I clarified my comment to him in a condescending manner. "That means *estoy aqui.*"

The uninvited guest leaned back in his chair, and I detected an eye twitch as he struggled to maintain his composure. I turned my attention back to the Ecuadorian.

"My 400,000 is only printed in two locations in the whole world. Your twenty grows wild everywhere, from the top of Colombia on down to the bottom of Bolivia. In every field, hillside, and deep brush. There are more sellers than there are buyers. Especially a buyer with $400,000 leaning against their leg as they sit here in front of you," I said.

The Ecuadorian picked up his water glass and took a sip. He then grabbed the bottle of wine by the neck and poured some into his wine glass, then filling the big guy's wine glass and the empty one in front of me as well.

"We have started our relationship in a manner unbecoming of the men we are. A peace offering. Your twenty is in that sack by the wine rack."

I looked to my left and glanced at a burlap sack bound by twine on the floor that had Girouard Coffee Company emblazoned across the side of it. I'd never heard of the brand. I looked back at the Ecuadorian and noticed an odd, perplexed look on his face.

Everything at first moved in surreal slow motion. The big guy rose from his chair and then a deafening explosion rocked the restaurant. I felt a percussion of energy and air streak past my right ear. There was a faint whistle as the first bullet came within inches of my ear from somewhere behind me. The big guy partially stood up from his chair and reeled backwards. The fugue of action snapped me to real time immediacy when blood splattered across the table. A smoking shell casing arched past my shoulder and bounced off the glass tabletop. The big guy had initially violently jolted backwards, but he was now falling towards me and the table like a lumbered redwood. The next bullet struck the big guy just above his left eye and blew the back of his scalp off. Blood and brains splashed across the decorative picture frame behind him and speckled widely along the wall. He hit the table with a resounding crash, the force of his body smashing down cracking the glass tabletop. It caused the table to tilt on its side and rise under his dead weight. The plates, wine bottle, and glasses all slid down upon him as he rolled onto the floor.

The table wavered and heaved under his enormous weight before righting itself as he slumped to the floor near my right leg and against his chair.

I instinctively sought somewhere low on the floor to get myself out of the shooter's aim. I pushed my chair back as I tried to get under the table. I wanted to make myself as small as I possibly could.

My chair hit the shooter in the shins. His next shot went into the Ecuadorian. I wasn't sure exactly where the bullet struck him, but I heard the Ecuadorian gasp. From beneath the table, I saw his legs stiffen.

I was on my knees, under the table with my back to the shooter. I drew my Glock from its secreted spot behind my back. There was broken glass on the floor and the big guy's leg was wedged up against me. I fell hard onto my right shoulder and pressed my head to the sticky Saltillo parquet floor. Miniscule glass shards ground into my cheek. I pulled my Glock quickly and maneuvered it under my bent body. My elbow, forearm and hand were pressed against the floor in front of me. I tilted the weapon up and fired reflexively a two-round burst. The rounds must have startled the shooter because I could see his black pant legs retreat towards the restaurant's vestibule area.

I scrambled from beneath the table and quickly rose to my feet, keeping my gun aimed in front of me. I caught a glimpse of him as he ran for the front door. It was the same restaurant patron in the dark suit with the combed-back blond hair. He was now nearing the threshold of the front door. I briefly looked back, and the Ecuadorian was slumped across the table. Blood oozed out from underneath him.

I was fully on my feet when the shooter opened the door. There was a combustion of noise and sound, and another shot was fired. I flinched and ducked behind the wine rack just on the other side of the vestibule and did a quick peek around the corner. I saw the tinted doors still open.

Scott Lew was sprawled on the asphalt parking lot. His leg was keeping the door open. Blood was trickling from his left temple. He still had his gun in his hand. I ran towards him, and was met by two windbreaker-clad DEA agents. They were frantic. They were trying to talk on their radios but due to fear and adrenaline were overmodulating. Nothing they said made any sense. One of the two started to assess Agent Lew for vital signs. I looked down at Lew—it didn't look very promising. I looked up again, still scanning the parking lot with my gun. An old Cuban man sitting on a bus bench on Palm Avenue just outside the parking lot was yelling desperately.

"*Rubio, rubio cruzó la calle!*"

[Blond, blond he crossed the street]

Across busy Palm Avenue I saw the shooter in a wild loping gait, dodging the last lane of cars, running north on the sidewalk.

I began chasing after him.

With a furtive glimpse at traffic, I ran onto Palm Avenue, putting all my effort into dodging the cars and trucks. Tires screeched all around me. A few dozen yards to my right I heard the tell-tale sound of a fender bender.

The blond kept running, his black jacket flapping behind him. As I ran towards him I thought of yelling, "Freeze, Police!" but that was pointless. Identifying myself wouldn't stop him. He'd just shot two people and a clearly identified DEA agent. Besides, I needed every gasp I had in me, and I just kept chasing him.

He spun and fired two shots at me. Both rounds struck the right rear quarter panel of a Pasteur Medical Clinic patient bus going north. I heard a symphony of screams from the senior citizen passengers erupt. The taillight from the bus splintered into little red plastic fragments no less than a foot from where I was running, the smaller pieces of shattered plastic hitting me in the chest and neck.

I rounded the bus, approached the east side of the sidewalk, and continued running right up against the bougainvillea-adorned fence of the racetrack. He reloaded his weapon as he ran. I saw the magazine from his gun flit and drop into the street. He wasn't looking back when he reloaded. He turned east into the property of the racetrack. I was still thirty yards behind him.

I cautiously entered the racetrack. I caught a fleeting glimpse of him running south through the grove of ficus and banyan trees, towards the jockey quarters and horse paddocks.

My heartbeat was surging. My breath was labored, short, spiked with adrenaline. Running with my gun in my right hand, I used my left hand to rummage across my body, searching for any bullet wounds.

The shooter didn't seem to be slowing down but he appeared to not know where he was running either. I saw him brushing away low-hanging branches from his path as he kept running. Sirens sounded behind us, getting louder and multiplying as I ran further south. Where there were small breaks in the bougainvillea on the fence line, I could see uniformed Hialeah police cars tearing north on Palm Avenue.

He was now entering the assembled two-story stucco duplexes where many jockeys and horse groomers lived during the racing season. The duplexes and bungalows were nearly seventy years old and showed the wear and tear of nomadic tenants and abuse. Lawn chairs, buckets, horse trailers, clotheslines with dingy clothing hanging from them and even a child's tricycle littered the dusty courtyard between the bungalows. I wasn't gaining on him, but I wasn't falling behind either. He approached a series of small circular paddocks, and briefly stopped to unlatch the metal wire loop of the paddock on his right. Twelve thoroughbreds were inside, grazing on hay bales hung from poles set into the center of the paddock.

The shooter turned towards me and from forty yards away leveled his handgun at me. He fired two shots at me. I dove to my left and rolled up against one of the bungalow's concrete porches.

The sound of the gunshots and the open gate were all the horses needed to create a frightened stampede out of the paddock. The horses large, strong, and terrified started running throughout the area between me and him. They were so frightened that two of them ran directly at me, causing me to dive back against the concrete porch as they thundered only feet away from me. One of the thoroughbreds got entangled in a clothesline. Many of the workers and jockeys who heard the gunshots came out of their doors to a sight of equine mayhem. I stood up. Through all the commotion I could no longer see the blond man in the dark suit.

He was gone.

This entire twenty kilo cocaine deal had imploded in the most horrendous way. I looked around unsuccessfully for anybody holding a cell phone. The need to get the horses back in the paddock was paramount to everyone except me. Everyone was running about with their arms extended trying to slow the horses and delude the scared animals into thinking they were fenced. I started quick walking, and then jogging back towards where I'd come in at. I was exhausted and sweating profusely. There was a tree line east of where I had come in at. On the other side was a large parking lot which was a direct feeder lot for the racetrack's famed clubhouse. I saw seven uniformed Hialeah police cars parked in a wide circle in the parking lot, their overhead red and blue lights flashing.

Landing zone.

The uniformed Hialeah police cars were creating a safe landing zone for the Miami Dade Fire Rescue helicopter. Often referred to as Air Rescue One, the flight crew and medics onboard were some of the best in the country. I knew this was where they'd be bringing Agent Lew to have him airlifted to Jackson Memorial Hospital's Trauma Unit. The trauma unit at JMH is one of the nation's finest.

I started making my way to the landing zone. In the distance I could hear the reverberating *thump thump* of the rotors as a small speck in the western sky became larger and larger. A Hialeah fire rescue truck came barreling through the gate, its light and sirens blaring. The helicopter and its multi green-colored paint scheme circled slowly above the landing zone. A helmeted and sun visored paramedic leaned out the open bay door looking for any telephone lines or obstructions that the officers may have overlooked when setting up the landing zone. The fire rescue truck stood ready to transport Agent Lew from their care to the care of the helicopter. The helicopter kept circling inching closer to landing.

One of the Hialeah uniformed officers exited his car upon seeing me and approached me aggressively. He had lieutenant's bars on his collar.

"*Oye pendejo regresa*."

["Hey asshole get back."]

With no badge on me and concerned he might see the gun tucked behind my back, I put my hands up in surrender.

"QRU I'm a cop. I'm a cop I'm with the Gables," I said.

"You're with who?" he shouted I as if the noise from the helicopter had clouded his hearing.

"Gables. Coral Gables. I'm Detective Cade Taylor, Vice Narcotics."

He glared at me, his anger not subsiding. He raised his voice even louder as the helicopter descended closer.

"Where's your I.D.? Are you part of this? Why can't you and these assholes stay in your own city? Aren't you supposed to advise us when you're in my city? I got half of my sector units here and the city calls are piling up. Are you the guy with the gun who just ran across Palm Avenue? We got three calls of a guy running with a gun. My captain is shitting flying pigs out of his ass because of this."

"The shooter ran across Palm Avenue, and I was chasing him," I yelled back trying to be heard despite the roar of the helicopter.

The helicopter was now hovering about forty feet above the landing zone.

"Listen, asshole. Don't you go anywhere. I got a score to settle with you. You and the DEA run like feral monkeys in my city, you don't tell any of us you're here. Then when all hell breaks loose you scream like babies for help. Don't go *anywhere*. You hear me? Stay right here," he said, pointing his finger directly at me, inches from my face.

He turned his attention to two of his officers. He ran towards them leaving me to stand beside his idling police cruiser.

There wasn't anything I could do for Agent Lew. Considering the circumstances, he was in the best capable hands he could possibly be in. As the Miami Dade paramedic was getting ready to step out of the now descending helicopter and help direct the pilot to touch down on the parking lot, I thought of what the lieutenant said to me. I opened his police cruiser door and pressed all four of the buttons inside the door to lower the windows and then closed the door. The rotor wash was beginning to kick up as the helicopter landed. In the hot swirling wind, I walked back towards *El Segundo Viajante*. The rotor wash from the helicopter filled the area with clouds of dust, stinging dirt, propelled gravel, loose papers, all of which were filling the interior of the lieutenant's car and beating against my back as I walked away.

Chapter Three

IT LOOKED APOCALYPTIC. On Palm Avenue, police cars with their revolving overhead lights were everywhere. There were deepening crowds of people growing. Many were under the Sunoco overhang seeking shade from the November Florida sun. The Sunoco was having brisk sales selling bottled water and Gatorades to the masses. Traffic was stopped in both directions on the busy artery. Crime scene tape was strung from the northern side of the gas station all the way across the road and affixed to the racetrack fence. Throngs of people were gathered outside the crime scene tape, all intently watching the action inside the cordoned area. Police and even some fire personnel were keeping the swelling pockets of people back. Inside the cordoned-off area was the Pasteur Medical Clinic patient bus. Two white-coat-clad medical men were leading the aged Latin passengers off the bus towards another bus awaiting them outside the crime scene tape. Two Hialeah Crime Scene technicians in dark blue BDU pants and light blue shirts adorned with HPD CSI across their backs were photographing and measuring the rear quarter panel of the medical bus. No one was monitoring the racetrack side of the sidewalk.

I bent at the waist and slipped in under the yellow tape. I walked into the crime scene and right to the two technicians.

"Sir, this is an active crime scene. You can't be in here," said the female crime scene tech.

"It's okay, I'm actually part of the scene. I'm Detective Cade Taylor, Coral Gables VIN."

"VIN what? Where's your I.D.?"

"VIN. Vice, Intelligence, Narcotics. I'm the U.C. from this deal." I said.

"VIN? From Coral Gables? Aren't you supposed to notify us when you're in our city?"

This was the second person to claim ownership of the City of Hialeah to me in the last five minutes. Which to me was like claiming ownership to the often-seen tattered abandoned lone shoe on the side of a freeway.

"What's your name?" I asked her.

My question must have stunned her from her own line of questioning. She almost instinctually answered.

"Hammy Garzon."

"Your parents named you Hammy?"

"Your parents named you Cade? Listen, strange-named guy, maybe you are part of this whole macho bullet fest but right now you're just a sweaty, dusty guy in my crime scene who has shown me no identification and is keeping me from my job. So once again, Mr. Coral Gables, get the fuck out."

"Well, I wanted to tell you there's an empty magazine there on the sidewalk. It's of prime importance that it gets processed way before anything else because it's small, liable to be picked up by one of your gloveless *compadres*, and it'll match the bullets you're pulling out of that fender. I should know since the bullets you're extracting were meant for me. He shot at me twice and those two bullets came from that magazine."

"You got some balls—"

Frustrated beyond compare, I cut her off.

"You want to hear about my balls, lady—"

At that moment we were both interrupted by someone near the restaurant, yelling my name across the crime scene.

"Taylor. Cade Taylor. Hey Taylor, come here."

It was a blondish brown-haired woman motioning for me to join her. She wore a dark oversized DEA windbreaker. I started to walk in her direction, relieved to be interrupted from saying something I'd invariably regret later. As I left, I said to Hammy Garzon:

"Now that I've been verified, can you or someone else, please process that magazine before it gets contaminated?"

I didn't need to anger *everyone* in the Hialeah Police Department. I could hear the sound of the helicopter rotors switching tone. Without looking back, I could tell by the rotor whine the craft was lifting and starting to move nose-forward across the racetrack towards Jackson Memorial Hospital. The landing zone would be breaking down and the lieutenant, who surely was still pissed as hell, might try and release some of his guys. I wasn't in the mood to be confronted by him again. I stopped and turned back towards Hammy Garzon.

"Hey, I'm not telling you what to do. But I was at LZ for the helicopter. You got a lieutenant out there with about nine units. The shooter shot two rounds in the paddock jockey quarters area. There are a lot of witnesses there and the shooter had his hands on the gates of the paddock. If you could notify the lieutenant, it would save a ton of time and keep the scene preserved. The shooter is tall with slicked-back blond hair, was wearing a dark suit. He's armed. He was last seen running north through the paddocks and duplexes. Let your units know."

She put the back of her gloved hand to her forehead for a moment. She looked down at the shattered fender light and then back at me. "I'll see who's there and let them know," she replied.

Inwardly pleased that I wouldn't have to see the lieutenant for the immediate future, I thanked Hammy and turned my attention to the waiting DEA agent. I scrutinized her face to see if I recognized her. She stood under the sloping overhang above the outside seating area. She was only about ten yards from the front door where Agent

Lew had been struck down. Behind her were discarded bloody gauze wrappings, used I.V. tubes, and crime scene markers. I'd never seen her before. She introduced herself.

"I'm Special Agent Marie Mandeville."

She didn't shake my hand. Agent Mandeville was experienced enough to know that shaking my hand might compromise any gunshot residue, or what we call "GSR," from my hands. She knew crime scene technicians would be checking me from head to toe sooner than later.

I asked her, "Were you part of my takedown team? I only heard Agent Lew mention Agents Marroquín and Agent Walker."

"No, they all work for me. I'm actually the Assistant Special Agent in Charge, you know the ASAC. I just got here, and I was wondering if you could help me understand how my agent got shot," she said.

"I don't know. I heard a commotion at the restaurant door and a shot. I got to the doorway and Agent Lew was down. There were two agents attending him and I chased the shooter."

With the helicopter now fully away and out of sight, the crime scene took on a solitary lonely silence. A large contingency of law enforcement was ardently processing the scene and speculating amongst themselves. Detectives, DEA agents, and crime scene technicians all dutifully worked around us. I wasn't sure who was leading the investigative team but knew from looking out past the crime scene tape that more people and more agencies would soon descend upon us. Just outside the yellow tape, I could see Florida Highway Patrol, Miami Dade, and Hialeah PD. I saw my first of what I guaranteed would soon be one of many agents from the Florida Department of Law Enforcement enter the area.

"ASAC Mandeville, may I ask a favor of you?"

She nodded as she tucked a pen behind her ear.

"I assume you have your gun and badge on you. I'm just here in these clothes with my gun tucked in my waistband behind my back. May I borrow your DEA windbreaker because everyone is asking me for I.D. and aggravating me, not believing I'm a cop. Without answering everyone's continual questions I think I can lead us through this step by step quicker and easier."

She looked at my shoulder length hair, goatee and earrings and recognized the implications of what I was asking of her. Without hesitation she removed her DEA windbreaker and handed it to me. I took off my jacket, briefly exposing the outline of my handgun concealed under my perspiration-soaked shirt, and I put her DEA windbreaker on. The DEA jacket was like an immediate invitation to the party. No more sideways glances, and no more questions about whether I belonged or not. This was my own George Jefferson moment as I immediately was "moving on up."

"Detective Taylor, I believe in information. Information sets us apart from most of the other intelligence and enforcement divisions of the Justice Department. It also helps us to further our investigations and right now I need as much information as I can get. Agent Lew and Agent Lew's family need this information as soon as possible. It's all we have to avenge what happened here. Justice be damned, one of my guys was shot and airlifted and I want answers *now*. Take me through this, from the beginning," she said with absolute serious conviction.

I looked at her, trying to gauge the trust factor. I knew that anything I said would help the investigation. I also knew that even though I'd fired my weapon, I didn't hit anyone. My status as an involved shooter in the investigation would be eventually glossed over. It wouldn't be a focal point.

I looked back over my shoulder towards Palm Avenue, at the bus bench where the old Cuban man had been sitting. He had correctly directed me to where the shooter was. Civic pride. He might still be here somewhere. I mulled her comment as I half-turned back to look at the people. I scanned the crowd outside the yellow tape and saw the old Cuban man there, animatedly talking to anyone who'd listen to him. A Hialeah police detective was a few feet away. I called out to him with authority.

"Hey. Get that guy in the turquoise shirt in the crowd. He's a witness, we need him. Hold him for us."

The detective immediately went to the tape and started calling to the man, speaking Spanish, to come to him. The old man now with a sense of importance and an "I told you so" smug look on his face, strode forward to the tape and the detective ushered him into the scene.

The power of the DEA windbreaker.

"Sorry, but he might be able to tell us what happened to Agent Lew. He was outside sitting on that bench," I said to ASAC Mandeville. "Did you see Lew's operation plan?"

"Not yet."

"Lew said he had a new source. I asked him who the source was. Lew said, 'he is reputable and comes from a family of reliable information.' So, we know the source is male, but Lew was concerned about case discovery at trial and didn't want to say anything—"

"So, if you were to be deposed as to why you were here today, you can just say information was provided to you by a law enforcement source, protecting the informant from discovery. Pretty standard," she said.

Standard.

They must learn that word at the Drug Enforcement Agency Special Agent Academy.

"Well, I don't know who his source was, but the plan was for me was to pick up 400,000 from our property evidence room and use it as buy money. He said his source had a seller looking to sell twenty kilos for twenty k each. All he said was that the seller was called 'the Ecuadorian.' I parked at the Masonic Lodge and Lew picked me up in his BMW. We waited because his source informed him the Ecuadorian was running late. Turns out our shooter pulled up in a taxi. That threw everything into a 'what if' situation, and Lew sent Agents Matias Marroquín and Vincent Walker off the surveillance take down detail to go try and pull the taxi over away from here. So, we were down at least two agents and Lew decided to go ahead with the deal. He drove me here and dropped me off behind the Sunoco station."

ASAC Mandeville had now pulled the pen from behind her ear and was taking notes on a pad.

"He let me out in the alley, and started to drive away. We tested the kel. He gave me a five-by-five affirmative on the reading. I walked in carrying the 400,000 in the satchel. I saw the shooter at a table off to the side. I didn't *know* he was the shooter; he was just the guy who matched the description of the passenger from the taxi. He was tall with slicked-back blond hair, kind of pale and wearing a dark suit. The Ecuadorian was at the table facing the door. He had some big guy with him. Lew never said anything about there being two of them. I was immediately a little pissed and not feeling too good about that. I sat down and we started to talk, and I just wanted to get it done and be finished with it. The Ecuadorian wanted it to be some sort of international play date, started pouring wine and all this crap. Next thing I know, I see the big guy starting to get up and he took two real fast. One in the chest and one in the head. He goes down. The table nearly topples. I hit the deck. I hear the Ecuadorian take one and I see the tall guy's legs and I returned fire from under the table. I got off two rounds and the tall blond guy starts running out of the restaurant. As he hit the door I heard what sounded like bodies colliding and another round. When I got to the door. Lew was down on his back. The agents were already on him helping him."

"Then what?" she interjected.

"I stepped out here in the parking lot and that old man we just secured was there sitting on the bench." I motioned to the bench with my arm. "He said in Spanish that the shooter ran across Palm Avenue. I saw the shooter running and took off after him. I get about halfway across Palm and he turns and lets off two rounds at me. They hit the Pasteur bus there. We keep running and near the racetrack gate he switches his magazine for a fresh one and drops the used magazine on the sidewalk. He got into the racetrack through the open gate and started running north. I chased him through the trees and duplexes and near the paddocks he opened a gate. He fired two more rounds at me and then all these horses came running out of the paddock towards me. I ducked down and he took off running north again. Between the horses and all the workers coming out it was a mess. That's when I lost him."

Hammy Garzon walked up to me and ASAC Mandeville. We both stopped talking and looked at her.

"Sorry to interrupt. Are you in charge of the DEA side of this?" she asked Mandeville.

"Yes. I'm Assistant Special Agent in Charge Marie Mandeville."

"Agent Mandeville, we have multiple scenes to process here, the least of which is the medical bus on Palm Avenue. We've already done all we need to do with the Pasteur medical bus. I'm CSI Hialeah Technician Garzon. If it's okay with you and any other lone incredibly rude impatient person who might have a difference of opinion," she said looking directly at me,

"we'd like to release the bus and open Palm Avenue. We have traffic backed up all the way for half a mile on Okeechobee Road and Red Road is gridlocked. We're going to have multiple scenes to process here and on the grounds of the racetrack. I've already ordered portable lights to be brought out because I think this will go well into the night."

"If you got all you need from the road then yes, open Palm Avenue. Technician Garzon, I have a request for own crime scene people to be dispatched here. They're coming down from a processing a meth lab in North Miami Beach. They should be here soon. When they get here, I hope you'll coordinate with them on all the fine work you're doing so we don't have duplication of efforts," said Mandeville.

"Hey Garzon, you speak Spanish, right?" I asked her.

With a disdainful "don't I have enough to do already" look on her face she said, "Yes."

"I want you to listen in when we interview this old guy here. It might help you get a better idea on how to approach and process the shooting scene here behind us," I said.

I called out to the Hialeah detective who was with the old Cuban man in the turquoise shirt. I asked him to bring the man to us. The old man was diminutive in size and missing some bottom teeth. His face was deeply tanned and creased with wrinkles. He had dark sunglasses on. His receding white hair was neat but slightly windblown. Up close his T-shirt was more aqua than turquoise. On the front in orange letters read the phrase, "I still call it Joe Robbie." Mandeville informed the detective that permission was granted to open Palm Avenue, and he could let his people know. The detective thanked her and walked away.

"Sir, do you speak English?" I asked the old man.

The old man looked at me than at Garzon.

"*Pruébalo en inglés primero,*" said Garzon in Spanish to the man.

[Try it in English first.]

Hearing Garzon encourage him to speak in English made the man lapse into a rapid-fire account of what he saw...all in Spanish.

"*Mi esposa me vuelve loco. Yo estaba a cargo de todos los wawas en La Habana. Me gusta ver pasar los autobuses en Palm Avenue. Me saca de la casa. Te juro que cuando me muera esa mujer va a ven a mi tumba todos los días solo para que ella pueda gritarme—*".

[My wife drives me crazy. I used to be in charge of all the buses in Havana. I like to watch the buses go by on Palm Avenue. It gets me out of the house. I swear when I die that woman is going to come to my grave every day just so she can yell at me.]

Garzon cut him off. Speaking again in Spanish she reminded him to tell us what he saw that day in English. The old man thought pensively for a moment looking for the right words to say.

"I was there," he said, pointing to the bus bench.

"It sounded like firecrackers in the restaurant. I looked back and I heard the *gomas* screaming," he said, pointing now back into the parking lot at Agent Lew's BMW.

"*La federale exito* and ran to the door. *Rubio* and *la federale choque a la puerte.* Boom! Bullet goes. I get to my hips," he said mimicking ducking behind the bus bench.

"*Veo Rubio y run to Palm and dos pistoles el y tu,*" he said now pointing at me.

"*De repente.* Boom boom! *Vidrio wawa explotó.*"

Garzon cleaned up the eyewitness account for ASAC Mandeville with a better translation.

"He's saying he heard shots fired in the restaurant and then he turned to see the tires squealing of the agent's car. The blond shooter and the agent collided at the door of the restaurant. He heard a single shot go off. Boom. He ducked down by the bus bench. He then saw Detective Taylor come out with a gun. The shooter still had his gun. Suddenly he heard two more shots, which is when the shooter shot at Detective Taylor, hitting the Pasteur medical bus."

DEA Special Agent Matias Marroquín joined us.

"Walker and I found the taxi at West 32nd Street in front of the Tarpoon Dive Center. We got all the driver's information. He said he picked up the shooter at the front entrance of Hialeah Hospital. Walker is there reviewing security footage from the hospital cameras," said Agent Marroquín.

"Good. Marroquín, our own CSI will be here soon. I want you to coordinate with Ms. Garzon here and oversee the collection of evidence with her team and ours. I need a liaison on this, and it's going to be you, Matias. You can start by getting in touch with Walker and advise him that the passenger may be heading back towards the hospital. He might be on foot and armed. Then I need you to get this gentleman's information," Mandeville said pointing to the old Cuban man.

Marroquín walked away with the old Cuban man while Mandeville, Garzon and I moved to where Agent Lew was struck down. Garzon put her notebook on the ground and got down on one knee on top of it.

"Our fire rescue has pretty much cleared from here. Before they left one of the paramedics told me that he didn't think your agent took a full bullet to the head. Based on these striations on the asphalt—he might be right."

"Agent Lew wasn't shot in the head?" asked Mandeville hopefully.

"I'm not saying that exactly. I didn't see him, and I wasn't here, but looking at these markings. It looks like the bullet may have either exited his head and impacted on the asphalt, or it hit the asphalt and he may have been fragmented by the bullet." Garzon continued studying the asphalt. She looked up from her kneeling position and gazed across the parking lot at the six-foot wall that ran the length of the restaurant's northern side. She rose, staring straight ahead and walked to the wall, where she rubbed along its surface with her gloved hands. She put her face close to the wall and continued surveying it. She looked back at me and Mandeville and smiled.

"I think I found it," she said triumphantly.

She radioed to another crime scene technician. The same male technician that had processed the Pasteur Medical bus with her arrived. The two of them measured, photographed, and made calculations. She eventually used a flat smooth tool and chipped the bullet out of the wall. She showed it to Mandeville and me. It was bronze colored and was flattened like a squished mushroom almost all the way around. A small piece of it was missing.

Within ten minutes the crime scene technicians from the DEA were on the scene. They gathered in the parking lot with their Tyvek suits as Mandeville spoke to them. I also briefed them about what had happened inside the restaurant. Garzon stood off to the side listening. Once the four person DEA team was fully donned in their evidence collection gear the decision was made to methodically enter the restaurant and start processing the murder scene of the Ecuadorian and the big guy. Mandeville, I, and Garzon waited outside as the four technicians entered the restaurant. As we waited, the male tech from Hialeah informed Garzon he'd processed and retrieved the magazine the shooter had dropped on Palm Avenue. He told her it was a magazine he'd never seen before.

After a few minutes had passed, an already perspiring DEA crime scene technician emerged from the restaurant.

"I thought you said there were two victims in here?" he said to Mandeville.

Mandeville looked at me.

"There are two victims. Both Latin males, both at the table by the window," I said to the technician.

He turned and looked behind him at the open doorway, then back to me.

"There's only one victim in there. A large Latin male with two bullet wounds. One in the upper torso the other in his head above his left eye."

I stood there, stunned, trying to reconcile what he was saying with what I had seen. My incredulous thinking was interrupted when I heard Garzon's voice.

"You still want to talk about your balls?"

Chapter Four

"THAT CAN'T BE right?" I stammered. "I saw them get shot. I saw them both get shot. First the big guy then the Ecuadorian."

"Didn't you say that you were down on the floor under the table, and you *heard* the Ecuadorian get shot?" asked Mandeville.

"You were under the table, and you got the nerve to talk about balls?" Garzon said softly to herself, almost inaudibly to me.

"It's not what you think," I snapped at her.

"You're sure there's only one body in there?" I asked the DEA technician.

He looked at Mandeville, then at Garzon before he wordlessly walked past us and went to a large tackle box-type kit the DEA team had left in the parking lot. He opened it and retrieved three sets of paper muslin shoe booties and two set of latex gloves which he dispersed to me and Mandeville. He gave Garzon the lone pair of shoe booties.

"You have gloves already," he said to Garzon.

"Let me remind you all, do *not* touch anything and do *not* aimlessly wander around in there. It's a tight space with all of us in there. Miami Dade and Hialeah will want to have their own homicide people also go in so at some time in the very near future. It's going to be a pig pile. Pardon the expression."

Fully geared up, I fell in line, following him inside, with Mandeville and Garzon behind me. Aside from the absence of the Ecuadorian I immediately realized the burlap sack with the twenty kilograms of cocaine and the $400,000 was also missing.

This whole fiasco in *la cuidad de progressia* had just progressed to a very unacceptable level. The calculation in my head of everything that had washed down the filthiest sewer pipe was tabulating.

The gut-sickening stacking of events started with an unknown informant, a DEA agent shot—that same DEA agent possibly dead, for all I knew—, a Latin male killed, an Ecuadorian I thought was dead who was actually missing, twenty kilograms of cocaine gone, $400,000 of Coral Gables money missing, a tall, determined shooter somewhere on the loose who shot the DEA agent and shot no less than four bullets at me too. This was a colossal mess beyond anything I'd ever experienced. Mandeville peeled off from the group with a worried look on her face.

"I'm going to need to make a *lot* of calls," she said, vacating the confusing murder scene as fast as she could.

"Can you call the Gables and just inform them that I had a firearm discharge so they can do their own slamming down hard on me about this?" I said less than enthusiastically as she was already nearly outside.

I looked at Garzon. An experienced crime scene technician, the calamity of broken glass, blood and the corpse of the big guy were not overwhelming, but were definitely not what she was expecting. The DEA technician looked at me for some frame of reference. I walked the few paces to where the shooter had been sitting.

"Let me try and take you through this because there will definitely be some major points of evidence here that we have to collect as soon as we can. The dead guy—unlike the other *dead guy*—isn't going anywhere. We need to find the guy who shot Agent Lew. Anything to do with him needs to be processed first. The shooter was sitting here at this table," I said motioning to a small table near a mounted facade of a wine barrel.

"Everything here needs to be printed. Check the seats for any fibers. I know. I know. Lots of people have sat here the past few weeks. But let's just hope that the tables were wiped clean, and he was the first customer to sit here today."

Two of the DEA technicians lifted the entire tabletop glass and carried it out to their crime processing van. They'd start with fingerprint dust, and if necessary, they would take it back to their laboratory and use cyanoacrylate fumes. Cyanoacrylate glue is the industrial name for what's commonly known as "Crazy Glue" or "Super Glue." Cyanoacrylate fuming is a method used to develop latent fingerprints, using the cyanoacrylate esters present in "super glue" vapors. The reaction forms a visible white polymer along the ridges of the fingerprint. It's useful for detecting fingerprints on smooth surfaces such as metal, plastic, and glass. All the stemware, and flatware were removed. They even took the vase of flowers, and the salt and pepper shakers were removed. They removed the cloth napkin and tablecloth for any of the shooter's secretions or DNA. That left just the high back lacquered black chairs. One of the DEA technicians started dusting the inside of the chairs where the shooter may have left fingerprints from pulling the chair out to sit in it.

"There was a burlap sack from some French coffee company right there. The twenty kilograms were inside the sack."

"If we find the sack, we may need to print you as an elimination print," said the DEA technician.

"I actually never opened it," I replied.

"They told you there were twenty kilograms in the sack. But you never saw them?"

This was not looking good for me in so many ways.

"We never got far enough into the deal for me to verify the kilos. As soon as they said where the kilos were the shooter came up from behind me and started firing," I said.

It was Garzon who spoke next.

"Why don't you let me help process the actual murder scene. That way you DEA guys can focus on the shooter, and I'll collect what I can from this homicide."

The DEA technicians agreed and dutifully, with incredible precision, continued their processing.

"So, tell me exactly how this went down. Who sat where and all of that," Garzon said to me.

I recounted the entire chain of events from the time I walked into the restaurant on up until the time I ran past Agent Lew outside. She looked at the assembled carnage and her eyes moved about the scene as I told her one fact after another. Straddling the body, she collected the wine bottle and wine glasses, because I specifically knew the Ecuadorian had touched those items. The tabletop was in shards, and she wouldn't have the luxury of pulling the whole glass top like her DEA contemporaries did. She tried to gauge which of the larger pieces might have fingerprints on them. I left her and the DEA technicians to gather all the evidence that they could and walked outside. Hialeah police officers were helping unload generators and portable lights from a low trailer. Mandeville was off to the side talking on the telephone and gesturing with her hands. It appeared that more federal agencies were now on the scene. Windbreakers were everywhere, all adorned with various three and four letter acronyms. ATF, OIG, FBI, FDLE.

Mandeville hung up her phone and in between calls said to me that Agent Lew was in the ICU at Jackson Memorial Hospital. There was a small fragment in his head very close to his brain, and there was a lot of swelling. For now the doctors were keeping Lew in a medically induced coma until the neurosurgeon could determine if the swelling would increase. She also said a Coral Gables contingency was on their way here. I expected that.

I noticed that the single hung door yards down from the main doors was partially open. When Agent Lew got shot the incoming takedown team of DEA agents rushed to his aid. I looked at the partially open, single hung door and wondered if perhaps in all the commotion of saving Agent Lew, the Ecuadorian went out through that door unnoticed.

I slowly approached the door. Looking through the open doorway, I scanned the interior floor. Three droplets of blood glistened on the floor.

I went back into the restaurant through the main doors and saw Garzon busily processing the murder scene of the heavy large man. She had secured the wine bottle and wine glasses in separate plastic evidence bags, and was on her knees looking at the body. I bent down to where she was.

"I suggest we get a blood tox on this guy and compare it with the blood on the tabletop. I'm pretty certain our other guy was shot and there should be two different types of blood samples. By the single door near the back, there are some blood drops on the floor. I think they belong to our guy who took off with the coke and money."

She nodded her head but in her eyes, I could see that I was one cop she wished she'd never met. The workload thrust upon her, and her contemporaries was mounting with each new discovery. Rather than challenge her reluctance, I just straightened up and walked away from the scene. I still had my little booties on my feet, so I took them off and threw them on the pile of gauze bandages, bandage wrappings, and discarded I.V. tubing by the doors. I decided to try and reconstruct the path the Ecuadorian took.

From the single hung door, I walked very slowly with my head primarily down looking at the ground in front of me, searching for blood drops or any other sign of where he might have gone. I walked past Lew's BMW which was now cordoned off with yellow crime scene tape. A young Hialeah uniform police officer stood just outside of the tape. He looked at me wordlessly. He didn't challenge me or ask me who I was. Once again, the power of the windbreaker. I turned north into the alley and immediately noticed how narrow it was. A car could barely get through it, but two cars could not pass through at the same time. This was due to the concrete and wooden telephone poles in the alley. Rather than take the antiquated wooden poles down, the utility company lazily inserted concrete poles into the ground feet away, creating pockets of narrowing within the alley. I looked at the roof lines for security cameras. There weren't any. The few windows in the two-story apartment buildings overlooking the alley were small, frosted bathroom windows. I looked north towards the Sunoco station and decided to walk to where Lew had dropped me off. Two cars were parked at the rear of the Sunoco station. There had been three—one was missing. There was also a surveillance camera at the rear of the Sunoco station. I recalled what I did when I got out of Lew's car and cut through the gas station on my way to the restaurant.

I'd touched the cars; in case they were related to the Ecuadorian. For forensic evidence—to verify that those cars were at the drug meet.

Chapter Five

I WALKED INTO THE Sunoco gas station. The crime scene tape had been moved to allow patrons in again, but the gas pumps were still inaccessible. I heard a few murmurs about *"La Migra"* and saw two wiry landscapers put their Pepsis and potato chips down. They hastily left the store with their heads down, eyes averting me.

The clerk was standing behind a large thick piece of plexiglass that I'm sure the gas station owner told him was bullet proof when in fact it most assuredly wasn't. Florida Lottery, RJ Reynolds, and Skoal stickers were plastered on the glass, vying for customer attention. The clerk was Cuban, six feet tall and overweight, though it was hard to be sure past all the stickers. I looked at him through the glass.

"No, I'm not Immigration...I'm uh DEA," I said as I looked down at the windbreaker for validation. "I need to see the tapes from the surveillance camera in the back please."

"Como?"

"I need to see the footage from your surveillance camera in the back."

"Eh? Como?" he said with a sly smile.

"You have a camera in the back that photographs the parking lot. I need to see the tape please."

He started laughing at his own joke of pretending to not know

English and called towards the rear of the station for a young man to come out and work the register while he went into the back with me. We went in the back through a hallway lined with boxes from floor to ceiling. In a small, cramped office was a TV monitor mounted just high enough above a desk strewn with papers, a telephone, and an ashtray with a half-stubbed cigar. The monitor had four images in a quad grid, all live feeds. Three of them depicted the activities of the gas pumps and the interior of the station. The fourth screen was the rear of the station. I asked him to roll it back to about 10:45am. The images blurred by, and as he neared 10:45am he slowed the tape and stopped it.

It showed the three cars that were in the parking lot. I asked him to go back further to 10am. When he did, there were only two cars in the back of the gas station. The young man called out to him from the front of the store.

"I can trust you, right?" he said, laughing again as he got up to leave.

I looked around. At the accumulated boxes and overall griminess of the rear office we were in.

"Yeah, scout's honor," I said sarcastically.

He walked out and I continued watching the screen. I sat down in the office chair. The armrests were torn from extreme overuse and wrapped in smudgy duct tape. I grabbed a loose pen from the desk and pulled a piece of paper from the dusty Minolta PagePro 6L printer, keeping my eyes on the screen. At 10:37am a silver 1997 Mercedes-Benz E320 entered the frame, backing into the spot between the other two cars. The angle the Mercedes took to park made it difficult to see the license plate.

The Ecuadorian was driving the Mercedes. The big guy was in the passenger seat.

The big guy exited the car and walked away out of camera range. The Ecuadorian stayed in the car. I could see his hands on the steering wheel, but his face was blurred by the morning glare. After four minutes the big guy came back to the car, opened the passenger door, and leaned into the car. They were talking. After another minute passed, the trunk opened remotely. The big guy closed the passenger door and went to the rear of the car. He pulled out the burlap sack of cocaine, leaving the trunk open.

It was nearing 10:39 on the tape counter.

The Ecuadorian exited the car and went to the back. The big guy pushed the trunk down, closing it. They both walked together. The big guy was clearly seen carrying the burlap sack. The Ecuadorian was almost unseen as he walked aside the big guy. It was just a matter of seconds they were on camera together.

Then they were out of camera range walking north in the alley. I made notations on the paper of the times.

At 11:14am Agent Lew's BMW is partially seen in the alley. He drives away and I can now be seen on camera walking across the parking lot. The camera clearly shows me placing my hand on the front of the three backed in cars. I walk out of the frame in a few steps.

At 11:23 The Ecuadorian is seen, looking panicked and disheveled. He's running to the Mercedes, the burlap sack clutched tight to his chest. The satchel with the money is pushed high up by the straps on his shoulder. He opens the driver's door and throws both the sack and satchel across the seat. His shirt is stained by a large black splotch. On the grainy monochromatic camera, it looks black but I'm certain it's blood.

I stopped the tape.

I left the office, nodded to the cashiers, and walked out of the gas station. I commandeered one of the uniformed Hialeah police officers who was pulling duty keeping the onlookers back from the taped off area near the pumps, and I brought him back in the gas station. I positioned him by the office door and informed him to not let anyone else in unless they were crime scene technicians or law enforcement.

The power of the windbreaker.

I walked back to the restaurant to find Lieutenant Charlie

Maddalone from the Coral Gables Police Department was now on the scene. He saw me and made a bee line straight for me.

"The sooner we do this the sooner I can leave," he said to me.

I walked with him to his vehicle, and he opened the trunk. There was an aluminum briefcase in the trunk. Lieutenant Maddalone asked for my Glock, which he put into the foam, rubber-lined case. He needed to take my gun back to the station to make sure it was functioning properly. At the station they'd test fire it, disassemble and reassemble it to make sure there were no manufacturing issues that may have led to an accidental discharge. Maddalone in turn gave me a different Glock from the case, which I holstered. The policy was they could ask you for your weapon in an investigation, but they could not leave you without one.

"Haven't we done these enough times with you, Taylor? There are others on the firearm discharge list, but I think you are definitely at the top of it," he said after we'd made the transition.

"Someone has to be at the top," I replied.

"Funny guy. I'll have the report on your weapon sent to Major Brunson," was all he said as he closed the trunk and got in his car.

Major Theodore "Ted" Brunson oversaw the Coral Gables Criminal Investigation Division (CID). That in and of itself made him my direct boss. Our VIN unit was without a lieutenant and Major Brunson was not only my current direct supervisor, but he was also the acting police chief. Our chief of police, Robert McIntyre, was convalescing from a near-fatal stroke he'd suffered nearly fourteen months ago, and our fiscally conservative city manager had decided to withhold filling both positions in a cost-cutting measure the city manager thought was beneficial to the city. Brunson was a fair man but a man of uncompromising ideals. He'd been with the agency longer than any other personnel. He often reminded those who opposed him that he sits in the largest office in the building for a reason: tenure, tenacity, temperament, and the ability to glean information from a wide array of unknown sources. The inflection in his voice was neither a pure southern accent nor any that could fully be defined. More like a subdued slower cadence of the cartoon character Foghorn Leghorn. He pronounced Miami "Mia-A-Muh," and was prone to profanity in such a haphazard way that it caused many a quizzical look when he went into one of his frequent tirades. He was a quick-tempered man, prone to kicking the standard department-issued army green metal wastebasket in his office He was fastidious about his perceived image, and out of guilt about an angry eruption, would try to swap out his dented waste basket with someone else's, on the odd chance the mayor or city manager should visit his office. He wore black western-style boots always under his suit and uniform pants and he had a strong inclination to sample hot sauces, of which there was usually one or two on his desk. They always had eye-catching names like "Hemorrhoid Helper Hot Sauce," or "Belligerent Blaze Habanero Gourmet Hot Sauce."

The restaurant was a highly energized bustle. There were agents and detectives from Hialeah and Miami Dade all milling about. Some were deep in phone conversations. Others were huddling together while a few walked about looking at rooflines, the hedges, and even the bus bench the old Cuban man had been sitting on. ASAC Mandeville was on her cell phone. She saw me and motioned to me to come to her. I walked to where she was. She hung up the cellphone.

"Crime Scene says there's a bullet hole in the wall where you say this 'Ecuadorian' was sitting. There's a fragmentation from the round. Hammy Garzon says it looks to her like the same type of bullet she pulled from the parking lot wall and from the medical bus. If she's right, we'll compare those rounds with what the medical examiner is able to find in the deceased. This should account for all the rounds the shooter shot here. A portion of our team is in the racetrack paddocks with Hialeah Crime Scene, printing the horse corral latch. They're processing the two bullets he fired at you there. Garzon thinks from the blood spatter there might be two types of blood inside. The big guy and the Ecuadorian you spoke of," she said.

I told her about my theory that while the agents were attending to Agent Lew, the Ecuadorian slipped out through the single hung door unseen. I walked her through the theory showing her the blood spots inside the door on the tile floor. We both walked north through the alley. I showed her where the 1997 Mercedes-Benz E320 had been parked. She and I then went into the gas station where the Hialeah officer was still at his post securing the back office. I introduced her to him, and she informed him that someone would be here very soon to retrieve the tape. We stepped outside and both surveyed the teeming pedestrians, and law enforcement activity. Media trucks were starting to set up on the north side of West 29th Street. The Sunoco gas station would get a lot of free publicity on the TV news tonight. With each turn of my head, I saw more and more detectives and agents from different agencies designated by the three initials on the back of their windbreakers. Ponytails were tucked up under ball caps, cell phones were in full use, small groups huddled and talked quietly in the fall breeze. Some of the agents who normally worked undercover toiled at their tasks on the scene wearing balaclavas, obscuring their faces from the public and media. The thought crossed my mind as well as I walked around draped in a DEA windbreaker. My standing here wasn't going to get the $400,000 back, nor was it going to keep the twenty kilograms from being sold somewhere else. I told ASAC Mandeville that I needed to get on my way and first return to Coral Gables and then get back into this investigation. She used her cell phone and spoke to Agent Marroquín. His car was not blocked in by anyone and she told him to give me a ride to my car. Marroquín walked up a few minutes later. I thanked ASAC Mandeville and handed her back her DEA windbreaker.

"Thanks for the raid jacket."

"We don't use that term anymore. We call them 'announcement apparel,'" she said.

I thanked her again nonetheless and followed Agent Marroquín to his car. He was in a state of obvious distress at seeing Agent Lew go down. His eyes were watery when he spoke about Lew, and he even mentioned him in the past tense.

"We don't know that yet. Mandeville said he was in a medically induced coma to stabilize swelling. The Hialeah crime scene technician and the Hialeah paramedics think he may have caught a fragment and not a full bullet. I know that's of very little comfort to you or his other coworkers, but I've seen these things before, and we have to remain positive until we know for sure otherwise," I said as gently as I could.

Marroquín pulled up to the Hialeah Masonic Lodge on Bright Drive. I exited his car and could feel the absence of the satchel and the $400,000 already. Driving back to Coral Gables to explain the details of today's events to Major Brunson was not going to be easy. Just two weeks earlier I'd visited Ramon from the rental agency and swapped out a midnight blue 1998 IROC Z28 Camaro that I'd been using for a few months. Ramon always seemed to keep a better car for me on the lot. He exchanged the IROC for what I was now climbing into; a 1999 black Acura RL. The car only had nine miles on it when Ramon handed me the keys. In the past year I'd driven a Ford Explorer, an Infiniti, the IROC, and now it looked like I might be closing 1998 in this roomy sedan.

The ride back to the Coral Gables was a series of stop and go traffic especially around the Miami International Airport area. The clock on the car's dashboard said 4:18 when I pulled into a parking space adjacent to the police station on Palermo Avenue. I parked right in front of Peppy's Restaurant. I grabbed my badge and my credentials. The four-story police and fire station was on Salzedo Street, sandwiched between Sevilla and Palermo Avenues. The building was a short, four block walk away from the bustling business and restaurant district of Miracle Mile. Each time I saw the police building, I was struck by the sheer lunacy and inept architectural design of it. The building was designed sometime in the early seventies and had a glass atrium on the west side that roasted all its inhabitants in the brutal South Florida afternoon sun. The result of this short-sighted design gaffe was the necessity of having an air conditioning system that was so frigid you could hang meat in the building. Every civilian employee wore a pilfered winter jacket from a road patrol officer, and they were constantly being mistaken as officers by the visiting public. The dispatch division had already fried two computer networks in the past two years simply because of ill-informed personnel plugging space heaters into orange designated hi-tech electrical outlets. The four-story building had been designed for a heliport until the poured concrete roof was deemed too weak to hold a helicopter. I think the strongest aspect of the building was the time capsule they buried in the concrete near the front door in 1976.

I used the staircase on the corner of the building. Many would call it an external staircase but since it was encased in a circular neo-modern funnel of cracking cement and flecking paint, I just considered it an external staircase. Requisite definition be dammed. I came out of the staircase and walked through the parking garage towards the north entrance of the third floor. The garage rumbled and shook slightly as a pick-up truck was coming down from the fourth floor. The driver was trying to maneuver the heavy truck through the narrow tight ramps of the dilapidated building. Although Coral Gables liked to call itself "The City Beautiful," there was absolutely nothing beautiful about this municipal building. Early in my police career the Human Resources director asked me if I wanted to lateral to the fire department. The idea of sleeping in and being inside this sickly building for twenty-four hours at a time was a deal breaker. Being in VIN afforded me the benefit of not needing to be in the building unless absolutely necessary.

Today a DEA agent was shot, we lost $400,000, and twenty kilograms of cocaine. This was an absolute necessary moment.

I used my credentials to card-swipe my way into the building. The third floor was unsettlingly quiet. Surely some semblance of what happened in Hialeah had been leaked out to everyone. Once the clock struck 4pm I could just imagine the exodus for the exits.

Outside of Major Brunson's office in the hallway was a dented waste basket laying on its side. I kept walking and approached the VIN office. There were only two people in the office on a full-time basis. Our VIN secretary, Ileana Portillo, was a Cuban American twice divorced, single mother of two, who worked in the center office, and it was she that visitors always saw first. Her obliteration of the English language and her penchant for watching Spanish language *telenovelas* was what most people knew about her. The second person was Gary Fowler, our in-house financial administrator. Gary had a surfer mentality and a Finance MBA from Florida International University. He had a blond buzz cut and the straightest whitest teeth I think I've ever seen. He also had a barcode tattoo at the base of the back of his neck and small tattoo of an "F" on his finger. He confided in me that the "F" was meant for the many times he was given an unpleasant task; he would wave his hand briefly. It was a silent "I don't give a flying fuck" moment for him when he did. I always called him "Big G' and it had nothing to do with his size or girth but simply a nickname I heard a guy once call his buddy in an elevator in Chicago.

Before I got to the VIN office door, I could tell the office would be empty. I didn't even look in to see if anyone was inside the VIN office. I knew they hightailed it as soon as they could. I sidestepped the dented trash can in the hallway and stood just outside the office door of Major Brunson. It was actually two offices. The smaller first office was where Charlene Muscanera, his secretary, sat. She was putting on a coat and grabbing her purse when I got there. She motioned with both her hands for me to stay out in the hallway, and she quickened her retreat even more to meet me out there. She got close to me, and in a hushed tone said:

"This is one of the worst I've seen him, and I've been working here a long time. I'm not even going to tell him you're here. Just go on in. He knows I'm leaving. I'm keeping it that way. Good luck."

She made for the exit as if her hair was on fire.

We'd changed to daylight savings time two weeks earlier. The waning light from the western sunset glinted off the double doors as she flung them open and made her way out of the building. I looked back at Major Brunson's office knowing that this was going to be an unpleasant encounter. I gingerly walked into Charlene's office, took a deep breath, and decided to meet the fray head on.

I stepped into Major Brunson's office. He was seated off to the side of his desk looking north out of his window at the afternoon traffic ebbing and flowing in the business district. His chair was pushed close to the large floor-to-ceiling window. The same simmering rays of sunset illuminated the left side of his face. He was motionless. I stood just inside of his doorway. He continued looking out the window. He didn't turn away from the view. He must have heard or sensed me in the office.

"My view used to be little businesses. The Italian restaurants Armando's and Cubby's, Gingiss Formal Wear, the Biscayne Cafeteria. Hell, I used to be able to tell by the outside lighting how busy La Palma's courtyard was. I knew right from sitting here. Right from here. Now look at this place. Towering corporate buildings and high-rise condos. I got DelMonte across the street and the Bacardi headquarters off to the west. My view at night is now fucking neon lit pineapples and bats," he said turning for the first time to look at me.

I stayed where I was, awaiting what he would say next.

"I was wondering when you were going to get here. Sit down, Cade. Anywhere. I don't fucking care what chair," he said.

He still stayed seated in his chair pushed up to the window. The space behind his desk seemed unfamiliar and foreign to me. I'd always seen him behind his desk like some sort of all-knowing village elder who dispersed discipline and profanity with equal ease. It was odd seeing him willfully abdicating the solid sanctuary of his desk. Sitting by the window in the fading light I could see the years and stress were starting to take their toll upon him. The pant leg of his left leg rode up, showing his black boot. The toe was scuffed, no doubt a byproduct of kicking the waste basket I saw in the hallway.

"I want you to look at that paper on the corner of my desk," he said.

There was a sheet of paper face down on his desk. I picked it up. It was the evidence property receipt I'd signed that morning when I checked out the $400,000. I scanned it, noting all the boxes checked and all the signatures on it. He continued looking out the window and hadn't yet even looked at me since I entered his office.

"You see your signature on it?" he asked me.

"Yes," I replied.

"What signature do you see below yours? The last one on the form?"

"Yours," I answered,

"Mine. Yup. Mine," he said as he finally faced me for the first time. "My fucking signature. Right fucking there. My 'I trust Cade so much I'll sign out nearly half a million dollars to him of the city's fucking money' signature. My ass on the line signature so Cade fucking Taylor can go to Hialeah and fucking nearly topple the whole law enforcement god forsaken universe. My phone has been ringing off the hook all day. The city manager is fit to be tied. His precious budget and financial allocations are in disarray. That's what he said: 'disarray.' Who the fuck even uses that word? I got the chief from Hialeah calling me every twenty minutes with more and more information about what a complete abomination today was. Do you have any idea why I have the biggest office in this place?"

"Because you're' the acting chief?" I said softly.

He rolled in his chair away from the window and positioned himself behind his desk.

"Do you know why I've survived this long?"

I just looked at him across the desk.

"It's because I treat this place the same way I treat going to the zoo. I'm just here to watch the monkeys fuck. Do you know that for thirty-one years I've watched the buffoons and baboons come through these doors and have had to deal with all of them? Never have I had a day like today," he said with exasperation. "Tell me about this agent who was shot."

"You mean Lew?"

"Lou? Who's Lou?"

"Lew."

"Like St. Louis?"

"No, like Lewis and Clark," I replied

"Goddamn it Cade, this ain't some vaudeville version of the Abbot and Costello Show, who the fuck is Lew?"

"Agent Scott Lew. The one who was shot. DEA Special Agent Lew."

"Tell me your version of what happened so I can fill in the blanks from what I've already heard."

"I was working with DEA Group Four, and we were going to buy twenty kilos for $400,000—"

"I know all that. Get to the part about Hialeah," he said, his face reddening with rising frustration.

"Agent Lew was the case agent, and I was the U.C. He said he had a new source—"

"Did he say who this source was?"

"No. All he said was the source was 'reputable and comes from a family of reliable information.'"

"Goddamn DEA. Go on," he said.

"Agent Lew pulled in behind the meet and dropped me off. I was supposed to meet a guy Agent Lew said was known as 'the Ecuadorian.' I went inside, and the Ecuadorian was there with some big hulking guy. The shooter was already seated at another table. We started talking and the Ecuadorian had the kilos in a French coffee burlap sack. Next thing I know the big guy takes one in the chest and one in the head. I hit the deck and hear the Ecuadorian take one. The shooter was behind me. I got off two rounds at the shooter and he books it for the door. He runs into Lew coming in and a shot went off. I got to the door and Lew was down. The rest of the takedown team was helping Lew. I chased the shooter across Palm Avenue. He cranked two rounds at me that hit a jitney medical bus thing. We kept running north. He turned and ran onto the racetrack grounds. He bent south towards the paddocks. I was still chasing him when he opened a paddock and shot two more rounds at me. The gunshots made about a dozen horses come charging out and I dove out of the way of the bullets and was delayed up against a porch as the horses were all running towards me. He got away in all of that."

Brunson thought about what I'd told him.

"No one secured the scene? No one secured the evidence? No one saw this Ecuadorian guy leave with the whole kit and caboodle of why we were there in the first fucking place?" he asked me in a rising voice.

Brunson was known for asking questions that he already knew the answers to.

"So, you spoke to someone with knowledge of the scene?" I asked him.

He looked at me like a parlor magician who has had one of his tricks revealed before he could finish it.

"Yeah, I spoke to ASAC Mandeville. Tell me Cade, what did Agent Lew say? Did he say anything else? What was the last thing he said as he dropped you off?"

"Actually, he said we were the good guys and that even in the shit he lets Jesus take the wheel."

"Jesus doesn't need to take the wheel; he needs to pull to the side of the road and smack some of you dumbshits with his flip flop," he said.

I inhaled sharply and looked down at the carpet. I looked back up and noticed the hot sauce on his desk.

Sphincter Shrinker XXX Hot Sauce.

"Well Cade, let me enlighten you. While you were sitting in a gas station looking at cameras, I was burning the phones here. I was on the phone with ASAC Mandeville and her boss SAC John Grayson. He's flying back from a conference in Jacksonville on a DEA plane. We have put an all-points bulletin for Miami and Fort Lauderdale airports for any solo male who buys a ticket at the last minute for any flight from Belize to on down to Macara, Ecuador. Specifically, any flights to Quito or Guayaquil. Every Emergency Room in South Florida has been alerted to notify us if anyone shows up with a gunshot wound. Every hospital with a trauma center has two uniformed officers assigned to them full time until further notice. A message was put on the narcotic wire from here to Pensacola to be on the lookout for a silver 1997 Mercedes-Benz E320 that may be abandoned or parked in one location too long. Conversely, all airport parking garages were also notified to copy and forward the license tag information of any 1997 silver Mercedes-Benz E320's that park in their lots. Every municipality that has a tow contract with a wrecker service has also notified their tow truck drivers to be on the lookout. As we speak, all the evidence gathered so far, and the evidence still being gathered is being catalogued and entered into a separate database to expedite the findings. The only thing I didn't know was the agent's name. Right now, he's in JMH. The DEA admitted him under a false name in case this shooter actually intended for Agent Lew to be his target."

I nodded my head in agreement.

"Cade, SAC Grayson, and I are going to form a task force for this. You're going to be a part of it. Be here at noon tomorrow. We should have people in place by then. In the meantime, go home shower and rest up. You look like hell."

I couldn't disagree with him. I knew the loss of the $400,000 would be a huge hurdle to get past the city manager. Twenty kilos of cocaine buys you nothing and besides we never even had possession of the twenty kilos to lose. But we'd be going to bed tonight $400,000 poorer than when we woke up today. I knew Brunson was hoping we'd recover the $400,000, get the twenty kilos, and find the Ecuadorian and the shooter but the odds of all that happening were slim at best.

It was a day for me that I most certainly did not want to repeat. I kept thinking about Agent Lew and was curious how he was doing. What his condition was, and would he live? Thoughts about today slammed against the inside of my head. I looked at Brunson and rose from my seat.

"Remember, be back here at noon," he said as a way of goodbye.

Everything he'd done and said I couldn't find any fault with. I made my way for the exit and was out of his office in just a few steps. I needed to be. I needed to go. I needed to start looking for the Ecuadorian.

Chapter Six

I WENT STRAIGHT DOWN to the VIN office and behind Gary's desk just under some telephone books was a strong box. It was where we kept petty cash for VIN incidentals, usually about $3000 was inside. We used the cash for last minute expenses. I withdrew $450 from the box. I scribbled a note to Gary and threw the note in the box. I tucked the cash into the front of my pants pocket. I went to Ileana's desk and picked up her office telephone. I dialed 305-888-8888—the telephone number boldly written across every yellow taxi in Miami. I told the dispatcher my car was broken down in front of Joe Peppy's restaurant on Palermo Avenue and I needed to go to the airport.

Hurriedly, I went out the same way I came in. The taxi would be arriving in less than five minutes. I used the same decrepit staircase to go down to the street level. On the way down I predialed the taxi company and had my cell phone ready to hit send. I stood by my car and waited. It was only about a minute when I saw a taxi approaching me as it rounded Fred Hartnett Park on Ponce DeLeon Boulevard. I hit send and the dispatcher picked up again just as the taxi was pulling up. I told her my name was Scott Lew. I told her to cancel the taxi but to know that the driver she dispatched would be calling her with a message. She was a bit confused, and I told her to wait to hear from her driver on Palermo Avenue in Coral Gables. Yellow taxi number 2951 pulled up next to me. I hung up the phone and motioned to the driver to roll down his window.

"What's your name?" I asked him.

"Eusebio Fortunato," he said.

"Eusebio Fortunato? Eusebio Fortunate? Well, I hope you are fortunate. I'm Scott Lew," I said holding my gold police badge out where he could clearly see it. "Your dispatcher is going to cancel this fare."

Just as I said those words, the dispatcher canceled the fare.

"Sir, I'm just a taxi driver I haven't done anything wrong, I—"

"Relax, Eusebio. I want you to write down what I'm about to tell you," I said. "I'm looking for a silver 1997 Mercedes-Benz E320. There might be some blood inside of it. I don't have the license plate number. Here's fifty dollars. This is for you," I said holding up the fifty-dollar bill in my hand. I continued, "On your alternate channel tell your dispatcher I have a hundred dollars for her. The dispatcher will need to put it out on the radio every hour for the next two days. We are looking for this car. If any of your taxi coworkers see a silver 1997 Mercedes-Benz E320 parked oddly, out of place, or ditched they are to call her or you. I'm going to give you my number. Whoever finds this car gets 200 dollars and you get an extra hundred. You understand? 200 to find it, a hundred for her and 150 for you for notifying me."

"*Si claro,* I mean yes I do, officer," he said.

"Okay. Contact her on the radio and the fifty is yours."

Eusebio picked up the console microphone and spoke to the dispatcher asking her to transfer to an alternate channel. He relayed the message exactly as he was instructed. He switched back to the main channel. He turned the volume on the radio to its highest level so I could hear from outside the taxi

"*Drivers. Drivers stand by for a message. Driver 2951 is with the Coral Gables Police. They are searching for a silver 1997 Mercedes-Benz E320. The Mercedes may have blood on the interior. If any driver discovers a silver 1997 Mercedes-Benz E320 parked in an out of the* *way place or abandoned notify this operator or driver 2951. There is a $200 cash reward for the recovery of this vehicle."*

I gave Eusebio the fifty dollar bill and my cell phone number. I instructed him that only he or the dispatcher were to contact me, and I reminded him if the car was located, he'd get an additional hundred dollars.

"What if I find it?" he asked with a broad smile.

"Then she gets her hundred and you get all the rest," I said.

As he drove off into the sunset, he waved out the car window. I'd told Eusebio my name was Scott Lew so that if anyone called my number I could tell immediately if they were calling about the Mercedes-Benz.

There are sixty-two police departments in Miami Dade County. Miami Dade County is the largest agency but some of these other smaller police departments have only nine or ten full time officers. Weighing the chance of one of those police officers discovering the Ecuadorian's Mercedes-Benz in addition to their normal course of duties, attention span, and the timeliness of information being delivered to them through roll calls was a low percentage play. I thought it was better to amass my own personal search party.

In Miami the yellow taxis are too numerous to count, and they're in motion twenty-four hours a day throughout all parts of the county. For fifty bucks I just purchased the biggest set of searchers I could possibly get, they were all notified at the same time and would be continually notified every hour on the hour. If one of them found the Mercedes-Benz, the additional $400 is well worth it.

From the sidewalk, I could see through the gauzy window draping the table settings for Joe Peppy's. I'm sure Joe and Sue Pappagallo were inside creating great Italian dishes for tonight's dinner crowd. As nice as it looked and as delicious as the wafting aromas filled the air were, I looked down at my sweat-stained shirt and dirty pants and opted to stay out of the restaurant.

I looked to the east. I knew just past the Arthur Murray Dance Studio was Christy's, one of Coral Gables' finest restaurants. I also knew they often gave large T-bone steak bones out the back kitchen door to our K-9 units. That was a bonus in my decision to patronize them. I could order their signature Caesar salad and French bread to go.

Some of the patrons waiting outside Christy's to be seated had spilled out of the restaurant's hostess area. They were milling about just outside the front door. It was a common occurrence. Wooden benches were provided for the overflow throng. Many of them had complimentary stem glasses of Chardonnay. I eased past the well-heeled assembly of people and stepped through the ornate wooden doors into the hostess area. As I went in, I could hear a few murmurs from the sidewalk crowd. One woman in a blue blouse quite audibly voiced to her companions her concerns about "the rising homelessness in Coral Gables."

The restaurant is very dark and adorned with deep mahogany wood vying with French red wallpaper to dominate the masculine décor of the long-established restaurant. The hostess was well trained in disguising her ambivalence to my appearance. I quickly ordered a Caesar salad with French bread to go. I paid with my credit card and told her I'd wait outside. She said it would be ready in twenty minutes.

Regardless of what you order or where you order in Miami it's always twenty minutes.

I stepped out into the dusk as the sun was now officially set. Personally, I'd given up on AM and PM a long time ago. As far as I was concerned it was either "coffee time" or "whiskey time." I decided to wait across the street at the empty municipal courthouse. I turned to the woman in the blue blouse holding her Chardonnay.

"The oakiness of the robust reds like Cabernet Sauvignon, although desired by many in the northeast, tends to wilt on the palate here in the warm days of Florida," I said to her as I kept walking.

I crossed Ponce De Leon Boulevard and sat on a bus bench directly across from the restaurant. Behind me was the short, concrete textured wall that enclosed the parking lot of the courthouse. I thought about a lot of things in those twenty minutes. I thought about Agent Lew, the predicament that Major Brunson was in, and I was mentally bombarding myself about what my role and purpose in all these events were. I could see the clean well-dressed clientele of the restaurant enjoying the prewinter balmy night air as they awaited the great food and service ahead of them. They seemed like the type of people who sit at restaurant tables and don't dive under them to evade bullets.

My life was in disarray. Yeah, I am one of those people that does use that word. Distressed, disastrous, detached, disenfranchised, and disillusioned; take your pick or circle that last bubble where it says all apply. Aside from my marriage flaming out in the most eviscerating way, the lifestyle of a VIN detective in Miami was challenging my sanity with each and every passing week. The ungodly hours and stress were killers by themselves, but in tandem with gun-toting drug dealers, money launderers, and gun runners it was surely an escalation to an early demise. The fact that there is a highway to Hell and a stairway to Heaven says a lot about anticipated traffic numbers.

The tree-shaded median was alive with engaged couples milling about with their full wine glasses. My life was nowhere near so carefree. To them I looked like a marginalized guy who society had left off the success train. Little did they know I was carrying $400,000 in cash earlier in the day and was now hell-bent on getting it back. The homeless population may be growing in Coral Gables. I don't know, but I'm not one of them—at least not yet. If there was a category for the displaced, well then yes, that would be another word beginning with "D" that would apply to me as well. I was definitely displaced both in body and mind.

Nine months ago, I was married and living in a quiet suburban house in southwest Miami Dade County. I'd thought I was recovering from the revelation that my wife, Gina, was having an affair with the landlord she rented an artist studio from. Gina was now living with him in northern Palm Beach Gardens, blissfully unaware of the carnage of my life.

The sense of failure that followed in the wake of my divorce was deeper than any swells that laid in front of me. I now know why storms are named after people. The divorce was a long, drawn-out barrage of legal filings and motions for discovery. I was actively still looking for a place to live. A doctor friend I'd met through a contact at the Miami Dade Medical Examiner's office had purchased a condominium in Paradise Point for his mother a few months ago. She was in the Dominican Republic. The day before his mother was to move to Miami, she broke her hip, and she was in daily physical therapy in the Dominican Republic for a few months trying to regain her autonomy. The doctor kindly offered me the unused, furnished condominium in Paradise Point until she was healthy enough to move. It was transitional but ideal for me where I was, and I leaped at the opportunity. I saw it as a good way to park myself while I tried to figure what it was, I intended to do with myself. The condominium is way down south in the county off Coral Reef Drive and Ludlum Road.

So homeless? No. Displaced? Yes.

To the diners waiting for their names to be called I must have looked like a guy looking for a handout. My pants had grass and dirt stains along the knees and hip from dodging bullets and stampeding horses. My shirt was dingy under my jacket. It had been twenty minutes since I had put in the order. I walked back across the boulevard and although the exact clientele outside had changed, the attitude and murmurs were sadly very similar. The hostess was delighted to see me, not so much because she liked me, but I would venture to say that the sooner she handed me my order the sooner I would leave the restaurant. I gathered my order and with my head lowered and avoiding eye contact, I left the restaurant. I ate the salad sitting on the bus bench. The salad was delicious, and I devoured it quickly. The city was becoming quiet. Commuters and workers were gone, and the big restaurant district was a few blocks north on Miracle Mile and Giralda Avenue. There's always a garbage can near a bus bench. Mass transit would prefer you leave your trash off their buses. I put the empty salad and bread containers in the trash and walked back to my car, replaying the events of the day in my head. I got in my car and listened to the car's newness call out to me. Little chimes and illuminated icons came to life with the turn of the key. I remembered what the Ecuadorian had said to me when he saw me approaching his table.

"Bienvenido, bienvenido, por favor siéntate. Los camarones al ajillo aquí es increíble, tienes que probarlo!"

[Welcome, welcome, please sit down. The garlic shrimp here is amazing, you have to try it!]

My mind started to click.

The Ecuadorian knew the restaurant. He had been there before. How else would he have known about the garlic shrimp? He was a Central Dade or North Dade guy. If we were going to find him or the Mercedes-Benz it would be somewhere north of Miami International Airport.

This was a monumental assumption but if I was correct, it would be a big swing in how we deploy resources. Miami Dade County is larger in size and population than the state of Rhode Island. That would be a large swath of geography eliminated. At the noon briefing I would let Major Brunson know of my theory.

I headed south on Ponce De Leon Boulevard. I turned east on Bird Road and took the heavily traveled road across U.S.-1 and continued through the center of Coconut Grove to Southwest 27th Avenue. I turned south and within a few blocks pulled into one of the small parking spaces in front of the Tiger Tail Lounge. My tires came to a halt on the parking lot's crushed pea gravel. The front façade of the entire lounge was cut flat coral rocks with wide and nonsensical concrete grout lines. It was as though the stone mason set the stones by what he picked up from the pile of rocks rather than any organized construction plan. The windows in the front of the drinking oasis were completely encased in shiplap boards all nailed tightly and close to each other. The boards framed the windows like big boxes. The wooden planks were so dense that once you were inside the lounge you'd never know if it was nighttime or streaming sunlight outside. To enhance the garish motif even more, the boards were painted in a muted cantaloupe color. Above the single hung door to the lounge was a generic but brightly lit sign. In a burnt orange cursive font at the top was "Tiger Tail Cocktail Lounge Liquor & Live Music." Although the street that angled right across Southwest 27th Avenue was called Tigertail Avenue, either by design or careless spelling the lounge was called "The Tiger Tail Lounge." The Tiger Tail Lounge was a serious dive bar. It was blocks away from the glitzy overpriced drinks, pretensions, and cover charges of the bars near the Shops of Mayfair on Virginia Street.

Former professional boxer Bobby Dykes opened the Tiger Tail Lounge in the 1960s as a place for him and his buddies to have a place to drink and socialize. The bar had gone through slow migrations through the years. Those changes were almost negligible to the untrained eye. The lack of aesthetic upgrades and an *if ain't broke don't fix it* mentality will do that. The bar remained the same, but the clientele had changed over the years. It had gone from a blue-collar sportsman's club where boxing matches were telecast on a small black and white TV over the bar, to a place where cocaine cowboys seeking a tucked-away spot away from the Mutiny Hotel and Regine's nightclub would finalize plans, debts, and death contracts. Currently it was doing double duty as a place for locals to get an inexpensive drink and a place for down on their luck shrimpers and fishermen to drown their poor career choices in frosted schooners of beer. There was always cold beer, usually a good band on the weekends, and a pool table that had just the right ripples in the felt to help a novice compete with a pool shark. Off to the side leaning against a palm tree, there was a rusty bicycle with a plastic milk crate wired to the handlebars. Mine was the only car in front of the lounge.

I got a glimpse of myself in the rearview mirror. Upon seeing my reflection, I got a sense of why the woman in the blue blouse made the remark she did. I went to the rear of the car and opened the trunk. I always keep a "go bag" ready with a change of clothes and toiletries. It's called a go bag because when it all falls apart, I can just get in the car and go. From the bag I pulled out a dark blue Hartford Whalers baseball hat. Although recently no longer a National Hockey League

(NHL) franchise, I still held out hope they'd be reconstituted. I put on the hat and tucked my shoulder length hair back under it. I went inside.

The place was dark and dank inside. My grass-stained pants and sweat-stained shirt fit right in. I was glad I had my jacket on because the continual darkness and cranking air conditioners made the place downright chilly. The lack of clientele and body heat also made it seem coldly deserted. An old man with longish white hair and beard was in the corner of the bar looking transfixed, deep into his beer. He wore a light green shirt. He was deeply tanned from probably spending his days outside. He looked like he could be Ernest Hemmingway's thinner, unkept, malnourished brother. I figured him to be the bike owner.

The bartender introduced herself as Betty Mae. Although beer was more than likely the drink of choice, I asked for a Jameson Irish Whiskey, neat. She had a nice pour and leveled the wonderful Irish whiskey to the brim of a shot glass with the Cutty Sark logo on it. I didn't concern myself with the irony of drinking from a different brand whiskey glass. I motioned to her to stay near with the bottle. I decided to just depth charge the first one hard and fast. I threw my head back and the Jameson shot went down smooth and warm in one quick swig. Unlike a typical college frat boy, I didn't slam the empty glass on the bar. I asked her to refill the glass and this next one I intended to savor slowly. She wasn't very interested in talking and I wasn't interested in talking to her or to the old guy at the bar. We had a little triangle of silence as he drank his beer, she tended bar, and I sipped the Jameson. There wasn't a band on this Wednesday night, and the jukebox was playing Concrete Blonde's *Joey.*

The warmth of the first shot was making me comfortable and a little pensive. The past nine months had been a lesson in personal upheaval and my own constitutional reunification of myself. Nearly everything that I'd once identified myself as being was either gone or eroding. I thought I was a pretty good husband. The divorce papers said an entirely different story. I thought I was a pretty good detective. Today said an entirely different story. I think the most difficult person to leave is the person you used to be. I was a long way from where I thought I was to where I really was. My life was organized chaos.

The door to the bar opened and I caught a glimpse of myself in the mirror behind the bar. My goatee was hardly noticeable in the low light. The only thing I could really see was the Hartford Whalers logo on my hat and my eyes under the brim. Two large guys walked in. I could see that one of them was wearing shrimper boots. They smelled of fish and diesel gasoline. They were loud, rambunctious, rude, and already inebriated. One of them went to the pool table near the empty stage and pumped a few quarters into it. A low rumble ensued as the billiard balls were released from their bracket. The fisherman started setting the table up for a game while the one in the shrimper boats leaned on the bar and ordered beers for the two of them.

Betty Mae set up two cold Miller Lites on the bar. He grabbed the beers with his grungy hands and told her to start a tab. Before the first pool game ended, they were into a third round of beers. At one point one of the men had the other in a headlock and jokingly said he was "a pussy." Their behavior was becoming increasingly more intolerable. Their language was foul, and they became more and more aggressive as they drank. The old man at the end of the bar had his hand wrapped around his beer. His head was slightly tossed back, and he seemed to be in a deep stupor with his eyes closed. The same fisherman in shrimper boots came to the bar and attempted to order another round of beers. Although nearly the only people in the bar, Betty Mae surmised the situation and cut him off. He slammed his hand down hard on the bar.

"Goddamn it 'Betty Mae I blow you' two more beers now!" he railed at her.

"It's Betty Mae. Period," she said tersely.

It was at this point that I asked Betty Mae for a third pour of Jameson. She looked at him sideways and stepped closer towards me and started to pour.

The shrimper became more volatile. "Oh, you serve this dickwad, but you won't serve us. What kind of shit is that?" he blurted at her.

"You're drunk, Danny James, and so is your brother. You know the house rules."

I just stared straight ahead sipping my fresh drink. It was apparent that these two were regulars and that there'd been some sort of admonishment about house rules laid out to them at least once before.

"Hey asshole," he said in my direction.

To answer would mean I'd inadvertently acknowledged that I was an asshole, and besides—I was just getting used to be referred to as a dickwad.

"Hey! I'm talking to you, asshole. You deaf or something?"

I turned in my low back bar stool to face him. Danny James was leaning on the bar and encroaching very close to me. There was spittle in his unkept beard. The other one that Betty Mae referred to as his brother was just off his right shoulder. Reaching around his brother in front of him he held the pool cue like a jousting pole. He literally put the tip of the pool cue on my left shoulder, leaving a smudgy blue chalk spot on my jacket. I could feel my Glock pressing against my back in the barstool. I could also just imagine Lieutenant Maddalone making a second trip out to retrieve my replacement Glock on the same day. I think even for me that would be a personal new best. As Danny James's brother put the pool cue on me, I could hear Maddalone's words from today in my ear.

"Haven't we done these enough times with you, Taylor? There are others on the firearm discharge list, but I think you're definitely at the top of it."

"So, your name is Danny James. I'm glad we got to meet like this instead of a few days from now at your brother's funeral," I said to him.

"Listen dickhead, I'm not interested in knowing who you are. You're aggravating me just by being in our bar. You don't belong here. We run this place and Betty Mae is just putting on a show for you. Hell, we get served till we say stop. Not her. There are two of us and one of you. You threatening my brother? Blood is thicker than water, asswipe."

With that comment he lifted his shirt. As he pulled out a Bic lighter from his pants pocket, he revealed a large fishing knife in a sheath on his belt. He pulled out a crumbled pack of Pall Mall cigarettes, lit one, and blew the bluish smoke in my face.

"Danny James, you know we trying to make this place better. You know smoking is for outside," Said Betty Mae.

"Well, pardon me," he said looking me directly in the eye as he put his cigarette out in my Jameson shot.

I said, "I think I've been sitting here long enough. I'm not going to anger Betty Mae. I'll go outside and light a smoke." I gingerly moved sideways away from Danny James and out of reach of the pool cue held by his brother.

Betty Mae watched me get up to leave with pleading eyes. In the low light I kept my eye on them in the mirror's reflection and by using the images of them cast by the glassware on top of the bar.

"That's right, pussy. Get the fuck out before we fuck you up. Get going, you loser piece of shit before I change my mind!" called Danny James to me as I left.

The door slammed shut behind me and even in the night air of Coconut Grove there was more visible light outside than there was inside the dark Tiger Tail Lounge. A few spaces from my car was an older white pickup truck with dents and auto repair bondo smudges all along the side in little haphazard swirls and splotches. The windows were down. I figured the truck belonged to Danny James and his imbecile brother. I went to my car and retrieved three roadside emergency stick flares from the trunk. I walked to the pickup truck. I unscrewed the gas cap and threw the cap in the debris-filled bed of the truck, and struck the flint on the top of one of the two-foot-long flares. The flare filled with strontium nitrate, potassium nitrate, potassium perchlorate mixed with charcoal, sulfur, sawdust, aluminum, and magnesium burst into a white-hot two-inch flame that cast me and the entire front of the Tiger Tail Lounge in a red pinkish light. I stuck the back end of the flare into the gas tank. It jutted out from the truck in a slanted angle, burning down towards the truck. The next two flares ignited immediately.

"I'll go outside and light a smoke."

It's not like I didn't warn them.

I strode back into the lounge, holding both flares. The brothers had their backs to me.

I think they saw the bar alight in the wide arc of illumination before they heard the sizzle and the acidic scent of burning chemicals hit their senses. I walked briskly at them, holding the burning flares straight out in front of me, my eyes locked on both brothers. Betty Mae let out a shriek of surprise. I have no idea if the old man in the corner even stirred from his stupor. I could see in the smokey pink light that Danny James' eyes were wide with disbelief and fear. He reached for his knife.

"Don't. Don't even think about it," I said to him as I jabbed the burning tip into his brother's shoulder. His brother shrieked in pain and stumbled backward, tripping on the pool cue he'd placed against the pool table. He landed on his back. A scarlet burn on his shoulder glared through his seared t shirt. I moved quickly and put one foot on his chest and held one flare down a few inches from his groin. I kept the other flare pointed at Danny James.

"Don't be jabbing people with sticks. You just might get jabbed back. One move out of you, or your shithead brother and I'll stub this fucker right into your balls," I yelled at him.

He did move just enough to squirm under me to open his legs as the hot ashes and flame droplets began to cascade down inches from the crouch of his ratty jeans.

"Okay, tough guy," I growled at Danny James. "You have a choice. Try and be a badass and do something bold and brave which I highly doubt you have the balls to do, or try and save your truck. I had three flares. The third one is burning down into your gas tank right now. I figure you got about two minutes before we all start begging Betty

Mae to show us where the back door is. You take one step in my direction and your brother will get the first ever vasectomy here in the Tiger Tail Lounge."

"Let my brother up." he said

"Truck's gonna burn," I said

"Let him up Goddamn it!" he yelled.

"Betty Mae you might want to move towards the back," I said.

"I'm telling you—"

"No, I'm telling you. Get the fuck out now and your brother here will be right behind you. Both of you nitwits get in that fucking thing you call a truck and get the hell out of here NOW!"

The old man was now leaving. As he opened the front door he yelled out, "Holy shit!"

Danny James heard that. He glanced at his brother on the ground and then at me. He started running for the front door. I took my foot of Danny James's brother and he scrambled to his feet, rubbing his shoulder.

"You. Move. Now," I commanded him.

He meekly staggered, arm across his chest, holding his shoulder. I marched him out of the bar holding both burning flares a few inches beyond his back.

"What's your name, asshole?" I asked him.

"Donny," he said softly

"Danny and Donny James. Jeez, your parents weren't big spellers, were they?"

I was directly behind Donny James as we stepped out into the parking lot. Danny had removed the third flare from his gas tank and thrown it down. It was on the ground, still burning. It was only about seven inches long now. I told Danny to get in the truck's driver seat. Donny quickly ran around the truck to get in the passenger side.

"I can't find my gas cap," Danny protested.

"I'm sure It'll tun up," I said.

I was down to one flare, and I held it near the opening of their gas tank.

"Start er' up and get going before I drop this in your tank," I said.

The truck showed signs of a faulty alternator but did spark enough to sputter and start up. He quickly put it in reverse, more so to get away from the flare than out of fear of me. He yanked the wheel and steered the truck away and south on Southwest 27th Avenue. He was missing one taillight. I watched until it faded from view then went back into the lounge.

"Can I get a refill on that Jameson please?" I asked Betty Mae as I slid into my exact same bar stool.

With a trembling hand she poured me a shot of Jameson.

"Obviously this is on the house. Mister, I don't know who you are, but you are some kind of crazy," she said as she poured the whiskey.

This time she didn't retreat to her corner of the bar. She lingered across from me, sizing me up. Her previous look of indifference was replaced by a look of willful acceptance and friendliness.

"Tell ya the truth, crazy can be sexy, and I kind of like crazy," she said, smiling at me.

I took a slow pull on the Jameson.

"I don't think you'd like *my* kind of crazy," I said.

Chapter Seven

I FINISHED THE DRINK rather quickly. The drive home was uneventful, and I soon was turning onto Coral Reef Drive. The short drive to the complex entrance is a South Florida horticulturist's dream. The narrow lane is bracketed on both sides with soft pink, luscious fuchsia, fiery orange, scarlet bougainvillea, fragrant frangipani, as well as billowing sea grape and mangrove trees. The official title of the gated community is Royal Harbour Yacht Club, but everyone knows it as Paradise Point. The guard at the gate was familiar with my odd comings and goings. He barely looked up as I used the remote attached on the passenger visor to open the gate. Midway down the stretch of road I pulled into my temporary dwelling: 6211 Paradise Point Drive. The community is essentially high-end row houses, each adjacent to the next by a shared external wall. Each residence has surprising depth, and each unit is, at a minimum, two stories high. Most, including my unit, have a third level used as an outdoor deck, from which manatees and dolphins are often seen swimming in the narrow channel that leads out to Biscayne Bay. My unit is on the south side of the lane. The view is an unobstructed spectacular vista of trees, mangroves, and Biscayne Bay looking south towards Boca Chita Key, Elliott Key, Chicken Key, and the rest of Biscayne National Park.

I parked in the courtyard driveway. I never park in the garage—it slows me down. The garage was under the entrance staircase and had a large oval kelly-green wooden door. My headlights illuminated the thick, climbing fig that covered nearly the entire arched exterior staircase. The unit is furnished very tastefully: oversized, comfortable couches and polished wood built-in shelves. There are some pre-Colombian art pieces; a few tastefully sized, imitation Botero pieces; paintings from Sebastian Spreng, Alberto Pancorbo, and Connie Lloveras hung on the walls. Even an imitation Wilfredo Lamb lithograph.. I only know this because the doctor left a folder denoting the various art pieces.

As soon as I was inside I wanted another pour of Jameson, but I really needed a shower. I grabbed the bottle from the top of the condo bar and decided to forestall neither—I'd drink in the shower. A veteran of one too many broken glasses in the shower, I knew to pour the Jameson into a plastic cup. The shower's spacious, and a testament to fine Italian marble and expert craftsmanship. The dual showerheads rained hot water down upon me, instantly revitalizing me. Away from the shower spray, I put the cup of Jameson on the interior shelf. After washing, I just let the water run down me, sitting in the shower on the tiled bench, savoring the whiskey.

Drinking alone can be a sign of a problem. Drinking in the shower can be sign of an even bigger problem.

I felt tore up from the floor up. This life I was leading was not intended to be lived this way. In the police academy they teach you the elements of a burglary, how to conduct a traffic stop, and how to write a traffic report. No one teaches you how to be a drug dealer or a money launderer. This world I lived in was predicated by the unconventional and the unlawful. The nefarious and untrustable. The ruthless and the conniving. I lived in a world of absolutes. There was no, "I'll have the sales report by Tuesday," or "the roofing shingles you chose are backordered." This universe was one of definite certainty. It's all about absolutes. Do you absolutely have the cocaine? Do you absolutely have the money? There is no forgiven aspect in this world.

Another absolute that I have always known. *Practically no one in my police department has any idea what it is exactly that I do.* Most of the police department have never seen me. I'm a ghost to them. A person they may have heard of or whose name is on a sheet of paper. I exist because they've been told I exist. I don't interact with many of them and the ones I do see all eye me suspiciously. It's the curse of the misunderstood and mislabeled. There's reluctant acceptance.

The liquor doesn't ask questions. It doesn't ask me how we lost $400,000. It doesn't ask me how Agent Lew got shot. It doesn't demand that I be somewhere at twelve noon. The liquor balances the imbalances. It comforts and understands. It rationalizes my brain and makes living in a world of absolutes seem normal. At least that is how I managed the delusional rhetoric in my head. I convinced myself that I was alone. I also convinced myself that I *needed* to be alone.

After the shower I laid down on the bed in the master bedroom. The moon cast a soft glow on the terrace outside. I watched it for a few minutes as if the scenery would change. It didn't. The bed covers and soft sheets felt good pulled up to my chin. For the first time all day I finally felt relieved and safe.

THE NIGHT CONTINUED, this time without me. My cell phone awoke me at 8:15am. Groggily, I reached for the phone on my nightstand. It was the VIN office.

"Hello," I croaked.

"Cade...eh *buenos dias*...Major *Broonsone* says to me to say to *ju* that the meeting is *reprogramado* for four o'clock today."

It was Ileana Portillo, our VIN secretary. She always spoke in a wild and divergent Spanish-English inflection we in Miami called "Spanglish." She also could never properly pronounce Major Brunson's name.

"Reprogramado?"

"*Ju* know like *eh* reset."

"Oh okay, did he say why they're rescheduling the meeting?" I asked her.

"*Yo no say es suthing* about someone in *Washintoone*," she said.

"Thank you, Ileana."

"Okay then *ju* have been told," she said as she hung up on me.

I hung up the phone, quietly loathing myself for not setting my cell phone to ring silently. I could have retrieved the message after I woke up properly. Now I lay there in bed, hungover. I tried to adjust my eyes to the morning light coming in from the terrace doors. I realized it would take more than just waking up to get me moving. I turned over slowly in bed and groaned at the soreness in my body from yesterday's running and rolling around in Hialeah.

Creakily I moved towards the shower. It didn't take long for the water to heat up. I tended to not only drink in the shower but also lay down under the shower heads and sleep on the tiled floor. I knew I needed to get going. Like a lobster being lowered into a pot I stepped cautiously into the shower. My whole body ached. The adrenaline and Jameson had worn off from yesterday, but the shower woke me up just as it had put me to sleep the night before. Within minutes I was driving away from the complex.

I went to Casa Larios in South Miami. The angled parking was filled, and I parked in the Winn Dixie supermarket parking lot across the street. I slipped the parking lot security guard a few dollars and a promise of *jamon croquettes* when I returned.

The restaurant's large oval bar had every type of bottle perched upon a center island. The multicolored liquors and bottles caught the morning light, casting rainbow shadows across the ceiling. Towards the back of the restaurant there's a small stage, as well as an impressive large map of Cuba set in wall tiles behind it.

I ordered a *café con leche* coffee and the breakfast special of scrambled eggs mixed with ham. It came with beautifully toasted, starchy Cuban toast. My shaking off of the hangover was made easier because the coffee was steamy and delicious, as was the breakfast. I put in an order of croquettes and a Colada of Cuban coffee to go. I provided the parking lot security guard with a white bag with the croquettes. We partook in a portion of the Colada in miniature ribbed plastic cups.

As soon as I got in my car and started the engine, my cell phone started ringing. I didn't recognize the number.

In the VIN world we don't have the luxury of ignoring calls from numbers we don't recognize. Any of these calls could be from burner phones, or informants and dopers who have switched numbers. I answered the call with a brusque greeting.

"Uh, hello? Is this officer Lew?" asked the voice on the line.

"I'm sorry? What?" I asked.

"Officer Lew, is this you? This is Eusebio from the cab company."

"Oh yes. Yes, it's me. Eusebio, how are you? Tell me you have good news," I said.

"Officer Lew, I think one of our guys found the Mercedes. He said he saw a Mercedes and it looks like it has blood inside. It's parked out of place, like you said."

"Okay. Okay. Excellent, where is it?" I asked with anticipation.

"He was on Bay Harbor Islands. He saw it an hour ago on West Bay Harbor Drive off 97th. He stopped the cab and got out and when he looked inside he saw blood on the seats and steering wheel," Eusebio said, his voice rising with delayed panic.

"Okay. Great. I'm kind of far away, it'll take me about forty-five minutes to get there. Tell him to continue working and see if he can meet me there in about an hour."

"He went off shift but I'm coming on. I can see you there," he said.

"Good. If it's the car we're looking for, I'll hook you all up," I said and hung up.

I took off towards West Bay Harbor Drive. I wasn't sure where it was located but I knew it was in the town of Bay Harbor Islands. The entire municipality is two small separate man-made islands and half of the Broad Causeway. I drove thinking to myself, who would I need to notify if in fact the cabbie found the Ecuadorian's car? I didn't want to put the calls out until I saw it for myself, and we could form an action plan.

I exited at Northwest 125th Street and got stuck at nearly every red light. It was the slowest part of my drive up to Bay Harbor Islands, and I was getting impatient. I finally made it to the Broad Causeway spanning across Biscayne Bay. I passed what should be considered one of the nation's most scenic gas stations. The Chevron station in the middle of the Broad Causeway has a 360-degree view of the blue aquamarine waters of the bay. Upon crossing onto the first island the Broad Causeway turns into the Kane Concourse. As I approached the commercial center of the town, West Bay Harbor Drive was clearly marked, and I turned north.

The Mercedes-Benz all but screamed to me on my right.

I kept driving past it and parked a block away. I found an ideal parking spot in front of 9761 West Bay Harbor Drive.

I walked back towards the Mercedes-Benz as casually as I could. I put on the Hartford Whalers hat and pulled it down on my head to try and hide my face in case the Ecuadorian was watching the car from a nearby lofty condo balcony. I kept my eyes on the neighboring townhouses and condominiums, scanning for the Ecuadorian.

The Mercedes was parked partially on the designated green painted bike path, very close to a fire hydrant. This was good news as it would provide the nexus needed to have the car towed away if we chose to do so.

I passed the car again. Although silver is a common color for a Mercedes it most certainly looked to be the same car from Hialeah. There was an almost continual openness of green space from 97th Street to the Kane Concourse. The green parks were bisected by a paved service alley that runs parallel to the Kane Concourse. It stops directly in front of the Bay Harbor Islands Police Department two blocks away.

I stayed in the grassy open park for a few minutes, studying the car from a distance all the while looking for any sign of the Ecuadorian. I walked back to my car, passing the Mercedes as I did. This time I walked on the street side so I could investigate the interior easier. I didn't linger too much, but I was there long enough to see obvious blood on the seats and steering wheel. It was exactly the way the cabbie reported it. The Florida license tag was DCH-328. I walked back to my car and sat inside. I adjusted my rearview mirror so that I could see the Mercedes. I kept watching the car when I called the communications center at the Coral Gables Police Department.

"Coral Gables Police and Fire, Operator J.R. Richards, how can I direct your call?"

"Jeanie Rae, this is Cade Taylor."

"Cade, please tell me you aren't in the middle of something again."

"No, Jeanie Rae, I need you to transfer me to teletype please."

"We're super short here so I'm doing both. What do you need?"

"Can you run a tag for me?"

"What's the tag and what's your number?"

"VIN 923, and the tag is a Florida tag DCH 328. Delta Charlie Hotel three two eight," I said, eyes still on the car.

There was a minute of silence as I waited on the line. She informed me that the tag was not on file with the DMV in Florida. I told her I would call back with a vehicle identification number for her to cross reference, thanked her and hung up. My next call was to ASAC Mandeville. She answered on the second ring.

"Mandeville."

"ASAC Mandeville this is Cade Taylor from the Gables. I think we found the Mercedes. It's parked in the 9700 block of West Bay Harbor Drive in Bay Harbor Islands."

"So, it's unoccupied?"

"Yeah, I'm down the road watching the car. It's got a Florida tag 'DCH 238' but my people say it's not on file," I said.

"By yourself? Sit tight. We have an SOG unit in the north part of Dade. I'll activate them and get you some more eyes on the Mercedes. I'll start Marroquín in your direction. Are you going to be at the briefing at four o clock?' she asked me.

"I'm scheduled to be there. How's Agent Lew?"

"SAC Grayson pivoted when he came in from Jacksonville. He went to the hospital to see him. Agent Lew is still in a medically induced coma. They removed a bullet fragment from his head. They have him listed as an improved state, but still in ICU," she said with a sigh.

"Okay. I'm here. I'll be waiting for Agent Marroquín and the SOG's." I said as I hung up.

The SOG unit was an acronym for "Special Operations Group." It sounds very intense and tactical. It's a supplementary unit comprised mostly of retired law enforcement professionals who augment the sworn agents in doing the mundane and less technical work. The big joke was that SOG was an acronym for "Some Old Guys."

After a half hour of watching the Mercedes, I saw a taxi driving slowly towards me on West Bay Harbor Drive. I flashed my lights at him, and he pulled up next to me. We were door to door. I lowered my window. It was Eusebio Fortunato. I handed him the $400.

"I don't want to be rude, but I'm in the middle of something. Thank you, Eusebio. Keep my number, okay?" I said to him.

He gladly took the cash, gave me a thumbs up and a broad smile, then drove away.

Within an hour I started seeing different cars come down the road and find parking. Each car was occupied with a lone driver. The SOG was arriving and setting up. Agent Marroquín drove by and lowered his window. He motioned for me to follow him. He continued south. I U-turned, and followed him to the Kane Concourse. He drove west out of the residential and business section of Bay Harbor Islands, then took the concourse to the Chevron where he parked in the small parking lot behind the gas station. I pulled in a few spaces from him. We both got out of our cars. We shook hands. The traffic was light and the expansive blue waters on either side of us was framed by the rustling coconut palms.

"Cade, how ya doing after yesterday?" he asked.

"I'm okay. I'm more concerned about Scott," I said.

"We all are. They're temporarily assigning more agents from Tampa and Orlando to help find the asshole who shot him," he said.

"I spoke to ASAC Mandeville, she said he's still in a medically induced coma."

"I talked with some hospital people directly," he said with a big sigh and a swipe of a hand through his hair. He was trying hard not to look frazzled. "They said that all things considered, he's lucky. The round hit the ground and splintered a little piece of it off, that's what hit him. Anytime there's head trauma the body goes into protective shutdown mode. With all the capillaries in the face and head it looked a lot worse than it was. Nonetheless, he had a foreign piece of metal go into his head, right? They think he'll recover with proper rest and maybe some rehab. The surgeon didn't have to go in too far to get the fragment. They got him under now because they don't want him thrashing about or having a post-surgical seizure."

I looked out at the slight chop of Biscayne Bay. Although this was encouraging news, I still had big concerns for him.

"He have any family?"

"He's got a wife and young twin sons."

My stomach knotted and I just looked away for a moment.

"We'll find this guy. We will. Right now, it looks like we got the Ecuadorian's car. I think we should sit on it for a bit, see if he goes to it. We need to get the VIN number off the car. The tag's unregistered," I said.

Marroquín called the Bay Harbor Islands Police Department and identified himself as a DEA agent. He asked for a uniformed officer to meet us at the Chevron station on the causeway. Within fifteen minutes an officer pulled into the gas station lot. Marroquín waved at him. The officer got out of his car and joined us. Marroquín made introductions. The officer looked at me and then at Marroquín.

"I'm Officer Oscar Chassimere. Everyone just calls me Chaz."

We asked Chaz if he'd ever seen the Mercedes-Benz before. He laughed, explaining that in Bay Harbor Islands a Mercedes-Benz was as common as liposuctions and tennis lessons. Marroquín explained that there was a surveillance team watching the Mercedes. He informed Chaz that the car was partially blocking the designated bike path and parked close to a fire hydrant. He asked Chaz to cite the Mercedes and get the vehicle identification number from the plate, visible on the dashboard through the front windshield. I suggested that he prewrite the citation here so that when he got to the Mercedes his exposure would be minimalized.

"Chaz, if this guy lives nearby, he might see the ticket on his windshield and come out to the car. If we don't see any sign of him in a few hours we're going to have it towed," I said.

"When I get the number, I'll just call you guys with it. I don't want to have to drive out here again." he said.

Marroquín provided his cell number to Chaz. As Chaz drove off, I wondered how arduous it must be to leave a town of 5100 residents and drive across a beautiful concourse?

Marroquín called one of the SOG members and told him to expect Bay Harbor Islands to be on scene to cite the vehicle. Fifteen minutes later Marroquín answered a call from Chaz and wrote down the car's information. I took the paper from him and called the Coral Gables Police Department. I got Jeanie Rae again. I gave her the car's identification number. She informed me it was not on file.

I had her read back the number to me and she read it back the way Marroquín had written it. I thanked her and hung up.

"My people are short today and she's really busy. Maybe she's not on her game today. Can you run it through DEA and see what you can find?" I asked him.

He made some calls, our eyes locked as he held the phone to his ear. He slowly shook his head. So his people were telling him the same thing that Jeanie Rae told me.

"You'll be at the four o'clock briefing?" I asked him.

"It's at your place in the Gables, right?"

"Yeah, you going?" I asked again.

"I'll be there. I'm mandated to be there. I'd rather be tracking leads like this but yes, I'll be there and so will SAC Grayson. So—how did you find the Mercedes so quickly?"

"Just fortunate I guess."

Chapter Eight

With the time for the meeting approaching, we decided at 2pm to have the Mercedes towed. Marroquín had called his crime scene technicians. Two of them would be at the meeting. Since the technicians would be there, it was a logical decision to have the car towed to the Coral Gables Police Department for processing. By 2:30pm the car was on a flatbed trailer heading to the police station. Two of the SOG members followed the tow truck to maintain crime scene integrity.

At the appointed hour myself and Agent Marroquín filed into the Emergency Operations Center on the fourth floor of the police department. The double doors were framed on either side with opaque green glass with the city seal etched into each one. The EOC was designed primarily for hurricanes. There were conference tables with triangular placards above them in the ceiling. The placards said things like "Recovery", and "Assessment" on them. Marroquín and I settled into seats under the placard "Critical Incidents." I couldn't help but think about the irony. Already seated were Major Brunson, DEA Special Agent Vincent Walker, and Hialeah Crime Scene Technician Hammy Garzon. She looked a little haggard from the long day she had yesterday. She still gave me a slight smile when she looked up from her cell phone, though.

We all sat in silence. I was wondering when Major Brunson was going to say something, but he remained quiet. A few minutes after 4pm two men in suits and three of the DEA crime scene technicians walked into the room. The last one in closed the door behind himself. Everyone found seats except the two men in suits. They went to Major Brunson and said some words to him in a hushed tone. He shook both of their hands and then they both took seats on either side of him. It was Major Brunson who spoke first.

"Men, we asked you to be here for this briefing on yesterday's event."

Hammy Garzon looked at me with a *What is wrong with you Coral Gables people* look. Major Brunson spied Garzon and quickly tried to correct his faux pas.

"I mean…I meant to say we've asked all of you here today to discuss the events yesterday in Hialeah. For those of you who are unfamiliar with Special Agent in Charge of the Miami field division of the DEA, John Grayson is here on my left."

SAC Grayson was in a tailored navy suit. He had an orange-colored necktie that stood out from his starched white shirt. I had no idea how much time he spent in the field, but being the SAC of Miami was a big position in the DEA. I'm sure through action and political moxie he found his way to the top of one of the DEA's biggest bureaus.

Turning to the man on his right, Brunson gave his last introduction. "Also with us is Mr. Robert McBride. Mr. McBride is from Washington D.C. He will be sitting in on this one with us."

Some guy from Washington D.C? He should have just called him Mr. Smith. It made no difference, whoever this guy was. He caused our briefing to be pushed back to 4pm to accommodate his airplane flight. He didn't want any of us knowing who he really was and who he really worked for.

Wonderful.

We're all here seeking a solution and Beltway Bob here is seeking an agenda. He wanted an answer to something totally unrelated to us. Whoever decided to start shooting up one of Hialeah's better

Spanish restaurants was more important to Washington D.C. than we were. That's one of the problems of dealing with government types. They want to know all you know but are like stingy children when exchanging information.

This guy McBride had CIA written all across him. Television likes to portray the men and women of the Central Intelligence Agency as highly patriotic and very efficient operatives. I've never met a CIA operative in Miami who didn't enrich his own bank account from overfunding and underspending on their operations. The acronym CIA should stand for "Criminals In Action."

I was beginning to feel like a show piece in this briefing. I was waiting for the inevitable, "Cade in your own words tell us exactly what happened yesterday." As I sat there mulling over those thoughts, I heard Major Brunson's voice.

"With us here is one of my VIN detectives, Cade Taylor. Cade was the undercover operative yesterday. Cade, in your own words tell us exactly what happened yesterday."

If it weren't for the benefits, I could quit this job and make just as much money being a mind reader at some sideshow carnival.

I glanced around the room, and except for SAC Grayson and Robert McBride from Washington D.C. everyone in the room knew what transpired yesterday and what my role in all of it was. This was a show and tell for two suits: one a light wool blend, for Miami's swampy climate, and the other a deeper tweed for Washington's inhospitable winter weather and even more inhospitable backstabbing.

With little fanfare and with minimal words I relayed how yesterday's events went down and where we were in the investigation process. The two suits either took me for a stoic reticent speaker or they figured me to be wallowing in some sort of recent PTSD concerning the whole affair, because neither of them asked any questions from me. It was Major Brunson who retook the master of ceremonies dais to stand up and speak.

"I think what we have here are two investigations, and we

should see where the intersection of these two investigations comes together," he said.

Major Brunson hadn't used any profanity. I felt like a new dad seeing little Johnny in his first baseball game waddle up to the plate, bat in hand, ready to hit a homer. I was almost proud.

"What frosts my ass the most is how this piece of shit got away," growled Brunson.

After fouling the first pitch and beaning the Sno-cone vender, little Johnny eventually struck out.

"Miss Hialeah—"

"It's Garzon. Hammy Garzon. Crime Scene Investigator Garzon from the Hialeah Police Department," said Hammy.

"Yes, of course. First, welcome, Miss Garzon. Could you please tell us what you've been able to determine so far?"

Hammy had a thick binder with her. She started shuffling through papers. She pulled out a stack of papers. Hammy opened the binder and she stood up. She leaned on the table and looked down at the binder. She began to speak.

"At approximately 12:30pm yesterday myself and other members of the Hialeah CSI unit were dispatched to 2846 Palm Avenue in reference to multiple gunshots fired and a possible law enforcement officer injured or shot. Upon arrival, Hialeah Police Department were on scene, as were federal agents from the Drug Enforcement Agency. Hialeah Fire Department paramedics were on scene treating a law enforcement officer with a serious head wound. HPD had secured a crime scene from 29th Avenue south to 27th Avenue. Within this crime scene was the restaurant, *El Segundo Viajante*, and Sunoco gas retailer number 4901. The first scene photographed and processed was the rear of Pasteur Medical transport vehicle number thirty-nine. Vehicle thirty-nine had two bullets embedded in its rear quarter panel and electrical system. Oral statement provided to this technician via Coral Gables VIN Unit 923, Detective Cade Taylor, stated that an unknown white male running from 2846 Palm Avenue shot two rounds from an undetermined handgun. Both rounds found final velocity termination in the vehicle. Detective Taylor also stated that approximately one eighth of a mile away, while in foot pursuit, the same unknown white male fired an additional two rounds at Detective Taylor in the paddocks area of Hialeah Racetrack."

She looked up from her report to see if she still had everyone's attention in the room. She continued.

"At 2025 hours last night both of those rounds were recovered in the paddock area. One round was found in the wall of bungalow seven and the other was recovered from the side panels of a feed supply room. Initial analysis shows the four rounds recovered are consistent with an additional round found in the parking lot of 2846 Palm Avenue. This round is believed to be the one that struck DEA Special Agent Scott Lew. The round was nearly intact, minus a small edging fragmentation. Ballistic analysis determined the round was fired into the ground and caromed into the parking lot wall. Five rounds recovered. None of the rounds were removed from any person, living or deceased."

"What about the rounds pulled from the dead guy inside?" asked Brunson.

"I was just getting to that. This morning the medical examiner released the two rounds from the autopsy of the deceased. With a cursory inspection they are all consistent. All recovered rounds were sent to the Walnut Creek California ATF laboratory for expert analysis."

She sure liked to use the word "recovered."

Major Brunson asked, "Miss Garzon, can you tell us aside from bullet recovery what else you did on the scene yesterday?"

"I assisted the DEA technicians with processing the scene inside the restaurant. Fingerprints have been sent to the Automated Fingerprint Identification System for comparisons. I'm still waiting to hear from AFIS. The deceased was killed by two equally lethal bullet wounds. Either one separate from the other would have killed him. I also processed the blood spatter pattern and concluded that two different people were shot at the table where Detective Taylor was sitting. The deceased had O-positive blood type. He had neither A nor B antigens in his red cells. With O-positive blood, the A and B antibodies are in the *plasma*. The deceased's blood type came from the toxicology report from the Medical Examiner. The other blood on the scene was type AB. The AB type has both A and B antigens in the red cells but neither A nor B *antibodies* in the plasma. That was gathered and tested by a portable hematology analysis kit. Detective Taylor fired two rounds inside the restaurant. We recovered both of those rounds. One impacted a wooden hostess stand. The other fragmented on a ceramic tile ledge by the kitchen window. Photographs and measurements were taken."

With that, Hammy sat down. Major Brunson asked DEA Special Agent Vincent Walker to stand up and speak next.

"We were able to determine that Agent Lew's shooter arrived at the location in a yellow taxi. Both myself and Agent Marroquín were able to contact the taxi driver. He stated that he picked up the shooter as a lone fare from the Hialeah Hospital emergency room. I went to Hialeah Hospital and reviewed the surveillance tapes but all that can be seen on the tape is the taxi pulling in. A diaper service truck pulled adjacent to the taxi and the camera view was blocked. All we could see is the taxi driving away."

How appropriate that a truck with shitty diapers just ruined any shitty camera capture we may have gotten of the shooter. Agent Walker continued with more information that caused at least me in the room to start taking notes.

"I spent the morning at the Medical Examiner's office. We have an I.D. on the deceased. He was Eberardo Rincon-Giraldez, age thirty-five. I checked his booking photos against his face. His fingerprints matched his lengthy arrest record. He's been arrested by Miami Dade, Hallandale, Surfside, and Aventura police departments for hard ball crimes. Aggravated Battery, Battery, Aggravated Assault, Assault, Weapons Violations…the list goes on. Everyone called him *Loco Curo*—The Crazy Cure. If the price was right and you had a problem, he was the remedy. He was the crazy cure to vanquish anyone bothering you."

"You're saying this guy was an enforcer?" asked SAC Grayson.

"He was the enforcer. More than likely an executioner and an unlicensed mortician too. According to sources, his reputation was unrivaled. He was the top pick for anyone who needed protection or needed to have an adversary or competition eliminated. He was as they all said, 'the crazy cure,'" said Walker.

I stopped taking notes momentarily. It seemed that Eberardo Rincon-Giraldez might have been everyone else's crazy cure, but he wasn't crazy enough to be a cure for himself.

Walker went on: "All the addresses listed with his arrests show his home as 8100 Hawthorne Avenue in Miami Beach. I guess nobody ever thought to check the validity of that. I went out there today. It's a sewage pump station."

The DEA technician gave his report. He said that the glass tabletop had large traces of Sodium Dodecylbenzenesulfonate, and Sodium Chloride. He attributed that to the common Spanish cleaner "Fabulousa." Aside from the traces of the cleaner there were some partial prints and those were sent off to AFIS for analysis.

"Did any of the spent cartridges form the rounds have fingerprints on them?" asked SAC Grayson.

"Yes," Hammy stepped in and answered. "The shell casings were all very clean, but we managed to get a partial thumb print. The magazine the shooter dropped on Palm Avenue was partially clean too, but we got some useable prints. He may have used gloves when loading his weapon but was careless somewhere along the way. Before you ask, we have *not* seen this type of magazine before and photographs of it were also sent to the ATF lab. I currently don't know who the gun manufacturer is."

Agent Marroquín stood up and spoke next.

"Today I assisted Detective Taylor with the recovery of the Mercedes Benz we think was at the scene yesterday. It was in Bay Harbor Islands."

Major Brunson immediately looked straight at me. I slowly

moved my hand in a sweeping gesture across the table conveying my message of *don't ask, we'll talk later.*

"It has visible blood on the interior, and we had it towed here for processing. Maybe Ms. Garzon will assist our DEA technicians and see if the AB blood she collected yesterday matches the blood in the Mercedes," suggested Marroquin.

The room became silent. I think Agents Marroquin and Walker were expecting some insightful investigative direction from their SAC Grayson, but it was not to be. Mr. X from Washington, Robert McBride, stood up and looked out at all of us.

"I want to thank you all for allowing me to be here today. Major Brunson and Special Agent in Charge Grayson, an especially sincere thank you to you both. In the beginning of this meeting, Major Brunson said, 'what we have here are two investigations and we should see where the intersection of these two investigations comes together.' Maybe so. Maybe not. It seems to me this was nothing more than a vengeful killing of Mr. Rincon-Giraldez. The 'Crazy Cure,' as you call him. As for Agent Lew, he may have just been the unlucky recipient of an accidental discharge."

After rolling in the grass and mud of Hialeah just twenty-fours ago, I couldn't contain my indignation.

"Did you not hear *anything* that was said here today? Accidental discharge? There was no A.D. out there!"

"Detective, what I heard was that a very bad man was murdered in a restaurant yesterday. His companion, we believe, was shot as well. We do not know if his companion was targeted or just an innocent bystander—"

"*Innocent bystander*? Are you out of your government-subsidized mind? He was selling twenty kilos of cocaine and he fled with the cocaine and the money. There's nothing innocent about him!" I blurted.

McBride presented a very calm composure.

"That may all be well and true, but from what I have read and from what I've just heard here today, *you,* Detective, never actually saw the cocaine. We don't know if there were twenty kilograms of cocaine in that sack. What we do know is that you fired two rounds recklessly and blindly behind you. One of which was found in a hostess stand, the other fragmented on a ceramic tile shelf. For all we know, your fragmentation may be what felled Agent Lew—"

"Hey, sport. You may be all high and mighty on Virginia Avenue in Washington D.C., but this is Miami. Down here we don't accuse people unless we have evidence, and the evidence says Lew was hit by our shooter. Now you may call it an A.D., but we have a witness who saw them collide in the door of the restaurant and heard the damn gunshot."

McBride was as cool as ice. He maintained a steady calm demeanor.

"Valid points, Detective. In the realm of jurisprudence wouldn't you agree that all avenues of exploration should be tried? This was an *alleged* drug transaction that went bad. It could be Los Angeles, Chicago, or New York City on any given day. It was Hialeah's day yesterday. That's all it was. Once again, I thank you all. I wish you success in your endeavor."

With that McBride strode out of the Emergency Operations Center. He turned right as he left the room. I stared straight at the door. I knew the dumbass had gone the wrong way. I got a little inward delight watching him walk past the etched windows, bewildered, then out of my sight.

"Who was that clown?" asked Walker to the room.

A valid question and one implying that McBride was indeed a clown and not even one of the better known clowns.

"He is a partner in another agency from Washington D.C," said SAC Grayson

"'*I wish you luck in your endeavor*.' Who the hell says that? An endeavor is trying to climb Mount Everest. This is a drug murder investigation with a DEA Agent severely wounded and $400,00 and twenty kilos loose on the streets," I said, temperature rising with every word.

SAC Grayson stood up and shook Major Brunson's hand. He then addressed us all.

"Walker and Marroquín, you both will be the point men on this investigation. I'm taking you off any other investigations until we can catch the shooter who shot Agent Lew. I also want this Ecuadorian found and the $400,000 recovered along with the twenty kilograms. Start working all your C. I's. See what you can develop. When Agent Lew can talk, I want to know who his informant was on this deal. You are both to work closely with Detective Taylor on this.' Looking to Hammy, he said, "Ms. Garzon, I've spoken to your police chief. He's made it known that you too will be brought onboard with this group until this is resolved. We at the DEA appreciate your skills and I think I speak for our technicians when I say we're thankful to have you with us, even if it is only temporary. I'm going back to the hospital. Marroquín, Walker, if you want to go with me, you can."

The two DEA agents filed out with their SAC leaving Garzon, Brunson, myself and the two DEA technicians in the room.

"If you three would please excuse myself and Detective Taylor he and I need to go to my office. Cade, will you direct these three to where the Mercedes is parked? I'll see you in my office in fifteen minutes," said Brunson.

I took Hammy and the DEA techs out to what we call the "third-floor apron." It's an exposed parking lot where many of our General Investigation detectives parked. The Mercedes was under a tarp near the fenced impound parking area on the apron. The sun was beginning to set. We pulled back the tarp and, in the orange, yellow sunlight the blood stains in the car were very evident.

"My handprint should be on the hood," I said.

I left the DEA technicians to it and walked with Hammy to her crime scene van.

"I'll need to print your hand to verify we do in fact have the exact same car here," she said.

She opened her I.D. kit. It looked like a fisherman's dream tackle box with all kinds of sliding drawers and lift-out trays. She produced a squeeze bottle with some black liquid in it and asked me to present my open palm to her. She put a dab of the black liquid in my palm. She used a soft felt roller to roll the liquid across my palm and my fingers. She then reached into a binder and pulled out a porous white sheet of paper. She put the paper on top of her case and asked me to press my hand onto it.

"Press hard. Get your entire palm and fingers on the paper. Don't wiggle. Just press hard. Let it settle for a second. I have cleaner for your hand. Don't touch anything, it's a bitch to get out of clothing," she said.

I reminded her to especially be sure to print the rearview mirror and the gas cap of the Mercedes. She looked at me with a tinge of anger in her eyes.

"It sounds to me like you're telling me how to do my job," she said.

"No. I just wanted to be sure those areas get printed," I said.

"Like I said. It sounds like you're telling me how to do my job. Do you think I've never done this before? Man, you are seriously condescending."

I didn't think I was being condescending, but I knew that Major Brunson was waiting on me and I needed to be going. I just chose to not engage anymore in the conversation. She told me to keep my hand steady. I did. She then told me to pull it away from the paper slowly.

"Okay, now hold your hand close to your chest," she ordered.

I didn't want to anger her anymore, so I did.

"No. Closer. Like three inches closer," she said.

I held my hand closer to my chest. It was then that she pushed the back of my hand up against my chest leaving a big dark handprint on my shirt.

"Fuck you, Cade Taylor," she said as she walked away.

Chapter Nine

I JUST LOOKED DOWN at my shirt and walked away, into the building. I used to be married to a feisty, argumentative person. I could handle her, and I could handle Hammy. Then again if I could handle anything maybe I'd still be married. Either way my interpersonal skills and confidence with the opposite sex were currently not very high.

Charlene had already gone home and there was no one in Major Brunson's outer office. I rapped on the door frame and stood in the doorway. Major Brunson looked up from his desk at me.

"Cade, normally I'd say come in but today I feel...what's the word I'm looking for? Sporty. Yup, that's the word. A little *sporty*, yeah, that's how I feel. Sporty. So, I'll say get your ass in here now. How's that? Sporty enough for you?"

"Major. I would like to say—"

"Say what? That you're a fucking asshole? Who do you think you are talking like that to one of our guests?" he said, raising his voice.

"One of our guests? This isn't a hotel here. That guy wasn't a guest. He was a spook right out of spook central, trying to gain some sort of information."

"Let me explain something to you that you may not fully under-fuckingstand. *I* called for the meeting today. *I* did. You have any idea how much I fucking hate meetings? Because some asshole fish crawled out of the water thirty-five million years ago and now thanks to him, we have meetings. Cade, you can avoid these meetings if you have a large sum of money in your bank account, have power here in the department, or have confidence in finding another job. But from where I sit and as you can see, I sit in the largest office in this shitbox of a police station, I don't think you have much money in the bank, I *know* you don't have power here, or a likeliness of being hired somewhere else. So you need to be in these fucking meetings. I *do* have power here, money in the bank, and I don't want to be fucking hired anywhere else and I still have to take my fat ass to the EOC for a meeting. One that I called!"

"It wasn't the meeting I had a problem with. It was that CIA guy, McBride."

"First of all, get your super-secret shithead organizations correct. He ain't CIA, he's NSA."

"So why is the National Security Agency interested in two Latin drug dealers in Hialeah?" I asked him.

"Good question. All I know is that SAC Grayson asked that we move the meeting back so that McBride could attend. Then you go and flatten all the tires on the welcome wagon saying he's out of his Goddamn government-subsidized mind."

"Didn't you see where none of what McBride was saying made any sense?"

"Cade, now tell me please, educate me. Actually, just humor me. What exactly do you mean by that?"

"McBride said that this was a drug deal gone bad. Well yeah, of course it was. We nearly lost a DEA Agent and did lose twenty kilos and $400,000. Commander Obvious from the NSA is accurate about that part. It's the other thing he said that made no sense," I said.

"What other thing?"

"The part about the big guy, Eberardo Rincon-Giraldez. The Crazy Cure. He said the Crazy Cure was the main target. That can't be," I said.

"Why not?"

"Because this Rincon-Giraldez was in the passenger seat when he and the Ecuadorian drove to the restaurant. We have it on closed circuit tape."

The Ecuadorian was driving the Mercedes.

"So?'

"So? So, he needed to be able to act quickly. He was the muscle on this deal, not the main player."

"No, Cade. He was just a passenger in a car driven by a little weasel who stole 400k from us and therefore put me in hot scalding water with the city manager."

"Major, he got out of the car and scouted the restaurant and upon declaring it safe came back and got the Ecuadorian. It's clear as gin on the tape."

I remembered, the big guy exited the car and walked away out of camera range. He opened the passenger door. He leaned into the car. They were talking. After another minute passed, the trunk opened remotely. The big guy closed the passenger door and went to the rear of the car. He pulled out the burlap sack with the twenty kilograms of cocaine in it.

"Cade, if McBride's theory is wrong then what kind of beef did this shooter have with the Ecuadorian and the Crazy Cure?"

"I don't know, but the shooter arrived just before the deal was about to go down. He knew we were going to do the deal at the restaurant. How did he know that? He knew the location and he knew the time. How? Tell me, how? I don't think he expected me to be on time. He may have intended to rip the two of them off. When I got there, he saw it was now three to a table and he had no idea if I was armed or if I'd bring someone with me. What's that expression? Three's a party, four's a crowd?"

"It's two's a party and three's a crowd. Tell ya the truth Cade, if two is a party I think I've had way too many parties with you, and they're not all so great. I'm not a party guy. When I was a young man, I snuck out of my house to go to parties. Now I sneak out of parties to go to my house. Cade, I think that playing pin the problem on the donkey with you is becoming fucking tiresome. What *is* it with you? It's like you're a continual shit magnet. It seems every time you're here in my office I watch another portion of my sanity and patience fly out the fucking window. There is no doubt you're good at what you do. You're very good. Sometimes you're *too* good. That kind of success comes with a price. I feel like every bad decision surrounding you lands right at my asshole. Like Buzz Fucking Aldrin on the moon, sticking a mechanical flag right up my butt."

"You think this is my fault?"

"No Cade, it's not your fault. It's not your fault, but the fact that you and $400,000 were in the middle of this and now just *you* are in the middle without the $400,000 makes it *my* fault. As was told to me by the city manager in three telephone calls, an email, and one direct face to face meeting. Did I tell you how much I hate meetings, Cade?"

"Yes, you did just a few minutes—"

"Cade, shut up, of course I know what I just said."

I sat there for a moment wondering where the conversation was heading next or would we continue lamenting the aspects of my career. Major Brunson had some very uncanny traits. One was being able to gather intelligence about nearly everything in the city. In a Yogi Berra sense, you never knew how he knew, but he knew what you thought he *didn't* know. His other notable trait was the ability to transition his mood and the conversation in a millisecond.

"Cade, tell me how you found the taxi today."

"I used some of the petty cash from VIN as a reward for any cab driver who discovered the Mercedes. I figured there were more of them spread across the county then there were of us."

Brunson slightly twisted his eyebrows, denoting an AH-HA moment in his head.

"Why do you think the Mercedes they're processing right now is the same one?"

"At the gas station next to the restaurant I saw three cars backed into spaces against a low hedge. I simply had a feeling walking into the restaurant, so I put my hand on each one's hood. You know in case the dopers inside were driving any of them. Surveillance camera showed them in the Mercedes. When they process the car, my handprint should be on the hood."

Brunson gave a hard look at the front of my shirt, concentrating on the greasy black handprint across it.

"I know you may think I'm against you sometimes," he said, "but I'm actually with you in many ways too."

That was neither an absolution nor affirmation that he was against me; nor was it a confirmation or detraction that he wasn't. Like I said: Yogi Berra.

"Listen, I'm not sure why John Grayson allowed that NSA guy to be in our meeting. My guess is he didn't have a choice in the matter. I can bet you a dozen dollars he didn't just fly down here to sit in our dinky meeting and drink our shitty coffee. He knows something more than he's saying. What his real name is doesn't matter. Half of Miami knows you as Cade Daniels, a pool liner company owner. It makes no difference. What matters is who you are at the end of the day. Who you truly are and what you truly believe in. What is real for you, Cade?"

"What do you mean?" I asked.

"I mean, what's your touchstone? Lieutenant Maddalone keeps a chart. You believe that? He keeps a running tab on all our shootings. Whether we kill a gunman, a charging vicious dog, or one of us accidentally shoots a toilet he keeps a chart of all firearm discharges. To him it's highly important. It's his touchstone. It's how he justifies his existence. It's his position in life. He sits in that very same chair you're sitting in right now and reads off velocity, bullet trajectory, calibration, what it hit, what it didn't hit, what it almost hit. I sit here and listen to him and just feel like putting a bullet in my own fucking brain from boredom. That's what he is and what he does. It validates him. For the record I must say I've heard way too many of these reports from him concerning you. He says you're at the—"

"Top of his list. I know I heard that from him already."

"Right. Everybody here has their role in the success of this police department. Truthfully, in many ways we're successful despite ourselves. But everyone has their role. You on the other hand seem to take your role to the outer boundaries of acceptability. I'd like to think it's the nature of being in VIN. But if I had a heart, I do believe you would be my cardiac arrest. It's been about a year now, hasn't it?"

"You mean since my divorce from Gina? No, it's been about ten months since we split up and about five months since we got divorced."

"A year, ten months, same thing. You're living like a vagabond. Cade, let me give you a little advice. Marriage means commitment. Of course, so does insanity."

I just blinked my eyes at the absurdity of this unsolicited advice.

"Do you know what's the best part about being married?" he asked me.

"No."

"It keeps you from getting married!"

"That's it. That's your theory on marriage?" I said.

"Not entirely. Someone in the relationship has to take the lead but that doesn't mean *you* have to always lead. It's never fifty-fifty. Sometimes it's sixty-forty, or even eighty-twenty, but there's an ebb and flow. I think my wife is gradually seizing control in my own marriage by asking me if I checked all the doors and windows each time we back out of the driveway. Bottom line is you have to live with the choices you make. You chose to get married and then either one or both of you chose to get divorced. That decision was made. She seems to have chosen her path quite clearly and you keep meandering and moping around here. You need to find yours. By finding your own path you need to stop looking at the bottom of a Jameson bottle or beer stein to find yourself."

Our momentary silence was broken when we heard Hammy Garzon's voice behind us.

"I'm sorry to disturb you both. I just wanted to let you know that we're still processing the Mercedes-Benz."

I turned in my chair and looked at her. I think Brunson was expecting more.

"Okay. Thank you. Anything else?" I asked her.

She stood there in the doorway waiting for an invitation from Brunson. He picked up on her reticence and asked her to sit down. She sat down next to me and adjusted her chair a little away from me. I noticed the slight.

She opened her binder. "The researcher at AFIS called me a few minutes ago. There was a positive I.D. on the fingerprints lifted from the wine bottle and wine glasses at the restaurant. I ran him through Hialeah's records section. Our runner with the kilos and cash is Dario Curbelo."

"The Ecuadorian?"

"He isn't Ecuadorian. He's from Paraguay."

"Paraguay?"

"Yup, born and raised in Ciudad del Este, Paraguay."

"Ciudad de what?" asked Brunson.

"East. The *City of the East,*" replied Garzon.

"Well, Agent Lew must have had his countries mixed up because he clearly said he was Ecuadorian," I said.

"I don't know what he told you but those fingerprints on the wine bottle and glass at *El Segundo Viajante* are definitely Dario Curbelo. He was arrested for protesting at the Summit of the Americas in 1994. A city of Miami cop arrested him on Biscayne Boulevard at the Torch of Freedom. He was blocking the sidewalk and refused to move. My people were able to get the arrest form and read it to me. It was a not obeying a lawful order charge, something about Clinton's motorcade coming sometime in the afternoon. I think the Miami cop got tired of being in the sun and chose to arrest Curbelo to get out of the detail. Charges were dropped within hours, but he was booked and that's how we got his prints in the system. Aside from that, he's been clean as a whistle," she said.

"I remember the Summit of the Americas. Every world leader in the hemisphere from Canada to Chile was here in Miami, many of them at the Biltmore Hotel here in the Gables. Fidel Castro was omitted and that caused a big ruckus, both pro and con. It was something like ten days of meetings, luncheons, and fancy events," I said.

"Well, there's no mention of Cuba in the arrest form. It just seems that Curbelo crossed the wrong cop that day and he spent a few hours at Miami P.D. He was transferred to Dade County jail and was bonded out pretty quickly."

"He was bonded out or did he bond himself out?" I asked.

"Does it make a difference?" she asked.

I let the question go and thought for a moment.

"Okay, okay let me get this straight. This so-called Paraguayan Boy Scout gets arrested in 1994 at the hemisphere's biggest world leader event. He never crosses the path of law enforcement for the last four years and now he shows up confidently looking to sell twenty kilograms. With him is a known enforcer in crime circles known as the 'Crazy Cure.' None of it lines up. I'm supposed to believe all of this?" I asked her.

"Well, here's something else for you to not believe. According to our records, Dario Curbelo from Ciudad de Estes Paraguay died in a 1996 housefire at 160 Northeast 164th Street in North Miami."

Chapter Ten

"WAIT. WHAT? ARE you telling me that the same fucking guy who fled with our 400k and twenty kilos is a charcoal briquet from a house fire three years earlier?" asked Brunson.

It wasn't the first time, and I'm most certain it wouldn't be the last time that Brunson's haphazard use of profanity embarrassed me or the police department. Hammy kept her composure.

"Major, I recognize that many things about Hialeah may seem inordinately true, including the incompetency of many city employees, but I'm telling you the truth. You're chasing a dead guy. The Miami Dade Medical Examiner has him listed as deceased in a housefire. They made the identification," she said.

"As far as we know unless yesterday's shooting was lethal to him, but since he drove across Miami Dade County and parked his car, I would guess he's actually still alive somewhere. In direct contradiction to what your people are telling you," I said.

"We have some very good prints from the Mercedes-Benz. The DEA guys are sending them to the same AFIS technician to make sure there is continuity on the comparisons. I'm confident they'll match. The blood type in the vehicle is also AB," she said.

"What about the rounds that were fired yesterday that hit the bus?" I asked her.

"ATF hasn't said anything yet and our own people don't know yet. There's something that did make our firearms people take notice, though."

"What was that?" asked Brunson.

"The shell casings. They aren't brass or aluminum—they're steel."

"Steel?"

"Yes. Our firearms people said they were steel-jacketed bullets. They also said they've never seen the magazine that was recovered on Palm Avenue before."

"Hammy," I started, hoping I wasn't wearing on her nerves, "has anything come back from AFIS on our shooter? DEA took the entire glass from the tabletop."

"Funny you should ask. They had the largest surface to work with and yet AFIS is saying that it's inconclusive. It doesn't make sense to me. I'm going back down to see where we are on the Mercedes," she said as she got up and walked out of Brunson's office.

"Inconclusive my ass!" bellowed Brunson.

"Someone knows something and doesn't want to share it," I said.

"I have a novel idea. I'm the Major. I do major things. She's the technician—she does technical things, and you're the detective. You do detective things. How about you continue to do detective things and keep me informed as you do?" said Brunson.

"You want me to leave?" I asked.

"Cade, in the worst possible way I'd love for you to leave. I've still got an hour of work in front of me here and I'm still missing $400,000. So yes, I'd like you to be off like a prom dress and get going."

"I'll see you tomorrow," I said as I walked out.

"Thanks for the warning," he yelled behind me.

I went down to the VIN office, straight to Ileana's desk. The fax machine was behind her desk and tucked under a shelf that had a hefty volume of *Robert's Rules of Order: Newly Revised.* I was at a complete loss as to why someone challenged with the most rudimentary aspects of the English language would have that type of book behind her desk. Thankfully that wasn't the book I was looking for. I was searching for the Yellow Pages.

I found the dog-eared, well-used issues of the *Miami and the Beaches Real Yellow Pages* books. I wondered how many cities in America were so big that they had to have an A-K and an L-Z issue of the phone book. Or for that matter, have the cover written in two languages. I picked up the *Las Verdaderas Paginas Amarillas* L-Z, and quickly found the pages I was looking for. I carefully tore out two pages from the book. The new books would be coming out in two months, and I hardly thought anyone would notice the missing pages. I folded the pages into a small square and tucked them in the back pocket of my pants, then headed out the door. I paused long enough to ask Hammy to have her people fax the information of Dario Curbelo's arrest to our VIN office. Her blank stare back at me I took as a yes, and I left the building. I was satisfied that we'd found the Mercedes-Benz that Curbelo had been driving, but I also felt no closer to finding him or the lovely parting gifts he took with him from the restaurant. Agent Lew was still in no condition to tell us anything and now I had a surprise visit from some government lackey who did everything to pretend interest and provided no assistance to us.

The sun had set, and time was running against us. The longer this investigation dragged on, the less chance we had at solving this case.

Time is not kind to police investigations. Suspects leave town, evidence gets concealed or destroyed, and resources get pulled away for other investigations. I was feeling a little helpless and more than a bit defeated on this one. I was also feeling hungry. I drove south from the station and continued on what we refer to as "deeper south" on Old Cutler Road. I was only a mile or so from the condominium at Paradise Point. I called Papa Ricco's Italian restaurant.

"Papa Ricco's," said the voice on the line.

"Hello, can I please get a pick-up for a large pizza with green peppers, sausage, and mushrooms?"

I gave him my info and he said, "Be ready in—"

"Twenty minutes. See you then," I answered for him.

Miami in late autumn on into the early spring has the most glorious weather. The evening air was toxifying and felt good through the open car window. I turned west and went to Papa Ricco's. The guy at the counter noticed the handprint across my shirt but politely said nothing of it. In just under twenty minutes from making my turn I was back on Mitchell Drive heading east straight to the condo. The aroma of the pizza heightened my hunger.

I was happy and relieved to be home. Even though it technically wasn't my own home it had been my home for the past few months. After all the events of the past few days it was good to be in a safe, secure place at a decent hour. I grabbed two Amstel Light beers from the refrigerator and took them with the pizza to the upper deck terrace. I sat down in one of the abundantly comfortable chaise lounge chairs. The beers were frosty cold and tasted wonderful. The pizza was very good, and I tore into it, polishing off three slices before I even realized it. The night air was scented with blooming jasmine. The sound of the soft lapping of the water against the boats and docks below was hypnotic. I finished all but one slice of the delicious pizza. I took the box and two empty bottles down to the kitchen garbage. I grabbed two more beers and went back up to the terrace, where I toasted the moon and drank the beers in the dark. When I finished, I still was in the mood to have a few more beers but I deferred to common sense, plopped into bed, and was soon fast asleep.

I AWOKE WITH a start. Although I slept soundly, my slumbering brain must have been doing cartwheels because I woke up already spinning. There was so much to do. I needed to get to the office as soon as I could. I showered and was on my way to the police department. I threw more clothes into my go bag in case I get another inky palm print on my shirt. I put on the same pants from yesterday and a different shirt. In the stop and go traffic of school buses and working commuters I ran through the list of things that needed to be done.

I needed to check in with DEA Agents Marroquín and Walker and see if Agent Lew was any closer to being brought out of the medically induced coma. I also needed to talk with them about what SAC Grayson had said about them being the point men on the investigation. I didn't directly want to have a conflict about that, but I was used to working alone and if I had to follow the DEA on every decision, I knew we'd never get anywhere.

I needed to see that arrest information on Dario Curbelo from the City of Miami. I needed to read it myself. I also needed to get my hands on the report about the 1996 house fire at 160 Northeast 164th Street in North Miami. If they found a body in the fire and it wasn't Curbelo...then who was it?

I needed to find out from Hammy if any of the prints on the glass tabletop had come back from AFIS. I also needed to talk to her about whatever else they may have found in the Mercedes-Benz.

Apparently, I *needed* a lot of things.

My mind reeled with these tasks as I drove on to the station. I parked in the alleyway between the department and the recently built Regions Bank next door. I took the same external staircase up to the third floor and entered the building from the seldomly used east door. I went into the VIN office to Ileana Portillo, who sat in the center reception area. It was she that visitors and detectives saw first when they entered the VIN office.

"Good morning, Ileana."

"*Aye* Cade, *ju* scared me. I not *especting ju* so early."

"Is Gary in yet?" I asked her.

"*El bano*," she said.

I poked my head back out the door and scanned the outer hallway, hoping to see Gary coming out of the bathroom. The hallway was empty. Off Ileana's left was the lieutenant's office. I went into the vacant lieutenant's office. The unit had been without a lieutenant since last February. The fiscally stingy city manager was in no hurry to fill the position.

The office was very sparse, but it had a desk, two chairs, and a telephone which was all I wanted for the time being. I saw Gary walk in through the door opening and I called out to him.

"Big G!"

Gary stepped into the office doorway.

"Come in, come in," I said to him.

"Why do I want to go in there? I have my own office. Why don't *you* come to *my* office? You want to talk to *me*. Come to *my* office."

I gaped at him, a little startled. He broke into that megawatt smile and stepped in and sat in the chair across from me.

"What's up, Kahuna?"

I just smiled and shook my head. Gary had a way of disarming tense moments with his humor and easy-going attitude.

"Gary, I need to ask if you'll do a favor for me?"

"Always. What you need?"

"I'm expecting a fax from Hialeah P.D. about an arrest made by the City of Miami in 1994. It's a simple misdemeanor charge but it has a lot of information I need. When it comes in can you check with Miami for the validity of it? I need to know how the defendant got out of jail. Did he bond out, or did someone bond him out? When the report comes in can you do the leg work on that for me? Please. I'm slammed with lots of other angles on this fiasco from Hialeah."

"Yeah, yeah, no problem, Cade. I heard you had a rolling time in Hialeah the other day," he said with a slight smile.

"It was a rolling time but not a rolling *good* time. My ass is in serious hot water with Brunson."

"Dude, that guy went totally ballistic. I mean like, seriously unhinged. I heard this banging garbage can and then saw the can go whizzing by our door. Ileana shut off her telenovela and said she didn't care about the show, she was getting out. I just stayed in my office 'till the cursing and yelling stopped. First chance I got, I boogied out of here, dude," he said.

"I guess I really set him off that day," I said.

"Dude, it was like Ralph Cramden was running this place. I swear. To the moon, Alice, to the moon!"

"Ah man, I don't know Big G," I said, feeling suddenly much sadder than I had before. "I don't know sometimes it just seems like it never ends."

"Hang in there Kemosabe, it's just a job. You were looking for a job when you found this one, right? Is there anything else I can do for you?"

I took a deep breath. "I don't know. I have to find a way to get a report on a house fire in North Miami in 1996."

"You know that the county has created a new incident report website," he said.

"No, I didn't know that." I replied.

"It's still being built out, but the website chronicles all Miami Dade Fire reports. I'll set us up with an account and see if your fire is in their uploaded database."

"Whoa, that would be *great*. It would save a ton of phone calls. The address is 160 Northeast 164th Street in North Miami. All I know is that it was in 1996. I don't have a date. Sorry."

"I got it, bro. I'll get back with you later," he said as he left the office.

Alone again, I started to write down the list that had been ruminating in my head onto paper. I called the Hialeah Police Department and left a message for Hammy to call me. I started calling various gun shops around Miami, asking if anyone sold steel jacketed ammunition. There was a lot of passing the phone around and asking coworkers, but it seemed that none of them sold steel jacketed ammunition. One shop said they'd never heard of anyone loading rounds in steel. I could hear Ileana on the telephone in the other office. She called out to me.

"*Oÿe,* Cade *de fronta* desk has a visitor for *ju*. I told them to send them up since *ju* are here."

"Ileana, you know we don't accept visitors up here. Why did you do that?" I said with a tinge of anger.

"*Aye* Cade, I can't keep up with all these rules. Too late. Next time, okay. They are on their way."

"Ileana it's not just *a* rule—it's one of our biggest rules."

Some idiots in the 1970s put black Saltillo tile in the hallways of the department. The cleaning crew's wheeled garbage cans always sound like a roller coaster falling off its tracks as the wheels tumble along the uneven grout lines and bumpy tiles. I could hear heels walking on the black Saltillo tile in the outer hallway. I could hear a woman's voice in the center office.

"Is this VIN? I'm looking for Detective Cade Taylor."

I heard Gary's chair squeak in his office as he must be leaning back to look at our visitor. Ileana didn't say much, and must have just pointed to the lieutenant's office.

The doorway to the lieutenant's office was quickly filled by a tall woman. She was wearing very snug black jeans tucked into black leather boots that had a high tongue. The boots had a half inch heel and a brass zipper that ran up only one side. She wore a lavender t shirt under her black leather jacket. Her curly, reddish-brown hair went past her shoulders. She was a very attractive woman. She narrowed her gaze at me for a second, then she spoke to me.

"Are you the joker that has my Mercedes?"

Chapter Eleven

I WAS TAKEN ABACK by her appearance and by her question. I just looked at her, stupefied. I probably looked at her a little longer than necessary.

"Save the cordial greetings for the Junior Orange Bowl Committee. Are you the guy who has my car?" she asked me again.

I snapped from my surprise and asked her who she was.

"Auburn McKenna. U.S. Marshal's office."

She unclipped her U.S. Marshals badge from her belt and tossed it onto the desk. I picked up her badge and inspected it before sliding it back across the desk towards her. She took that as an invitation and sat across from me in the same seat Gary had just been in minutes ago.

"Your office could use some decorating," she said as she looked around at the bare walls, loose cables and phone lines poorly tacked along the baseboards.

"Marshall, you want to tell me why you're here again?" I asked her.

"I'm here because of you. You *are* Cade Taylor, right?"

"Yeah, I'm Cade Taylor," I said.

She pulled out a piece of off-white paper from the inside pocket of her jacket.

"Cade Taylor, Unit 923 Vice Intelligence Narcotics from the—"

She paused to look around at the water-stained ceiling tiles and well-worn carpet and then she finished.

"Coral Gables Police Department."

I wondered what she was reading from.

"You ran the vehicle identification number in the system of the very same Mercedes-Benz we have spent *months* looking for."

"You've been looking for the Mercedes? Why?"

"Is there a place we can talk that has a little more ambience?" she said, flickering her gaze around. "Like maybe a bus terminal bathroom? Or a cramped janitorial closet with a leaky sink?"

"I'm not a fan of the building either. I am a fan of breakfast. Do you know Sergio's Café on Coral Way? Care to meet me there and we can talk?" I asked her.

"Breakfast? Absolutely! I'll follow you. Where are you parked?"

"I'm in the alley between the bank and the station. I'll be in a black Acura RL. I'll wait for you," I said as we parted ways outside the VIN office door.

I was in my car only a few minutes when a blue Chevrolet Blazer pulled in behind me. U.S. Marshal Auburn McKenna was wearing sunglasses, but it was her. She followed me to Sergio's Café on Coral Way.

The parking lot in the rear is bigger than the restaurant. I pulled into a crudely painted parking space, and she pulled in beside me. I noticed the door lock on her driver's door was scratched all around the cylindrical lock. Too many times fumbling in the dark with the keys in her hand, obviously. We walked in together. The hostess sat us at a booth and placed two laminated menus in front of us.

"So, tell me why this Mercedes is so important to the U.S. Marshal's office," I said.

"You tell me first why you chose to run the vehicle identification number of the Mercedes and where the car is now."

I said nothing. The waitress came to the table to take our order. I told her we would need a few minutes.

Auburn McKenna could tell I wasn't going to budge so she drew the mental short straw and spoke first.

"The person who owns that car is being sought by the U.S, Marshals for protocol indiscretions."

"Protocol indiscretions? What the hell does that mean?"

"It means I'm not playing around here with you. I'm asking you for the last time, nicely—where is the car now?"

"Listen, lady. You got a real nice looking circular star badge, but I'm not impressed by it or you. I used to be married to one just like you. She was shorter and meaner and if I could handle her I sure as hell can handle you."

"If you could handle her than you would still be married to her," she said.

When the waitress returned to the table, I requested she bring me the Sergio's special "Country Breakfast *revuelto y jamon*." I never took my eyes off Auburn, and McKenna just stared back at me and told the waitress she'd have the same thing I was having. The waitress walked away, probably thinking to herself she was witnessing a divorce.

"You don't even know what Country Breakfast *revuelto y jamon* is," I said to her.

"My Spanish is pretty good. Good enough to know scrambled eggs with ham," she said.

"Your car is in my care and custody."

"Let me hear you correctly. You not only ran the Mercedes in the system, but you towed it back to that dumpy building?"

"Originally? Yes. Now it's probably in one of our contracted tow yards," I fibbed to her.

"Who do you have contracts with?" she asked.

"Mostly we use Southland Towing."

"I can see how inappropriate this may seem, but I really need to make a call about this. My cell crapped out. It's in factory reset mode. It's useless. Can I borrow your phone for a minute? Please?" She didn't blink, didn't waver.

"How do I know you'll be back with my phone?" I said sarcastically.

"You know I'll be back with it because I'm a U.S Marshal and more importantly because I'm hungry." she said.

I gave her my cell phone and she left through the front door of the restaurant as she was dialing. All eyes in the cafe were on her as she walked out. As I said, she was a very attractive woman. A little demanding, but attractive. Upon seeing her leave, the waitress asked me if I wanted any coffee. I ordered a café con leche. The coffee came to the table sooner than McKenna did, ten minutes later. She passed my phone back to me. She'd cleared the most recent number dialed.

Smooth.

"Let's get back on track. What made you decide to run the Mercedes?" she asked me.

"It's part of an active investigation. Why are you so interested in it?" I asked her.

"The same," she vaguely replied.

"Are we investigating the same person and for the same reason?" I asked her.

"Depends. Who and what are you investigating?"

"Okay," I said, leaning back in the booth. "I've had a real good time here playing some sort of U.S. Marshal's home version of 'What's my Line' but as far as I'm concerned, I have an investigation to do, and I have the Mercedes. I think the cards in my hand trump yours. So either start talking or you can continue to either keep looking for the Mercedes or you can watch it through a chain link fence for the next four months. Your call. Talk."

"Okay, Mr. Cade Taylor. I *am* Deputy U.S. Marshal Auburn McKenna. Yes, that is my name. My father hated his in-laws, you know my grandparents. They were big University of Alabama football fans. You know the whole Bear Bryant thing. So, my dad named me Auburn because he knew they would have to say Auburn for the rest of their lives. Twisty. I know. I used to be assigned to the Witness Security Program. We call it WITSEC in case you need a basic lesson on federal law enforcement. For the past three years I've been in a fugitive investigative strike team, recovering fugitives and assets. Myself and my team work primarily in Tampa rounding up all the bad guys, but we do work as far west as New Orleans and as far north as Atlanta. The owner of that Mercedes has been on our list. He's been on the list for too long. Way too long. Now, you. Talk!"

"Me? My name is Cade Taylor and I've been with the Gables about twelve years. The last nine years have been in VIN. I've been detached to the DEA for about six years. Myself and my team work primarily in Miami but do work from time to time out of town. I don't know why my parents named me Cade. I don't remember what I wanted to be when I grew up but I'm pretty sure it wasn't this. I don't follow college football. I'm divorced and a Scorpio."

"Every psycho I've ever dated was a Scorpio."

"Every psycho I've ever dated believed in Astrology," I said.

"We're not getting anywhere here. I can have you subpoenaed to tell me everything."

"Listen Marshal, you might be cozy with a ton of judges but as of last night I'm on a designated Justice Department task force. Since I didn't see *you* at last night's parent-teacher open house, that makes you not a member of the class. Now I can lobby to have you enrolled in our little club but as of now…no dice. As far as subpoenas, well good luck with the orthopedic surgeon who sets your damaged arm because you'll be writing a lot. Not just for me but for lots of people here in Miami and Washington. So do you want to play nice, or do you want to go the long way around the sun here?"

Our plates arrived. The waitress was still sensing the tension at the table and softly asked me if I wanted a refill on my café con leche. I gladly said yes. She also asked Auburn if she would like some coffee. She declined.

"How do you drink that swill?" Auburn asked me.

"What? I like Cuban coffee. You don't?"

"You mean like Pilon or Bustillo? No way. No how. Last summer a whole contingency of us had to go to Europe for the world cup in France. There was a threat concerning CONMEBOL. I spent a lot of time in Belgium and France. Now *that* is real coffee, not this dishwater shit you all drink from these little windows all over Miami."

"What is CONMEBOL?"

"It is one of FIFA's six continental confederations. You know, the soccer governing body? CONMEBOL is responsible for the organization of South American soccer's major international teams and tournaments. You follow soccer? You know, the world's game?"

"I just told you I don't follow college football, what makes you think I'd know anything about soccer?"

"I bet you're a really boring guy. Actually, I shouldn't bet since I've already got some quick inside information that you *are* boring."

"Where did you get your winning personality? In a car crash?" I asked her.

"You're really funny," she said, no smile. "Let's get back on track. Why did you run the Mercedes and why did you tow it?" she said.

"Did you hear about the DEA agent being shot in Hialeah two days ago?"

"Yes."

"We're looking for the shooter. He wasn't driving the Mercedes, but he shot the driver of the Mercedes before he shot the DEA agent," I said.

"The driver of the Mercedes, was he killed?"

"We don't think so."

"What makes you say that?"

"Because he drove away and ditched the car somewhere near Miami Beach."

"Near Miami Beach? Like where exactly?"

"Are you interested where the car is or where it was? Because I have it."

"The car. How did you find it?"

"Same thing I told DEA. Just fortunate. The blood in the car is consistent with what crime scene technicians gathered at the scene in Hialeah."

"You think the driver is alive? Have you checked the hospitals?"

"We have every ER on alert and officers stationed in every trauma center."

"Good. That's good. It's a good start. The Marshals' service has resources to find people. We can help. Open the door for me or any of my fellow Marshals to get in on this with you."

"No offense, but if your resources are so good how come you've been looking for this car for months?"

"Because it hasn't been a big priority, but seeing as one of our DEA agents has been shot, finding the driver is now our priority."

"Cars don't drive themselves. Why are you so interested in *this* car, though?"

"Like I said, the driver violated some protocol indiscretions."

"You're being evasive and vague. That's no way to get me to get you on the task force. You want to play games? Then go play by yourself. We'll figure this out without you or the U.S. Marshals."

"Cade, we have certain levels of confidentiality that we just can't break. Not for you. Not for a DEA agent who was shot. It is a tenet of our judicial system."

"We *are* the judicial system. Ever hear of the thin blue line? You're no different than that cretin from Washington last night—"

"Wait. They had someone come in from Washington on this?

"Yeah, some suit who pompously sat in our meeting then left.

Typical seagull manager. He came flying in, made a bunch of noise, shit on everything, then left."

She looked out the window and kept quiet for a moment. She then looked at me.

"Okay. I'm going to tell you something. It stays between us. I told you I was previously WITSEC. The owner of the Mercedes is in our house. We created him. I can't say if he's the driver you're looking for—but the owner of the Mercedes was conjured up by us. He's gotten off the team bus and stopped checking in months ago. It happens. About ninety-five percent of witnesses in the program are criminals. They don't always change their spots. Yes, some of the people we put in WITSEC are witnesses that testified against other criminals. So, before you ask, I can't tell you if the owner of the Mercedes is a criminal or a witness. All I can say is we put him in that car."

"The owner? But we don't know if the driver from Hialeah is the owner or not."

"Do you have any fingerprints or identifying items?" she asked eagerly.

"No. The car was clean, and we're at a standstill," I lied.

"How do you know it was the same Mercedes from the DEA shooting in Hialeah?" she asked me again.

"Because I was there. I was there when he got shot and I was there when the DEA agent got shot. I put my handprint on the hood of the Mercedes before I walked into that hellfire. My print came back positive on the hood."

"I'm sorry you had to go through that," she said.

"So, who is this guy? The Mercedes owner?"

"Cade, we gave him a new identity and place to live. We've checked his address and it looks like he moved out weeks, maybe even months ago. He stopped paying the utilities. He hasn't used a credit card in six months. No traceable records. We had a license plate verification notice put on the car. No parking tickets, no tolls, nothing—until *you* ran the car in the system. We had a silent alert on it. When we saw somebody named Jeanie Rae Richards from the Coral Gables Police Department ran the tag for Detective Cade Taylor, I got told to drop everything and get to the Gables and find this Taylor guy. That's you, and here we are."

"If he hasn't done anything since he was in WITSEC, why the urgency?"

"Because he's vital to other things related to our work."

"So, he was a witness in protection?"

She suddenly slammed her hand on the table, startling the waitress who snapped her head up from another table. Auburn leaned across the table. She spoke in a low voice.

"I didn't say that. What I *said* is he's vital to our work. Stop hearing what I'm saying and start listening to what I'm saying."

I just looked at her and took a sip of the delicious café con leche.

I put the cup down. "Is drama a big thing with you Marshals? Because I've had enough hard times and excitement in my life, especially in the past few days, to last me a lifetime. How about you dial it down a little." Now I leaned across the table. "Who. Is. The owner of the Mercedes?" I spelled out slowly. "It would help us, and it would help you in the end to tell me."

"He's protected. I can't tell you that. Let's just refer to him as 57."

"57?"

"Yes, 57. I can't reveal his identity to you or anyone unless his file is directly requested by a high court and that would take months and even then, there's a snowball's chance in hell it would get released. The justice system would fight the release of that information on principle for months. You'd have one law entity challenging another law entity, just making attorneys rich as they both burn through legal fees."

"So, 57. Like Heinz 57. You make it real hard to trust you, you know that?" I said.

"I know. I'm a woman and I'm a woman with a gun. Trust was never part of the manufacturer's fine print. Cade, I would suggest that rather than continuing to lock horns with me, you find a way to work with me and I'll find a way to work with you. I'm sure there's someone above you that I can convince with less aggravation."

I thought about what had transpired over breakfast. Auburn knew the identity of the owner of the Mercedes-Benz. Whoever he is, he now has a new name and identity complete with government-manufactured credit cards, social security number, driver's license, a secreted home location and an unregistered vehicle. If I worked off the assumption that the Benz's driver was also the owner, then I knew his true identity: Dario Curbelo. This was a nugget of insight I wasn't going to share with her. Not now, at least.

She wants to play coy. I can play dumb.

Aside from knowing his true name I could also physically identify him. At this moment it didn't matter what his assumed name was—he was off the grid with the Marshals, and they knew his new identity. U.S. Marshal Auburn McKenna probably didn't know Curbelo was arrested in 1994 by Miami P.D. She was going to staunchly keep her information to herself, and I was going to do the same.

Brunson wanted the 400k returned immediately, and wanted to get the twenty kilograms of cocaine off the street—but the focus was still on who shot Agent Lew.

I decided to keep McKenna away from Hammy Garzon, as well as DEA agents Matias Marroquín and Vincent Walker for as long as I could. I'd let her spin on the car, and I'd focus on finding Curbelo, or as she called him, "57."

"When you get your cell phone fixed, call me so we can get on the right side of all of this," I said to her.

I threw a twenty down on the table and walked out.

Chapter Twelve

I DROVE BACK TO the station. I hated being in the building but today I needed to get some things squared away. I needed to start plotting the best method to approach this investigation.

I went back in the vacant lieutenant office. Gary saw me walk in and he retrieved from the fax machine the arrest report filed by the Miami Police Department on Dario Curbelo. He sat down across me as I read through it. The report had a very short and perfunctory narrative. It did list Curbelo's address, 12 Cape Florida Drive on Key Biscayne. I read it twice. It most certainly appeared that Dario Curbelo was arrested for a minor infraction that most cops and police departments wouldn't have arrested someone for. It was very ticky tack Mickey Mouse. The officer wrote that Curbelo was asked to step back on the sidewalk, and he didn't move in a timely manner, so he was arrested for disobeying a lawful order. The arresting officer was Denny Byrne, city identification number 3263. I used the desk telephone and called the City of Miami Police Department. I identified myself and asked the operations center if they still had an Officer Byrne. They informed he was now a sergeant. I provided my cell phone number and asked them to have Sergeant Byrne call me.

"Dude, who was the biker chick?" Gary asked me.

I sighed. "She was wearing a leather jacket. That hardly makes her a biker chick. She is a U.S. Deputy Marshall."

"For real? I mean, she was smoking hot. What's her name?'

"Her name is Auburn McKenna. I'm sure she may appreciate you thinking she's smoking hot and would probably appreciate it more if you found a way to express that sentiment in a language that was more conference room than locker room," I said.

"Dude I'm just saying—"

"I know what you're saying," I said holding my hand up. "I hear you. Big G, what sign are you anyway?"

"Scorpio. Why?"

"Never mind. Thank you for getting this fax. Anything on the house fire in North Miami?" I asked him.

"Interesting you should ask. The county website does have the fire listed. I was able to pull the report up. I haven't read it yet but it's on my desk, let me go get it."

He came back holding some papers fresh off the printer, which he perused for a few seconds and then started reading from the first page.

"On this day and date at the above approximate times—"

"Hold on. What day and date and times?"

"January 28, 1996, at 21:52. So that's what? 9:52pm, right?"

"Yeah, so go on Big G."

"On this day and date at the above approximate times North Miami police units 4123 and 4128 were dispatched to 160 Northeast 164th Street regarding a complaint of smoke in the area. Upon arrival both police units discovered the entire residence at 160 Northeast 164th Street engulfed in flames. Miami Dade Fire was notified via the North Miami Police Department. Incident Command was informed that the concrete structure was, by police estimates, in full inferno. Incident Command dispatched two extension ladder trucks, one fire rescue truck, and one battalion supervisor from Miami Dade Fire station twenty. First responding fire personnel observed a single structure with flames emanating from all windows and exceeding the roofline. Weather conditions were partially cloudy with winds out of the northeast at fourteen miles per hour. Adverse weather does not appear to be a contributing factor to the origin of the fire. Point of origin was not established until six hours later. Arson investigator Jeff Baggett unit D6012 determined the initial point of origin was a liquid accelerant that was distributed copiously amongst the interior of the structure."

"Sounds like arson to me," I said.

Gary continued reading, "Fire containment took thirty-five minutes. Fire extinguishment was within ten minutes of containment. Arson Investigator Baggett established incendiary cause through physical evidence at scene. Low rise char and extensive burn patterns were seen throughout the house, most evident at the four foot or below level. Accelerant was uninformedly spread throughout the floor level of the residence and flame crawl among the walls and ceiling were created from the floor up. Intense smoke and gasses from plastics and woods rendered the air quality within the structure to be unsurvivable. Within the embers a lone human remain was located in the front foyer area of the structure. It was determined the remains were that of a male. Burn ratio to the body was at 100%. Pelvis size indicates a male. Remains were sent to the Dade County Medical Examiner's office for final analysis. Neighborhood canvass determined from neighbors that the structure had been vacant for an extensive period of time, and it was speculated the remains may be those of a squatter or a person residentially challenged. The structure is considered a complete loss."

If there was a lone squatter or someone who was potentially unaccounted for in society it would be very easy for the U.S. Marshals' office to say that the victim of the fire was Dario Curbelo. If the U.S. Marshals could get Dario Curbelo listed as deceased, it would keep anybody who'd been looking for Curbelo from finding him. The big question was did the Marshals give him an entirely new identity, or did they have him assume the identity of the deceased person in the fire?

I thanked Gary as he left the office, then I called the Dade County Medical Examiner's office. The former medical examiner had left earlier in the year to take a position in Toronto. I knew there was an office assistant named Arum who'd been assigned to the intake portion of the Medical Examiner's office. After a few telephone connections I reached him.

"Hello."

"Arum, this is Cade Taylor from the Coral Gables Police, do you remember me?"

"Detective Taylor! Of course I remember you. How could I forget all the overtime you created here last winter?"

"You're a funny guy, Arum."

"Actually, I'm not. How can I help you, Detective?"

"Arum, there was a house fire a few years ago and I wanted to get some details."

"Details?"

"Yes, I need to get some details," I said.

"Details."

"Arum, I just said that—"

"No. Details. As in give me the information so I can look it up, the details," he said.

"Oh, sorry. It was a house fire on January 28, 1996. The location was 160 Northeast 164th Street in North Miami."

I could hear the clicking of a keyboard and his breathing on the telephone.

"Hang on, it's coming up. This system is really slow. We used a grant to upgrade to a new system with MCI and it has not been a good match for us."

"I recall you being all excited about it when you first got it," I said.

"That was then. This is now," he said with a tinge of exasperation in his voice.

I heard more keystrokes. There was about a minute of silence then I heard him say, more to himself than to me, "Well, that's odd."

"What's odd?"

"It has a hold for release on it."

"What does that mean?" I asked him.

"It's kind of a misnomer. It means I can't access the report and I can't release any information even if I could. It's like when a celebrity dies, and the family wishes for the autopsy photos and report to not be released. Or when there's an open investigation and pertinent information cannot be released. Not as common as people think but it does happen, and well Detective Cade Taylor, it has happened to you today. I wish I could help you, but I can't get into the file."

"Well, who can release it from the hold?'

"Whoever or whatever put the hold on it in the first place."

"Does it say who put the hold on it?"

"No. It's one of those things where it will be sealed forever. Then one day, we'll look into it and suddenly the hold will be released. I think you can deduce what I'm telling you here. Someone or something high up on the food chain doesn't *want* this released."

"Thank you, Arum, sorry to bother you."

"No bother. Goodbye."

I stared at the telephone and let out a deep exhale. I leaned back in the chair and interlocked my fingers behind my head as I looked up at the ceiling, contemplating the complexity of this mess, and how in a short span of time my life had become a quagmire of dead ends and obstructed passages.

I picked up the fire report and reread it. Sometimes reading something can open a train of thought different from having something read to you. Something leapt off the pages at me. Arson Investigator Jeff Baggett Unit D6102 said in his report that the "Burn ratio to the body was at 100%. Pelvis size indicates a male." I know it's possible to get fingerprints from cadavers in many stages of decay and deterioration, but Baggett said the body was 100% burned. He even had to use the measurement of the pelvis to determine the sex. Dental records would be the best way to identify the body. Hammy Garzon said, "According to our records Dario Curbelo from Ciudad de Estes Paraguay died in a 1996 housefire at 160 Northeast 164th Street in North Miami."

If the fire at 160 Northeast 164th Street in North Miami was indeed arson as Baggett stated in his report, then they may have been *too* good at setting the fire. If they intended to have a lost soul burn in that inferno and then claim it was Dario Curbelo, they may have done a great job of sealing the report at the Medical Examiner's office, but neglected to get Baggett's report. I added tracking down and talking to Arson Investigator Jeff Baggett to my list of things to do.

I pulled the two pages I'd taken from the phone book from my back pocket, unfolded them and placed them on the desk. I decided to go down to Major Brunson's office and update him on where I was in the investigation. I hadn't really made any progress, so it wouldn't be a very long or fruitful conversation. I steadied myself for the profanity barrage I was going to get.

Charlene was sitting behind her desk in the outer office. She looked above the lens of her reading glasses at me. I began to speak when my cell phone started ringing. I put up the universally understood one finger to hold hand gesture and backed out of the office to take the call.

"Hello."

"Is this Detective Taylor?" said a man's voice on the line.

"Who's this?"

"This is Sergeant Byrne from Miami P.D."

"Oh, yes, sorry. Yes, this is Cade Taylor. Sergeant, thank you for calling me back," I said.

"Do you have the ticket number and location?" he asked me.

"I'm sorry, what?" I said.

"The citation. I only get calls from outside agencies because someone's wife or relative got a ticket. What is the citation number?" he said.

"No. Actually...um, no, I called because I want to talk to you about an arrest you made a few years ago," I said.

"A few years ago? Are you serious? How would I remember anything like that? I don't know about the Gables, but we arrest a lot of people here in the so-called Magic City," he said, starting to laugh.

"It was during the Summit of the Americas at the Torch of Freedom on Biscayne Boulevard," I said.

The phone was unsettlingly quiet. I assumed he was trying to remember the inconsequential minor misdemeanor arrest. I asked him if he was still on the line.

"Yeah, I'm here. Look buddy, I don't know who I'm talking to here. You're just a voice on the line. I work Coral Way and I'm out here now. If you are really with the Gables, meet me at Plate. It's a restaurant in the 2200 block. I'll be there in twenty minutes."

The line went dead. He didn't even say goodbye. He also didn't ask me if I was nearby or available. Fortunately, I was. Meet him at Plate in twenty minutes. This wasn't even a to-go order. Maybe all restaurant connections in Miami are twenty minutes. I wasn't going to waste time thinking about his brusque manner or the food in twenty minutes phenomena in Miami. The restaurant with light traffic was easily fifteen minutes away and parking would be a mess. It was just down the road from Sergio's Café where I'd dined with Marshal Auburn McKenna earlier. Today I was getting a heavy dose of restaurants on Coral Way.

It didn't take long to find the restaurant but as I predicted finding a parking space would be the bigger challenge. A UPS truck was just finishing up a delivery near Our Lady of Lebanon Catholic Church. As he pulled away from the curb, he revealed an open parking space which I slipped into. Within seconds I was walking towards the small restaurant.

Crossing 21st Avenue I saw it. The restaurant was a small place directly next to the Uruguayan Consulate. The crest of the Consulate General was prominently displayed above the building entrance.

Consulado General del Uruguay.

Sitting at one of the outside tables was Sergeant Byrne. He looked very slender in his Miami police uniform. His most distinguishing feature was his shocking white hair. A coffee cup and saucer was in front of him. On the table near the coffee cup was a copy of C.S Lewis' book, *Out of the Silent Planet.* I locked eyes with him as I strode towards him. I shook his hand, presented my detective badge to him, and sat down across from him.

"I don't usually meet uniforms in public, especially outside," I said, looking around.

"You didn't say you were U.C. If you'd said that you were U.C., we could've met somewhere else," was all he said very casually.

"I didn't really have a choice in the location. You hung up quickly," I said.

"You going to have anything?" he asked, ignoring my comment.

"No, I ate earlier. This shouldn't take too long." I watched the moderately heavy traffic on Coral Way. Being outside like this was unnerving. "So do you recall making an arrest at the Torch of Freedom during the Summit of the Americas?"

He lowered his voice a little as he leaned in across the table.

"I don't remember his name but yes, I made an arrest. I got slammed by the brass because it left my squad short that day. We had a bunch of protestors at the Torch, most of them easy and friendly just holding signs, blowing whistles, waving flags. You know. The usual."

I didn't say anything I just nodded in understanding.

"So anyway, this typical fed in a suit comes up to me and says he's with the State Department. They wanted this one protestor removed so they could I.D. him. He pointed this guy out to me. I went to talk to him and with all the shouting and whistles I don't think he heard me too well. It was a good opportunity to get him separated from everyone else and I made the arrest for disobeying a lawful order. Well, from the ass-chewing I got from my people, I sure learned a lesson. Some of the other protestors started getting agitated when he was placed in cuffs, and it caused a little tension out there. I took him back to Miami P.D., processed him, and never thought of it again until you called today. I mean it was nothing. Or is it something?"

"No, it's nothing unless you're the guy who got arrested. Do you remember his name?"

"Seriously? Hey buddy, *you* obviously know his name because you know I arrested him. So why don't you shoot straight with me here. What's the angle on this?"

"His name is Dario Curbelo. There's no angle, he just came across our intelligence network, and we're trying to get as much information about him as we can. Do you remember him saying anything about his home or friends or anything?"

"No. It was a real in and out, super easy arrest. I wish I could tell you more but no. Sorry."

"Was he transported to Dade County Jail or just held at Miami P.D.?" I asked him.

"You know, I don't know. We have intake people for our arrests and if we're expecting mass arrests like a demonstration, we have arrest teams. We didn't have teams that day. He might have been transported or he might have just been held and then released," he said.

"What about the guy from the State Department, you ever hear from him again?" I asked.

"Nope. Typical Washington asshole. Short hair, sunglasses, not used to the heat and sweating even though it was December," he replied.

"Can I ask a favor of you? Since you were the arresting officer, can you see if there was any follow-up? I'm curious how long he stayed in jail, either with you or with the county. I'm wondering if he was bonded out and who bonded him. Can you look into that for me, please?"

"Absolutely. I'll let you know when I know," he said.

As I got ready to leave, I shifted gears. "Thank you and thank you for your time. I appreciate it. You like the South District?"

"I'd rather be in the Grove or the Roads, but Coral Way is okay. Mostly we get a minimum of three bomb threats a week across the street at that Cuban radio station. Some crazy exile gets on the airwaves and says something construed as pro-Fidel Castro and the whole place erupts in high ratings Hispanic hysteria."

Coral Way is two lanes each way with tall, street-shading Banyan trees in the center median. I looked across Coral Way at the 2100 building. A sign for the radio station, *"CARACOL 1260 AM WUSA"* was prominently displayed on the building's façade. Parked in front of the building was a dark Chrysler 300M. Two guys were inside of it, looking towards me. Typical Washington assholes. Short hair, sunglasses, not used to the heat and sweating, even though it was November.

Chapter Thirteen

I DIDN'T SEE A readily accessible rear exit inside the restaurant. I thanked Sergeant Byrne again as I left and started walking north on Coral Way. When I looked back at him, he was already sipping his coffee, reading his book, oblivious to the Chrysler across the street.

There was a man standing in front of the Uruguayan Consulate, smoking a cigarette. I asked him for directions to Coral Gables just to buy time as I watched the occupants of the Chrysler reflected in the Consulate building's smokey glass windows. The man still with cigarette in hand, pointed west down Coral Way. I made a grand gesture of nodding my head and giving him a thumbs up as I walked away towards 21st Street.

Whoever those guys were, they were either watching the consulate or me. If they were watching me, they'd be waiting for me to get in my car and drive west.

I walked to my car parked in front of the church. Unless they moved their own car, I was too far down for them to see me. Traffic had eased on the street, and I was able to throw the car quickly into reverse, cut the wheel and rapidly back into the church parking lot. I threw the car into drive and drove east through the asphalt parking lot into a vacant overflow lot. The transition went from asphalt to flattened grass and I tore across the grassy lot and out the black wrought iron gates. I turned north on Southwest 19th and hit the gas, past Shenandoah Middle School. I didn't let off the speed until I got to the intersection at Southwest 16th Street. I turned east and slowly meandered my way east. I pulled over a few times and checked my mirrors, but it didn't seem like anyone was following me.

I arrived back at the police department without a tail following me. I knew I'd have to talk with Major Brunson, so I went to his office. I once again steadied myself for the profanity barrage I was going to get. I walked into the outer office and saw Charlene sitting behind her desk. She adjusted her head so she could see me better. I began to speak when she put up the universally understood one finger gesture which uses a different finger and has nothing to do with "hold on one minute."

"What's that for?" I asked her.

"It's all for you. You make my life miserable. You get him riled up and he starts kicking garbage cans and stuff."

"I... I... I—"

"No, 'I don't mean to,' or no, 'I don't know what you mean, Charlene.' Whatever it is you do Cade, I don't understand it—but whatever it is it sure pisses him off," she snapped.

I just chose to ignore her own barrage. Although not profane, it really was nothing compared to Major Brunson.

"Is he in?" I asked her.

"Is he in? Of course not, you dolt. Do you think we'd be having this conversation if he could hear us? He went to lunch. Where? I don't know, but if I had to guess he's probably at Uncle Tom's Barbecue eating a pulled pork sandwich, secretly hoping a car crashes through the front window and ends his aggravation."

The hostility was moving into the creative mind space, and I figured it was better I just use the same door I came in through to go back out. In law enforcement you work off the three "R's." Respond, Report, and Respect. I decided to employ the little known unspoken fourth "R."

Retreat.

I went back to the VIN office. I started jotting down timeline notes on a legal pad. I needed to keep the events of the past days clearly understood. I wrote:

An unknown new informant had set the deal up with DEA Group 4 to sell twenty kilos of cocaine for $400,000. The seller of the cocaine set the deal up to take place in a restaurant in Hialeah. DEA Agent Scott Lew was the case agent. He was in contact with the informant. I was asked to be the U.C. As the meet was about to begin a pale stranger arrived at the restaurant in a taxi. He went inside the restaurant. Two DEA agents Walker and Marroquín chased down the taxi to get any passenger information. I went into the restaurant alone with the $400,000 but not before following my gut instincts and putting my hand on the front hoods of three nearby parked cars. I went in and was surprised to see the dealer that I knew only as "the Ecuadorian" sitting with a very large, imposing Latin male. The Latin male turned out to be Bernardo Ricon Giraldez, a heavyweight muscle nicknamed the "Crazy Cure." Within minutes of sitting down the pale stranger shot both the Crazy Cure and the Ecuadorian. I shot at the pale stranger. He ran out and collided with Agent Lew who was running in. Lew suffered a gunshot ricochet wound to the head and is still in a medically induced coma. I chased the pale stranger and he fired twice at me on the street and twice more near the paddocks of Hialeah Racetrack. Upon returning to the scene Giraldez was dead and the Ecuadorian, the cocaine and the money were gone. Surveillance cameras from the gas station next door showed the Ecuadorian leaving the scene in a Mercedes-Benz. He was wounded and had the cocaine and money with him. The car was located the next day in Bay Harbor Islands. Giraldez, aka the "Crazy Cure," had been arrested multiple times and each of his booking addresses came back to a sewage pump station on Miami Beach. Currently a dead end. The Ecuadorian was arrested in 1994 by Miami Police Sergeant Denny Byrne. Home address 12 Cape Florida Drive Key Biscayne. Turns out he isn't from Ecuador but is from Paraguay. His name is Dario Curbelo. According to computer records Hialeah police discovered that he died in a North Miami housefire. Arson Investigator Jeff Baggett stated the body in the fire *was 100% emolliated. U.S Marshall Auburn Mckenna informed me that Dario Curbelo was in the WITSEC program and had stopped communicating with the U.S Marshals' office. They'd been looking for him when my recovery of his Mercedes-Benz set off an alarm in their system and she was now demanding to know all that I knew and to be put on the task force looking for him. On top of that we have a stuffed suit from Washington pretending to be a paper pusher when he is in fact an operator.*

It helped me to keep abreast of the developments if I wrote them down, especially if Major Brunson was going to be on a continual Defcon Four status because of the missing money and cocaine. The afternoon was getting away from me. I still hadn't heard from Arson Investigator Baggett. I was curious about Agent Lew's medical condition, so I made a call to ASAC Mandeville. She informed me that he was still in the coma, but the doctors were starting to test his brain recovery. They wanted to pull him out of the coma maybe as early as tonight. The goal of a medically induced coma is to reach a level of sedation called "burst suppression." When the brain is in this state, it's completely quiet for several seconds, alternating with very short snippets of activity. The period when the brain is quiet gives it critical time to rest and heal. This is a medical procedure that cannot be rushed. It just can't be *hurried*, no matter how badly I needed to know who his new informant was. The informant set this deal up and the informant should be able to help us find Dario Curbelo.

The calls I needed to make from the pages I'd ripped out of the phone book were still awaiting. Flattening out the two sheets of pages, I knew I wouldn't be able to get through both pages with the afternoon getting away from me like it was. I started dialing the very first business on the page. The phone rang three times before someone picked it up.

"Aamco."

"Hello, my wife was just there for an oil change, and I think your technician didn't put the plug back in tightly. There's some oil dripping on the floor of our garage."

"What? What's your wife's name?"

"Actually her secretary brought the car in for her, so I don't know if she used her name, our name, or the company name," I said.

"Do you have the license tag, I can check it that way," he said, the exasperation clear in his voice.

Bingo! Just what I was hoping for.

"Yes, its DCH-328."

"No buddy, that car didn't come through here today."

"Well maybe she has her dates mixed up. Do you show it in your system at all?" I pushed.

"Nope. Never been here. Maybe she took it to a different Aamco?"

"Yeah, I'm getting the whole story second-hand here. Thank you. I'll check with other Aamcos," I said and hung up.

The call went exactly the way I expected it to go. Many people don't realize that chain oil change service centers retain an in-house database for marketing and customer retention reasons. Since they're usually franchised, each oil change service center keeps their own database of customers and customer cars. This was a complete fishing expedition. I was hoping that maybe Dario Curbelo got careless and although his car wasn't in the Florida DMV records it may have been in the proprietary private sector records of Aamco, Jiffy Lube, Sears, or another oil change service center.

I called five more oil change centers and told the same story practically verbatim. None of them had any record of any cars with license tag DCH-328 in their system. I made little check marks next to each number I called. I looked at the clock and thought about traffic building and knew I needed to get out to Key Biscayne and check the address that had been provided to the Miami Police Department when Dario Curbelo was arrested. I slipped out of the VIN office, avoiding Ileana and Charlene as well as Major Brunson. I reasoned that I'd *tried* to see him today. It wasn't my fault he was knee-deep in hot sauce and barbecue brisket when I showed up.

I worked my way east through Coral Gables and used some of the side streets in Miami that ran parallel to U.S. 1 in Miami. By urban design and neighborhood enhanced traffic calming dead-end streets I was eventually forced into the U.S. 1 bumper-to-bumper traffic of commuters all aiming for I-95. As U.S. 1 terminated at the on ramp to I-95, I veered hard right on Brickell Avenue, then onto the Rickenbacker Causeway. I passed the revolving shark display advertising the Miami Seaqaurium and went through the wide toll booth. The pedestrian walkways and bicycle lanes were already teeming with cyclists, joggers, and sightseers all vying for their personal fitness level records, moderate exercise, or simply taking in the view. Although us long time Miamians will always refer to the entire stretch of causeway as the Rickenbacker, it is now known as the Rickenbacker Causeway and the Powell Bridge that spans the incredible aqua marine colored Biscayne Bay.

The view to the idyllic, but burgeoning island of Key Biscayne is one of the most picturesque drives in the United States. As I passed Hobie Beach and began the climb up the Powell Bridge, the vistas to my left encompassed all of downtown Miami, Fisher Island, and even peeking through the bridges and trees in the far distance the southern portions of Miami Beach. To my right was the lush green shoreline of Coconut Grove, all the way down towards Cutler Bay. At the apex of the bridge the view of Virginia Key and Key Biscayne were like two shining green emeralds in a blue Heaven sea. On the backside of the Powell Bridge I passed the now shuttered Miami Marine Stadium. It had some marvelous glory years prior to Hurricane Andrew blowing submerged debris into the channel. Some of the world's finest powerboat races took place at the stadium. Singer-songwriter Jimmy Buffet recorded a concert there that helped put the Marine stadium on the map as a fun tropical show venue for entrainers. The famed Miami Seaqaurium with its gold dome, aquatic research buildings, and animal shows were a blur as I whizzed by it. I crossed the flat bridge spanning Bear Cut. Once across Bear Cut the road bisects Crandon Park.

The entire island had been an inhospitable mangrove preserve and mosquito-plagued working coconut plantation one hundred years ago. At the very southeastern tip of the island was the Cape Florida lighthouse which had been attacked in 1836 by Seminole

Indian raiders and nearly destroyed by fire. The lighthouse was restored and is still a major feature of Key Biscayne. The island and its beaches are stunningly beautiful. A tropical paradise on a barrier island just a few miles from the mainland of Miami Dade County. It wasn't until the Mackle Brothers and other developers started building affordable housing for returning G. I.s in the late 1940s and early 1950s that the island caught on in popularity.

I drove down scenic Crandon Boulevard past Crandon Park Beach and the Key Biscayne Golf Course. I went to nearly the very end of the island. Across from the post office I made a turn onto Knollwood Drive which within a few yards led me right to Island Drive. I thought I'd drive past the house at 12 Cape Florida Drive a few times before I approached it. I wanted to see if there were any cars or people in front of it first. Island Drive took me to a T intersection, and I turned onto Cape Florida Drive back towards Crandon Boulevard. I quickly realized that I needn't worry about any cars or people—Cape Florida Drive went into a cul-de-sac. The road circled back out.

There *was* no 12 Cape Florida Drive.

Where 12 Cape Florida Drive should have been was a thin patch of grass and a water and sewer meter. The grassy strip abutted a wall and was sandwiched between 15 and 10 Cape Florida Drive.

This was literally and figuratively a dead end. Both Bernardo Ricon Giraldez, aka the "Crazy Cure," and Dario Curbelo had found clever ways to use the Miami Dade Water and Sewer locations as home addresses.

Shit. Literally shit.

This entire ordeal was grinding on me. This case was becoming more than exasperating—it was becoming unwinnable. False turns and leads everywhere, and me spinning wheels in my head and driving up and down God's green earth chasing half-assed leads and hopeful wishes. This was becoming a wish case. A case where you wish for this, and you wish for that, hoping that your wishes would lead to an outcome. At the very least a $400,000 outcome.

I hadn't heard from DEA agents Walker and Marroquín since late yesterday when they walked out with SAC Grayson. I guarantee they decided to forge ahead on their own and keep me out of the circle of information. There was no task force. That was just to appease that Washington honcho, Robert McBride. Understandably their first priority was to find the pale stranger who shot Agent Lew. Twenty kilos of cocaine and 400,000 come and go in the DEA system every day. I'm sure they thought Dario Curbelo would show up again at some point. As for me, I wanted to try and get all the wonky parts of this case in order.

Getting wonky parts in order was truthfully not my forté. My own personal life was a careening downhill shopping cart full of mismatches, misspokens, misunderstoods, and misforgottens. There wasn't anything about my life that had a deeper purpose aside from this woeful job in this woe begotten city. Gina couldn't wait to be rid of me. She abhorred the life I'd brought across our threshold. She said the VIN lifestyle had changed me.

Cute. Real cute. I was already in VIN when I met her that fateful day at the Old Cutler Oyster Bar.

My life was an abundance of scarcity. There was just way too much of nothing. There wasn't enough tranquility or any sense of ease in my life. Even meeting Marshal McKenna, why does it all have to be so contentious? It's as though there has to be gauntlet of bullshit, bluster, bravado, and backstops before I'll let anyone get close to me.

Not that the Marshal intended to be close to me in any way, but even Charlene blaming me for every hissy fit Brunson goes into was just emblematic of where the entire VIN existence was hardening me with each and every passing day. It was an armament of defensiveness I used to keep anybody and anything from being too close to me. I had become a master of deflection, deference, and detachment.

I sat in the car listening to the sea breeze rustle the palm fronds and waft amongst the sea grape trees. Former president Richard Nixon had once owned a home a few blocks behind me. It came to be known as the Southern White House during his presidency. Now just off its property line it was known more for the boaters and their wild weekend *pachangas* on the Mashta flats also known as the Nixon Sandbar. The sun would be setting soon and there would be no maritime parties on the sandbars today. Tomorrow would be a different story as the weekend boaters would be on the sandbars as soon as low tide started rolling out.

As I turned onto Crandon Boulevard, I sensed the energy of the Friday afternoon crowd beginning to take hold. It was in the way they drove off Key Biscayne and more importantly the way they drove onto Key Biscayne. In days past the parking lots of long-established bastions of Key Biscayne drink and food like Stefano's, Sundays on the Bay, Linda B's, and the Jamaica Inn would be swelling with happy hour revelers. Those famed restaurants were now gone. Many of them seized by the feds for money laundering.

Miami. It's criminality par excellence in pastels, soft fabrics, and an amazing wine list.

There were plenty of new restaurants many of them Italian, Argentine, or Peruvian matching the changing demographics of the island's residents. I considered stopping off at the bar, Cherries, for a drink. It had been fifteen years since Ricardo "Monkey" Morales, a DEA informant and all-around scummy intelligence whore was killed in the bar. Many of us in the drug trade on both sides of the cocaine corridor avoided Cherries. It was just a bad karma thing. The Miami Dade police report described Morales as "the spy, counterspy, mercenary, confessed murderer, bomber, informer, dope dealer and operator extraordinary who was shot in a vulgar bar brawl." Claims to fame and notoriety in the drug business can lead to mythological interpretations of simple ordinariness. Fighting the good fight doesn't preclude you from being another Miami drug-related homicide. Too many undercover agents had been killed in the bright sunlight of Miami. In the end it didn't always matter the circumstances of the urgency or severity of the case they were on. Scott Lew had nearly become another bronze plaque hanging in the lobby of the DEA's Washington headquarters.

The Friday sunset was splashing red and orange across the bay and the rays danced through the tree-shrouded streets of Key

Biscayne. It had been a long week and I was looking forward to going home and getting lit like a plastic Jesus. I also hadn't eaten since having breakfast with U.S. Marshal Auburn McKenna. I saw wave after wave of bicyclists and motorists coming onto the Key to start their weekend festivities of late autumn fun. I went in the opposite direction. I left Key Biscayne and traveling across the Bear Cut bridge I saw the Miami Marine Stadium looming on my right. The stadium is an architectural wonder. The entire cantilevered roof is formed entirely in concrete. The Miami Marine Stadium's dramatic roof is supported by eight enormous, angled columns which are anchored in the ground through the center grandstand. The columns are set back to afford spectators unobstructed views of the racing course, floating stages and even the occasional Easter service on the bay. I made an impromptu decision and turned into the gates of the Miami Marine Stadium.

The parking lot is vast. It stretches the length of the stadium and then extends in both directions even further. On the east side is a small marina with postcard views of downtown Miami across the bay. Tucked into the deepest corner of the parking lot, wedged against the boat storage racks, is a little out-of-the-way restaurant. Known to the locals as Bayside, it's been there for years, long before the mega giant retail developer Rouse Corporation created a waterside Marina and retail venue in the downtown Miami Marina, aptly titled "Bayside." The mighty Rouse Corporation took the little restaurant to court alleging the name similarity and the confusion it caused for vacationers who can't read a map cost them business. Justifiably, the Rouse Corporation had their butt handed to them by the judge. Plus attorney's fees.

The little restaurant had a quaintness to it that was sorely missing in the rapidly developing Miami. Its wraparound wooden porch ran along the front of the restaurant underneath interlocking chickee huts. The seafood was always incredibly fresh, purchased hours earlier from the recreational anglers. The fishermen often dock up to the marina with a larger haul of fish than they could stock in their freezer. They have some of the best conch salad, steak, and fritters west of the Bahamas. You can eat inside or go outside under the chickees. On Sundays the normal house band at Bayside is the reggae-calypso Spice Roots Band. I liked the place because in addition to the tasty menu there's jazz and blues on Friday nights. I settled into a little table deep under the chickee. I could see the parking lot and the masts of the sailboats in the marina. As the sun set even more in the western sky a very soft ambient light from downtown Miami bathed the outside areas of the restaurant. Some very good jazz musicians call Miami home. Ed Calle, Billy Marcus, Nicole Henry, and Nestor Torres are all residents. I wasn't familiar with the band tonight but the tight foursome on the stage were playing some wonderful jazzy rifts. I ordered a basket of conch fritters and a grouper sandwich. I also had a small ice bucket with three Red Stripe Jamaican lager beers on the table in front of me. The place was filling with patrons quickly. I passed the time savoring the chilly lagers and taking in the sounds from the band. The food took longer than twenty minutes to be served but when it did arrive it was absolutely delicious. The conch fritters were meaty morsels of plump pieces of conch in a flavorful deep fried seasoned to perfection batter. I had just polished the fritters off when an immaculate grouper sandwich arrived at my table. I had already had two Red Stripe lagers and with one left bobbing in the ice bucket I was debating whether getting wonderfully soused should start and end here at this magnificent spot or would I indulge in serious home deck drinking. I cracked open the remaining Red Stripe and had just taken a refreshing swig of the beer when I glanced out into the parking lot. It was now just past dusk, and the parking lot was partially illuminated by the lights of the restaurant. I saw a car parked amongst a row of other cars. It stood out because of its large size but also because the engine was running.

I continued to enjoy the remnants of my meal amongst the many people in the restaurant. The drinks and music were affecting a few brave souls who danced on the small dance floor by the band. The continual movement of people getting up and down made my sitting position ideal to keep my eye on the idling car. Just as the band launched into a deep saxophone rendition of Gato Barbieri's *Europa,*

I saw one of the occupants of the idling car get out of the passenger side and walk towards the restaurant.

He looked like one of the men I saw on Coral Way earlier watching me and Sergeant Byrne at the café. *Europa* had always been an adopted love anthem in Miami, and it was as though every couple in the place got up to dance. Chairs were moved, tables pushed against walls, bodies up against each other overspilling from the cramped dance floor. I used all that rising, heaving movement to conceal myself as I made a bee line right for the kitchen.

I assumed that the two men in the car from earlier in the day were outside the restaurant but had lost sight of me. One of them was coming into the restaurant to surreptitiously confirm that I was still here. I pushed open the kitchen doors and stepped into the hot and brightly-lit work area. Water puddled under the honeycomb rubber mats that ran between the cooking stations and counters. I could see through the kitchen straight to the back screened door. It was old and weathered with dull green paint along its wooden frame. I walked briskly through the kitchen, catching the eye of one of the Bahamian cooks. He went right back to plating the dishes in front of him. I passed a large gas stove. There were some pots on the stove that had visible signs of years of use. I grabbed the handle of a simmering lid off of a dented 8-quart stock pot. I kept moving and pushed through the screen door. There was another cook outside by a stack of plastic crates taking a cigarette break. He didn't pay any attention to me as I quickly walked past him, still holding the lid with dripping condensation on its underside. I rounded the corner of the restaurant. The sounds of conversation, dinnerware, and music filled the night air. I avoided the lights being cast out from the restaurant, keeping to the darkened parts of the parking lot. I'd only have about four minutes before the sentry sent in to find me discovered I wasn't inside.

I walked stealthily between a Pontiac Sunbird convertible and a pickup truck with a camper top. The idling car was a dark Chrysler 300M. It had a temporary paper tag affixed to its rear with duct tape on the corners. With long strides I walked up to the passenger side and quickly pulled on the door handle swinging the door open.

"Was he inside?" was all I heard the driver say as I slid into the passenger seat, shocking the driver. Before he could say anything else or acknowledge I was not his confederate, I slammed the flat wide pot lid hard against the right side of his face and head. With my left shoulder and hip against the seat, I struck him rapidly three more times with the lid. On the fourth blow I pushed his head up against the driver's window and seat post. I held his head against the glass and leaned across the padded arm rest, putting my body weight on him. His head was held in place by the lid and his face was smooshed against the glass. I leaned in even harder using my legs to push against the floorboard. My left foot was on some sort of DVR type box plugged into the cigarette lighter. My right foot was outside the car using the ground for leverage.

"Who the fuck are you?" I yelled at him.

He tried to reply but his mouth was contorted from the lid up against his face. He gave a muffled reply. I released the pressure slightly and then pushed the lid against his face again.

"You don't start talking now I'm going to put a bullet right through your ribs and hold you against this door until you bleed out," I growled.

Pulling my right foot inside the car and pressing it against the floorboard, I bent my left leg and pushed my knee into his side locking his right arm against his body. I could feel he didn't have a gun on his right side. I relented and pulled the lid off his face just enough for him to talk. He tried to catch his breath and stem the pain of my knee grinding into his ribs. He panted out a quick response.

"P.I. I'm a P.I.," he said almost inaudibly.

"Private Investigator?" I quizzed him back, shoving the lid hard up against his face again.

"Yefgf a Pwiate Investigaer," he mumbled against the glass.

"I.D. Now!" I demanded, knowing full well my time before his partner returned was becoming short.

"Riyhte pajnts pocquet."

I kept the pressure of the lid hard up against his face. I used my left hand and ripped his right pants pocket away and down from his slacks. A small black billfold was exposed in the cotton lining of his pocket. With my left hand I dumped the contents of the billfold on the seat. His Private Investigator identification fell out. It had his picture on it.

Franklin G. McCarron.

"Why are you following me?" I demanded to know.

I pulled back the lid just enough so he could speak clearly.

"You know that I can't tell you."

"Why are you following me and who hired you?" I hissed at him through clenched teeth.

"There are confidentiality issues with my client!"

"Bullshit you tell me now or I'm going to push your face through that A.C vent. You want to remember what it feels like to be born? I'll push all of you right through that narrow opening!"

"I can't, it's client investigator privileges. I can't. There are certain levels of confidentiality that we just can't break!" he wailed.

Through the windshield I saw his partner exiting the restaurant. I needed to get out of the car fast. Just because the driver didn't have a gun didn't mean his partner didn't have one.

My car was a few rows away and obscured from the restaurant lights. I snatched his keys out of the ignition, gave him one more hard shove with the lid and then pushed off of him, dashing out of the car.

"Keys are in the center median," I shouted back as I ran away. I ran through the rows of cars, unseen by his partner. I made it to my car and hurriedly got into it. I peeled away from the restaurant out to the Rickenbacker Causeway. I made the right turn towards the Powell Bridge. I had told him the keys would be in the center median. I didn't say where. I drove a good seventy-five yards before I tossed the car keys into the center median.

As I neared the top off the bridge, Miami was a shimmering

conglomeration of artfully lit buildings, streaming multitudes of rooftop accent lights, and neon.

I was angry. I wanted to know more and wasn't able to learn as much as I could about the two guys following me. I chided myself for not holding them both at gunpoint and demanding more information. I was also mad because the joyful feeling of having a few beers and listening to good music was gone. Franklin G. McCarron and his unknown partner seriously interfered with my wanting to drink about things I won't remember.

Chapter Fourteen

I WAS ALREADY UP on the flyover that would drop me into U.S. 1, and I was fuming. I started trying to clearly piece it all together. A P.I.? Why would private investigators be interested in me? There was no reason why my ex-wife Gina or her dipshit attorney Phillip Gilot would see a need to hire private investigators to follow me.

I was sure Franklin G McCarron P.I. was going to have a sore neck and face for a while, and it made me smile. Perhaps my anger at the guy was a little misplaced, but it still felt good to be angry at someone.

At Southwest 17th Avenue I pulled into a gas station. I parked by the vacuum and tire pressure station and took a deep breath. I needed to think about what just occurred. Something wasn't right. I just kept staring out the windshield trying to figure out where those guys had come from, and more importantly, who hired them. My thoughts went back to my ex-wife Gina. As far as I knew there was nothing left to contest in the divorce. I *was* divorced. It was completely done and final. I'd heard of former spouses dragging each other back into court post-finalization, but that didn't fit here. I don't know why it was even at the top of mind for me.

I eased my seat back a little and looked out at the comings and goings of the gas station. For a Friday night it was moderately quiet. The club scene on South Beach was still hours from being in full swing. Soon there would be throngs of cars coming from West Kendall, lining up on South Beach in multi-block-long traffic jams just to park their hand-me-down cars next to well-polished Porsches and Corvettes. They'd all be vying to get into hot night clubs like Liquid, China Grill, Red Square, Groove Jet, and Joia. The night would be full of scantily-clad, barely old enough ladies posing and primping with stylized clueless guys looking for a quick ascension to manhood. They would fill gas stations just like this one on their way to South Beach as they load up on beers, wine coolers, and gasoline. Like Rodney Crowell says: "This mean old world runs on sex and gasoline." The partying antics of a narrow demographic of Miami's large population was the least of my concerns.

I kept looking out of my windshield. I watched the club goers and occasional service industry types pull up to the gas pumps. Everyone it seemed was holding a cell phone to their ear. Just less than ten years earlier there were very few cell phones. Those that were available were nicknamed "bricks" for their large size. Now I saw all types of phones being used by everyone as they went in and out of the gas station. They were infinitely cheaper and smaller with all types of features. I looked at my own phone on the seat next to me. It emitted a soft little green light that flashed approximately every twenty seconds as it sent a receiving signal out to the nearby cell towers.

I replayed in my head what McCarron said exactly. He said he was a private investigator, and he couldn't reveal who hired him due to confidentiality clauses. How did he know I was going to meet Sergeant Byrnes at the café on Coral Way? How could they have known I was on Key Biscayne? How did they know I was at the Bayside restaurant having beers and conch fritters? I kept thinking about Franklin G. McCarron and the car. Whoever hired him and his partner must have very deep pockets. Two investigators in one car are not very efficient and highly expensive. I seriously doubt Gina, or her wacka-doodle attorney would spend that kind of money when I had nothing to hide and nothing to offer her. The Chrysler 300 M had a temporary tag, and it was held in place with duct tape.

Duct tape?

If car dealerships all used duct tape instead of cellophane tape to affix tags on cars it would be a drag on their profit bottom lines.

That was no dealership car. Franklin G McCarron covered his car with a temporary license tag, and he did it for a reason. What the reason, aside from cloaked anonymity was, I couldn't fathom.

The consistency of the changing types of people outside my car was startling in their flawed perception of originality. They were all rooted in their need for acceptance, thus creating more similarity than they probably realized. Every single one unendingly using their cell phones.

I again looked back down at my own phone on the car seat. The green light emitted its flash steadily, like clockwork. You could almost set a watch for when the light would flash.

Then it hit me.

In the P.I.'s car, when I pulled my leg inside, I leaned in even harder pushing against the floorboard. My left foot had been on some sort of DVR-type box that had been plugged into the cigarette lighter.

That was it.

The box plugged into the cigarette lighter was a triggerfish. They were tracking the Equipment Serial Number (ESM) of my cell phone. Serial numbers are usually located on the back of the cell phone under the battery. The ESM uniquely identifies equipment and is embedded electronically by the manufacturer. Triggerfish machines are electronic devices that can capture a cell phone's ESM. Once the triggerfish has the ESM locked it can mimic cell phone towers, allowing the triggerfish monitor to pinpoint a phone's location, sometimes even before it makes a call or text. Franklin G McCarron, P.I., and his partner were tracking me with a triggerfish.

They still had the triggerfish, and I still had my cell phone.

Albert Einstein said: "The definition of insanity is doing the same thing over and over again and expecting a different result."

Sitting here at the gas station all I was doing was providing a stationary target for them while they were in the median of the Rickenbacker Causeway looking for the car keys. Once they found their keys, they'd be tracking me again and I was sure pothead McCarron would be looking to exact some revenge.

I switched the phone to silent privacy mode so its ring wouldn't be audible. I put the car in drive and weaved around the club goers and walking pedestrians at the gas station, caught an open seam in traffic and merged in. I headed into Coconut Grove and pulled up quickly to the Tiger Tail Lounge.

Parked out in front of the lounge was the same crappy, dented, white pick-up truck belonging to the shitbird James brothers. The gas tank had a rag stuffed into it. The nitwits never even looked through the junk in the bed of their truck to find the gas cap.

I dashed out of my car and went to the back of their truck. I shoved my cell phone deep into the paint cans, splintered boards, empty Natural Lite beer cans, Styrofoam buoys, and drywall pieces in the truck bed. If McCarron and his partner decided to get back up on the triggerfish and search for me, they'd be following Danny and Donny James instead.

Then I headed home. I was cautious as I drew near the condominium at Paradise Point. I had no idea how long McCarron and his partner had been following me. I also had no idea who they worked for and if there was another team of private investigators watching me. If there were two, there could be a lot more.

Making the turn onto Coral Reef Drive, I went through the guard gate at the entrance and drove to the end of the complex, all the way to the eastern point near the Cutler Channel. I got out of the car and stood on the dock. Looking east a few miles across the bay, I could see the Cape Florida lighthouse with its roving beacon light. I may not have been attacked in 1836 by Seminole Indian raiders, yet I felt a solid strong kinship with the lighthouse out there on a spit of land by itself, still doing its job. I was still here on a small precipice of my own, still doing my job. Obviously, DEA Agents Walker and

Marroquín had decided to forgo working with me. I hadn't heard from them all day.

Remembering to drink so I could forget would have to wait. It was time to start looking for Dario Curbelo and Agent Lew's shooter by myself. The day was finished and even though the next day was Saturday, it made no difference. It was time to get busy and get it done.

In an abundance of caution I parked at the community swimming pool and walked the few addresses back to the condo. I checked the entire interior of the condominium for signs of entry. When I felt sure enough, I shut all the lights off and went up to the rooftop deck. I felt in many ways like the lighthouse keeper at Cape Florida in 1836. He knew there were adversaries out there somewhere. He couldn't have known that they'd come for him under cover of darkness from the mainland in low profile dugout canoes. I'm sure he'd have loved to extinguish the light of the lighthouse and not foretell the Seminole raiders where he was, but he had to maintain the line. He had to do what was right. He had to be a beacon for the ships trying to navigate the shallow shoals, coral reefs, and feather banks off the coastline.

Similarly, I needed to stay in the frame of what I needed to do. Agent Lew was fighting for his life, the Crazy Cure was dead, and the same gunman had tried to kill me. There were too many fractured parts. There was no synergy in the investigation. The left hand didn't know what the right hand was doing. Everyone seemed to have the desire for a final outcome, but it was as though the participants all had a different idea of what the outcome should be, or at the very least, should look like. Major Brunson had his objective, which was to recoup the lost $400,000 and placate the penny-pinching city manager. Marshal McKenna wanted to find Dario Curbelo. ASAC Mandeville wanted to arrest the shooter who shot Agent Lew. We all wanted that. That was the common denominator we all shared.

I wanted it all.

I wanted the shooter who shot Agent Lew badly. I especially wanted the blond-haired shooter because he tried to kill me too. I wanted the twenty kilograms of cocaine off the streets of Miami. I wanted the $400,000 that was essentially stolen from me. I wanted drug trafficking Dario Curbelo for the aggravation he was causing. The death of Bernardo Ricon Giraldez, the *Crazy Cure,* was not of my concern. He was a potted plant to me. It was as though this was a hundred-yard dash for people with no sense of direction. There wasn't any coordination. Collaboration was strained at best. There was no clearing house or traffic manager to triage information. This was the most disorganized task force I had ever been a part of. The investigation was in parcels.

I needed to be my own task force. If they weren't too engaged to play with me then I'd shove myself right into their huddle, right into their dugout. I'd make it nearly impossible to not work with me. I'd be that guy in the Bermuda shorts and black socks who sits in a lawn chair in the middle of an urban park and although the softball league wants to have a game, he sits there reminding everyone "the park is for all." I'd be that guy. Deal with me. This was not the time to divvy up the investigation regardless of what SAC Grayson said. And I remembered what he said, word for word.

"Walker and Marroquín, you both will be the point men on this investigation. I am taking you off any other investigations until we can catch the shooter who shot Agent Lew. I also want this Ecuadorian found and the $400,000 recovered along with the twenty kilograms. Start working all your C. I's. See what you can develop. When Agent Lew can talk, I want to know who his informant was on this deal. You are both to work closely with Detective Taylor on this."

Hammy Garzon was also in the wind. Grayson said she was onboard with our nonexistent task force, and that he was thankful to have her there, as I recalled. I'm sure SAC Grayson was sincere when he said those words but the last twenty-four hours either demonstrated a seismic shift from that mindset, or the DEA had decided to go about the investigation their own way. The night was still. Unfortunately my sensibilities were not. My mind was misfiring with convoluted thoughts. I was angry, agitated, stymied, and a little confused about the way the past few days had played out. Things that were normally routine were not so rote anymore.

Tomorrow is Saturday, I thought with a brief clear of brain fog. But Saturday meant nothing this time. I relish my days off. *I'm sure Agent Scott Lew's family relish their time with him.*

There would be no days of until we found the shooter. I made that vow to myself and planned to keep it. The night was still somewhat young. I looked at the bottle of Jameson Irish Whiskey on the bar. The slightly cool night air softly billowing through the upstairs open patio doors was definitely beckoning to me. I could rest, for a few hours anyway.

I TRIED TO shield my eyes from the bright Saturday morning sunshine creeping through the valances. I slowly felt around the bed for the bottle for Jameson Irish Whiskey. Many a morning I had awoken to the feel of bone-dry bottle of Jameson up against my leg or my back. I widened my feel around, a blind search pattern in the bed for the bottle of Jameson. I couldn't find the bottle. I tried to remember my activities last night. I was now worried the bottle might be in the bottom of the Roman-sized jacuzzi tub or in the Italian tiled shower. I checked in both places. Empty. I went downstairs to the bar. The bottle was still on top of the bar. Untouched. Proof positive that I don't need alcohol to make bad decisions, trip over nothing, say inappropriate things, or wake up with puffy eyes. That was one of the problems of drinking as an at-home pain management plan or to keep the rampant psyche in check. You sometimes forget how much you drank the night before and on rare occasions, like now, you'd forget if you actually drank at all.

After showering and getting dressed, my hair was still wet and would look like a rat's nest by midday. I donned one of my many dark blue Hartford Whalers hats to keep that from happening. I retrieved a dish towel from the kitchen and draped it over my hand, holding my Glock under the towel. It concealed the gun nicely. I didn't want to alarm any of my neighbors who may be out walking dogs, pushing baby strollers, or doing that dreaded thing called exercise. I went outside and did a walkaround before going to my car. I scanned all the parked cars making sure they were unoccupied and there was no sign of Franklin G. McCarron or his equally dead wood head partner.

The drive out of the complex gates was leisurely and slow as I checked each and every car on the way out. I was soon northbound on Old Cutler Road. The morning was still early, and vehicle traffic was very light. The biggest obstacles I faced on my way towards Coral Gables was passing the multitudes of bicycle dudes. Road cyclists on Old Cutler Road can be tricky to get past as they all seem to be different body shapes and sizes, yet they wear the same type of unflattering tight lycra biking gear. It's a local Tour de France that plays out all across south Florida roadways on the weekend.

No sign of anyone following me. I continually checked my rearview mirrors. I gave hard looks at any parked cars on the side of the road. I made a few "heat runs" to make sure I wasn't being tailed. At Cartagena Circle I veered slightly west, took Granada Boulevard north through Coral Gables. A few of the houses had orange and green banners and University of Miami flags in front of them. The Miami Hurricanes football team was playing Temple University at Veteran's Stadium in Philadelphia. Kickoff was at 4pm. The afternoon should be quiet for the uniform patrol division of the police department. All of South Florida, especially Coral Gables, would be in their comfortable homes and Miami Hurricane-friendly bars watching the game.

I continued north on Granada, passing the east side of the University of Miami. The campus was quiet as students were sleeping off pregame hangovers only to rally for the game and do it all over again. I took Granada as far north as I could. I passed under the coral rock archway at the Granada entrance to the city. Oddly it has always been called the Granada entrance and never the Granada exit. My destination was just a few yards in front of me across Southwest 8th Street in the city of Miami. I found a parking spot easily and walked into the Cellular One cellphone store. I explained to the young clerk behind the counter that my cellphone was lost in Coral Gables. I told him I had lost my cell phone at the Denny's restaurant located at 1 Miracle Mile in Coral Gables. The Coral Gables Police Department stupidly considers themselves a service-oriented police department. That means that they'll write a report for anything for anybody to appease the needs of the public. Every cellular telephone company demands a location and a police report number for replacing lost or stolen cell phones. Every cellular telephone employee at every competing cellular telephone company tells their customers to go to the Coral Gables police station and tell the front desk officer they lost their cell phone in Coral Gables. Whether it occurred in Coral Gables or not was immaterial to them. The easiest address to remember is the Denny's Restaurant at 1 Miracle Mile. The Denny's has become the black hole of Calcutta for cellular telephones in Miami Dade County. According to our uniform crime reports, Denny's is the number one location for lost or stolen cell phones. All fabricated, but nonetheless dutifully documented. Thus inflating our property crime and property loss statistics to such an extent that we added two detectives to the property crimes section of the department who truthfully had nothing to do but read the same unfounded bogus reports.

The clerk was surprised that I beat him to the punch with the Denny's address. I told him my case number was 98-923. The current year and my unit number. He didn't need to see, nor did he ask for the actual police report. He just wanted a number. I could have told him 98-E-I-E-I-O and it wouldn't have mattered. He went to the back of the store and quickly returned with a new Nokia 6110.

"It's going to take me about thirty minutes to get all your data switched to the new phone," he said as he took the Nokia out of the box.

"I'll be back then," I said

I stepped outside of the Cellular One store. On the corner of the shopping plaza was Roma Bakery and Cafe, a lovely Cuban restaurant masquerading as an Italian bakery. It had the requisite walk-up coffee window and all the signage in Spanish. There was a large sign in the window that to their credit was printed in Italian colors, but that's where any semblance to Italy ended.

"Estimados Clientes,

Desayuno diariamente desde las 6:00 A.M.- 1:00 P.M

$3.95 Por Personas"

"Dear Customers,

Breakfast daily from 6:00 A.M.- 1:00 P.M.

$3.95 Per Person"

I sat at one of the tables across from the glass display that had stacks of ready-made Cuban sandwiches, Midnight Sandwiches (*Medianoches*) and loaves of freshly baked Cuban bread.

Viva Italia!

The waitress was friendly, and my breakfast order arrived quickly with a steaming café con leche. There were *Diario Las Américas* and *El Nuevo Herald* newspapers on top of the counter near the cash register. When I was finished, I went back to the Cellular One store and retrieved my new cell phone and more importantly, its new ESM number. I drove to the police station, this time adding the precaution of parking in the alley just outside of Joe Peppy's back door. I used the grassy path between the restaurant and the mortgage escrow company to walk to the external staircase and up to the third floor of the police department. The third floor was very quiet. Most, if not all of the detectives, were off for the weekend. I went into the empty VIN office and sat down again in the vacant lieutenant's office. There was a message on the desk, written in Ileana's scrabbly script. It was Arson Inspector Jeff Baggett's phone number. He must have called Friday. I was tempted to try out my new cellphone, but held off; besides, it needed a good charge first. I made sure the cell phone was turned off to accelerate the charging process and plugged the charger into the wall outlet. I picked up the telephone on the desk and trying to decipher Ileana's handwriting, I called the number in the message. After a few rings a man's voice answered.

"Hello?"

"Hi. This is Cade Taylor, I'm a detective with the Coral Gables Police Department. I'm looking for Jeff Baggett."

"If you want to talk to me, then okay. If you're *looking* for me than I'm going to hang up," The man said jokingly.

"Mr. Baggett, I can assure you I just want to talk and am not looking for you," I said.

"I'm just messing with ya. What can I do for you, Detective?"

"I know you've handled a lot of arson cases, but I was wondering if you have any recollection about a housefire in North Miami in 1996?"

"Two years ago? I should. What was the address?"

"160 Northeast 164th Street in North Miami. There was a lone victim in the fire. Your report stated you made an assessment the victim was male based on the pelvis size of the deceased and that he was severely burned. Does that ring a bell?" I asked him.

"Yeah. Yeah, I think I know what one you're talking about. The fire department used their pumper trucks in the front of the structure and then drafted the water from the swimming pool in the backyard to create two extinguish points."

"What exactly does that mean?" I asked him.

He sighed. "It's basically fighting the fire from two directions to come to a middle ground, keeps the fire from raging in one area while another part gets extinguished. Drafting is pulling water from a non-pressurized source, like a lake or swimming pool. They do it by using hard suction hoses and a special priming motor that can pump air, creates negative pressure by pulling the air out of the hose, causing the water to be pulled into the void in the pump. Once they get the water in the pump, they can use the pressurized water to fight fires," he explained.

"So you do remember this fire?" I asked him again.

"Yeah, I got there about 10:30 at night. You could smell it for blocks. Just getting out of the car I knew their insurance adjusters would deem it a total loss. I mean it was bad. The entire roof had burned in from the rafters down. There were burnt shingles in the living room. Anything made of plastic or soft aluminum was puddled. I got called in because the battalion chief could see by the fire's consistent intensity, it was arson. Normally a fire spreads from one combustible to another combustible. It jumps and travels that way. Like the curtains catch on fire and that burns the curtain rods and then the window frames. You get the idea. It's a progression thing. Not here. It was from floor to ceiling. It was a massive inferno," he said.

"What can you tell me about the body inside?"

"Off the record?" he said. "He was burned to nearly nothing. On the record—he was burned to nearly nothing," he said.

"What exactly do you think happened to him?" I asked.

"I think he was an extreme dumbass. He may have been hired to do an arson job and the little firebug got caught up in his own fire."

"So you don't think he was a homeless person using the house as a shelter or squatter in the house?"

"We don't use the term 'homeless' anymore," he corrected me. "We call them *residentially challenged*. I personally think of them as perpetual outdoorsmen, myself," he said with a chuckle.

"So help me understand why he was an arsonist?" I said.

"Many fire-causing accelerants are hydrocarbon-based fuels. Your most common hydrocarbon fuels are gasoline, diesel fuel, kerosene, turpentine, and—rarely, but still used oddly enough—butane. There are also combinational chemicals that by themselves are inert but when combined with other flammable solvents called volatile organic compounds are ignitable. In the fire business we call them VOCs. Miami Dade Fire's after-action analysis showed the fire to be created by gasoline as an accelerant. Actually, a lot of gasoline. The body was found pushed up against a locked interior door. The door was nearly disintegrated by the time the fire was extinguished, but the door lock and knob were found. The knob was in the lock position. Many amateur arsonists don't realize the flammability of gasoline fumes *in addition* to the high flammability of the gas itself. Our arsonist dropped a flame source to the gasoline he'd spread throughout the house. When it ignited it startled him with a big unanticipated eruption. You know that *whoosh,* for lack of a better term. That ignition knocked him back. He fell backward, and he closed the door with his body. He was locked in with the fire he started, and it was a pretty horrible death for him."

"Man. What a way to go," I murmured.

"I can't tell you if it was quick or slow, but I'm sure once the fire started, he seared his lungs and trachea and was probably out cold within seconds. In fire training we don't measure the time in minutes or seconds, but in breaths. Very often people don't 'burn to death' in a house fire. They die from smoke inhalation, they die because they took a breath of super-heated toxic gases, singed all the alveolar sacs in their lungs causing them to succumb to unconsciousness as they suffocate."

"Your report said the body was burned badly. In fact it said the 'burn ratio to the body was at 100%,' I said as I read the words from his report to him. "What happens to your body if you're burned alive?"

"I think we should start with what actually happens inside the body first. Fire is agnostic. It will burn any of three things: a combustible like paper, a liquid like gasoline, or a gas like hydrogen. It doesn't care as long as it has a source to burn. Once you know what it's burning then you know how to fight it. In a structure fire, a chemical reaction of extremely hot air starts breaking down material, turning that material into cinder, ash, and smoke. If you breathe this arid, acidic air in, it will quickly dry out your respiratory system. It will burn, singe, and obstruct your mouth, throat, and lungs, quickly making your body oxygen-deprived. Your muscles and brain function diminish quickly but won't completely shut down at first due to endorphins and the adrenaline rush going through your body. This won't last very long though as you fall unconscious from lack of oxygen, or in the absolute worst case, from the pain of being burned alive," he said matter-of-factly.

"Wow, are you serious?"

"Detective, I'm serious like a bus driver with third graders on a field trip," said Baggett. "Your muscles, tissues, and skin don't burn as readily as you might think. You have to remember our bodies are 80% water. The fire will evaporate the water within your skin. When that happens, the burning and deterioration within the body is quick. Once the heat has reached your blood, arteries, and veins, it causes the blood compounds to quickly clot, blocking off much of your blood flow. The arteries and veins kind of melt more than burn, so that starts destroying your circulatory system. It's not a matter of a lack of blood, it's just the circulatory highway of your body has no way to *carry* the blood. You're dead for sure now. Most marginally-fit people have some muscle tone, and muscles are quite dense, so the fire will have a harder time burning though them—but with enough time, it will. You can bet the ranch it sure will. From the inside out your organs will burn faster and before the muscles do. The organs get rapidly dried out from the smoke and heat from the external and internal burning of your body. Lastly, both muscle and bone are harder for fire to burn. It takes a little more time, but both muscle and bone will burn, and with bones they'll just crack. That's the very end stage."

"So in this case...there was no way to make an identification on the deceased. What I mean is there were no fingerprints to be taken or anything like that," I said.

"Well, there's always dental. Charred human dentition can be identified because of the very unique individual types of filling materials. That's the easiest way. Although burned, residual restorative material and dental work is valuable in the presumptive identification of a burned victim. Anything a dentist puts in your mouth—gold, silver amalgam, silicate restoration, and so on—have a different resistance to prolonged high temperature. Most of the dental examination relies heavily on the presence of the restoration. If he's been to a dentist, especially one in the U.S., there is a chance of identification."

"You sound like you could have been a dentist yourself," I said.

"Me? Nah, I barely made it out of college. I went to Oklahoma

State University. When I bombed out of aviation classes I moved back to Pensacola where I grew up. My dad was a fighter pilot. I got into arson investigation. From there I got hired by Miami Dade. I moved down here nineteen years ago."

"Interesting. I hear what you're saying but in the case of your arsonist at 160 Northeast 164th Street, just for clarification's sake—the body *was* burned beyond fingerprints or any other identifiers. Correct?"

"Oh yeah, it was pretty bad. He was down to the bones and even some of them were splitting open."

Arson Investigator Bagget and myself talked a little more about our jobs and then I hung up with him, promising that I'd follow up with him if I needed to.

Hammy Garzon told me and Major Brunson that Dario Curbelo was listed as the victim found in the fire in 1996 at 160 Northeast 164th Street.

Someone somewhere was lying or covering something up.

"Major, I recognize that many things about Hialeah may seem inordinately true including the incompetency of many city employees, but I'm telling you the truth. You're chasing a dead guy. The Miami Dade Medical Examiner has him listed as deceased in a housefire. They made the identification," Hammy had said.

When I tried to get the file from the Miami Dade Medical Examiner, I spoke with Arum who clearly stated the file was sealed. He said it was similar to when a celebrity dies and the family wishes for autopsy photos to not be released, that it was protected. He said he couldn't get into the file.

U.S Marshal Auburn McKenna informed me that Dario Curbelo was indeed alive and living under an assumed name. *"We created him,"* she told me. She said the owner of the Mercedes was made, that he'd gotten off the team bus and stopped checking in months before. Something else she said stuck with me:

"I can't tell you if the owner of the Mercedes is a criminal or a witness. All I can say is we put him in that car."

I needed to see this from a position of reputation and credibility. Arson Investigator Jeff Baggett was the most credible person in this equation. He had no stake in the investigation, and he was clearly recanting to me from his observations two years earlier. When I read back to him portions of his own report over the telephone, he didn't disagree with me. He also attested to what he wrote about the body in the fire being burned beyond normal recognition. He confirmed fingerprints could not have been used to identify the body.

The next person in the equation was Hammy Garzon. Hammy said that that the prints from the shooting at *El Segundo Viajante* matched Dario Curbelo's, which also matched those from when Curbelo was arrested in Miami in 1994 at the Torch of Freedom.

Officer Byrne confirmed he did arrest Curbelo in 1994. Hammy also stated that the Miami Dade M.E. identified Curbelo as the victim of a house fire in North Miami in 1996, but she never said how the identification was made. Arum from the Miami Dade Examiner's office told me the file was sealed.

I looked at my newly acquired cellphone and could see it was still charging. I decided to make more telephone calls to the oil change centers listed on the pages I tore out of the phone book. With each one I went into almost the exact spiel I'd used yesterday, that my wife had taken the car in and now the oil plug wasn't tight, and the car was leaking oil in the garage. Each manager I spoke with was certain that his team would not have been that careless and in their zeal to assure me, they each looked up in their computer system the license tag I provided them.

"DCH-328."

The better part of the morning was getting away from me. So far, I was striking out in the most horrendous way. It was tedious looking up each oil change center on the pages and then calling and reciting the same story. It felt like I was barely making any progress. I decided to take a break from the calls. For the life of me I could not imagine being a telephone cold-call salesperson. It must be so defeating in so many ways.

My new cell phone was fully charged. I removed it from the charger and turned it on. Already there were some voice messages on it. I played them back in the order they came in. The first message was from Hammy Garzon. I hadn't set up any greeting on the cell phone and she sounded hesitant that she might not have the right number. Another byproduct of the VIN lifestyle is never having a voice greeting on your cell phone—a trait that I was sure Hammy wasn't aware of. I called her back from the phone, primarily to test its functionality, but so that she might recognize the number and accept my call.

"Hello?"

"Hammy, it's Cade Taylor. I'm calling you back," I said.

"You're calling me back. Wow, thanks so much for letting me know that's what you're doing exactly at this moment, otherwise I'd have never figured that out on my own," she said, her voice dripping with sarcasm

I looked across the room at the blank wall and secretly wondered why I even try sometimes.

"So Hammy, I apologize for calling you on a Saturday. I switched out my phone and I don't know when you left the message to call. I just got it so I'm calling you back."

"Your gallantry still astounds me. Is there somewhere we can meet?"

I picked up and dropped the pages of numbers in front of me in an absentmindedly way. I was tired of the monotony of chasing a needle in a haystack calling the oil change centers. I also wasn't in the mood to traipse to Hialeah on a Saturday.

"I'd love to, but I don't know if I can make it to Hialeah," I said.

"You are such a nimrod sometimes. I work in Hialeah, but I don't live in Hialeah. It's kind of important that we talk. Can you meet me somewhere?" she implored of me.

"Yeah, sure. I'm sorry. What part of the county are you in?"

"I live in Saga Bay, is that anywhere near you?"

"Saga Bay? Didn't that get pulverized by Hurricane Andrew?"

"Well, that was six years ago and in the rebuild I was able to get in. Homeownership. The American dream. Even if it comes with astronomical insurance rates. So are you anywhere near me?" she said.

"Actually I'm in the Gables right now. Do you know Walter's Coffee Shop?"

"I practically live there on the weekends. How about I meet you there in an hour?" she said.

After hanging up, I checked my other voice messages. The next call to come up was from Marshal Auburn McKenna. She left a lengthy voice message.

"Cade, hey it's Auburn McKenna. I got my cell fixed. Listen, I'm going to be out of pocket a few days, I've been TDY'ed back to Tampa for some fugitive pick-ups with Florid Marine Patrol. They got a big problem with poaching in state and federal waters. When I get back, I want to get on this situation in Miami. I don't care about the WITSEC shit, he's part of the reason why a DEA agent was shot. That's all I care about. Let me know if you spoke to anybody about getting me in with you guys so we can catch this little shitling. My bosses are up my ass about finding him. This is my cell number so put it in your contacts. I'll reach out when I get back in a day or two. Bye."

She must have already been gone because she said when she gets back, she wants to get into it with us to find Curbelo. "TDY" is often used by people with military experience. It's military jargon for Temporary Duty Assignment. She provided me her number. She also asked again if I had made any headway in getting her temporarily detached to the task force. Her bosses, she said, were "up her ass" and they wanted Dario Curbelo found immediately.

I added her number to my contacts. I didn't even call her back. How was I supposed to tell her that as of this moment we weren't a functional task force? We were just spinning wheels coming off a flaming race car. There was no information at all from the DEA.

The last voice message was from Cellular One welcoming me to the "Cellular One family, where the emphasis is on you being the one." I retraced my steps and was back in my car in a few minutes. It felt as though all I'd done in the past few days was drive the entire boundary of Greater Miami.

Walter's Coffee Shop was easily twenty blocks south of the condominium in Paradise Point. Once I decided to go that far I wasn't going to be coming back up towards Coral Gables. Whatever Hammy needed to talk about would have to wait until Monday. I drove south on U.S. 1 and traffic was light until around Southwest 104th Street where the spirit club of Miami Palmetto High School was having a car wash. Once I got past the soaking wet teenagers holding their poster board signs , the traffic started flowing much easier. Approaching Coral Reef Drive I could see the demarcation line of where Hurricane Andrew scoured Miami Dade County. Although being rebuilt tenaciously, there was still a few reminders of the carnage the big hurricane caused. Many locals jokingly started calling any part of Miami Dade County south of Coral Reef Drive the "Dirty South." Walter's Coffee Shop was still another twelve blocks south. Former residents who moved north post-hurricane to the pristine new communities of Weston, Parkland, and western Davie in Broward County refused to even make the trek back to their old neighborhoods. They acted as though they'd escaped from some sort of hovel of despair. I guess seeking shelter in a bathtub as you hold a mattress against your head praying for your life while a category five hurricane roars above you would make you think differently about returning.

Walter's had become a little more upscale from what I remembered prior to Hurricane Andrew. Walter's was more than a coffee shop. It has an extensive menu with many breakfast and lunch options. I went inside. Hammy was already seated. She looked less antagonistic out of her work uniform.

"Took you long enough," she said as a way of greeting as I slid into the booth across from her.

Like I said, she *looked* less antagonistic. It doesn't mean that she was.

"If you take that kind of attitude with me, I won't let you buy me lunch," I said to her.

"I'm a civil servant, just like you. You know what that means? It means I can afford anything, but I can't afford everything."

"Contending with the tension for the pension," I said.

Hammy ordered the "Sailor's Melt," a quirky name for a tuna melt sandwich. The all-too-familiar American black coffee was the only coffee option on the menu. I opted for an iced tea with extra ice. Hammy reached into a knapsack she'd brought with her and pulled out a manila folder.

"I haven't heard word 'boo' from any of you macho mantatstic dingalings," she said. "I made a copy of what I've found so far." She slid the file across the table towards me.

"If it makes you feel any better, I haven't heard a word from anyone either. Before I open this, do you want to tell me what I'm looking at first?" I asked her.

"I'm not sure. It just seems like there's way more going on here than meets the eye. Didn't your incredibly pleasant Major say we should all be working together? You're telling me you haven't heard anything from the DEA either?"

"It's been crickets the past two days. I got a surprise visit from the U.S. Marshal's office though. They say that Dario Curbelo is in WITSEC, but he's pulled a Houdini on them, and they can't find him," I said.

"So they have a relationship with him?" she asked, astonished.

"I don't know if it's a relationship or some sort of prior involvement. Whatever it is, he's out of touch with no forwarding address," I said.

"So you're in the dark too?" she asked me.

"Very much so. Agents Marroquín and Walker walked out with SAC Grayson, and I haven't heard from them since. I spoke with

ASAC Mandeville, and she said they're trying to slowly pull Scott Lew out of the coma. I don't know where the medical team is with that or how successful they've been or haven't been. It's been a tangled mess. I did speak with the arson investigator from the house fire in North Miami. He said there was no way that the medical examiner could make a body identification from fingerprints. He said the body was burned to nearly nothing. Do you know how your people were able to say that Dario Curbelo was identified as the body in the housefire?"

"No. I just got a read out that the prints from the shooting matched a cadaver found in the fire. I was just relaying the information to you," she said.

"Somewhere in the information chain a very much alive Dario Curbelo was listed as deceased in the house fire, but identification wasn't made with fingerprints—yet using *only* fingerprints, he's identified as the victim of the fire. By the way, the house fire victim autopsy and reports are sealed at the Dade Medical Examiner's office."

"The report is sealed?" she said with her mouth actually agape in disbelief.

"I'm telling you, something's up with the U.S. Marshal's office. As soon as Dario Curbelo's Mercedes-Benz was located, they started showing up demanding to know whatever they could find out about Curbelo." "Let me give you the *CliffsNotes* version of what's in that file. I processed the dropped gun magazine on Palm Avenue. You know, the one the shooter dropped from his gun when he was shooting at you—"

"How could I forget?" I said, interrupting her.

"As I was saying, the magazine had prints on them. The prints aren't in AFIS, and we've entered them into the system. Each time we enter them into AFIS, within eight to ten hours they disappear, and we have to reenter them."

My turn to let my mouth hang open. "Are you telling me each time you enter the prints into the Automated Fingerprint Identification

System, the national registry for *all* fingerprints, they're being wiped out of the system within a few hours?"

"For a native speaker, you pick up on the English language well," she said, rolling her eyes sarcastically.

"Have you ever seen anything like that before?" I asked her.

"No. Absolutely not, never. I mean it's like some sort of computer glitch but only with *these* fingerprints. Our I.T. people are stumped. So are our clerks who work with the system every day. The fingerprints were legible, and we were able to pull them easily. It's not like we're sending them smudges or smears. But there's more."

"More?" *Than that?*

"Lots more. Check this out. So we got fingerprints from the gun magazine and a partial thumbprint on the shell casings in the restaurant. The rounds aren't normal by U.S. criteria. The second weird thing about this is that the magazine doesn't fit a conventional gun and—"

"A conventional gun?" I asked her just as the waitress was putting down her sandwich and my iced tea. The waitress gave me a sideways glance as she obviously heard what I said.

"Its' something our armorer isn't familiar with. We put an inquiry to the ATF lab in Walnut Creek, California, for some assistance. They got back to us late last night."

"I've dealt with the ATF lab in Walnut Creek before. They're pretty good at deep digging on these kinds of things," I said.

"What do you want to hear first? The rounds or the gun?" she said.

I was holding the file but was more interested in hearing what she had to say first. I could read the file later. I kept it closed and eagerly asked her to tell me about the gun first. Between bites of her sandwich she began to relay the information to me.

"It's not an American gun," she said with a mouthful and wide eyes, like she was giving me some juicy gossip. "It's *Russian*."

"Russian?"

"Yes, it's Russian. It's made by the KBP firearm company. I'm not even going to try and pronounce what KBP stands for, but it's in the report you're holding."

I opened the report and quickly found the company known as KBP.

Konstruktorskoe Buro Priborostroeniya.

I decided I too wouldn't even try to pronounce it. I let her know that I found it in the report, urging her to continue.

"So this Russian company, KBP, has been around for a long time. After President Reagan and Soviet premier Mikhail Gorbachev instituted Glasnost in 1985 the Russian military and police orders for the KBP firearms dropped significantly. Change finally caught up to KBP around 1991. KBP had a huge reduction in gun manufacturing. It nearly killed them. They had to up their game and start making a line of firearms that was appealing to the western world and not just the Kremlin. The problem was between Colt, Sig Sauer, Glock, and the rest, there wasn't a lot of room to break into the gun market. So KBP designed a gun called a Tula P-96. Tula is the manufacturing town where it's made and 96 represents the year it was introduced into the market."

Hammy's thoroughness was growing on me. I was impressed with how much of the report she'd retained.

"You know this stuff pretty well," I said.

"I've had to since all you *cabios* left me back at the corral. I've been reading it to myself since I got it."

"I'll read this while you eat," I said as I opened the file fully.

> *The Tula P-96 in its present form does not possess reliable means of adaptive firepower for law enforcement. The Tula P-96 has the appearance of modern pistol construction development trends, including matt-black polymeric material with embedded steel slide rails. The Tula P-96 is market-initiated, and its reliability and range applications are not fully known by this technician. Cursory examination by ATF field*

*agents and data received from said agents are consistent that the construction is at the level of an improving prototype. The trigger of the Tula P-96 is similar to what is used in the Austrian Glock. There is a striker trigger, dependent upon the weapon being constantly in the preliminary cocked and fully retracted mode. It is only effective when the trigger is pressed. Most notably, all surfaces are rounded, as it is theorized to keep the gun from catching on clothing. The firearm was designed as a concealed weapon. The Tula P-96 is the first KBP (*Konstruktorskoe Buro Priborostroeniya*) of small arms designed for the international market.*

The cartridge is 9 x 17mm. The 9 x 17mm cartridge is generally known in Europe as a 9mm as a Kurz or Corto which just means "short" in Slavic languages. The 9 x 17mm cartridge is unpopular as a service round. It is commonly referred to as a small arms round. It meets minimum functional chambering for self-defense. In Europe, the round was favored by many military and police forces. It was adopted as a standard military pistol round in countries like Czech Republic, Italy, Serbia, Bosnia Herzegovina, and Montenegro. There is a multitude of possibilities of loadings, with military-type jacketed bullets or police loads with hollow point bullets. The shell casings are rigid, and they are usually made of brass or steel cases (made in Russia).

Fraternally,

Special Agent Robert Ainley, Senior Firearms Inspector.

Bureau of Alcohol Tobacco and Firearms ATF Forensics Laboratory.

355 North Wiget Lane, Walnut Creek, CA 94598

I stopped reading and looked up at Hammy. She looked back at me with a knowing look.

"Like I said, there is *way* more going on here than meets the eye. How does a cocaine dealer and his thug buddy get shot by a Russian who doesn't show up in any systems, and when we put him in the system he continually gets deleted *out* of the system?" she said.

I thought about her words and recognized right away where she made the conclusion our shooter was Russian. The report said that the handgun was Russian and when the bullets are in steel jackets, they are Russian-made. I remembered what Hammy had said days earlier to me and Major Brunson.

"Yes. Our firearms people are saying they were steel jacketed bullets. They also said they've never seen the magazine that was recovered on Palm Avenue before."

"You assisted the DEA crime scene technicians. Have you heard from them?"

She shook her head a little. "I'm not sure if you walked into this movie in the middle but I think I was pretty clear when I said that I haven't heard from any of you at all."

I nodded my head in submissive agreement.

"Cade, I was able to get a lot done with very little. I had shards of a glass tabletop, the neck of a bottle of wine, and singular wine glass to work with. We both know any good defense attorney could just pull the employee records at *El Segundo Viajante* and show high attrition of kitchen workers, nonexistent cleaning policies, and antiquated dishwashers and say that the prints are inadmissible. As far as you and your case is concerned, Dario Curbelo was never at the restaurant. Even his DNA can be explained away in similar fashion. The DEA. *The DEA*? They walked out of there with an entire glass tabletop from the shooter's table. Yet as I sit here questioning why I even got a tuna melt; I've heard nothing from them about what fingerprints they retrieved. They haven't asked to compare prints from the shell casings or the gun magazine. Nothing. It's like poof! They just disappeared. By the way, the prints on the Mercedes-Benz, including the gas cap, matched those at the restaurant. Same guy. My guy. Oh, and for the record I'm sorry about your shirt and the inky handprint. I get frustrated sometimes."

I had already forgotten about that little stunt. "It's okay. I didn't really like that shirt anyway."

The waitress cleared Hammy's plate away and left a check on the table. Before Hammy could pick it up I snatched it off the table. I pulled a twenty dollar bill out of my wallet, much to Hammy's protestations.

"We may not be able to afford everything, but we can afford everything on this menu," I said as we both walked out.

Chapter Fifteen

It had been a hell of a week. That was the main thought going through my head as I walked Hammy to her car. I was still holding the manila folder she'd given me.

"Are you responsible enough to hang onto that?" she asked me.

"Of course I am," I said, knowing full well that there are many times in my life when I'm not even responsible enough to own white pants.

She drove off and I got in my car. I was tired. I was just bushed. It had been a whacked-out week. A wave of exhaustion crested on top of me. I knew I'd need to get dinner, but I really wanted to go home and lock it all down. Just put it all somewhere for a while.

The drive from Walter's Coffee shop to the condo at Paradise Point wasn't very far. The car clock radio said it was 3:45pm. Papa Ricco's was just a few blocks north of Walter's. On Saturday they don't open until 4pm. I drove to the Kings Bay strip shopping plaza and pulled in front of the amazing French bakery *Delices de France*. I can never remember the name of the bakery. I just always called it "Patrick's." My former neighbor always called it Patrick's. I simply assumed that was the name of the wonderful bakery. I get tongue-twisted butchering my way through my usage of Miami Spanish—I had no hope of ever speaking French. On weekend mornings the line for the bakery stretches out the door for the amazing baked goods and coffee. At this late hour there were very few patrons. I ordered a latte. It was superbly made and served in an insulated corrugated paper cup that kept the coffee piping hot. I sat outside in front of the bakery at a small bistro table. The western sky behind me was turning pinkish orange with the approaching sunset. I could see Papa Ricco's from where I was sitting. It wasn't exactly 4pm yet. Within a few minutes someone from inside the little Italian restaurant turned on the neon 'open' sign in the front window.

The coffee tasted so good. I was too comfortable, and I was too tired to walk down and place my order face to face. From the little bistro table and just a few storefronts away, I called Papa Ricco's from my phone. It would be my second Papa Ricco's order placed within a few days.

"Papa Ricco's."

"Hello. Can I please get a pick-up for a baked ziti with a side order of two meatballs?"

"You want two meatballs and the ziti?" he asked me.

"Yes. To go."

"Anything else? Maybe bruschetta?"

People who know the correct way to pronounce bruschetta can't wait for you to hear them pronounce it.

"No, just the ziti and the meatballs will do."

"Is that it?"

"Yup, that's it."

"Twenty minutes."

I picked up the order. I just wanted to get home, but I did a little heat run on the way, pulling into the parking lot of the elementary side of Westminster Christian School. I sat there for a minute or two. There didn't appear to be anybody following me. I went through the gatehouse at the complex. This time I dared to park in front of my unit and dragged my feet up the stairs with my delicious-smelling meal. Papa Ricco's had the University of Miami versus Temple University football game playing on their TV. I put the food on the kitchen counter and plopped down into the oversized comfortable couch and tuned the big screen TV to the game. Miami was wearing their road white uniforms and the announcers were a little dull. Before I knew it, I had fallen asleep. I awoke late in the fourth quarter of the game. Miami was winning 47-0 when the Hurricanes let a quick pass get past them for a touchdown. Final score 47-7. I guess everyone needs to save face I thought to myself as I rubbed the sleep from my eyes and tried to wake up.

Saving face. I hadn't given it too much thought but maybe that's what a lot of this was. When you cut it down to its last tendrils of the sinewy muscle that's left on the bone, maybe that's what we're all doing. Everyone is trying to save face. Major Brunson needs to save face with the city manager and show him that we can responsibly use $400,000 as flash money on drug deals and not lose the entire amount. ASAC Marie Mandeville wanted to save face because her agents deviated from an ops plan, and the entire team lost twenty kilograms of cocaine by not covering the exits properly. SAC John Grayson had one of his agents shot by a fragmented bullet and finding the shooter would save face for the DEA. Marshal Auburn McKenna needed Dario Curbelo found to save face for the U.S Marshals, since they entrusted him to be back in society under an assumed name. This was all one big circle copulation. Even the National Security Agency lackey Robert McBride was trying to poke into this quagmire of a case and get in front of whatever went wrong in Hialeah rather than try and work from being behind it. Everyone working for their own known or cloaked agendas, but none of them working together. All of them trying to save face.

McBride is woefully the epitome of why there is so much insincerity in politics. A class A jerk who's spent more time making decisions on carpet than on concrete. He's a classic "Washington handshake." The Washington handshake is when you're shaking someone's hand but kind of looking over their shoulder to see who else is in the room. You're always looking to further yourself, strike a deal or cover your own ass. Continually looking to see if there's someone in the room who could help your career. The only face I was trying to save was my own actual face. I laid face-down in the dirt and patchy grass of the Hialeah Racetrack when some Russian decided to make me his own moving target range.

I was still feeling sleep deprived, but was also hungry. I reheated the baked ziti and meatballs and ate them in silence as the weekend slipped away from me. I'd been working too hard this past year. It was all catching up to me. The VIN lifestyle had pulverized me into a physical and emotional mess. Just when I thought I had it all figured out it's as though the dynamics of probability and the rules of engagement change on me. I finished eating. There wasn't much more for me to do. I checked the door locks and I headed up stairs. This time I took the bottle of Jameson with me

---

SUNDAY WAS RATHER uneventful. Assisted by one too many snorts of Jameson, I slept in longer than I normally do. I had a bear of a time getting my day underway. I was unmotivated to do anything. Still very fatigued from the previous week, my Sunday consisted of me dozing on the couch with the Miami Dolphins versus the Carolina Panthers game on TV. It was a pretty dull game. Without Dolphins kicker Olindo Mare and his field goal accuracy, the Dolphins would have lost this snoozer of a football game. It gave me plenty of opportunity to think about the things I needed to do, starting tomorrow morning. There were so many investigative things that needed to be done. If we didn't get any more assistance from the DEA or any information from Agent Lew, I'd start hitting the known locations where informants and dopers congregate in Miami and start putting feelers out that I wanted to buy twenty kilograms. Maybe I could flush out Dario Curbelo that way. I was going to try to find a way to assert a little more pressure on U.S. Marshal Mckenna and see if there was anything in Curbelo's file that she may have overlooked that would help us locate him. I went down to my car and pulled my go bag from the trunk. I took many of the clothes out of it and repacked it with different clothes. My toiletries and spare Hartford Whalers hat were still good to go. I put the bag near the front door and let the rest of Sunday slip away.

Monday morning I was in the VIN office before Ileana or Gary got in. I relished the quiet of the morning. At 8am I started dialing the oil change centers. I told my same fictionalized story about my wife. Each time I was met with the news that the center couldn't have been the one to service my wife's car, nor did they have any record of her ever being there. It was nearly 10:30am when I was getting down to the bottom of the list. Then there was that one. The one I was looking for.

"Tire Choice."

"Hello, my wife was just there, and I think your technician didn't put the plug back in tightly. There is some oil dripping on the floor of our garage."

"Here? Are you sure? This is the Biscayne location," he said.

"I'm pretty sure. I mean, that's where I told her to go."

"What time was she here? We've been doing mostly tires here today," he said.

"I don't know, can you look her up by her name or car or something?" I said.

"What's your wife's name?"

"Actually her secretary brought the car in for her, so I don't know if she used her name our name or the company name," I said.

That line was the one that I'm sure caused more eye rolls and exasperation than any other.

"Without a name I can't help you, buddy," he said, getting ready to hang up.

"Hold on! I have the license tag. Can you check it that way?" I asked him, feigning excitement.

With a heavy sigh he asked for the license plate number.

"It's DCH-328."

I could hear some keystrokes on his computer.

"You sure about today, because that car hasn't been here since last January."

Adrenaline surged right through me. I wanted to jump right out of my chair. I didn't want to spook the guy, so I kept my real excitement in check and tried to keep my composure. I hastily reached for a pencil on the desk and knocked the cup holding the pens and pencils onto the floor.

"January? Are you sure we have the right car? What's the address?" I asked him.

"9032 Froude Avenue."

I scribbled the address down on a piece of paper. I decided to try and throw a Hail Mary long bomb while I was still holding the ball.

"Yeah, that's the old address. You don't have the new address in your system. If you did, then I'd know for sure she went to your franchise," I said.

"That's it, buddy. Whatever oil problems you got it ain't because of us. Your car hasn't been here since January."

"No, No I hear you. What's your name by the way?" I said as I looked out the doorway of the office right across Ileana's desk at Gary working at his desk.

"Wayne Street."

"Mr. Street, she constantly kills me at tax time. She mixes up our company billing with our private billing. I am so sorry to bother you one last time. By any chance, does your system show our company name or our name? The company name is Big G Enterprises."

"Says here Ricardo Sanabria," he said.

"Well that's me. I don't understand her sometimes. Thanks for your help, Mr. Street. I'll have to ask her again to tell me for sure where she took the car. Thank you. Sorry to bother you."

"No bother at all," he said as he hung up.

I leapt up from the desk and fist-pumped the air a few times. Throwing down the pencil on the desk, I grabbed the sheet of paper that I'd written down the address on. *I don't care if your mother named you Dario Curbelo or the U.S. government renamed you Ricardo Sanabria. I'm on to you*, I thought to myself as I walked down the hallway to Major Brunson's office. I turned into his doorway and made eye contact with Charlene. She must have been able to read the look on my face. Wordlessly she picked up the telephone and dialed the Major.

"Cade Taylor is here," she said into the mouthpiece.

She hung up and with both hands, straightened the sweater on her shoulders.

"He'll see you. Go in, Cade," she said to me.

I felt the swoosh of the carpet from under the door as I opened it. Inside, Major Brunson was at his desk. In front of him was a large stack of papers. Many of them he was signing. He looked up at me.

"I don't recall you being on my calendar, but then again when has that ever stopped you before?"

I took that as an invitation and sat in the chair across from his desk. He moved the pile of papers off to the side with a facial expression of displeasure and exasperation that surely wasn't about the paperwork.

"Okay, Cade. What is it?" he said.

"I think we might have a good lead on the Paraguayan from the shooting."

"Go on, I'm listening."

"I did detective things," I said.

"I'm sorry, what?" he said with narrowed eyes and a curled lip.

"You said you're the Major and you do major things. Hammy Garzon is the technician—she does technical things, and I'm the detective. I do detective things."

"Cade, as a kid did you get hit in the head by the teeter totter on the playground? What are you babbling about?"

"You wanted me to continue to do detective things and keep you informed as I do."

"When this is all said and done, I'm going to sit down with Lieutenant Maddalone and see about getting a different psychologist to help with our hiring practices. That's what *I'm* going to do. So aside from telling me things I've said and already forgotten, why are you here?"

Dario Curbelo. The Paraguayan? I may have a solid lead on where he is. I received a visit from a U.S. Marshal named Auburn McKenna. She had a records hold on the Mercedes-Benz and license tag that Curbelo was driving. When I asked Jeanie Rae to run the tag it set off a tripwire in the system at the U.S Marshal's office. McKenna told me that Curbelo had been in WITSEC, but he's been out where the mailman doesn't deliver for the past couple of months. The Marshals have been looking for him ever since. She said they gave him a new identity and he bolted on them."

"What's his new identity?"

"She wouldn't say."

"What?" he said, his voice rising.

"She said they 'have certain levels of confidentiality that we just can't break.'" I told him with air quotes. "Not for me and not for a DEA agent who was shot. That it's a 'tenet of our judicial system.'"

"A *tenet of our judicial system*?" he said, his face turning red. "Is creating a new identity for every New York mafia mobster and putting them in Scottsdale Arizona a tenet of our judicial system? You ever been there, Cade? It's like *Vito's Italian* in North Miami all over again, except it's every restaurant on every corner. In the fucking desert, no less!"

"Yeah, I wasn't feeling the love for sure," I said.

"All right. I can get around that Marshal secret handshake clubhouse bullshit. Go on," he said.

"I don't think you'll need to. I think the Marshals renamed him Ricardo Sanabria. His last address might be 9032 Froude Avenue in Surfside."

“Where did you get that from?” he asked me as he leaned closer, his chair creaking.

He’d been surprised by my use of the taxis to find the Mercedes. I needed to keep some of my methodology to myself.

“Word from the street,” I said, referring to Wayne Street, the oil change center manager.

“Okay, just as well, I don’t want to know all your sources. It’s better that way for me,” he said.

“Major, the bigger issue is I haven’t heard a single word from the DEA since they all followed SAC Grayson out of here like a bunch of little ducklings. Is there or is there not a task force on this? Because I spoke with Hammy Garzon, and she hasn’t heard a word either.”

“You haven’t heard anything?” he said as he stood up and put both his hands on the desktop. He slowly studied the contents of his desk. I was expecting the sweep of the papers across the room to be followed by a series of unrivaled profanity. Although not unseen before, when he opted to kick his garbage can, I for one was partially surprised. The vein on the left side of his forehead pulsed.

“Cade, listen to me clearly. I want you to go out to that address—”

“9032 Froude Avenue in Surfside.”

“Yeah. Go out to the address in Surfside and get a good scope on it, but do not do *anything* by yourself. Do you understand me? I’ll call Grayson and I’ll get some people out there.”

I started to get up and leave but he held his hand up motioning for me to wait for one more set of instructions, or maybe even an admonishment.

“I’m telling you, Cade. Do *not* take any action by yourself. Just get set up on the house. Come up with an action plan for surveillance. I will talk with our city attorney about whether or not your information is enough to get a warrant for the house. Believe me you, I am from the fuck around and find out generation. Grayson will get an earful and there *will* be a cavalry coming. You just need to hold it down ‘til we get people in place.”

I nodded my head affirmatively as I stood fully from the chair to leave.

"I'm going to give you one good reason to be careful, aside from the other 399,000 obvious reasons. Cade, only you have seen this Curbelo or Sanabria or whatever the fuck his name is. Remember—he knows what you look like. He's seen *you*, too."

Chapter Sixteen

SURFSIDE WAS ONE on those small towns in Miami Dade County that I'd spent very little time in. I knew it was adjacent to the archipelago that's essentially the northern tip of Miami Beach. I also know that post World War II Winston Churchill vacationed often at the famous Surf Club. That was about the extent of my knowledge of Surfside. I never fully understood why Carl Fisher and the other developers of Miami Beach didn't just continue the entire sand marsh and muck they dredged from Biscayne Bay and make the entire island Miami Beach. It was very confusing. Even more confusing was that Froude Avenue turned into Bay Avenue without any demarcation or reasonable reason why. I drove past the house first and was briefly confused when the road changed names. I circled back and once again drove by the house, this time a lot slower.

I would surmise the house was built sometime in the 1950s. It was in the middle of a residential street. It wasn't a large house and had a single car driveway on the northern side. There was a three-foot tiered and columned brick wall in front of the house, both low-slung and painted white. There was with weathered black wrought iron between the columns. It had all the formidable aspects of a child's scrap wood-built tree house. There was a decorative wrought iron sign driven into the front walkway column featuring two bowing palm trees bending inward toward each other. The numbers 9032 were between them. The house was painted in a muted peach color with Spanish tile roof. The front door was a non-descript single hung painted white door. There were eight silver Bismarck palms in front of the house.

Lots of palm trees of various types dotted all along the street. Through the years and the hurricanes of South Florida, palms were the most hearty and resilient and were obvious choices to plant and propagate to return a semblance of life that couldn't be destroyed. The houses on the street were very similar in appearance although many had obviously gone through some extensive renovations. This was a definitely an older established neighborhood that I'd venture to guess had a long history of being desirable and affordable housing for many decades of people who worked in Miami and Miami Beach. I don't think the builders of these homes ever environed two or more cars per household. There was a lot of street parking by the neighboring residents. Parking had caused small choke points in traffic where only one car could pass easily by. Luckily the street didn't appear to be very heavily trafficked, with the exception of an occasional UPS truck, or Zephyrhills water delivery truck.

The luck was going to run out if Major Brunson delivered on his promise to get "the calvary" out here.

Additional bodies would be great for surveillance but would seriously tax the viability of the street. There'd have to be a single car keeping an eye on the house and other surveillance units staged elsewhere. I was in place and set up a few houses down where I could see the house. There weren't any cars there, and I was watching to see if Curbelo or anyone else came or left from the house.

As more law enforcement people started arriving in the area, slowly the calls started coming into my cell phone. I used a legal pad and wrote down their telephone numbers, names, and the types and colors of cars. DEA Agents Walker and Marroquín were part of the cavalry that Brunson had mustered up. The arriving personnel all found little places to park and wait out of sight and off of Froude Avenue. I continued with the surveillance of the house, vigilantly watching the house for nearly four hours. One of the DEA agents relieved me of the responsibility so I could meet with DEA Agent Marroquín a few blocks away.

"Where ya been? I haven't heard anything from you in days," I said to him.

"They got us pulling all kinds of stupid stuff. Checking hospitals, chasing down old informants, going through Scott Lew's desk. It's just a waste of time. Finding the Mercedes and now this address are the two biggest leads we've had so far."

"Have you talked to Hammy Garzon from Hialeah?" I asked him.

"No."

"Well, she and her people are saying the bullet and the gun used to shoot Scott was Russian."

"Russian?" he said, astonished.

"Yeah, it's called a Tula P-96, and the rounds are steel jacketed."

"All the evidence we gathered went to a DEA lab and we haven't heard anything at all."

"You need to not be so dark and start playing with the rest of us. Hammy's busting it and getting all kinds of breakthroughs and linkage. I can tell you from chasing the shooter, he sure could pass for a Russian."

"So how do you think this Russian knew to be at the restaurant in Hialeah the same time we were doing the deal?" he asked me.

"I have no clue, but I think if we can figure out who the C.I. was on the deal, we'll have a better idea of where to start looking," I said looking intently at him. "I think you and Walker, and a few others need to get on the winning team here. Hammy and I are digging up these nuggets and you guys are checking bedpans at hospitals. Where are Mandeville and Grayson in all of this?

"They're flipping their shit because of this. So is our crime lab director. Everything we pulled from the scene went off to a second lab and as of now the results are either 'inconclusive' or 'not back yet.'"

"What about Lew? I never heard if they were able to pull him out of the coma. What's his condition so far?" I asked him.

Marroquín breathed a sigh of relief, though he came across as troubled. "They got him to sit up. He's still sleeping a lot. He hasn't said anything yet, but they think he recognized his wife and sons. He got more emotional and animated when he saw them. But as of yet, still not talking," he said.

Marroquín and I set up a schedule for round the clock, twenty-four hour surveillance on the house. Alternating agents kept an eye on the house until around 10pm. At 10pm the SOG squad would cover the house until 6am. The next day we'd take up the surveillance again and as the day progressed, we'd then decide if this information received about 9032 Froude Avenue as being the house that Dario Curbelo was living in was worth pursuing.

By 9pm I was pulling into the condominium at Paradise Point. The Surfside location was in the capable hands of the last remaining DEA agents and the oncoming SOG members. It had been a very long day. A very long, boring day. There'd been no activity at 9032 Froude Avenue.

I went upstairs to the master bathroom and turned the hot water on in the large jacuzzi bathtub. As the tub filled with warm bubbly water, I went back downstairs and retrieved four Amstel Light beers from the refrigerator, went back upstairs and was undressed and in the tub within minutes. I started relishing the first frosty cold beer. I must have been in the bathtub for well past an hour. The water was very relaxing and the effects of four beers were settling in nicely with me too. The beer bottles bobbed in the water. I crawled out of the bathtub leaving the empty bottles to slowly sink down to the bottom with the draining water. Barely dried off, I collapsed into bed, my cell phone alarm set for 5:10am.

At a quarter to six the next morning I was searching for an open Cuban café, looking to get an eye-opening hit of café Cubano. I needed the potent caffeine to help boost me into the day. I was seriously dragging. One of the DEA agents relieved the SOG member and the entire SOG squad went home. At 8:30 am my cell phone rang.

"Hello?"

"Is this Detective Taylor?"

"Who's this?" I asked.

"This is Sergeant Denny Byrne from the Miami Police Department."

"Oh yes. Sorry. Yes, this is me. Good morning, Sergeant," I said as I sat more upright in my car seat.

"You asked me to look into the follow-up on the arrest I made at the Torch of Freedom. I got the paperwork here in front of me. It was buried deep in records, it being practically a nonevent and all," he said, trying to downplay the arrest and still distance himself from it all.

"Yes, I'd be interested in what you were able to find out," I said.

"Well I know you already saw the arrest form, so there's nothing new there. He never was transported to Dade County Jail. He was released at our station. Like I said, not much of an arrest and I caught all kinds of hell because of it."

"So he just was let go and walked out?"

"No, a friend came and got him and signed him out. I can't really make out the signature, but they must have made him print his name under it. Aroldo Cordozo DDS. I love how these doctors and dentists put their title in everything they sign."

"Wait. Are you telling me the guy who signed him out of your custody is a *dentist*?" I asked.

"Apparently so. I never heard of him, but he must be a dentist. Doesn't DDS mean Doctor of Dental Surgery?"

"It sure does. Thank you, Sergeant. I appreciate you getting this information to me."

I quickly hung up and called the VIN office. Ileana picked up on the third ring.

"*Veen.*"

"Ileana, it's Cade. I need you do me a favor and look up a dentist for me."

"*Ju* need a *denteest*? *Coño* Cade, I know is not what *ju* think but I know a guy who in *Cúba* was a great *denteest pero*, he can't get his license in the United States but he's good. He's in Westchester and he works in *he's* garage *pero* he is *bery* good."

"No, No *I* don't need a dentist. I just need you to look up a particular dentist for me. Aroldo Cordozo."

"*Espere.*" Wait. I could hear the audio from her TV. She was watching one of her telenovelas. There was a brief fumbling as she came back on the line.

"Aroldo Cordozo. 1140 96th Street, Bay Harbor Island, Florida."

I almost dropped the phone in my excitement.

1140 96th Street was only a block or two from where Curbelo's Mercedes-Benz was found. I quickly hung up with Ileana, then asked both agents Walker and Marroquín to meet with me away from the house on Froude Avenue.

When I saw them, I could hardly wait to tell them that the dentist who bailed Curbelo out of jail had an office only two blocks from where the Mercedes-Benz had been located. There were enough people to cover the house here in Surfside. We all agreed to go pay a visit to the dentist, each of us taking our own cars. We'd meet up again outside the dentist's office less than two miles away. We had a brief discussion in front of a plastic surgeon's office where we formulated a plan. It was agreed I would go in first and see if the doctor was in. They'd give me ten minutes and then follow in behind me.

We crossed the landscaped median, and I went into the office building. The directory was posted in the lobby, and I quickly saw on the board the doctor's suite. He was in suite 311.

The elevator chimed when it reached the third floor and the

doors opened up to an expansive hallway. Suite 311 was at the end of the hallway. I look at the name stenciled on the frosted window of the door.

Dr. Aroldo Cordozo D.D.S.

Diplomate, American Board of Oral Implantology/ Implant Dentistry

ABOI member since 1993

Se Habla Español

I stepped into the inner office of the dental practice. There were three empty chairs in the lobby, a coffee table with neat stacks of current magazines and the right amount of large indoor plants to make the most nervous patient feel at ease. A pretty young receptionist called to me from an open window. I could see past her all the filing cabinets and rudimentary office equipment. It looked as though the office continued past her workstation down a hallway.

"May I help you?" she said with a smile of perfect veneers.

"Good Morning," I said in my most cheery voice. "I'm Cade Daniels and I'm the membership coordinator for the Florida Dental Association. Is Doctor Cordozo available?"

"I'm sorry, you're with who?"

"Cade Daniels. Membership coordinator for the Florida Dental Association. Is Doctor Cordozo available? His membership has lapsed, and I happened to be here in Bay Harbor Islands. At the FDA we try to keep retention before we have deletion. I'd like to talk with him about getting him back in good stead before he loses the benefits of the FDA."

I had hoped to confuse her enough with the jargon of the Florida Dental Association and the continual use of the initials, thinking she might forget the organization and refer to me as being from the FDA—the same initials as the Food and Drug Administration. Dentists and lab technicians do not want to run afoul of the bigger, more well-known FDA. She looked at me with a furrow in her eyebrows and picked up the telephone. I heard her say under her breath that a man from the FDA is here.

Bingo!

"Dr. Cordozo will be with you in a minute," she said, flashing her ultra-white teeth.

"Thank you. Could I get a piece of paper from you please?"

She pulled a blank sheet from the office copier and handed it to me through the window. I folded it in half. There was no one in the waiting room and the morning was still early. There was a better than average chance the doctor, although I'm sure busy, would be able to turn aside whatever he was doing to see me, especially if he thought I was from the FDA. My intonations were correct when I saw a glimpse of him through the receptionist's open window. The door leading to the hallway and examination rooms opened. A slight man with wire-rimmed glasses and dark hair with tinges of gray on the temples opened the door.

"Mr. Daniels. I'm Dr. Cordozo. Please come inside. My office is just down the hall," he said.

I followed him down the hallway past the receptionist. He was wearing a thin white medical coat over a light blue dress shirt and patterned necktie. His office was functional and comfortable. Behind his desk were framed diplomas from The University of Puerto Rico School of Dental Medicine and The University of Florida College of Dentistry. There were framed pictures. One in particular of him in front of the Eifel Tower. He sat at his desk, and I sat across from him.

"I must say you don't look like any of the employees I've met from the FDA before," he said, looking at my scruffy unshaven face, longish hair, jeans, and t-shirt.

"Well, Doctor, I just happened to be down here for a an out-of-office event, and I thought I'd chance dropping by to see you. It's a miracle I can even get out of my cubicle sometimes and we're very liberal about in-office attire and appearance. Getting out of the office is important. I see you do from to time to time, by your pictures behind you." I said

He briefly turned in his chair and glanced at the pictures on the credenza behind his desk. “Yes, Europe is a pleasure. Last summer it was beautiful. So exactly what is this about?” he asked me.

“Well, we at the FDA not only handle membership and retention of our members but we also must respond to egregious complaints too. May I?” I said as I rose to close the office door. “You may not want your staff to hear what I’m about to say.”

His eyes showed that he was a little alarmed, but he nodded his head. I closed the door and sat back down. I put the folded sheet of paper on the edge of the desk closest to me.

“Is this your signature?” I said, motioning with my head to the paper.

He leaned forward in his seat and reached for the paper, bending low across the flat surface of the desk as he grasped the paper.

I moved very quickly. I jumped up and yanked aggressively on his necktie with my left hand. I pulled him even further off balance and across his desk. His glasses fell off his face and bounced across the surface. I unholstered my gun from under my shirt and stuck the barrel right up against his forehead. He was immediately stunned and frightened, his eyes wide with fear, hands scrabbling at the air as he whimpered.

I hissed down low at him, “You scream? You yell? You make a *sound* and I’ll blast you right here.”

“Who are you?” he said through trembling lips, his eyes starting to water.

“Right now? I’m just a guy with a gun and I’ll be the last thing you see if you don’t start talking.”

‘Talking? Talking about what?” he said, his eyes definitely welling up now.

I took a gamble and bluffed my next comments.

“The morphine. We know about the high amounts of morphine you used last week. Where is he? The man you treated for a gunshot. Where is he?”

"I…I …I don't know what you're talking about. What man?" he blubbered.

If I was incorrect in my belief that Dr. Cordozo treated Dario Curbelo for his gunshot wound, this was going to go disastrously wrong for me.

"You have a choice. You can tell me now or my associates who will be here any minute will either shoot you in the head for lying to me, or they'll shoot you in both hands and you'll never practice dentistry again."

"Associates? What? I'm…I'm confused." He was now full out crying. At that moment the quiet chime of his outer office door was heard, and muffled conversations came from the door between his receptionist and whoever had come in the office. My hope was it was Walker and Marroquín.

"They're here. I can't save you now. You should have told me about Dario Curbelo before they got here. I can't save you now. Say your prayers, Doc. It's finished for you."

"Curbelo?" he stammered.

His eyes were pouring tears and the fear was creased across his face. His phone started buzzing from the receptionist.

I pulled his tie tighter around my fist. "Right! Curbelo! You think I'm going to come in here and ask you questions I don't already know the answers to?" I tugged on his tie even more, tightening it around his neck as I drew him even further off balance. The phone was still buzzing. I used my gun to knock the receiver off the cradle. I leaned down and calmly said into the mouthpiece, "Send them in."

"Please. Please. I have a wife and kids."

"Yeah, you and about 64 million other people in this country. Last chance, Doc," I said as the shadowy figures of Walker and Marroquín started to obscure the opaque glass of his office door.

"I'll talk! I'll talk! I'll tell you everything. Whatever you want. I'll tell you." He was bawling anguished tears. There was a rap on the office door. He dragged his head slightly on his desk looking towards the door.

"Just a second!" I yelled towards the door. I released the tight hold I had on his necktie and pushed him back into his chair.

"Get yourself together," I said through clenched teeth, still pointing the gun at him. He hastily wiped his face with his sleeve and adjusted his necktie. He tentatively reached for his glasses and put them back on. I holstered my gun and sat back down across from him.

"Come in!" I yelled to the door.

Walker and Marroquín filed into the office. The office immediately no longer seemed spacious with the four of his inside. Both agents stood on either side of me looking at the Paraguayan dentist.

"Doc. You have one chance. Talk."

"Dar…Dario, I have known for a few years. We were introduced by people in our home country—"

He stopped to look at the three of us. I'm sure he was having one final thought go through his head about lying to us.

"I'm telling you now, Doc. Both. Hands," I said slowly.

He nodded and then began to slowly talk.

"We are both from Ciudad del Este, Paraguay. We did not know each other growing up, we were introduced here in the States. I was asked to pick him up at the Miami Police station a few years ago. Since then I became his dentist, but we also started socializing. You know just shared interests like futból and food. Not American football. Futból, like soccer. Last Wednesday it was near the end of the day, and he called me. He said he was in trouble and could I come get him."

He briefly stopped talking and looked at the three of us. I leaned forward and locked eyes with him. He felt the intensity of my gaze and began speaking again.

"I asked him where he was. He said he was just across the street, and he was hurt very bad. He said he was shot, and he wanted me to go get him. He begged me to not call the paramedics or the police. I was stunned, I didn't know what to do. I stood up and looked out the window. I was still on the phone. He said he was just past the park, and he was bleeding badly. He begged me again to come get him—"

"Is that what you did?" asked Walker.

"He was my friend. He was hurt. What would you do? Of course I did. I grabbed some towels form the hall closet and went down to my car and I drove to where he was—"

"On West Bay Harbor Drive," confirmed Marroquín.

The dentist spoke quickly. "Yes. It's across the street, just past the park. He was nearly passed out in his car. I gave him a shot of adrenaline, and he perked up enough to be able to help me get him out of his car. I put him in my car and drove him back here. I practically carried him up here. He swore to me no doctors and no police. He had a gun tucked into his waistband. I was scared, I never knew Dario to carry a gun. He kept one hand on it as I shot him with four milligrams of morphine. I had to give him three more injections within about ten minutes. I used whatever tools I had here to open the wound and I was able to pull the bullet out. He was shot just below his left clavicle. I filled his wound with a liquid antibiotic and then gave him about fifty-three sutures to close it. He rested for about forty-five minutes. He'd lost blood. He was weak. I don't have blood here. While he was resting, I was torn. I was scared. I was scared if I called the police, he might shoot me or one of the police. I didn't know what to do."

His eyes filled with tears again. Once again, he looked back and forth between the three of us, seeking some sort of compassion. We just stared back at him.

"If he didn't get a transfusion his recovery would be slower as his body would need to create more blood. I told him. I told him that. He waved me off. I begged him to let me take him to a hospital. He just kept clutching the gun and saying no. After about two hours of monitoring him he asked me to take him home."

"Where's that?" I asked, trying to conceal my anxiousness.

"I don't know if it's home, but he had me take him to 1036 Northeast 89th Street."

I took a pen off his desk and jotted the address down on the piece of paper I'd walked in with.

"That's it?" I asked him.

"Yes. I drove him to that address and that's it," he said, his voice near hysterical.

"I'm telling you for the last time, Doc. Both hands. You lie to me again it's going to be *both hands*. I told you already I won't ask you any questions I don't know the answers to already. Now tell us about the coffee sack and the bag or I swear to God I'm going to turn these two animals on you."

He blinked hard and fast at me and then at both Walker and Marroquín. He slumped back even further in his chair.

"When Dario was recovered enough that I could get him in my car he had me drive back to his car. He had me take the coffee and the bag out of the backseat and put them in my car. I took him home and helped him into bed. I carried the sack and bag into the house for him."

"How much?" I asked him.

"How much what?" he asked me back.

"How much did he pay you and where is it now?"

For the first time the good doctor seemed like he'd played out his last card in the deck. He exhaled out of his nostrils and stared at me for a second or two, measuring me up. He swiveled around in his chair, his back to us as he pulled a cigar box-shaped decorative case from the credenza behind him. He opened it and withdrew the entire contents of the box. With his body partially turned to the desk he flung a banded stack of $20,000 onto the desk. The fifty dollar bill on the top was smeared with bloody fingerprints.

I stood up. I spied a box of latex gloves off to the side on top of a small table. I withdrew a glove and put it on my hand, and I pulled the fifty with the bloody fingerprints from the stack.

"Hammy Garzon already has Curbelo's prints on file. Let's get her to process this and check for comparisons."

Both agents nodded. It was Walker who spoke first. He looked directly at Doctor Cordozo.

"Doctor. I'm Special Agent Vincent Walker with the DEA."

"You guys are cops!" Dr. Cordozo shrieked.

"Doctor, you are under arrest for not reporting a gunshot victim to the authorities, practicing trauma medicine without a medical license, administering a known opioid to a non-dental, in-need patient, money laundering, and for conspiracy to traffic in twenty kilograms of cocaine."

"Wait. Wait. I didn't know the money was drug money! I didn't know there was cocaine involved! I was just helping Dario!" he pleaded.

"Doctor, my advice is to not say anything more until you meet with an attorney," Walker said knowingly as he went behind Dr. Cordozo. He had him stand up and then Walker placed him in handcuffs. Walker then turned to me and Agent Marroquín.

"I'll call for an intake team to take him to the Miami Detention Center. I'm going to call my buddy at the Office of Inspector General and see if he wants a piece of this case and I'll stay here with him until they get here. I'll make sure he doesn't make any calls until I hear from you guys. Why don't you two get going to the address he just gave us, see if you can find our guy. Let's get more bodies out there, too. I think we can shut down from the Surfside location for now. We'll leave just two people on it in case, but everyone else can start setting up on this new address."

"You don't need to tell us twice," said Marroquín.

Both Marroquín and I made for our cars and started driving east across the causeway. We went past the Chevron gas station where we'd met last week. Once on the mainland we veered south on San Souci Boulevard. We both breezed through the green the light at Biscayne Boulevard and powered south on the heavily traveled corridor. I could see Marroquín in his car in front of me. He had the cell phone to his ear constantly. I was doing the same thing. I put a call into Hammy and was unable to reach her. I relayed Walker's cell phone to her and asked her to call him about processing the fifty dollar bill. I tried to reach Major Brunson, but he was at City Hall in a meeting with the city manager. I asked Charlene to have him call me when he returned. In a giddy sense of fair play I also called Marshal McKenna, but I was 0 for 3 in contacting anyone. She must have still been in Tampa assisting the Florida Marine Patrol. I left a voice message on her phone asking her to call me.

We made the turn on East 96th Street and then barreled through the next turn at Northeast 10th Avenue. I was right behind Marroquín when he slowed down considerably and put his flashers on. He stuck his hand out the window and motioned for me to pull aside him. We were side by side at the wide intersection of East 90th and 10th Avenue. I rolled down my passenger window.

"I'm going to go in and do a little recon run. You hang here and I'll call you about where we can set up 'til everyone else gets here."

Before I could answer he was driving off towards the address. I parked and sat in my car, waiting. I was beginning to get impatient when my cell phone rang. It was Marroquín.

"This is a big house."

"What do you think?" I asked him.

"I think we need to have eyes on it until we can get a warrant. This house has lots of windows and faces the intersection with unobstructed views. It has a side driveway in addition to the front driveway. This place is *really* big. There's a little finger marina directly across the street with direct access to the bay. It could be tricky."

"I got no problem setting up on it, but keep in mind he has seen me—but it doesn't matter if he comes out walking a dog or going to a car. We're just going to hard bang him right there anyway," I said.

"My thoughts exactly. I'm going to set up east, more towards this finger basin thing. The street dead ends two houses to the south. You back into that. I should see any activity coming from the front of the house and you'll be in place to move on it if I do," he said.

"What about the side driveway?" I asked him.

"We'll have to chance it 'til we get more people here."

"Okay. I'm coming in," I said before I hung up.

When I turned down the street towards the house, I could see what Marroquín meant by it being a large house with windows. The house faced due east and had commanding views of the small marina basin; a little finger channel called Lake Belmer. The view continued out to Biscayne Bay, and most portions of the street. The house looks as though it was built in the 1930s. It has multiple banks of white framed hurricane impact windows. There was a side covered portico where the front door is. The front door had protective security bars framed around it. Under the portico it was barely noticeable and did not detract from the beauty of the house. The style of the house was peach-colored rough stucco with a Spanish tiled roof. The window frames, rooflines, and archways above the doors had a Moorish accent. The stucco had been poured, formed, and applied by a very good mason. The passage of time had created opportunities for the house to have multiple additions added to it. It was a beautiful sprawling home that has been restored and maintained very nicely.

I saw the south end of the street. I backed my car into the dead end. I positioned myself so that I could see if there was any activity at the house. Getting a warrant could take a few hours. I settled in for the long haul. Within the hour we had pulled nearly everyone from the Froude address in Surfside. Agents were positioned to the west of Marroquín and I. After a few hours of watching the house and seeing no activity, both Marroquín and I left our positions as we were relieved by other surveillance agents. There was a Burger King at Biscayne Boulevard and 90th Street, a two minute drive away. Marroquín and I met at the fast food burger restaurant. We found an isolated booth to sit in as we discussed what we needed to do.

Agent Marroquín started. "Walker called me. He said the dentist is crying like a baby. They still haven't provided him a phone call yet—they don't want him tipping off Dario Curbelo. Our legal division says the fact that the dentist saw Curbelo with a gun and he did at the very least conspire to traffic in cocaine, we have enough for a warrant. ASAC Mandeville said we should have the warrant by 6pm tonight. What do you think?"

"Do we have a tactical team?" I asked him.

"This guy was part of the reason Scott Lew got shot. We want in on this all the way. We're going to do it ourselves. Walker, myself, and three other agents will do the take-down. We want you on the scene to I.D. him."

"When do you plan to hit the house?"

"Four in the morning. We think he'll be tucked in asleep. The whole element of surprise thing. We got good people on the house now. Let's you and I bug out and meet back here in the parking lot at two in the morning," he said.

Chapter Seventeen

WITH VERY LITTLE sleep I was back at the Burger King at 2am. Walker and Marroquín were at the back of Walker's SUV, both donning DEA tactical Kevlar vests. Undoubtedly, they'd be wearing the vests under their "announcement apparel." There were three other agents there as well. I'd brought my own jet-black Kevlar vest that had Velcro-attached name plates that said "Police/Policia" on the front and back. There had been a gold badge on the front of the left chest plate. I cut that off with a razor blade months ago. People are instinctual. They're especially instinctual with a gun. A standout gold color can be an easy target for a skilled marksman, or just a novice shooter when they fire a gun. I didn't need that placed on my heart. I donned my vest as we gathered. The plan was laid out rather simply. The whole operation relied on a trio of elements working together:

Surprise.

Speed.

Violence of Action.

These three elements in concert are considered the triangle of success, with surprise being the biggest element. Surprise is the base of the triangle. Without surprise no amount of speed or violence of action can compensate for its loss. Surprise was the key. Which explained why we were gearing up at 2am for a 4am raid on the house. Speed in an operation like this is measured by how fast you can make entry and dominate the residence. Clear rooms, search for subjects, and apprehend those inside. Violence of action is nothing more than controlled aggression to achieve your objective. The violence of action in this operation might just exceed what was needed to achieve the objective. The DEA agents were angry, and with good cause. The DEA agents would align themselves in a standard DEA five-man entry team formation.

Standard.

The plan was explained by Marroquín. He started the briefing talking about the security bars around the front door. I thought about the disparity of nomenclature. In Hialeah a restaurant has "anti-burglary bars," but here in the posh northeast bayside corridor they're "security bars." A tow truck would be brought in with its lights turned off. It would drive down the street and park out of sight of the house. The agents had fifty feet of tensile-strength, tightly wound cable. One end of the cable had a hook and a sliding clasp, the other end had a heavy-duty hook attached to it. The heavy-duty hook would be tethered to the tow truck. An agent would quietly walk the cable up to the front door. He'd loop the cable through the security bars and attach the hook to the sliding clasp. On the go signal the tow truck would rev up and drive off. The cable would instantly become taut and rip the security bars off the exterior of the house.

At least in theory.

The agents would be aligned in a single formation consisting of the five of them. They would cover windows and any other portals with their weapons until the bars were shorn away by the tow truck. The last agent in the group would have a large sledgehammer. With the bars gone he'd quickly step forward in front of the group and break the door lock. He'd then step aside, and the team would then rapidly enter the house through the broken open door.

At least in theory.

Marroquín and Walker pulled me aside away from the other three agents who were quietly donning their gear.

"Cade, we don't normally do this with locals. You've been in on this from the start, and you deserve to be here. Plus, we need you here to help identify Curbelo. Scott Lew may not have been shot by Curbelo but nonetheless, one of our brother agents is in the hospital because of this guy. We're going to ask you to step off on this one Cade," said Walker.

"I'm sorry… *What*?" I said, bordering on indignation.

"Listen man, it'll be dark in there and lots of things can happen. We can handle our own internal investigation, but we don't need FDLE or the Miami Dade State Attorney's office looking into our shit too. Something goes down deeper than we anticipate, it's better that you aren't there as a participant *or* an observer," said Marroquín.

"Cade, we're going to have you cover the rear side gate. Just in case on the odd chance we get a runner or something," said Walker.

They were telling me they didn't want me on the inside team because they wanted it to be all DEA. If something went wrong, they wanted to huddle amongst themselves and make sure they all agreed on the same chain of events and have a collaborating story. They want to be congruent with each other. No dissenting members or non-DEA allowed who may not go along with fabricated post-operation accounts they agreed upon. No one to deny what truly happened inside the house.

There was an undertone of vengeance in the way they spoke and having an "outsider" who might not share their exact feelings. Or an outsider who'd be subject to an investigation outside of the DEA's Office of Professional Responsibility was not the baggage they wanted on this mission. I was being left out so that they could have agency continuity.

At least in theory.

"You get it, bro. You know the drill. You know we need to go in with *just us*. The guys who worked every day with Scotty," said Walker.

After forty minutes of checking gear and small talk the agents were ready to drive to the house. I checked my cell phone one last time. No calls from Hammy or from Marshal McKenna.

Neighborhoods have rhythm and when that rhythm is altered slumbering residents do take notice. To avoid the oddness and noise of multiple cars driving down the very quiet streets, we left our cars parked at the Burger King. We locked our cars. The five agents loaded up into one Cadillac Escalade. Since I'd be dropped off first, I rode in standing on the running board. As they neared the house to the rear of Curbelo's they slowed enough for me to hop off the running board. They killed their lights and drove very quietly on. I slipped down the dark street as quietly as I could. All it would take was one constantly yapping dog to throw everything off.

Without surprise no amount of speed or violence of action can compensate for its loss. Surprise was the key.

Very few trees overhang entire streets. I walked in the middle of the street. This minimized my chance of stepping on a crunchy pod of berries, or the errant aluminum can that had fallen from a bin awaiting the morning garbage pickup. Every house had multiple large black garbage collection bins and green recycling bins out on the curb for pick up, each with the Miami Dade County logo on them. I wondered who on the street was that guy who puts his bins out before anybody else? The first one.

The *binstigator*, or the *binfluencer.*

On the corner, across from Curbelo's house was a very modern, alabaster-poured, concrete house. Even the house numbers were carved in three-foot-high vertical digits in a concrete column.

1025.

Wide steps led up to the front door and a concrete bench at the top of the stairs. The stairs and the bench would be an ideal place to sit and wait for the DEA to call me in and identify Dario Curbelo.

The wall around Curbelo's house, in conjunction with the densely packed tall palm trees and jungle-like foliage, rendered me unseen from his house. The other surveillance units had moved away to locations further away from the front of the house. This was going to be the DEA Entry Team Show from here on out.

The Escalade glided in neutral to a slow, silent stop just around the corner on the bayside of the house whose steps I was now sitting on. Everyone was being very quiet. Most of the communication that I was able to see was in hand signals from the entry team members. Like me, they were north of the house, deftly tucked out of sight. I looked to the west of my spot on the house steps and saw a truck turning the corner.

It was coming in my direction.

As soon as the truck made the turn, it shut off its headlights. I breathed a sigh of relief—it was the tow truck. It too glided in and past me, almost soundless. The driver had put the tow truck in neutral and turned north going past the entry team. The driver then turned off his engine. This allowed the entry team to move even further north. They must have spoken to the driver in whispers.

From my vantage point I could see east towards the marina basin and out towards Biscayne Bay. The moon cast romantic shadows on the water although I didn't foresee a lot of affection tonight. One lone entry team member crossed the street in front of me. He was walking backwards, uncoiling the cable. As he drew close to the property line of Curbelo's house he stopped. I could see him. He stayed in one place and uncoiled the line even more from where he was standing.

The entry team member unspooling the cable looked towards the house, then quietly laid the cable down and walked back towards the others. Whatever it was, he had a hitch in his step that forewarned he'd seen something he didn't like. Although the portico was attached to the north side of the house the front door actually faced north as well. The tow truck driver would have to pull the security bars from the north side of the house. Within a few minutes, four of the entry team members moved in tight formation across the street to my left. The agent leading the team had both hands on his gun. He was in a shooting position as he led the team. The three agents behind him each had a hand on each other's shoulders as they moved in a synchronistic straight line towards Curbelo's house.

The agent with the sledgehammer then came into view. He bent down and picked up the cable, then used a palm-sized flashlight to signal the tow truck driver with short pulses of light. He walked out of my sight, carrying the sledgehammer in one hand and the cable in the other.

Although being as quiet as he could be, I heard the tow truck engine getting closer, until it came into my view. He rounded the corner, right past me, westbound. The cable clattered briefly on the street before quickly going taut. The DEA Agent with the sledgehammer must have affixed the other end of the cable to the security bars—the tow truck's engine groaned under the strain. I was worried about the cable snapping.

I quickly moved behind the house's concrete column with 1025 chiseled into it. There was a momentary rigidity to the cable, than a loud, shrieking crash from the house. The cable must have held as the bars were ripped from their bolted position in the stucco of the house.

The cable went slack as the framework of the bars hit the portico's concrete surface. The tow truck lurched forward and then with a withering groan, stalled. The cable went firm again. The driver gunned the engine even more. Whitish blue smoke started to rise up from the undercarriage of the tow truck. The driver eased up on the torque and the line stayed rigid. He put the tow truck into reverse, and the cable dropped to the street. He then put the truck into a lower gear. He attempted to go forward. Once again, the cable became a tightrope walker's dream, and there was a sound of crunching and crashing from somewhere near the house. The horsepower of the truck was no match for whatever was on the other end of the cable. Engines burn out and die. Poured concrete houses that have withstood sixty years of storms and weather are more formidable.

Something wasn't right. Anxious shouts erupted from the entry team. Something wasn't going as planned.

I ran towards the tow truck even though I was worried the cable would snap and whipsaw me in half as it recoiled back. The driver was super task-driven on pulling the heavy bars away. Revving the engine, he tried to move forward. The RPMs were screeched. I ran to the passenger side of the tow truck, stepped up to the passenger window and banged on it. The driver was a slight young Hispanic man. His eyes were filled with determination, and he was staring straight ahead. He looked at me and immediately let up on the gas. The smoke from the burning tires and shivering transmission wafted above and around me.

"*Basta, basta, alto. Atra!*" ["Enough, enough, stop. Back!"]

He eased the tow truck into reverse, backed up about seven feet and got out, leaving the driver's door open and the engine running. At first the engine was essentially hiccupping from the ordeal but with the RPMs now at zero the engine started to compose and recalibrate while he and I worked feverishly at the back of the truck to unclasp the cable.

It was at that time that we both heard a long series of gunshots come from the house.

A panicked look of fear lit up his eyes. He became distracted. He lost his concentration and started fumbling with the cable, which started sporadically vibrating. That was not a good sign, especially after hearing gunshots. That vibrating, it meant people were walking on the cable. The DEA agents were either still making their entry or they were retreating. Something in the timing of their entry into the house was askew.

Without surprise no amount of speed or violence of action can compensate for its loss. Surprise was the key.

The cable had shredded in sharp, wiry strands near the clasp. The tow truck driver put on gloves to make it easier to unfasten the cable. It was at that moment that we both flinched.

Another explosion of gunfire came from the house.

There was a brief pause and then a short staccato round of gunshots, followed by shattering glass.

He nearly had the cable unhooked. His hands shook and he muttered to himself—it was obvious he was scared. He wanted to be out of there as soon as he could. The cable was mercifully finally unhooked. Within seconds, the side gate was flung open with a loud bang, the gate smacked against its mooring post. The gate nearly came off its hinges from the forceful opening.

Dario Curbelo in sweatpants and a rumpled shirt ran out of the gate. He looked like he'd been just woken up and threw on whatever clothes he had near his bed. The look in his eyes was as wild as his hair. His left arm was in a sling that was wrapped across his body.

He started running right at us.

Using his free hand Curbelo unleashed a torrent of bullets from a cheap nine-millimeter TEC-9 machine pistol. Regardless of how cheaply a gun is made, it's still made for a singular purpose.

At that moment, we were the purpose.

The TEC-9 machine pistol holds seventy-two rounds. Disheveled Curbelo fired at least ten of them right at me and the tow truck driver. The tow truck driver, being so slight of build and in this the most desperate moment of his life, dove under the tow truck. I propelled myself back and tried to get behind the rear fender of the idling truck as the driver skittered underneath it and crawled out the other side. He was up and running before I could even get myself fully behind the truck for cover. The driver was at a full sprint running east back towards the bay.

I could hear Curbelo, but I couldn't see him. The street was darkened by the trees obscuring the moon and low-light streetlights. My ears were perked listening for any sound that could tell me where he was, my eyes scanning wildly looking for him. My heart was pounding. My head was filled with so many thoughts: *Where is he? Did he actually see me? Does he know where I am? Can my vest absorb and stop multiple rounds? If I have to medically tourniquet myself, can I get my belt off in time to do so?*

Primarily, I just needed to know where he was. I had no idea where he was. I lost sight of him as I was ducking for cover.

As I dashed behind the tow truck, I skinned my left knee, ripping a hole right through my jeans. I hit the curb on my way down. The tow truck's cab and light bar took the majority of rounds he fired at us. The light bar's amber lens shattered into little pieces that rained down across the street and windshield. The frame and interior of the truck definitely took rounds. I heard them ping and carom off the surface areas of the truck.

There was a large Australian pine tree on the swale. It was gnarled at the rotund base. The tree was right off the rear of the tow truck. I wedged myself between the truck and the tree, trying to minimize my exposure. A telephone pole was ten feet away. Steel guide wire cables for the pole ran at an angle and were anchored to the ground. My setting was less than ideal with the cables diminishing my ability to turn and shoot if I needed to. Everything was happening so fast. I heard the tow truck door slam shut. The overworked transmission clunked into drive. I don't know if it was instincts or stupidity, but I rose from my crouched position and I flung myself across the rear tire well, right into the shallow bed of the tow truck.

I hit the grimy back area of the tow truck as it lurched forward. I shared the space with an upturned hubcap that held loose lug nuts and screws. The little metal pieces became suspended in the air like miniature satellites searching for their orbital path, as the torque from the acceleration lifted the hub cap up in the air. The contents spilled out and flew behind us. I grabbed one of the winching cables to try and steady myself.

Immediately the tree canopy partially across the road was whooshing by overhead. Curbelo was speeding as fast as he could, trying to get as far away as he could. The tow truck's main winching cables were rigid and locked into place, the boom of the truck held in place by the hydraulic rods. The boom was knifing through the night air like a small, angled mast on what was now a mechanical war beast. I caught a brief glimpse of Curbelo through the rear window of the truck. He was holding the wheel with his right hand and leaning forward. I stayed as low as I could to the greasy, dirty truck bed. I squirmed on my side. I pulled myself closer to the back of the cab area of the truck by pulling myself along on the cables and boom. The main hydraulic winch box was above me, and a smaller secondary winch just off to the side of the main one.

I was able to get up on my knees. I was directly behind Curbelo—the only barrier between us was the cab's rear glass. Flashing him my badge to try and get him to stop was pointless. The man just fled from a swarm of DEA agents storming into his house. Me and my badge were not going to sway him in the least. Shooting him through the glass could result in both of us being killed in the ensuing crash. I was able to retrieve a very worn and chipped crowbar from the bed of the truck.

I used my left hand to hold the winching cables and steady myself. Still on my knees I swung the crowbar against the back window. The first blow resulted in a lightning-like crack in the glass that sprawled a few inches from the initial impact. It also alerted Curbelo that I was behind him. I swung the crowbar again with disastrously the same results. A loud thump, a miniscule crack, and an even more agitated driver. Curbelo leaned forward and used his left hand in the sling to hold the bottom of the steering wheel. He fully extended his right arm and turned his hand back towards the rear glass.

In his hand was the TEC-9 machine pistol.

I dropped the crowbar and threw myself down into the bed of the truck and right up against the cab with the dirt, metal shavings and rusty tools; the glass was directly above me. Curbelo fired and bullets penetrated the glass above me. Against the moving tree canopy and night sky the bullets looked like a Roman fountain spurting bluish-white eruptions of fine granular glass particles. If I hit the glass again with the crowbar, I was very confident it would shatter now that the bullets had breached the glass's strength.. It would also expose me to gunfire.

I pulled my Glock from my holster and still lying partially on my left side, I put the muzzle of the gun right against the glass, and I shot three rounds into the cab of the truck. Neither of us could see the other as we shot. My only slight advantage was that my rounds had the potential to ricochet inside the cab.

The truck came to a screeching, tire-burning halt, pressing me even further against the cab. I felt myself being lifted up from the sudden change in inertia. I held onto my gun tightly and slammed against the cab and the rear window. My body weight forcefully effected a complete spider webbing of the glass with fissures throughout the entire window. The sudden stop nearly took my breath away.

The driver's door flung open. A wafting, noxious-smelling dusty smoke curled out of the open door. Curbelo staggered out of the truck. Still holding the machine pistol, he used his right hand to hang briefly against the yawning open truck door. One of my rounds must have pierced the driver's side airbag deployment spring. When the airbag went off it blew out with a rapid explosiveness and crushed him back strongly against the seat. Curbelo locked up the brakes. In doing so, he threw me against the glass. I crumbled against it with such force that I was concerned I may have broken a rib.

I slid down from being thrown against the damaged glass and tumbled out of the truck bed on the passenger side. I hit the hard ground and was partially stunned. If I hadn't broken a rib in the sudden stop, I surely must have done so then.

We were both dazed and hurting. He started staggering away from the truck. I felt broken, and I ached everywhere. I rolled onto my side. I managed to get on my knees, bent at the waist. Curbelo kept moving unsteadily away from the truck. I used the running board on the truck to help raise myself up from the ground until I was leaning against the side of the truck. Through the cab I could see the airbag had deployed. The entire air around the truck smelled like the soaked chemicals used in the muslin of the air bag. Using the left side of my body and my left arm to steady myself against the front of the truck, I raised my Glock in my right hand.

"Curbelo!" I yelled.

He kept walking away unsteadily.

"Curbelo!" I yelled again.

He stopped and looked back over his shoulder at me, the truck headlights illuminating his face. I stayed pressed against the truck on my left side. My right arm was nearly fully across my body as I steadied my gun on the truck's hood. The engine was still running, and the hood felt hot under my hand.

He wavered briefly. His left arm was still in the battered sling although it was a little rip-shorn from his body. He held the TEC-9 machine pistol in his hand. I'm not sure if he was confused or if it was an act of overt aggression, but he raised the gun and fired at me. The bullets tore into the front grill and windshield of the truck. Fortunately for me, the truck headlights illuminated him. I fired three rounds at him.

All three rounds hit him. His arms were thrown up into the air from the force and he staggered backwards. He fell against three garbage bins on the curbside. The plastic bins toppled like building blocks under his weight. I kept my gun pointed at him, both hands clasping it as I painfully moved away from the truck and approached him.

He wasn't moving. He was barely alive. My bullets had torn into his lower abdomen, left rib cage, and his pelvis. I shuffled closer. I could see the machine pistol a few feet from his hand. The gun laid amongst the strewn garbage from the spewed-open bins. Curbelo himself was sprawled across the overturned garbage in what looked like to be the most uncomfortable of positions. His head and neck were propped up awkwardly on one of the bins. He looked at me with unsteady eyes. He blinked. He tried to focus. It was as if he briefly recognized me.

"We have started our relationship…in a manner unbecoming… of the men we are," he said in a hoarse, dying whisper.

Just before his eyes closed for good.

Chapter Eighteen

IT WAS HOURS later. The sun had risen twenty minutes ago. The day's light was just taking hold. I was now back at the scene at Curbelo's house, sitting in the back of an ambulance. The rear doors were open to the sunrise over Biscayne Bay. Marroquín was sitting next to me.

"We messed up big time, Cade. This one's on us," he said.

I was underwhelmed by his obvious understatement. I kept my gaze fixated on the tranquil waters of the little marina basin called Lake Belmer.

"So what happened? What happened with the entry?" I asked him.

"We ran the cable from the tow truck through the portico's arched doorway. We should've run it through the garage opening, it's wider and further from the door. When the bars ripped off, they kept clattering against the concrete columns of the portico, they were too big to fit through the opening. Every time we tried to make any steps closer to the door, they'd swing back around at us. You ever see any of those documentaries about commercial fishing in Alaska and one of those steel cages breaks away? All the deck hands are trying to settle it before it crushes them. I'm telling you; it was just like that. It was crashing against the concrete making all kinds of noise. That damn tow truck driver didn't have enough common sense to know it wasn't working and he kept trying to pull away, making it crash even more and more. Walker cut his hand and his forearm trying to get around it."

Silently I remembered telling the driver to stop pulling the cable and back up so we could unhitch the damn thing.

"Basta, basta, alto. Atra!" ["Enough, enough, stop. Back!"]

"The noise was horrific. It woke Curbelo up before we could make entry. He started shooting immediately. Bullets were everywhere. We had to retreat even further back," he said in a defeated tone.

Without surprise no amount of speed or violence of action can compensate for its loss. Surprise was the key.

"Curbelo nearly cut us all in half. He knew we were at the front door. He didn't stay to fight. He blew out the French doors of his master bedroom and he took off out the rear side gate. I guess that's where you saw him," he said.

I watched the sunrise dance on the water in the basin and the bay. It was so peaceful if you could look past all the police vehicles, DEA agents, and the coffee cup-holding cops from Miami Dade County, and the Miami Shores police departments. They were both on the scene since Curbelo's house was in an isolated, three block area of Miami Dade County that touches the City of Miami's most northeastern point, and Miami Shores' most eastern boundary. It's literally sandwiched between both jurisdictions. I caught a glimpse of Hammy walking by. Hours earlier, I made it a point to Marroquín that she needed to be on the scene. She needed to process the shooting of Curbelo. She'd worked hard on the Hialeah scene, and she made the connections in Hialeah. She needed professional closure. She also had his exact blood type and fingerprints. She would be the best person for case continuity to process his death. If there was to be a trial for anything, it's better to have one person testifying than a bunch of people confusing the jury. Marroquín saw Major Brunson approaching the ambulance and he gave me a knowing look.

"We'll finish our talk in a few minutes," he said as he stepped down from the ambulance.

"Morning, Major," he said as Brunson brushed past him and took the now-empty seat in the ambulance.

"Jesus Christ! You okay?" he asked me.

"Yeah, I'm okay."

"Jesus Christ! What the fuck's *wrong* with you Cade?"

"What's wrong with me? I love when movies end with the lead actor sitting in the back of an ambulance with a ratty Motel 6 blanket and non-lethal wounds," I shot back at him.

"Seriously. I thought the last time I sat in the back of an ambulance with you would be the *last time!* Here we are again," he said.

"How did you make it here so fast from the office?" I asked him.

"I haven't been to the office. I live in Miami Shores. Nancy Ward is their Assistant Police Chief; she plays canasta with my wife. She knocked on my door and told me as I was getting ready to go to work."

"What's canasta?"

"Cade, I don't know, it's some sort of fucking card game. All I know is it gives me a reprieve and I can get out of the damn house. So did they find our 400k in the house? What about the kilos?"

"I don't know, I haven't been inside."

Major Brunson tried to hide his disappointment and his anxiousness.

"Well, do you think you're well enough to get up and go inside with me?" he said, semi-sarcastically.

We stepped down from the ambulance. The ambulance driver was outside the ambulance killing time smoking a cigarette.

"Hey buddy, save my seat," I said to him as we walked by.

As we approached the house there was a flurry of activity. People were milling about with a measurable amount of less care than at the Hialeah restaurant scene. There had been no action by law enforcement or the DEA at the house, so the normal protocols were tossed out the bullet-shattered window. Curbelo had done all of the shooting and damage. With him lying dead a block away, the focus was more on what was inside the house than what forensically occurred. This was a recovery and information mission. Although from the looks on everyone's faces, it wasn't much of a recovery or an information windfall. Miami Dade Crime Scene technicians were processing the house. I asked one of the DEA agents standing outside why their own people weren't processing the scene.

"We didn't do anything. We served the warrant but *el stiffo* down the street shot up his own house. As far as we're concerned this is just a firearm discharge. Multiple discharges actually, but in the county. This isn't our show," he said.

Brunson huffed next to me. "Let's hope we find something because I'd hate to have you on administrative leave for two years while some cagey attorney milks the city for millions as he represents some grieving widow who says her husband was killed by *you* because he was scared and ran for his life from what he *thought* was home invaders," said Brunson to me in a low voice.

We stepped through the front door. The house had immaculate dark walnut floors, there wasn't a single knot to be seen. When the house was built in the 1930s it was as though the carpenter stood at the back of the lumber yard delivery truck and selected only the very best boards. The fireplace was comprised of tightly packed coral rocks painted white, and it went all the way up to the celling in a fluted angle. The hearth was broad and there was a large painting placed on the hearth, leaning against the stack of the fireplace. Every room had deep dark wooden beams interspaced with three feet of white painted lathe and plaster ceilings. The master bedroom told a different story. The wooden French doors were splintered, and bullet-ridden. I couldn't be sure if Curbelo had been in such a haste to leave that he impulsively chose to crazily empty bullets from his gun into the doors to get out. He may have also feared there were agents outside the door, and his intention was to shoot his way out, quite literally. One of the Miami Dade technicians found a set of keys on the armoire. With his gloved hand he picked up the set and inserted one of the keys into the damaged locking mechanism of the bullet-raked French door. The lock turned.

"Guy was probably in such a hurry to get out he didn't want to mess with the keys," said the technician to me and Brunson.

Marroquín walked in. He came to where me and Brunson were standing. He too, spoke in a hushed tone. "I got to tell ya gentlemen, we got a serious problem here. We've run a Miami Dade, Miami Shores, and a Florida Highway Patrol dog through here. Three dogs. Three handlers. None of them alerted to anything. No drugs. No money. Nothing. We got nothing. We're okay on the warrant based on what Cade saw at the restaurant in Hialeah, and the dentist, Cordozo, said he saw a gun. Yeah, we're good on the warrant, and the fact he fired on all of us you should be okay with this too, Cade. But we still are out the money and out the kilograms. ASAC Mandeville and SAC Grayson are gonna go ballistic when they hear about this."

Major Brunson just nodded in understanding. Marroquin's cell phone rang, and he walked away to take the call. Although starting to steam due to the current events, Major Brunson kept his composure for the most part. He stood in front of me but looked past me when he spoke softly again.

"I'm going to chew galvanized nails and shit out a barbed wire fence over this. There has to be more to this than 'we got three dogs and fucking nothing.' I don't care if they have to call Doctor fucking Seuss himself and get every dog from *Go, Dog, Go!* in here, and the dogs shit on the carpet. We need answers!"

"*Go, Dog, Go!*?" I asked him, arching my eyebrow.

"Cade, I got fucking grandkids. The little ankle biters have their crap everywhere in my house," he said as I followed him outside. We stood on the front lawn looking at the assembled police cars, gawking neighbors, and the occasional agitated garbage man upset he couldn't finish his route. Hammy stepped across the lawn towards us.

"Good morning, Major," she said to Brunson.

He reciprocated the greeting. She just nodded at me in the barest form of acknowledgement.

"Cade."

"Hammy."

"Well, let me give you some of the highlights. Many of them you know already. Miami Dade was a little frosty with me working in their homicide scene, but the DEA smoothed that out. Dead guy down the street? To my eye looks like the same prints from the restaurant. They're on their way to AFIS for confirmation. Cause of death is certainly multiple gunshots. The M.E. took possession of the body thirty minutes ago. Autopsy should confirm the obvious. Blood samples were retained, and duplicates sent off with the Medical Examiner. Checked his pockets—no I.D. Only this." She held up a single key looped by a stainless-steel ring to a common marine foam floating keychain.

These types of keychains are popular for maritime use. The keychain is made of polyurethane foam material, so it can float. It keeps boat keys from sinking in case a boater drops their keys overboard.

My eyes lit up when I saw the key and keychain.

"Miami Dade know you have that?" asked Brunson.

"Major, I'm Hialeah. What do you think?" she said with a sly smile.

"Can I have that please?" I asked her.

She put the key and keychain in my hand. I scanned the assembled people, looking for Marroquín. I found him still on his cell phone off to the side by the damaged portico. I made a beeline for him. Brunson and Hammy both had puzzled looks on their face as I briskly walked away from them. I stood in front of him making those frantic gestures one makes when they want someone to hang up their phone. Marroquín saw my urgency and told whoever he was talking to that he'd call them back.

"What? What?" he said.

"Call your legal team and get them on the phone with whatever judge signed the search warrant. See if the judge will sign an addendum to the warrant for us to search a boat related to Curbelo. Once we find the boat, we just need to add a paragraph or two. The judge has to agree via the phone to sign so we can do it *now*. I don't know which one it is yet, but I think it's going to be one of these boats here," I said gesturing to the basin.

He looked at me a little perplexed.

"Hammy found this on Curbelo," I said, holding the key and keychain up for him to see. "No I.D. No cash. But this boat key. We need to see which boat the key fits."

Marroquín beamed with delight.

"I'm on it. I should have an answer in about ten minutes. Start looking at the boats and think about which ones we should try first," he said excitedly.

Returning to Major Brunson and Hammy, I said, "Let's all take a walk." I led them towards the marina.

"If you were Curbelo, which of these boats would you want to own?" I asked them.

Hammy was shielding her eyes from the morning sun with her large binder. Brunson's eyes roved up and down the marina.

"He'd need a boat with two engines in case one conks out. Preferably dual Mercs or more, at least. It needs to have the range to get to the Bahamas. Bimini at the very minimum. He needs to be able to live aboard if he has to. He needs speed and range," I rattled off.

My comments lowered the field of possible boats from the nearest twelve boats to the house down to three. One was docked directly in front of the house to a concrete dock, just within the curved coral rock stairway leading down to the water's edge. The other two were moored to a wooden dock off the starboard side of the boat at the dock. The names on the boats were eye catching.

Unsinkable II.

Sea Señor.

Cassiopeia.

"It doesn't really matter which boat it is. The key will determine that. I'm thinking it's one of these three. Seeing as the house was built in the 1930s, it was probably here first, and it was granted mooring rights. I think it's going to be the one right here in front of us," I said.

The boat I was betting on was *The Cassiopeia*. The vessel was a 1997 Baia Cantieri, fifty feet long and nearly brand new. The Baia Cantieri is internationally known for boasting exhilarating performance, full comfort, and opulent elegance wrapped within a high-performance hull. The boats are outfitted with twin inboard 1000hp MTU 12-volt engines that can hit a top cruising speed of forty-five knots. The fuel capacity is easily 600 gallons.

Marroquín joined us on the starboard side of the vessel. He affirmed that the judge would sign the addendum to the warrant. He read to us from a note he'd written: "... as pursuant to any all actions enacted and gained from the search and discovery." Before he and I stepped aboard the sleek boat, Hammy had us both put on gloves.

"If I have to process this too, I don't need you guys muddying up the prints," she said.

The boat had a beautiful paint scheme. The bottom hull was turquoise with gradient dark blue and white up to the bow and stern. Hammy and Brunson stayed on the dock as Marroquín, and I boarded the boat. Marroquín inserted the key and turned it to the right.

It fit.

The cockpit dials and gauges came to life, backlit by a soft blue glow. With inboard gasoline engines, you need to turn on the blower for four full minutes before starting the boat to remove any fumes that could be lingering in the bilge.

As we waited, even Major Brunson seemed to smile.

The boat was very neat and orderly. Nothing seemed out of place. No buckets with cleaning rags in the stern, or any unkept areas. The captain's chair was neatly adorned with a thick white vinyl cover. The deck lines were new and showed no sign of fraying or misuse. I leaned over the sunpad covering the engine compartment and looked at the still stationary props of the engines. They looked well-maintained and regularly serviced, and coated with anti-fouling paint.

We were now past the four-minute mark and Marroquín turned the key further to the right. The engines stoked and highly calibrated, sprung to life with the roar of an aquatic lion. The engines were in complete synchronistic harmony with each other. It left no doubt to us and to all the investigators who were now looking our way that this boat was intended for pleasure and built for performance. The boating enthusiasts in the gathered police personnel start walking our way. I didn't want to see Hammy get lost in their gaggling cooing and fawning over the boat.

"Hammy, put on some gloves and get onboard with us," I said my voice raised to be heard over the engines.

A few of the investigators and some of the police started descending the coral rock staircase down to our water's edge. Major Brunson took a position to keep them from boarding the boat. This would be a look but don't touch event for them. I'm sure he was thinking like me that we didn't need all types of people crawling around the interior and then claiming a portion of any money or drugs we might find.

The lower compartments of the boat were exquisite. The salon was spacious with an open galley and entertainment center. Interior cabinets and bulkheads were made from maple, anigre, and cherry wood. There were color coordinated soft textures blending superbly with the luxurious accommodations. The en suite was in the most forward part of the stern. There was a separate guest suite.

We stood together in the narrow cabin hallway. I spoke first. "This is what I'm thinking. If he still has the money and the dope, he was smart enough to not keep it in his house. If you guys had made entry like you planned, he might've been tucked in bed, and we'd have no idea about this boat. So maybe there really is a reason for everything happening the way it did. Curbelo had enough time to get the TEC-9 and grab the boat keys. He wasn't concerned about anything else in the house. If he had gotten away, he might have later come back here and been on the high seas before we knew anything. So if he was putting distance between himself and anything I'll give you two to one odds, nothing is in the main stateroom. I'm betting it's in the guest suite. The boat is too small for us to split up, let's just all search the rooms together."

The guest suite was on the port side. The suite's narrow door was beside Hammy. She opened the door and we all looked in from the doorway.

It was comfortable but cramped. Every inch of the room was designed to maximize storage and space. There was a narrow closet behind the door. I opened the closet door.

Immediately I saw the brown leather satchel that I'd been carrying into the restaurant in Hialeah. It had bloody handprints on it.

A huge wave of relief swept over me. Internally, I was giddy with happiness. I looked back at Marroquín and told him and Hammy to step back a few feet. I pulled the satchel out of the closet. I unzipped it and saw the cash still inside.

"Hammy would you be so kind as to take this up on deck and give it to Major Brunson?" I said calmly, though I was jumping for joy inside, as I handed her the satchel. She took it up the stairs. I could barely hear her over the idling engines as she handed it to Major Brunson. Although I had a difficulty hearing her, I definitely heard Major Brunson once he realized what she'd given him.

"Hot damn. Buddy. Buddy. Yes! Oh, heck yes!"

There wasn't anything else in the closet. I looked at the cabin's bunk. It looked as though the headboard had been pulled away from the stateroom wall. Both Marroquín and I pulled the mattress back, then pulled the bed frame away from the wall. There was only a foot of clearance to maneuver with and we used every inch of it. Wedged between the bed and the wall was the burlap sack bound with twine. There was visible blood residue on the sack. We both tugged on the sack, but it was wedged in the space very tightly. Marroquín unwound the twine from where he was with difficulty.

He took seven of the kilograms of cocaine out of the sack. This made the sack more pliable. With me pulling the mattress back, he was able to extract the rest of the sack from behind the bed. There were thirteen kilograms in the sack. The seven kilograms on the bed amounted to the twenty from the restaurant. The sack had the Girouard Coffee Company emblazoned across the side of it.

"I told you it was some French coffee company," I said with proud vindication.

We stuffed the kilograms of cocaine into the sack and brought it topside. I handed the coffee sack over the side of the boat to a waiting DEA agent on the dock. I caught a glimpse of Major Brunson, and he had an enormous grin on his face.

"Are you happy?' I asked him.

"I am very happy," he said.

"You're not lying to me. Are you?"

"Cade, There are a lot of things I would lie to you about but this ain't one of them."

I asked one of the K-9 handlers to get his canine partner and come aboard to search for any additional hidden cocaine. The three of us sat on the sunpad at the back of the boat while the handler and his dog searched. The dog alerted his handler to the area where we'd found the burlap sack. Aside from that, the boat appeared to be clean.

Hammy was in the main cabin for at least twenty minutes photographing and measuring the room. She discovered a manila envelope in the bedside cabinetry. She placed the items from the envelope on the bed. Fanned out on top of a manila envelope were Curbelo's Florida driver's license and a Paraguayan passport, both with Dario Curbelo's name and face on them. Two credit cards with Dario Curbelo's name on them were there as well—a Mastercard and an American Express Platinum. In the top drawer there had been a second envelope, too, containing another Mastercard and American Express Platinum—this time with the name Ricardo Sanabria. A second Florida driver's license showed the same picture of Dario

Curbelo but with the name Ricardo Sanabria. A U.S. passport—Curbelo's picture, the name Ricardo Sanabria. The entry and exit stamps were primarily between Asuncion and Miami, but there were a few departure and entry stamps from Guaraní International Airport in Ciudad del Este. There was also three gold bars minted as being 100 grams of 99.99% pure gold.

"What's this?" she said motioning to the gold bars and documents she'd spread across the bed. I studied the small gold bars briefly. I was more interested in the passports and driver's licenses.

"Looks like we got Curbelo's escape contingency plan here. Hammy, after you photograph everything, I'm going to hold onto this Sanabria passport."

"You mean you're going to withhold evidence?" she said.

"No, you'll have it documented. I'm not withholding evidence. I'm seizing a forged document as nexus to an ongoing narcotic investigation," I said to her with a smile.

I went back topside then stepped off of the boat. I saw ASAC Mandeville walking towards the concrete steps leading down to the dock. Marroquín saw her too.

"Let's get this over with and go talk to her before she talks to us," he said, and we walked towards her, meeting her before she reached the boat.

"Good morning, gentlemen. I hear this was a real rooting tooting shooting time for everyone today."

Marroquín began to speak but Mandeville held up her hand and stopped him.

"Let's focus on the positive things here, shall we? We got the twenty kilos, and Major Brunson is happy Coral Gables got their buy money back. We got one doper dead, but we also have Agent Walker needing stitches in his forearm because of a flawed tactical entry. Those are odds of success that I can live with. If I can live with them, I think I can get SAC Grayson to live with them too. Mathias, give me a second alone with Detective Taylor if you will please?" she said staring at Marroquín.

Marroquin looked at me with the look of a school child released from the principal's office. She watched him walk away and then turned her attention back to me.

"You look like you rolled around in a greasy rusty barrel."

"The morning light complements you, too," I said.

"Funny. Detective Taylor, thank you for your assistance on this case. Both SAC Grayson and I want to convey our appreciation to you. We still have the problem of the shooter who shot up the Hialeah restaurant and killed *Loco Curo* and shot Agent Lew. All of the evidence we gathered at the scene is taking an inordinate amount of time to be processed. We're waiting to get the prints back from the glass tabletop and all the other evidence. Do you have any idea why that could be?"

Throughout this entire investigation keeping information to myself had served me well. Not trying to surmise things I know nothing about as also served me well. My gut told me to keep on that track. What I knew about the house fire in North Miami, Marshal McKenna's WITSEC program, and the arrest and reidentifying of Dario Curbelo to Ricardo Sanabria, I decided to keep to myself. At least for now. That would be the best practice. It would be better that way.

At least in theory.

I feigned a level of ignorance that was commensurate with my perceived involvement of this case. I just shrugged my shoulders. I gave her a standard reply.

Standard.

"Inordinate amount of time? How's that?"

"I don't know. None of this makes sense at all. SAC Grayson is on the phone constantly with our field labs. Something's up. In all my years I've never seen this. Even when I was a field agent in Connecticut, I never saw anything like this."

"Connecticut? You were in Connecticut? Ever get to a Hartford Whalers game?"

"No, I was a field agent in New Haven. What a bucket of blood that was. Good ol' gun waving New Haven. Lots of stabbing and grabbing, too," she said, gazing out at the marina.

"Has Agent Lew said anything yet?" I asked her.

"Very little. It's slow, but he is much better. They have him sitting up. He's working with a memory specialist, helping him to know the names of his sons and his wife. They have a lot of occupational therapists working with him on shapes, colors, geography, all those kinds of things, and he's accelerating very quickly. I mean, like lightning fast. They're very happy, and surprised at his recovery. Everyone is optimistic but it's going to take a little time. They think he will be nearly fully back by the end of Thanksgiving or early December."

"If Grayson is working the phones, I'm sure you'll get some answers soon," I said.

"I hope so. Today was only half the problem. We want the shooter. We've always wanted the shooter. Today takes care of a lot of the investigation, but hear me for the third time: We. Want. The shooter," she said through gritted teeth.

I nodded my head in total agreement.

"If you'll excuse me, I need to review the after-action report from my team and hear their version of why the entry into the house was so tragically flawed," she said as she turned to go back up the coral rock concrete stairs.

I saw Hammy stepping off of the boat. She had Dario Curbelo's gold bars and documents in sealed plastic zip lock bags. Including the Ricardo Sanabria passport. She saw my displeasure immediately.

"Don't be getting all pissy with me. I can't separate recovered evidence in some sort of 'I trust you so much to get this back to you' sort of VIN game here. I discovered it. I'm responsible for it. So before you stomp your feet and act all macho 'I'm the cop, you're the lowly tech' with me, I took the liberty to snap two Polaroids of it for you," she said as she handed me the photographs of the passport. All the details of the passport were clearly visible. In actuality it would be an easier way of seeking information or verification with people.

She actually was doing me a favor in addition to the favor I asked of her.

"I see your point. Can I ask a favor of you? Can you just keep this in your Hialeah property room for a while? Take the extra step to limit access to anyone other than you and me for at least a few days? I'm going to need to have a chat with the U.S. Marshals about how this all came to be, so I can count on you to do that for me?" I asked her.

"Okay, Cade. I can do that. Subpoenas, proper media requests, and high-ranking nosy police commanders outrank your pleading favor. You know that, right?" she said.

I spotted Lieutenant Maddalone walking with Major Brunson, heading in my direction.

"Please excuse me for a minute," I said to her as I went to meet them midway to the boat.

"Cade, we're thinking of sending our range master back to the road since you seem perversely committed to firing every gun we have in the department," snapped Maddalone.

I just sighed, feeling the air fill and then leave my lungs. I looked off to the side.

"I'm going to give you your assigned weapon back. You can give me the loaner we gave you just last week when you decided to shoot up Hialeah. I'm going to ask you to save me the aggravation of cleaning this gun. Can you let me know in advance if you plan to shoot anybody soon?" he said as he opened the same foam, rubber-lined case from last week. We made the gun exchange right there on the dock.

"I'll keep your number on speed dial," I said with a dismissive smirk.

Brunson said, "We have the money in Lieutenant Maddalone's car trunk. I'll be following him back to Coral Gables. I put a call into Gary Fowler to set up in the vacant office in VIN so that we can count the money and then put it back in our evidence room. I also called our sorry, piss-ant city manager and told him I think we have all—or at least nearly all—of the money recovered." With hands on hips, Brunson steeled himself and stared me down. "Cade, go home. I mean seriously, get out of here and go home. I'm telling you take a few days off. We'll sort out the shooting with Miami Dade Homicide. It was a good shoot. He shot at you, and he shot at the DEA first. Put it out of your mind and go take a few days off."

With that comment they both walked away. All of a sudden, the administrative and investigative typhoon of today's activity had spit me out on the proverbial rocky shoreline. I wasn't really needed or asked to be a part of any of the activity anymore.

I stood on the dock. Alone. The house on one side of me and the boat on the other side of me, representative of the beginning and the end of a whirlwind saga that had started in Hialeah. It would have been convenient if that truly was the end of it all. In many ways it was just the beginning. ASAC Mandeville was correct. There was a shooter out there who killed *Loco Curo.* He shot Dario Curbelo. He shot DEA Special Agent Scott Lew and the most aggravating thing in my eyes—he tried to shoot me.

Repeatedly.

Chapter Nineteen

NO MISSED CALLS on my cell phone.

I tried to call U.S. Marshal Auburn McKenna. After five rings it went to her voicemail, and I left her a message to call me as soon as she got my message. I hung the phone up and slipped it into the rear pocket of my jeans. I was tired, and the adrenaline rush within me was dissipating very quickly. Steady waves of cortisol flushed out of my arteries, and I was suddenly feeling very fatigued. A Miami Shores police detective was talking with one of the SOGs from the DEA. I asked him if he could take me to my car parked at the Burger King. The SOG in turn asked me if I could take him back to the Froude Avenue address in Surfside. He had doubled down on my favor. The SOG had ridden in with another agent here, and now he needed to get to his car. Although feeling wiped out and bushed, it was a tit for tat existence.

The Miami Shores detective drove us both to my car, where the SOG agent and I got in my car, and I drove him to 9032 Froude Avenue in Surfside. I was honestly having a hard time keeping my eyes open. The crash down from the events of last night had caught up to me. Thankfully traffic was very light and the drive to Surfside was uneventful.

Uneventful until I made the turn on Froude Avenue.

I pulled up to the curb on the corner and let the SOG out of my car. With a wave and wish of good luck he was quickly driving away. Through my bleary eyes I could see 9032 a few houses down. For the past few days until we pulled off the targeted address, there'd been no activity at the house. I could now see a vehicle was parked in the driveway. I was too far to know the type and model but there was definitely something in the driveway. Once we realized that Dario Curbelo was living somewhere else, 9032 Froude Avenue had become a secondary address. The presence of a vehicle in the driveway piqued my interest. I pulled away from the curb and eased down the avenue very slowly. As I drew closer to the address I pulled over to the side of the road. I exited my car and walked cautiously but steadily down the avenue. There are no sidewalks, and the swale areas of the neighboring homes abut right against the street. I stopped in front of the next-door neighbor's house. I could see the vehicle more clearly now—it was a blue Chevrolet Blazer. Creeping closer to the house, I could see the license plate.

ZAQ-178.

Although I'd never seen the license tag before, the Chevrolet Blazer seemed oddly to me to be very similar to the Blazer I had seen Marshal McKenna driving. I looked around. The street was quiet. I walked onto the next-door neighbor's property. From that vantage point I stared intently at 9032. I crossed around from the neighbor's thick boundary of palms and ferns and crept swiftly onto a sliver of the side yard. I put my hand on the Blazer's engine hood. It was cool to the touch. The car hadn't been driven in a while. I glanced into the passenger window. There was nothing distinguishable about the vehicle to tell me anything about the owner.

Without appearing any more suspicious than I already was, I quickly walked around the rear of the SUV. I didn't want to be on the driver's side of the vehicle in clear view to anyone inside the house. Unfortunately, it was unavoidable. I wanted to see the exterior of the driver's door. I saw that there were scratches in the door handle area of the Blazer. I remembered seeing the telltale markings on Marshal Mckenna's Blazer when she parked next to me in the Sergio's parking lot.

I'd noticed the lock on her driver's door had been scratched all up.

I turned on my heels and walked briskly back to my car. With a deep sigh, I started the engine and started to drive home.

There were a couple of things that were going through my head. The house at 9032 Froude Avenue might be a U.S Marshal's property, either as a residence or as a safe house. Agent McKenna might be staying there since Tampa is her normal duty station.

The other unavoidable question was what if she'd been involved with Curbelo? Her questioning of me might have been personal in nature.

I called the Coral Gables Police Department's main number from my cell phone. I was transferred to teletype. Jeanie Rae answered the phone once again.

"Coral Gables Police and Fire, Operator J.R. Richards, how can I direct your call?"

"Jeanie Rae, this is Cade Taylor."

"Cade, I think you call us more than any other detective."

"Someone has to be at the top of the list. Jeanie Rae, I need you to transfer me to teletype please."

"Do you recall me telling you we have nobody here since this hiring freeze? You want teletype? Well, you got her. What do you need?"

"Can you run a tag for me?"

"What's the tag and what's your number?"

"VIN 923, and the tag is a Florida tag, ZAQ-178. Zulu Alpha Quebec One Seven Eight," I said.

There was a minute of no conversation while I waited, a knot in my stomach.

"Florida tag ZAQ-178 comes back to a 1997 Chevrolet Blazer registered to Alamo Rental Car, 2400 Yankee Clipper Dr, Jacksonville, FL 32218."

"Thank you, Jeanie Rae."

"Do you want a hard copy of this?"

"Yes, if you could just print it and send it to my box, I'd appreciate that. Thank you again," I said as I hung up the phone.

I continued driving home. It was nearing twelve noon. I couldn't have cared less if it was bright sunshine or the darkest night, I needed to get to sleep. I pulled in front of the condo at Paradise Point. All I could think about was getting cleaned up and swan-diving into bed. My legs felt heavy as I trudged up the stairs and went inside. I locked the door behind me. I grabbed two Amstel Lights from the refrigerator, relishing that the condo was pleasantly cool from the air conditioning. It was also very quiet. I went upstairs into the master bathroom. I turned the faucets on full bore in the large Roman tub and stripped off my clothes. Before the bathtub had sufficiently filled, I eased into it. Steadily it was filling with the hot steamy water. I watched the water rise up over my body, then laid my head back against the back of the tub. The water had filled to just below the top of the tub. I used my foot to turn off the water, and just soaked, letting the day's grime slough off of me. The beers went down fast, helping to take the edge off. I was nearly asleep when my cell phone on the tub's edge started ringing. I shook as much water as I could off of my hand and picked up the phone.

It was U.S. Marshal Auburn Mckenna. I put the phone to my ear and answered it.

"Hello?"

"Is this Cade Taylor's Mercedes-Benz towing service?"

"Very funny. How was Orlando?" I purposely said Orlando when I knew she said she was going to be in Tampa. I wanted to see how she would answer.

"It's Tampa actually. I was in Tampa. I thought you knew that?"

"Yeah, I get mixed up sometimes. So how was Tampa?"

"Tampa was fine. The Marine Patrol is happy. We got to bag and tag some bad guys for them."

"So are you back yet?" I asked her.

"No, not yet. I'm still on highway I-75, the infamous Alligator Alley. I swear I've driven this road so many times I could tell you about every weed-choked crack in the asphalt. Any word on our shared interest? Have you been able to talk to your people about getting me on with you guys? Trust me, we want him found just as much as you guys do."

Events of the past year had taught me to trust no one. She was lying to me. Even in my fatigued state I could tell she was lying to me. I was fully convinced the Chevy Blazer at the house in Surfside was hers. I was certain she had been in Miami for at least the last twelve hours.

"Actually Marshal, I've been trying to call you about our *shared interest*, as you call him. We aren't very interested in him anymore."

"Huh? What are you talking about? Didn't you say he was a main priority for all of you? We could use your help finding him. Without you guys in the mix…that leaves us back where we were before. That's not very neighborly of you to your big sister Marshal Mckenna." Her voice grew far more ominous. "Pissing off the U.S Marshal's office is no way to seek future favors, Cade. Need I remind you; we are an extension of the court? You may want to realign your priorities, bucko. You seemed pretty dead-set on finding him. Why the change?"

"Our priorities are aligned pretty clearly. Seeing as our shared mutual interest is already dead-set himself, he's no longer a hot item. In fact, he is a…room temperature item."

"Wait. Whoa, right there. What are you saying?" she asked, the ire in her voice rising.

"I'm saying Bachelor Number Two wasn't chosen for the honeymoon package. Your interest—not ours—is no longer a concern. He's dead. As of about 4am today."

"What?" she shrieked into the phone. "Are…are you fucking serious? Please tell me you're joking. Please tell me this is some sort of sick prank. You can't be serious."

"I'd like to tell you I'm sorry to be the bearer of bad news, but actually I don't see this as bad news. We make choices in life. He made a choice that wasn't conducive to his staying alive."

"I can't believe you're saying this. No. No way. How? How did this happen?" She was nearing hysteria.

"Early this morning the DEA hit a house he was staying in, and he shot at them. When it was over, he was shot and killed."

An ungodly wail blasted through the earpiece of my phone, followed by muffled gasping and what sounded like dry heaving or hyperventilating.

"You there? Marshal McKenna, you there?"

I sat further up in the bathtub. After a moment of silence, a very soft, almost meek-sounding Marshal McKenna softly answered, "Yes, I'm here. So you're telling me the DEA shot him this morning?" she asked quietly.

I thought of the best way to answer her, as it was becoming obvious that Marshal McKenna was having a disproportionate reaction to the news of a wanted cocaine trafficker being killed. I was perplexed, but also recognized that even when truth is hard to take, it is still the truth.

"No. He fired on the DEA team making an entry into the house. I shot and killed him."

"Oh. My. God. I can't believe what you're saying. What happened? How did you find him? Why wasn't I notified? I mean, why weren't we notified?"

"Marshal, you know any shooting is still an ongoing investigation. Besides, you're an extension of the court. I just can't discuss it."

"You sanctimonious prick," she hissed. "You shoot and kill a man, you take a life from the surface of the earth, a man you don't even know, and you act like you just threw out yesterday's newspaper. You fucking asshole—"

"Obviously you knew him better than I did, and it means more to you personally than it does to the DEA. The DEA are trying to find the person who shot Agent Lew in Hialeah. I think keeping you off the team was a good call. Speaking of calls, I left plenty of voice messages on your phone. Some of them before the shooting. So before you start calling people names, think about checking your messages. Maybe this could have been averted—especially if you had information to share."

"What? What information? What would I have been able to share? I told you, you fucking ignorant local yokel, we wanted him as much as you did," she yelled, her voice rising above her emotions.

"For starters, you could've told us his name was Dario Curbelo before you and your Marshal buddies changed him into Ricardo Sanabria."

"Cade, you know way more than you should. Way too much. I'm telling you now. You're on thin ice with me and the agency!"

I sat even further up, splashing water over the side where it spread across the floor. I searched for the right words to say. Then it hit me. I recalled my first sighting of the burlap sack in the restaurant in Hialeah, and then the same burlap sack containing the kilograms of cocaine found on the boat.

"There was a burlap sack from some French coffee company right over there. The twenty kilograms were inside the sack."

It was as though there were fast shooting microbursts of clarity filling my head. I recalled the conversation between myself and Marshall Mckenna in Sergio's café.

"How do you drink that swill?" she'd asked me.

"What? I like Cuban coffee. You don't?"

"You mean like Pilon or Bustillo? No way. No how. Last summer a whole contingency of us had to go to Europe for the world cup in France. There was a threat concerning CONMEBOL. I spent a lot of time in Belgium and France. Now that *is real coffee, not this dishwater shit you all drink from these little windows all over Miami."*

"What was the name of that soccer thing you did in France last summer?" I asked her.

"What? Are you some kind of a fucking mentally challenged simpleton? You killed a man today and you're asking me about the World Cup?" she yelled.

"Not the World Cup. That organization with the problem. 'CONME…' something?"

"CONMEBOL? What about them?" she said, agitation and anger straining her voice.

"Where are their headquarters at?"

"Asunción, Paraguay. Actually in Luque, a suburb of Asunción. Why?" she answered, exasperated.

"We have both of Dario Curbelo's passports, including his Ricardo Sanabria passport. I was just wondering if we looked at his passport stamps and compared them to your own passports stamps if there would be any matches. You know like a commonality. A commonality, like even sharing a house in Surfside."

"Fuck you, Cade Taylor! You have no idea what you're up against. You're out of your league, you scuzzy VIN piece of shit," she said as she hung up the phone abruptly.

I wanted to throw the phone across the room. I wanted to see it shatter into a thousand little pieces of plastic and metal. This phone still reeked of newness. I'd only had it a few days. In a moment of composure, I leaned over the side of the bathtub. More water trickled onto the bathroom floor. I placed the phone down on a dry spot and pushed it across the floor like a child's Matchbox car. I eased back into a prone position even deeper in the tub than I'd started, the warm sudsy water lapping at my collarbones. Not busting up my cell phone out of anger felt good.

It was the only thing I felt good about in the last twenty-four hours.

Chapter Twenty

My whole body ached. I let the water drain down and then refilled the tub twice. Each time as the water got cooler it woke me up. My neck started to hurt from pressing against the rim of the tub. I figured it to be about 2:30pm. I had no idea of knowing the time since my phone was on the floor across the room.

I kind of clambered and partially slithered out of the bathtub and picked up my phone. I was surprised to see it was nearing 4pm. I'd been in and out of a slumbering stupor in the bathtub for much longer than I had thought. Still damp, I pulled back the bedcovers and climbed into bed. I tried to silence the voices and nullify the images running through my head. I wasn't entirely sure how to stop the rampant cacophony in my mind. My whole body ached from being slammed against the tow truck glass. Hitting the ground right afterwards I would also classify as a contributing factor to my soreness.

I kept visualizing the way Curbelo's arms flung up when I shot him. It was as if he was heaving his soul to Heaven, or at least somewhere high above himself.

I told Marshal McKenna that Dario Curbelo made a choice. This I believe to be true. I wondered if he was nudged into that choice when a tow truck tried to yank off a portion of his house as men with guns screamed at him.

The lifestyle of a drug trafficker and the men and women who are entrusted to stop them run parallel lines of emotional despair and satisfaction born from desperation. We see the world through our own colored and sometimes cloudy lenses. Righteous justification and self-articulation kept the engines of our lives stoked as we slog ahead, not considering the ancillary damage our actions forge upon others.

I could feel myself finally starting to doze off and soon I was asleep. In bed. Before the sun set.

I SLEPT THROUGH the entire night and into the late morning. Many physicians say that sleep helps heal the body. If that is absolutely the truth, then I needed to be somewhere in the Rip Van Winkle category. Everything still ached. It hurt to raise my arm above my head. I sat on the edge of the bed trying to collect myself. Although I had slept for what to me is considered an extremely inordinate amount of time, I was still groggy. The Jameson bottle was still on the nightstand from the other night. I opened the bottle and took a large swallow. It turned my halitosis breath to that of a drunkard. I didn't care.

Easing out of the bed slowly, I went into the bathroom and turned on the shower. While I waited for the hot water I took another hit from the bottle. I left the bottle on the sink vanity and stepped gingerly into the shower, moving slowly and with deliberate purpose. After a few minutes I could feel the synapsis of my brain start to awaken more. My muscles reacted to the hot water. I became loose. I started moving with less pain. I was partially dressed soon after.

I went downstairs carrying my shirt in my hand. In my other hand I carried the Jameson bottle. In the kitchen I ground three Tylenol caplets in a shot glass and poured the Irish whiskey on top of them, instantly creating a mocha brown cloudy mixture. I dipped two of my fingers into the shot glass and started rubbing the

Jameson-Tylenol mixture on my shoulders and arms, massaging it into all of my body parts that ached. Alcohol is an instant absorber. The Tylenol is a pure analgesic. Instead of swallowing the pills and hoping my bloodstream and digestive system knew where to send the pain reliver, I learned a long time ago that this method takes the pain relief right to the muscles. I fingerpainted the remnants of the shot glass across my body. The last drops of the powdery residue I slurped with my tongue.

With the glass whistle dry, I washed it in the sink. I put on my shirt. I had my badge and gun with me, and I left the condo. The warm November sunshine felt good on my face. I looked around at the scarlet and fuchsia blooming bougainvillea crawling across the front of the condominium. The tiled address with the blue numbered tiles 6211 was becoming hard to see. I made a mental note to clip some of the thick vines back. The rustle of the palms was in the background as I walked to my car. Although I'd heard the rustle of palms my entire life, I never tired of hearing the soft sounds they created. I drove into Coconut Grove. I drove right past Ristorante Buccione at 2833 Bird Avenue. There was a time when many of us in VIN would pop in for a light Italian lunch, but since its owner killed a Florida Department of Revenue employee over back taxes, it was now shuttered. The owner fled to Italy where he was arrested and tried in absentia. Because well…that's just Miami.

I continued on Bird Avenue a few more blocks. I found a parking spot in front of Flanigan's Loggerhead Seafood Bar and Grill. The vibrant white exterior with green accented paint, even bolder green painted roof line, and subtle green neon, although in contrast to each other, were calling to me. The family-owned business has many locations in South Florida. They originally started as package liquor stores and lounges named "Big Daddy's." The nickname of the chain's founder, Jim Flanigan, was Big Daddy. The enterprise changed their name to Flanigan's. Jim Flanigan was a gregarious affable restauranteur. He was also an avid angler who saw the profit and stability of being a family restaurant over the headache and aggravation of being a liquor-driven business. The switch was a no-brainer.

The motif inside was two separate decorating styles, appealing to two separate segments of the dining market. It was a prodigious sports bar with TVs tuned to all sorts of sports games—yet nearly every inch of the wall space was covered with nautical items. Picture frame after picture frame of sun-burned anglers, caught fish, sun-splashed docks, and fishing boats adorned the walls. Many of the dining areas are separated by live aquariums with colorful tropical fish swimming in them. I chose to sit at the large oval bar, selecting a seat near the bathrooms. It wasn't that I liked being near the foot traffic of the bathroom, but from this darkened corner I could see almost the entire bar, front entrance, and dining room.

There wasn't anything on the menu that's not always delicious and bountiful. I'd caught the backend of the lunch crowd, and the place was full of people, some of them lingering and others like me, just arriving. I ordered the Big Daddy cheeseburger and curly fries with barbecue sauce.

The bar was filled with a diverse mixture. There were blue collar workers reluctant to get back up on the ladder, splice the wires, or install the piping. A few professional types had bellied up to the bar as well, leaving the banking spread sheets, insurance policies, and law briefs behind them for the rest of the day. Amongst them were pockets of insightful conversations about the 6-2 Miami Hurricanes football team. Many theorized if they'd finish the season with more wins making them Bowl-eligible, and wondering if they'd retain head coach Butch Davis. The conversation held very little interest to me. My interest was in satiating my hunger.

Marshal Mckenna was coy on the phone yesterday, referring to Dario Curbelo as "our shared interest." We may have shared an interest, but we had totally different agendas. It was now very obvious her agenda was vastly different from my own.

My burger arrived. Ten ounces of seared perfection. It was so good I was tempted to order another. The restaurant and bar are open until 4:30am. Rather than make a gluttonous wreck of myself, with reluctance, I abstained. I could always come back later. I paid my tab and stepped out into the beginning of another beautiful sunset and the amassing traffic. I recalled exactly what Major Brunson said to me:

"Cade, go home. I mean seriously, get out of here and go home. I'm telling you, take a few days off."

I had already gone home. I satisfied that requirement. I was now looking forward to making the most of taking some time off. I drove over to the heart of the commercial district in Coconut Grove past the venerable Coconut Grove Playhouse. I parked on Franklin Street just off of Main Highway. One of the caveats of being a long-established local resident is knowing where to park in Miami. It was just a short jaunt on Main Highway, and I was now in front of the Taurus Bar.

The Taurus had gone through some subtle changes over the years but has relatively stayed the same from when an old ship salvager's house was converted into the bar in 1926. Back then it was a little clapboard cottage that served as a gathering place for locals, salvagers, and sea merchants. It has steadfastly always been Coconut Grove's favorite spot to drink beer and indulge in the house special hamburgers. In the late 1960s it wasn't uncommon to walk in and see songwriters like John Sebastian and Fred Neil holding court at the bar, discussing the pitfalls of the music industry. Sebastian became most known for his hit theme song for the ABC TV show "Welcome Back Kotter." Fred, or Freddie as everyone called him, was most known for penning the hit song "Everybody's Talking at Me" from the movie *Midnight Cowboy.* The Taurus has a very wide selection of libations and a "Chug Burger" on the menu fostered on the beloved Martin Burger that were served from an open grill on the patio area in the 1980s. Happy hour drinkers, domestic home avoiders, college students, and the Taurus neighborhood regulars affectionately called "Grovites" milled about on the sidewalk and covered front patio of the bar. I side-stepped the assembled revelers and drinkers and walked into the bar area of the cozy establishment. The stools at the bar were predominantly filled and I wasn't in the mood to sidle up next to anyone. To my left was the decades-old functional fireplace. Very similar to the fireplace at Dario Curbelo's house, the

Taurus fireplace was tightly packed coral rock with natural limestone grout lines. It too was painted a bright white with a storied solid wooden header running across it. Gabled roofs were at the east and west ends of the bar, and neatly-spaced dark rafters were overhead. The bar wasn't exceptionally big, but it accommodated a fun and alcohol-addled crowd. The header over the bar was neatly stacked with aligned bottles of Jack Daniels, Chivas Regal Scotch, Johnnie Walker Black, and my beloved Jameson. I was fortunate to get an unattended small table just off of the fireplace. My seat was in the corner. I could actually feel the cool oolite, coral, and limestone of the wall and adjoining fireplace. Above my table was a metallic-framed mirror with a multi-color graphic of a Jameson Irish whiskey bottle in the center of it. If there was ever an omen and an out of the way corner table designed just for me, this was definitely it. There was a large flatscreen television over the fireplace. I couldn't see it from my seating angle, but I could hear it. The bar TV was tuned to the same channel—the Florida Panthers and Pittsburgh Penguins pregame show. This whole arrangement was working out very nicely for me.

A waitress came over and introduced herself as "Kristen with a K."

"I'm Cade with a C," I said.

"Well, Mr. C, can I get you started with a drink? Would you like to hear our specials?"

"No, Miss K, I'll just have one of those. Neat please," I said pointing above my head.

She was disturbingly confused as she looked into the Jameson mirror and then kept looking behind her as if something in the mirror's reflection was what I actually wanted. I decided to quash the confusion and simultaneously put my hunger to rest.

"Kristen, I'll have a Jameson neat, with a Chug Burger and fries please."

"Oh right. Duh! Silly me I get it, the Jameson in the mirror. Sorry. Do you want that all together?"

Here we go again.

"No Kristen, if you would be so kind to bring the Jameson first and I'll sip on that as I wait for the burger."

"Oh right, double duh!" she said as she made a little head shake and eye roll that spoke to her own self-effacing opinion of herself.

I felt very relieved to be tucked into the little corner here in the bar. As it got darker outside less light was filtering in through the Bahamian shutters and the restaurant lights were turned up a little. Even with the lights near the bar and the glow of the TVs, I felt it was adequately dark enough for me to see my burger but also drink in the shadows. I was on my second Jameson when the juicy burger arrived. I devoured it much like I did the first one at Flannigan's. When the dishes were cleared away, I decided to make this a longer rest stop than I initially had intended. I ordered a third Jameson. The hockey game wasn't going very well for the Panthers. Stu Barnes got the first goal for the Penguins. The Panthers should have never traded him to the Penguins. Revenge was sweet for Stu tonight.

My cell phone started ringing. I didn't recognize the number. I answered the phone.

"Hello?"

"Cade, This is Robert McBride. I hope you don't mind; I got your number from ASAC Mandeville. How are you doing?"

I was surprised to hear from "Mr. I'm from the Government and I'm here to help you." I wasn't comfortable that Mandeville provided my cell phone number to him. I also knew he couldn't care less about how I was doing. I hid my displeasure by being abrupt, but cordial.

"I'm okay. How about you?"

"Personally? I'm fine, but we're still dealing with what happened to Agent Lew. Though more and more it looks like he'll recover and be back to himself soon. Cade, where are you right now?"

"Right now?" I said, reflexively looking around the bar. "I'm in the Grove."

"Good, I'm not too far away. Can you meet me at Greenstreet Cafe on the corner of Main Highway and Commodore Plaza?"

"I'm already settled in here at the Taurus and—"

"Even better. I'll meet you there in a few," he said as he hung up.

I had no chance to veto seeing him. I could get up from my comfortable spot and book it out the door, but I wasn't inclined to leave nor run from a Brooks Brothers-suit-wearing jackball. He wants to come in here and see me? He can bring it on. Talk about a buzzkill. Nothing like having a duplicitous NSA spook sit across from you and pretend to be your confederate all the while trying to manipulate the conversation for his own cloaked machinations. I put his number in my contacts so that if he ever called me again, I wouldn't be surprised. I could have the discretion in the future to accept his call or let it go to voicemail.

My third Jameson arrived. Although I was building up to a steady inebriation, I held off on the third until McBride arrived. The hockey game was in the second period. The Panthers were down 3-0, even Penguins goalkeeper Tom Barrasso got an assist. This wasn't looking promising for the Panthers. Or for me. I wasn't feeling good about Robert McBride wanting to talk to me.

Twenty minutes later, in walked McBride. He scanned the bar area looking for me. It was obvious he'd forgotten what I looked like. He was now hoping I'd stand up and wave at him like some moonstruck lover at the arrivals area of Miami International Airport. I stayed seated in the partial darkness, just watching him. He kept looking around and was becoming apprehensive that either he was in the wrong bar or that I had intentionally misled him. He finally looked in my direction and decided to take a chance and approach my table. As he drew closer our eyes locked. It was a now or never moment for him and he played it off as though he recognized me from the start.

"Hey there, Cade," he said with a tight smile.

I stayed quiet, just long enough to make him question if he was talking to me or maybe he was chatting up a total stranger. His facial expression started to morph from confidence to confusion. I decided to let him off the hook.

"Mr. McBride. What can I do for you?"

"Mind if I sit down?" he asked me as he was already pulling out the vacant chair across from me at the table.

He looked at the shot of Jameson in front of me. I could imagine what he was thinking. He was probably registering how many drinks I may have had and questioning if he should have a drink as well. Kristen ambled over and inquired if he wanted a drink or to see a menu. McBride eyed the full shot in front of me and must have surmised I'd be staying for a while. He ordered a gin and tonic, specifying that the gin be Bombay Sapphire. I power charged the Jameson shot down and this time like a typical college frat boy, I did slam the empty glass on the table. Immediately McBride was probably inwardly wondering if he just ordered a drink so he could watch me walk out or he was surmising that maybe I was tipsy enough that he could snow me with whatever story he was here to tell me. I ordered another shot and saw McBride's shoulders relax as he sat even further back in his chair.

"Cade, thank you for indulging me with your time and allowing me to sit with you. I apologize for intruding," he said.

The soft sell always works best when said with a dose of reality within it.

"No problem, Mr. McBride."

"Please, call me Robert," he said with a smile. He looked around the Taurus and it was evident by the look on his face that he felt comfortable and liked the vibe of the bar. "Cade, you have been an invaluable part of this investigation and you have surprised many of us."

"Many of us?" I asked him, feeling my eyebrow raise.

He smiled as he took out his phone and dialed a number. He said into the phone, "Come in," then hung up and placed the phone on the table. Kristen brought both drinks to the table. He just continued with that smug, yet blank smile. I stared at him across the table doing a slow burn.

I was feeling set up.

A beat or two later in walked private investigator Franklin G.

McCarron and U.S. Marshal Auburn McKenna. McCarron said something to Kristen, and she nodded. He sat in a chair at the table across from us, but close enough to be in the conversation. McKenna sat next to McBride.

"This is the strangest intervention I've ever seen," I said.

"Hey smartass, next time someone tells you they're a U.S. Marshal, maybe instead of staring at their tits and being bedazzled by their badge you should ask for some identification, too," said McKenna.

I recalled when she first walked into the VIN office unannounced.

She'd unclipped her U.S. Marshals badge from her belt and tossed it onto the desk. I picked up, I looked at it before sliding it back across the desk towards her.

"Don't flatter yourself. Both your badge and tits aren't as impressive as you might think," I said.

"Fuck you, Cade Taylor."

In the past few days those exact words, spoken more than once to me by both Auburn Mckenna and Hammy Garzon, were becoming a repeated theme.

"Fuck me? Honey, you wouldn't like it. I just lay there wondering what color to paint the ceiling," I said.

Off to my side I could see McCarron shift in his seat, getting agitated.

"What? You got something to say, too?" I said to him.

"Just five minutes. I just want five minutes alone in a room with you," he said menacingly.

"You had three minutes alone with me in a car. How'd that work out for ya? Pardon the expression—but put a lid on it," I said.

He was about to retort something as he rose out of his chair when at that moment Kristen came over with two drinks on an oval tray. All conversation awkwardly stopped. She put a drink in front of McKenna and McCarron and walked away.

McBride.

McKenna.

McCarron.

"McBride, McKenna, McCarron. I get it now. Here's a novel idea. Why don't the three of you go McFuck yourselves?"

"Cade. Like a lot of things in life, not everything is what we initially perceive it to be. Auburn here, as you now know, is not a U.S Marshal, and Frank here isn't a private investigator—"

"I don't give a damn who they are," I said pointing at McKenna. "What she is to me is someone who impersonated a federal agent. She compromised me and an official DEA investigation. Those are criminal acts. I hope she enjoys McJail because that's where she's going before this Mcnight is over."

"Cade, listen to me Cade. I can understand your anger but before you get all Miami crazy here, she isn't a federal agent, as you said. She supersedes that designation. To what extent, I'm not at liberty to say, but I can assure you that even attempting to arrest her would be an extreme exercise in futility and possibly humility for you. Now, we are all gathered here to discuss a few things. We all have drinks in front of us and I'd like to consider this a social outing. How about you allow me to talk first, then you can pass judgment or as you must be thinking, Mcjudgement," said McBride.

"I don't care if she's the Secretary of State, she put us in harm's way. She knew the identity of Dario Curbelo and withheld that information, impersonating a U.S Marshal. She even shared a home with him at some time in whatever their relationship was. I got a DEA agent in Jackson Memorial Hospital whose kids are wondering if he'll ever throw a baseball with them, and you bring her in here expecting me to not do anything? She was sleeping with Curbelo and neither of you state department secret squirrels see something wrong with that?"

McBride started talking again.

"Cade. Once again let's have a chat before you get even more riled up. Yes McBride, McKenna, and McCarron are not our real names. It doesn't matter what are names are. What matters is that we are here in front of you. Yes, we are a branch of the government that isn't often discussed. Yes, we do work many operations using aliases, false documents, or anything else necessary to accomplish our objectives. Yes, we work both internationally and domestically. Whether Auburn here had any type of relationship with Dario Curbelo is no concern of yours. Part of what we do is gather assets. McKenna is an asset gatherer. Curbelo was an asset. He was an asset that went rogue. Regardless, he was a key piece to what we're trying to accomplish—"

"And you shot him like he was some sort of street dog. Do you have any *idea* how far you set us back? Do you even care about the damage you've done?" interrupted McKenna, her eyes watering.

"I think Curbelo may have set something on the ass of your asset gatherer. She might have gotten to close to the asset," I said staring at her.

Mckenna sat there fuming shooting daggers at me with her eyes. McBride kept his continual tact. Even and cool.

"Cade, we lost touch with Dario Curbelo for a few months. Both Auburn, whose responsibility it was to keep him close in the fold, and myself who oversees the operation, failed in our mission. We didn't know if he was Dario Curbelo. We didn't know if he was using the identity, we gave him—Ricardo Sanabria. He surprised us. His going dark on us was very detrimental to our overall objective. We need to know a few things. We're very concerned about the integrity of what we need to accomplish. How were you able to find him both as Dario Curbelo and by his new identity, Ricardo Sanabria?"

The three of them had neglected recalling that someone in their organization had Curbelo arrested by Sergeant Denny Byrne of the Miami Police Department. It was probably a good idea back during the Summit of the Americas in 1994, but that arrest and the mistake of not sealing Arson Investigator Jeff Baggett's arson report of the North Miami house fire unraveled their plans. I remembered what both McKenna and McCarron had said to me on separate occasions.

"There are certain levels of confidentiality that we just can't break."

"You know Robert, I'd like to tell you how I found him but there are certain levels of confidentiality that I just can't break," I said smugly.

The color slowly drained from his face.

"Cade, I recognize you may be a bit angry—"

"Angry? You send one of your team into my office posing as a federal agent. She in turn borrows my cell phone to make a telephone call. She steps outside and instead of making a call she forwards my ESN number to Joe Bazooka over here. He puts it into a trigger fish and then joins up with someone just as stupid as he is and the two of them start following me all over greater Miami. Angry? I'm beyond angry."

McBride tried to play the great conciliator.

"Cade, how can I make this up to you? I'd be agog to make this up to you."

"*Agog*? What the hell is that?" I asked him.

Before he could answer McCarron spoke up.

"It means eager. Maybe if you had some sort of formal education, you'd know that," he said.

"Is he supposed to be helping? Because if he is, he's about as useful as a screen door on a submarine," I said to McBride. I turned my attention back to McCarron.

"You don't know anything about my education. I may not have graduated from the college of leaflets, pamphlets, and brochures like you, but I can assure you I am far from the lowly municipal worker you three seem to think I am. If I recall correctly, the conversation was how did *I* find your guy, not how did you *not* find your guy," I said.

"Yes, that is the reason we are having this discussion," chimed in McBride. "Cade, how *did* you find Dario Curbelo?"

"I'm sure that for some sort of after-action report that you'd like to doctor, that's important. But to me what's important is the unauthorized eavesdropping on my cell phone, which put me and everyone I work with in a very precarious situation. There is still a shooter out there who shot DEA Agent Scott Lew. You and your Washington cronies keep interfering with the DEA's investigation. You took possession of physical evidence from the scene and every time Hammy Garzon enters fingerprints in AFIS they disappear in a matter of hours. That's you guys all the way. I can smell it. So no dice, chief," I said.

"Cade, are you familiar with the noble lie?"

"Is that one of your Washington Houdini parlor tricks?" I asked, growing tired of this tedious, unforeseen, and unwanted meeting.

"Well not exactly. The *noble lie* was created by Socrates in Book III of Plato's Republic. You see, Plato realized that many people in society were starting to demand the same privileges and ascensions that the highest nobility in society enjoyed. Plato determined that the masses were unfit to rule themselves. He felt that people should be ruled by those with knowledge. We have knowledge, Cade. *We* have knowledge," he said gesturing to himself, McKenna, and McCarron. "So Plato came up with a myth that all people were derived from the earth but were infused with a certain metal endemic to them and where they were in society. The myth is propagated by the premise that there were three types of people. At the top were the ruling class. They were the most noble and they were comprised of gold. Warriors were silver, and artisans were bronze and iron. Now, because these three types of people had innate compositions of metal that were purely aligned with their status in society; the people in society were more apt to happily stay at their status and not aspire to rise higher. Plato called this a noble lie because it was in the best interest for the republic as a whole if everyone stayed at their perceived level. With a noble lie comes justifiable truths, propaganda, policies, and actions. Do you understand, Cade?"

"Keeping people down," I said as I looked at him and nodded my head disgustedly.

"The noble lie is necessary for a functioning government. It's necessary for a stabilizing government. When the populace is at ease, the government can direct their attention to running the government. When there's dissension or questioning by the masses, the government must divert its attention from governing society to defending itself. The lie is only efficient if it makes people feel content and happy with their lives."

"That's why they don't talk about UFOs, and they manipulate inflation numbers," I said.

"Exactly. There are things that we, the government, do on behalf of all of *you* to keep the country running smoothly. We have to essentially cripple critical thinking. If individuals start questioning everything in society then the lies become ineffective. The masses become unhappy. So we create constructs that hold them to the lie. We *bind* them to the lie. Multi-year mortgages, health care expenses, energy costs, things like that to keep them busy and spinning in their day to day lives. We don't want them to pay attention to what we're actually doing to keep society running," he explained.

I began to dislike the three of them even more.

"As generations grow older, they become wiser. We must keep the myth alive by creating intermixing truths and lies. The generation that supported the war efforts in World War II were vastly different than the support seen by the generation in the Vietnam War. There must be constant tweaking of the myth to keep what we consider the high ideals of the American dream."

"If every household in China had an air conditioner there would be no ozone layer," interjected McCarron.

"So Cade, consider us economic hitmen. We create friends and enemies in the world to further our own democratic agenda. We promise and deliver, and sometimes we promise and don't deliver. As long as we get what we want, we don't care," McBride said with a lighthearted smile. "We aren't concerned with their outcome. But by keeping the world disadvantaged, off-balanced, we can secure our societal future. It's our job to create scarcity, supply, demand, needs, and wants. We must be the gatekeepers of what is tolerable in society and what is intolerable," said McBride.

"Including drugs like cocaine," I said with anger rising in me.

"Cocaine, like any other thing, is just a commodity to us. If it props up a dictator who's agreeable to our agenda, then we're all in! If it creates an insurgency that destroys a regime which is a threat to our economic stability, we're all in on that too. We have no issues playing on both sides of the fence."

"So just like the Iran-Contra situation you don't care if you flood our streets with cocaine smuggled in through intermediaries so long as you get what you want?" I retorted.

"Our CIA brethren took the hit on that one. Even Fawn Hall's wardrobe and her hairstyle were designed to keep the public talking about her and Colonel Oliver North. It kept people from seeing more than what was really at stake. The noble lie depends on manipulation, subterfuge, sleight of hand, if you will. We know what's best for the United States and we are *always* five steps ahead. Cade, look at the total economic model of cocaine. Quit looking at it like it's a local Miami scourge, think of the counteractive drugs for drug addiction, the job placement centers, the marriage counselors, the construction of prisons, the rise in law school enrollments, the federal loans for the aspiring lawyers, the hospitals, the swelling of medical staffs, the proliferation of urgent care centers, the advances in law enforcement, even the casket makers"

"Your own fucking overtime. You dumbass," snarled McCarron.

"Well thanks for the civics lesson, professor, but I don't see how interfering with a DEA investigation is relevant to what I'm trying to do here," I said.

McBride looked at me and then he looked at both McKenna and McCarron. McKenna was raging inside, her eyes shining bright with fury, but I noticed a slight head nod to McBride as though she knew what he was going to do, and she was agreeing to it.

"The U.S. dollar is the king of all currencies. Dollar bills, specifically 100 dollar bills, are in circulation *outside* the U.S. more than *inside* the U.S. In underdeveloped financial systems, poorer countries, countries lacking financial infrastructure, there's an unquenchable thirst for the almighty dollar. U.S. dollars represent a stored value to them. Many of our foreign partners consider English the language of prosperity. They believe in the noble lie. The message we put out globally is 'wealth.' Attainable wealth. We cultivate the positive aspects of a free and democratic world—so long as you do it our way," he said, smiling at me just like a doctor holding a syringe behind his back would. "Cade, we have had a sizable, growing problem down south of here."

"How far south of here?" I asked him.

"I know in your world you think *down south* always means Colombia, but I can assure you there is a lot more to South America than Colombia."

"He's talking about deep south near Argentina and Paraguay, you moron," Mckenna hissed at me.

McBride looked briefly at her as if to say, "Relax, I got this." McBride continued with his explanation.

"As I was saying, we have a growing problem in South America. Four years ago on the morning of July 18th a van was seen in Buenos Aires cruising the streets. It pulled up to the Argentine Israelite Mutual Association headquarters. Inside the van were 275 kilograms of fertilizer and TNT. The explosion was incredible. It destroyed the seven-story building, killing eighty-five people, some of them children. There were 300 more extensively injured. There were rare books, artifacts, and important documents in the building, all lost in the explosion. There's a clandestine organization in Argentina called 'Project Witness.' They operated from offices in the building. This group has been linking Argentine sympathizers with Nazis. The driver of the van was killed in the explosion. We were able to identify him as Ibrahim Hussein Berro, a Lebanese citizen with ties to Hezbollah. This was our first indication of anti-Semitism, and anti-American dissidents in the TBA."

"What's the TBA?" I asked him.

McCarron scoffed and shook his head, looking down at the floor. "I told you this was bad idea. This dumbass is clueless," he said to McBride.

Once again McBride kept his composure and his demeanor never wavered.

"Cade, there is dissension in our ranks, and you have an aptitude for finding information. So I think you can help us," he said, glancing over at McCarron.

"The TBA is an acronym for the Tri-Border Area. The triple frontier. Believe me when I tell you, it is a frontier in every sense of the word. It's where southern Brazil, Paraguay, and northern Argentina all share borders with each other. In this tri-border area the Iguazú and Paraná rivers converge. Where the rivers join are the cities of Puerto Iguazú in Argentina, Foz do Iguaçu in Brazil, and Ciudad del Este in Paraguay. Since 1996, the three of us have been part of the Tripartite Command of the Triple Frontier. We like to say we 'help coordinate monitoring tasks among the three bordering countries.' The geography of the border region is a transnational organized crime paradise. There is rampant political corruption and weak, almost nonexistent judicial systems, making it very difficult to monitor organized crime and all the illegal activities connected with them. The three of us are intimately familiar with the region. We know there are Iranian-backed Hezbollah militia groups and encampments in the dense hill areas. These groups have been bolstering high financed forces of Islamist radicals in the world. In Ciudad del Este there are no controls on the amount of currency that can be brought in or out of the country, and there are no cross-border reporting requirements. Little personal background information is required to open a bank account or to make financial transactions in Paraguay. Therefore, there is a high incidence of money laundering activity," he said.

"Dario was one of our biggest assets in the area. You fucking *killed* one of the strongest connections we had in the region, you low-life, ignorant *cop*," McKenna said, her voice rising.

"Your biggest asset was selling cocaine here in Miami. Maybe if you guys hadn't lost track of him this would be a moot point. Ever think of that? *You* low-life, ignorant bureaucrat?" I said back to her.

She started rising out of her chair and although I was not one to hit a woman, I wasn't opposed to it either, at least in this situation. McBride extended his arm out from his chair blocking her from rising up. He kept it there until she was sufficiently fully seated.

"We know you have experience in the money laundering arena. This is part of why we're having this discussion. The full extent of narcotics trafficking in the TBA is unclear although the estimates are high. Very high. Criminals in Ciudad del Este and Foz do Iguaçu are extreme specialists in laundering drug money. We peg the amount of money being laundered in the TBA to be averaging twelve billion per year. Foz do Iguaçu appears to be the principal money laundering center, followed closely by Ciudad del Este. The most popular method they use for laundering in the TBA appears to be CC-5 accounts, with a Brazilian CC-5 that belongs to someone residing outside the country. The possibilities are endless for laundering drug money. They open the accounts with fake identity documents, making investigations difficult. Earlier this year, Squadron 51 of Argentina's National Gendarmerie detained a Paraguayan woman in the Chaco Province in northeastern Argentina. She was in possession of false passports. Lots of them. She was also carrying official Paraguayan judicial order seals and visa applications seals. With Curbelo's help we were able to trace the seals and documents to an interim Paraguayan consul. The consul was part of a group that belonged to an organization specializing in illegal documents. In a quick six months, this consul issued more than 500 illegal visas, many of them Russian." McBride presented his information so carefully it was impossible not to be riveted, especially if you were me.

When he said Russian, my ears immediately perked up.

Hammy Garzon had determined that Agent Lew was shot with a Russian handgun and with Russian ammunition. The shooter was tall, pale, and blond. He definitely could have easily been Russian.

I played my peaked interest cool. I took a healthy swig of the Jameson in front of me. I held the nearly empty shot glass up so that Kristen could see it. She nodded her head, and I knew that another shot would be coming my way. I wanted the three of them to think that none of what they were saying was outwardly having an impact on me. Inwardly, I was keenly listening.

"Two years ago the Russian mafia began exploring Paraguay, just like they did in Colombia, Argentina, and Brazil. Russian mafia groups are seeking out contacts with crime groups, principally those operating from the drug-trafficking zones of Pedro Juan Caballero-Ponta Porã and Ciudad del Este-Foz do Iguaçu. The intention of the Russians is to ally themselves with the bosses of the South American drug cartels in order to maximize the distribution of cocaine in Europe. This is not good for us. Not good at all. A strong Russian-controlled drug trade in Europe would hamper our missions in Europe. Those dollars circulating outside the U.S. can't end up in Russian hands. The Russians started by ousting the Brazilian and Nigerian cartels in border towns like Pedro Juan Caballero. The Russian mafia presence in Argentina, specifically Chechen gangs, has been linked primarily to the use of Argentina as a transit country for Andean cocaine shipments to Europe, arms trafficking to Brazil and Colombia, and money laundering. Curbelo had been reporting to us that Chechen separatist groups and Islamic terrorists are in the TBA."

My cool was momentarily uncooled. "*Terrorists?* Separatists and terrorists." I just had to say the words out loud.

McBride didn't skip a beat. "We suspect Chechen use of these networks for arms-smuggling and cocaine trafficking purposes. Once again this is not good for our interests in the global theater."

"Your interests in the global theater? What you're trying to say is if the U.S. government loses control of the cocaine trade in Europe you'll lose leverage in other parts of the world. As they get bigger, we get smaller, and the big noble lie is no longer believable," I said as Kristen set the shot glass of Jameson in front of me.

"There is a micro view of the world *and* a macro view of the world. We like to be the ones who adjust the optics," he said with skewed diplomacy.

I facetiously raised the shot glass to the three of them.

"Once again thank you for the civics lesson and the state of the union address but I'm not seeing what some mudholes in South America have to do with me?"

"They aren't *mudholes* you moron, they're full-fledged cities. We're talking about population centers of hundreds of thousands of people. Didn't you hear the man? Twelve billion dollars and Russian and Islamic groups!" McCarron spat furiously.

People who are unfamiliar with fishing for dolphin in the Florida Keys don't realize that the dolphin like to swim beneath a weed line or under a piece of floating wood. It keeps the school of dolphins out of the glare of the sun. You don't land the very first one you get on a fishing line from a school of dolphin. You keep that dolphin on the line and reel him close to the boat. The other dolphins will follow him and come closer as well. As long as you keep at least one on the line in the water, it's just a matter of easily hooking the others.

McCarron was my dolphin on the line. I baited him and pulled him out of the shade and close in by feigning ignorance.

"I still don't see what this has to do with me," I said.

"Well, let me put it this way..." said McBride.

Here come the rest of the dolphins.

"Other members of our team took possession of the glass tabletop at the Hialeah restaurant. Each time Ms. Garzon submitted the prints from the gun magazine we were able to intercept them in the AFIS system and use them as comparisons to what we gathered from the tabletop. She submitted great prints. The prints matched a known and feared Russian crime lord named Viktor Moshienko. He was in the Interpol system under a green notice."

I took a sip of the Jameson.

"A green notice means that we're aware of who he is, but he's just to be monitored for criminal activity or a threat to national security," interjected McKenna, the second dolphin.

"So, this guy is a known Russian criminal. Actually one you say that is feared, yet Interpol only had him classified as a green notice?" I said to none of them in particular.

It was McBride who continued talking.

"Cade, after the events of the past few days Interpol has bumped his status to a red notice, meaning we need to locate him and arrest him for extradition or imprisonment. Viktor Moshienko rose through the ranks of the KGB in Moscow. When Glasnost spelled the end of the KGB's tyranny, he like many other well-trained spies and assassins started freelancing their skills to the highest bidders. He's suspected in the death of a diplomatic courier in Budapest, a businessman in Paris, and for the last two years we think he's been down in South America in the TBA running a large cocaine and money laundering organization. We want to know how he ended up in your drug deal in Hialeah."

"I don't know. The bigger question is how did he end up in the United States?" I said.

"I just told you about a detained Paraguayan woman in the Chaco Province in northeastern Argentina. One of the passports she had was a copy of his original Russian passport. We think he came into the United States on a Lan Chile flight from Ciudad de Este to Panama. From Panama he came here to Miami under a false passport in the name of Yury Rudakov. Viktor Moshienko is a ruthless brute whose rise in the cocaine and money laundering trade is bordering on meteoric. This guy would kill his own mother if he thought it would be to his advantage. Curbelo was off our radar, and we were looking for him. You know that already. We were also trying to find Moshienko for entirely different reasons. How they both came to be in a tiny Hialeah restaurant and with you there, trying to buy twenty kilos of flake has us stumped."

"Does the DEA know that Moshienko shot Agent Lew?"

McBride looked at his watch.

"In about an hour from now you're going to call Hammy Garzon and ask her to resubmit the prints in AFIS. This time they'll go in and stay in. The match will come up. You can expect her to call you and the DEA. We bought as much time as we could with the delay. Interpol is going to jump all over this. SAC Grayson and the rest of the Boy Scouts at DEA will be jumping through hoops for Interpol. That will more than likely lead to nothing. At least we can say we did our part. You seem very good at finding people. You found Dario Curbelo. You even found Curbelo when he was Ricardo Sanabria. We're hoping you'll find Viktor Moshienko too."

"And if I do find him?" I asked.

"Then call us," he said.

"And if I do find him and I don't call you?"

"Then we're going to call you," he said with a threatening tone.

Chapter Twenty-One

I walked out, leaving the McWhoevers to pick up the tab. I left the Taurus looking over my shoulder and simultaneously was keeping a keen eye in front of me for any of the McCrew I might have overlooked.

The Jameson shots were having a very acute effect on me. I decided the best practice would be to let the alcohol subside before I called Hammy Garzon or even attempted to do anything significant. I "bent my run" as we used to say in my sports playing days. I walked down the leafy street directly behind the Taurus. Across from the backside of the Taurus was the E.W.F. Stirrup House. The Stirrup House was originally built in 1897, by E.W.F. Stirrup, who built over 100 homes in Coconut Grove during his lifetime. The local Coconut Grove preservationists were trying to get the home designated as a historic site. The house was long vacant and was in serious need of repair. A crudely erected chain link fence surrounded the old two-story wooden house. I breeched the faltering chain link fence. At first, I intended to sit down on the creaky steps of the front porch. There was a weathered, time-beaten couch on the shaded porch, protected from the elements. I sat on the couch. I laid my head back, listening to the soft rustling of the palm trees. Above me, the porch ceiling was lined with tightly placed one-by-four boards, now peeling down in flat decaying strips. The night was quiet. Just before dozing off I reasoned to myself the historic preservation board would be happy to have an armed cop watching over their next designation, even if he himself was inebriated and asleep.

For almost forty-five minutes, I drifted in and out of a fitful slumber. The thought of a homeless person using the same couch as a resting spot or a roving cockroach crawling over me kept jolting me up from the deep sleep that my mind demanded. I was sober enough to get in my car and drive home. Any police officer who might pull me over would have to decide whether I was or wasn't by their standard policy.

Standard

That didn't happen. The journey home down Old Cutler Road with the windows rolled down and the radio blasting either enabled my ability to properly handle shots of whiskey or was yet another foolish behavior to add to my expanding list of foolish acts. I drove past the guardhouse at Paradise Pint. The interior of the guard house was lit only by the bright monitor inside. The security cameras affixed to the outside of the guard house captured moving footage of my car as I drove into the complex.

I made my way up the condo's stairs and into the unit. The art pieces and the high-end décor touches were starting to grow on me and although my former marital home was good and gone this was becoming good and home to me. I wrestled with the belt on my pants until finally giving in and just leaving it partially on my waist. I very quickly fell asleep with my clothes on.

The brightness of the morning light is what stirred me from my sleep. I assessed the success I had in taking my clothes off the night before. If half a belt and one shoe qualifies, than I was in the medalist round for sure. There was nothing in the rules book that said I had to be undressed in one sitting. Still laying on my back I continued getting undressed pulling my shirt up over my head which resulted in me pulling my head forcefully off the pillow. I made a mental note to not do that again. I was soon undressed and in the shower. The shower felt good although I'd have hoped for a quicker revitalization as I was still feeling the effects of last night when I redressed for the day. I called Hammy. She didn't answer. I left a message telling her that our I.T. people and our teletype people had informed me that the AFIS system was down for days because of system upgrading. I suggested she resubmit the prints from the gun magazine again. I didn't mention Viktor Moshienko. I decided to see if it played out like McBride said it would. The DEA would get all hot and bothered with Interpol and maybe someone would have a lead on Moshienko. I also couldn't trust that McBride was telling me the truth. There may not *be* a Viktor Moshienko, and there may not be an alias Yury Rudakov in Miami. McBride and McKenna went to great lengths to protect Dario Curbelo. What would keep them from protecting the Russian shooter too? If they were telling the truth about Moshienko amassing a bigger stake in the cocaine trade, especially in the drug trade in Europe, it could be very disadvantageous to whatever McBride and his government buddies were doing. The best answer was to get Hammy to submit the prints again into AFIS, sit back and see what happens. That's just what I did.

I wasn't very hungry, but I was very hungover. I found the initiative to actually change out of my clothes and into a bathing suit. I went down to the community pool, which was heated and sat down in the still water near the pool's entrance steps. A purple float in the shape of a miniature raft has been left by a child. I laid over it and dozed off in the water, bobbing against the pool's edge. The pool skimmer's gentle hum was the only sound. Soon I was deeply asleep, rocked by the soft jets of the pool. An hour had passed, and I could faintly hear my cell phone ringing. I didn't want to get off of the raft. I tried to paddle to the edge of the pool, where my phone was, with my legs straddling the raft and my butt waddling in the water. Whoever it was they were insistent on either reaching me or leaving a voicemail as the phone rang for at least seven times before I was able answer it. It was the VIN office.

"Hello."

"Cade. *Aye Coño ju* always sound like *ju* are in sleepy dream land."

"Hi Ileana."

"*Jes ju* are talking but whatever it is *ju* need to wake up. *Borracho!*"

"Ileana I am off work."

"Okay then what *je* lady from *je* DEA said I will tell *ju* when *ju* are working."

"No Ileana. I'm here on the phone with you now. Who called and what did they say, please?"

"Ok *espere. I* need my *ojos.*"

"Eyes?"

"*Si,* my *ojos!* My glasses."

There was a brief pause while she retrieved her glasses from somewhere on her desk. I wondered why she didn't have her glasses with her before she dialed. Before I could put that thought out to the universe she came back on the line.

"Cade a SACA Mandeville—"

"It's ASAC. ASAC Mandeville."

"Dios mío, ¿es realmente tan importante?"

"Go on, Ileana."

"Irregardless. *Des* Mandeville called. She said to tell *ju* Scott *Loo* said *eh de informante* was Guillermo Fonseca. Whatever that means."

"Guillermo Fonseca?"

"*Si*. Guillermo Fonseca."

"Thank you, Ileana."

"Okay, then *ju* have been told," she said and hung up on me.

I'd tethered myself to the pool's edge with my free hand and put the phone back down on the ground. I thought back to what Scott Lew had said to me about his informant.

"He's reputable and comes from a family of reliable information. But you know, for discovery purposes, I need to keep that to myself."

Guillermo Fonseca.

Fonseca?

There was only one Fonseca I knew, and he was definitely reputable in the information business.

Santiago Fonseca.

Santiago was someone I'd known for roughly six years. I met him on Michigan Avenue in Miami Beach when he acted as an intermediary in a cocaine deal we'd arranged with three Panamanians and the Miami Beach PD. From there, our connection evolved into one of favors and information sharing. He knew the drug business thoroughly. He also knew many of the players, not just in Miami but elsewhere across the Caribbean. Santiago was intimate with the traders and sellers in the business. He was well-versed in the restaurant and seafood industries. The seafood business was what many considered to be his legitimate business. He was an expert on fish. He understood everything about snapper, cobia, grouper, and even square grouper.

Square grouper was a moniker for dumped marijuana bales on the high seas.

When the U.S. Coast Guard was well-funded, the maritime interdiction groups were at their peak. Santiago eluded them on each and every run he ever made. He was a sea ninja. He knew the countless inlets, deep dark canals, back hidden channels, and vast southern Biscayne Bay better than anyone I know. On one night when we both had way too many drinks, Santiago claimed that he'd once been a smuggler but was now "retired from the import business." Although still claiming his retirement status, he was still immersed in the comings and goings in the cocaine trade.

I had tapped into his information pipeline a few times. He was definitely reputable for his reliable information. Santiago was Cuban American. He was fiercely loyal to the United States and equally passionate about one day seeing a democratic, free Cuba. This business is full of shady characters. He was open with me about his information. I would stop short of saying Santiago was shady. If you could draw a fine line between shady and smudgy then I guess, I'd have to lean into smudgy. Santiago was a black bag. There are people who have certain skill sets or connections that they carry in their proverbial black bag. Every day, black bag people walk amongst us with seemingly normal lives and employment, but when help is needed, they either do what many others won't do, or they know who will do it for a fee. Santiago has always worked in the food industry. His work lends itself for him to know a lot of the goings-on in Miami. Some in the illegal narcotic business would refer to him as a confidential informant. Someone like Santiago you don't officially document as a C.I. They're a caliber above that. When reward or payment is asked for, it usually comes in the form of favors, or assistance. I wouldn't categorize us as 'friends.' Friends ask questions. Friends want to know how you are and what you've been doing lately. Santiago was someone I like to think of as a "fixer." He employs his immense clout, contacts, and savvy to solve difficulties and avoid unpleasant situations. You wouldn't ask a plumber what kind of wrenches he uses on your pipes, and you shouldn't ask a fixer how they do their work. You simply pay for the services you received, relieved and confident that the job was completed correctly and that you won't have to deal with it again.

The day was so peaceful and quiet. There was no one at the swimming pool. It was almost impossible to pull myself away from the relaxing floating and buffering on the pool float. I hesitated in deciding and then reluctantly exited the pool. I went back upstairs to the condominium. I changed out of my bathing suit. I redressed for the second time today. Once dressed, I went down to my car, opened the trunk, and gave my go bag a quick perusal. I had most everything I might need if I had to, as they say in the advertisements for Taco Bell, "make a run for the border."

I eased myself behind the wheel. I was soon on my way to where I usually could find Santiago. I drove north on Old Cutler Road. I opened the sunroof and occasionally looked up in awe at the canopy over the road of banyan trees flanking each side. My travels were becoming almost routine as I once again drove on Main Highway in Coconut Grove. I drove right past the Taurus and shook my head in bewilderment that I'd just been in there last night with our government's finest. I continued past the Barnacle House and turned south onto Bayshore Drive. The road languidly curves and bends like a silky ribbon painted with brushes dabbed into a spectrum of tropical colors. Each passage along its way is an unfolding arching curve into color popping splendor. High-rise residences and hotels line the left side of the road, each one an architectural marvel unto themselves. Some are concrete, some are steel and glass, but each one is a highly desired place to live. Gigantic Royal Palm trees, splashy fountains, detailed landscaped hedges, and tropical vines and plants abundantly cover the grounds. Some of the structures are round, square, or clustered in identical towers, all of which give breathtaking views of Biscayne Bay. The picturesque journey took my mind off of the hangover that was trying to overtake me. The grandeur of Peacock Park on my right, as well as the occasional vistas of the sparkling blue water of Biscayne Bay, are the mental bandages for whatever ails you. I continued south on Pan American Drive, passing the Regatta Park and Miami City Hall signs, leaving the open green expanse of Peacock Park behind me. Miami City Hall is located at the end of the road with Biscayne Bay directly outside the back door of city hall. If you're a smoker, I would challenge anyone to have a better office to step out of and suck down a lung dart.

Miami City Hall once served as the Pan American Airlines Air-Sea Terminal. It was homebase for their floating airplanes, known as the clipper class. They were large, multi-engine planes with wing spans that testified to the competency of determined engineering calculations. These "floating boats," as they were nicknamed, left this exact shoreline for exotic South American destinations in the 1930s. It was a time when Pan American was the premier airline in the world. There are still remnants of the terminal's glory days in City Hall. It's evident in the terrazzo floors, banks of ornate windows, fine detailed woodworking in the crown cornices, and the use of Brazilian hardwoods in the paneling and parts of the roof. A grassy oval median rimmed in parking spaces is in front of city hall. Although some parking spaces are designated for certain local leaders there are plenty of visitor spaces. I pulled into one of the visitor spots. I exited the car.

The air was scented with a mixture of salt, diesel fuel, and something deep-frying in peanut oil. Adjacent to City Hall is a full-fledged working marina. The two are separated by a chain link fence. In the marina are four massive concrete and aluminum structures that previously served as the hangars for the clipper ships during the Pan American era. They are now utilized to dry dock boats in multi-tiered racks that reach up to the very top of the building's rafters. The diesel forklifts are in constant motion. They're gigantic, smoke-spewing, nimble machines used to retrieve recreational boats from their lofty perches for their eager boat owners. The former clipper ship launching ramps can still be seen on the other side of the chain link fence. The poured concrete ramps that once launched aviation dreams and anticipating vacationers into the bay can still be seen from the topside sea walls. I walked through an intentional opening in the fence line designed to let city hall workers go next door for lunch a few more steps across the dirty, oil-stained parking lot to Scotty's Landing, a bayside restaurant favored by locals.

As I crossed under the orchid-laden trellis of the open-air restaurant, I saw a calypso band setting up their equipment on the stage in front of me. Soon the afternoon would be filled with the sound of conscious rhythms and steel drums. Beyond them, the view of the restaurant captured my sightline. It was a mesmerizing view on out to the sunny sky above Miami and the aquamarine water of Biscayne Bay. Unlike many other outdoor bars and restaurants in Miami, Scotty's Landing does not have thatched roof chickee huts. Scotty's is a singular wooden structure housing the kitchen and the bar. The dining area is under a green and white vinyl tent affixed to the wooden roofline of the kitchen and bar. There are enough white plastic chairs and tables under the tent to easily seat 150 people. The chairs and tables are very interchangeable, functional, nondescript, durable, and are no different than what can normally be found on a summer day in the backyard of a New Jersey split-level ranch house. High above the tables are whirling fans keeping the warm bay breezes circulating. The salty air has rusted nearly each and every one of them, but they work, and they're quiet. When it comes to the fans, I think I speak for every patron when I say no one cares how they look, just so long as they work. The bar is large and imposing. It runs the length of the front of the restaurant. There are green padded barstools aligned along the full length of the bar. The shiplap boards affixed to the bar's façade show incredible wear and tear at ankle height where many a bare foot and flip flop have pushed against them. The restaurant is directly adjacent to the former launching ramps for the clipper ships. While their parents indulge themselves at the restaurant, children often wander down near the ramps looking at the mullet, needle fish, and crabs that swim and live near the water's edge. The youngsters having no idea the history they're standing upon.

The restaurant was moderately full, and the atmosphere was light and breezy. I looked for Santiago, but I didn't see him. A waitress was maneuvering through the scattered misaligned tables and pulled-out chairs towards me. When I asked her if Santiago was working, she said he was in the back somewhere.

"If it's okay with you, I'm going to take that table by the edge, near the water. Can you please tell him Cade is here?" I said to her.

"*¡Cómo?*" she said.

"Cade. Cade Taylor."

She nodded her head and then went to the back of the restaurant while I too, maneuvered through the same maze of tables and chairs. I sat down at a table near the edge of the restaurant, very close to the bay. There was a lawn of recently mowed thick green Bermuda grass between the fringe of the restaurant and the seawall. I felt lucky to be seated at such a prime table. Draping one arm over the back of the chair, I leaned back and admired the wonderful vista mere yards from where I was sitting. The view was a pageantry of colors as sailboats with unfurled sails and flags dotted the blue waters of the bay.

The very same waitress reappeared a few minutes later, carrying four ice-cold bottles of Kalik Bahamian beer wedged into a plastic bucket of ice. She placed the imported and difficult-to-find beer on the table. Kalik was one of my favorite beers. Despite the fact that the nearest Bahamian island, Bimini, is only fifty-seven miles from Miami, finding Kalik Beer in the area was nearly impossible. Santiago always had his fish suppliers include a few cases of Kalik beer with the seafood he bought from the Nassau and Freeport seafood brokers. He kept a few on ice for his closest friends and regular customers. I felt privileged to have the same status as some of our local judges, politicians, drug smugglers and gun runners.

"Santiago he be out. He say to you. Fried shrimp is *excellente*," she said in faltering English.

I remembered what Dario Curbelo had said to me as I entered the restaurant in Hialeah. I was beginning to wonder if shrimp recommendations from Latin men were a cultural cliché.

"Thank you. I'll go with his recommendation. I'll have the fried shrimp with fries please."

She smiled as she reached into her front apron. She pulled out a cheap bottle opener and placed it on the table before turning away to go back in the kitchen. I pulled a very cold Kalik from the icy bucket and used the opener to uncap the beer. The beer tasted wonderful, and it complemented the view superbly. When I heard Santiago's voice, I don't know what I was savoring more, the view or the beer.

"Cade Taylor. The man, the myth, the legend."

I looked at Santiago as he pulled up a chair and sat across from me.

"Yeah, that's me. The older I get, the better I was."

He smiled and chuckled as he withdrew a Kalik from the bucket.

"That could be both of us, *amigo*. Both of us. We used to run like the wind. Now we run like the winded," he said, popping the top off the beer.

We clicked both bottles together in a ceremonial toast to ourselves and our longevity in one of the most volatile businesses there is. To me it was symbolic of our relationship and our current gratitude to be able to sit down across from each other. There was a time we could have been extreme adversaries. The turbulent business of contraband and the long passage of time has softened the hard edges of our lives to a point of understanding without asking. We never let our conversations wander under the emotional fences of our lives. There are two main reasons why people don't talk about certain things: either it means nothing to them, or it means everything to them. There had been a symbiosis to our lives. Our lives were glancing blows to each other. Head feints, sharp elbows in the ribs, and collided sweat stains under the basketball rim of life.

"Any new news?" I asked him.

"Nothing on my end. There's always talk of some developer wanting to come in here and literally tear the tent down and build a multi-use building with a fitness center with Stairmasters looking out over the bay. That shit looks great in commercials but even with a view like this you'd either be staring at the TVs in the corners or the asses in front of you," he said.

"You think they'll do that?" I asked him.

"Who knows? It's Miami. If it doesn't have a construction fence, forty guys in hard hats, and a roach coach pulling up blaring some crazy horn that either sounds like the Cuban national anthem or the changing of the guard in Nepal, it isn't considered relevant. We spend more time knocking things down so we can build unaffordable unattainable things in their place."

I took a cold swig of the beer.

"Thanks for the Kalik's, you always make a guy feel welcome. Is business going strong? I mean, do you think they'll try and move you out?"

"Who knows? You think those half-brain dimwits next door at city hall have any idea what's going on in Miami? Ever been to one of those city hall meetings? It's a come to life larger than life banana republic. I kid you not. They make decisions based on who's lining their pockets or kissing their asses. If they ever do knock this place down, they'll probably build another Margaritaville-type restaurant trying to replicate the feel of an old established waterside bar. Even you can see the absolute irony in that, can't you?"

I held up my hands in mock surrender.

"It's as though they make it harder and harder on all of us," he said.

"Us?"

"I'm trying to give the family a leg up. I got a nephew and niece working here now. My sister's kids. I don't know how they feel about the restaurant business. It becomes a pain or pleasure thing. Do you want the pleasure of earning money or the pain of being broke?" he said.

"I don't know much about kids. That's something I haven't experienced yet," I said.

"Cade. Look at me," he said for emphasis. "They're like locusts. I swear. That's no exaggeration. They eat everything. Hilary Clinton said it 'takes a village to raise a child,' I'd like to get some directions to that village and drop the little monsters off."

The same waitress dropped off my lunch order to the table. I thanked her before she walked away.

"Is that one of your nieces?" I asked him.

"Her? No she's been with us about three months now. She's Venezuelan. She's good. Shows up on time. Does her shifts. My nephew and niece think this is some sort of casual show-up at *Tio Santiago's* whenever the hell they feel like it. If they weren't my sister's kids, I'd have fired them weeks ago."

"Any other news you might have heard?" I asked him as I dug into the fried shrimp platter.

"Nothing really. What about you?" he asked me.

Part of the neurolinguistics of the drug trade is the ability to be vague, evasive, and non-committal within a conversation. There's a circular rhythm that swings like pendulum between the participants until it's either abruptly stopped by one of the conversationalists or it runs out of the inertia needed to keep it moving.

"I heard something the other day," I said.

"What did you hear?" he said.

"DEA agent got shot in Hialeah," I said in between bites.

“The TV news said it was an accidental discharge,” he replied.

“Is that what you think?” I said.

“It was on TV. It must be true. Right?”

I momentarily stopped eating and looked at him. He gave me a slight smile. He then looked off past me at the bay. I was nearly finished eating. I felt a headache coming on. I devoured the shrimp in an attempt to stave it off.

“Accidental discharge?” I said. “That would be kind of hard to do as you're falling backwards—especially with someone else's gun,” I said, dabbing the corners of my mouth with a paper napkin.

“Sounds like you were there,” he said.

“Like you said, it was on TV.” I replied.

We were both now into a second beer each and the bottom of the empty bucket was a slurry of ice and water. Santiago looked at the condensation on the bucket. Adding salt to the ice will cause the melting ice water to stay colder.

“I keep telling them to add salt to the tableside ice buckets. It keeps the beer colder,” he said.

The conversational pendulum had stopped swinging.

“Who is Guillermo Fonseca?”

“Guillermo Fonseca?” he repeated with no hint of any expression on his face.

“Yes. Who is Guillermo Fonseca?” I asked him again.

“Cade, I know you didn't grow up in Havana, but Fonseca is a very common Spanish last name. Still not nearly as common as Taylor. Why? What did this Guillermo Fonseca do?” he asked.

“Nothing. Forget I even asked. I've got to be going. Thank you for the Kalik's and the time. Next time we need to meet somewhere you don't work,” I said rising up from my chair.

“Where I don't work? That's easy. Finding someplace in Miami *you* don't work, now *that's* going to be difficult,” he said smiling at me.

I patted him on the shoulder and smiled before weaving once again through the chairs left askew and the tables in need of cleaning. The calypso band was set up and looked like they'd be starting soon. I was nearly away from the restaurant when I spied the waitress by an open side door that leads to the kitchen. She looked like she was taking a much needed, but unscheduled break. She was drinking a soda from a cup with a straw. I stopped and drew close to her. I pressed a ten dollar bill in her hand. Santiago always comps my meals, but I feel inclined to take care of the staff. She thanked me. Her heavy accent was definitely not Cuban. I asked her if she was from Caracas. She shook her said no.

"Barquisimeto," she said.

"Where's that?" I asked her.

"Eh...oeste de Caracas."

"West of Caracas, oh okay. What's your name?"

"Alondra."

I had a difficult time understanding her because of her accent.

"I'm sorry. What?"

"Alondra."

"How do you spell that?"

She sheepishly smiled and looked behind her. There were timecards in a rack above a paint-chipped, wall-mounted timeclock. She pulled her timecard from a slot and presented it to me. Alondra Briceño was written on the top of the card.

"Okay. Alondra Briceño," I said, reading her timecard.

I stepped past her and put her card back in the open slot. There were about twenty cards in their respective places. One in particular caught my eye.

Guille Fonseca.

Chapter Twenty-Two

GUILLE.

Santiago pointed out that I didn't grow up in Havana. That may be true, but I know enough Spanish to know that "Guille" is a common nickname for Guillermo. Granted, there could be more than one Guillermo Fonseca in Miami—in fact, a safe wager would say that there are many. Scott Lew said about his source that he was "reputable," and came from a family of "reliable information."

This was not passing the smell test.

It would be easy to turn right around and march back into Scotty's Landing and accuse Santiago of lying to me and demand answers from him. That would have gotten me nowhere. People like Santiago cycle in a world of information, loyalties, and severities. He may have a measure of loyalty to me, but the power of his loyalty to his sister's son would be stronger. It would be easy to spend a little time in the Coconut Grove area and spot-check back in when Guillermo "Guille" Fonseca was working. If Santiago was as cagey as I thought he was, then he'd probably already called Guille and either fired him or told him to stay away from Scotty's Landing. Santiago more than likely thought I knew more then I said. This would need to be a high-wire walk of not upsetting Santiago, locating Guille, and keeping my responsibility to the DEA. It's a lot like having a rat in your house. You may not know where the rat is exactly, but by closing doors and eliminating water sources you can force him into a smaller space. The rat's easier to locate in a smaller space.

I needed to get Guille into a smaller space.

Tipping his uncle off that I knew of him would put him in the wide-open spaces. Wide open like an airplane trip to Houston, Mexico City or somewhere else he could lay low for months.

As far as I knew Guille wasn't a reason why Scott Lew was in the hospital. He might be a contributing factor, but I really just needed to talk to him, to know if he knew how to find Viktor Moshienko. The situation with Guille was in my limited span of control. I had time. How much time I wasn't sure, but I had time to focus on what was in my span of control.

Back in my car I put the air conditioning on high and lowered all the windows. I did a few laps around the large parking oval in front of city hall and let the car's hot interior air blow out. Trying to air condition air is easier than trying to air condition hot air. In the process of doing this very Miami hack is when my cell phone rang.

"Hello."

"Hey, it's me Hammy," she said somewhat breathlessly.

"Did you get my message?" I asked.

"Yes, I did. I ran the prints through AFIS…again! You're I.T. people must be right because this time they came back with a match. Are you ready for this? They come back to a Russian named Yury Rudakov."

I needed to play this off as though I was hearing it for the first time. Surely McBride and the other McWhoevers wouldn't want me to reveal anything about our conversation in the Taurus last night.

"I'll save you the aggravation of spelling it for me. Just text me his name please. What do you know about him?"

"I know it makes more sense why our shooter used a KBP Tula P-96 gun. Russian shooter, Russian gun. That's pretty logical, no?"

"Has this Rudakov guy ever been arrested?"

"No, his prints were part of his passport package. He came to

Miami from Panama. I sent this information over to the DEA. They want to meet in two hours at their offices in the Seattle Building at the Koger Center. Can you make it?"

I saw the wheels starting to turn. I just didn't want to get crushed under them.

"Yeah. I'll see you there," I said.

TWO HOURS LATER I was walking through the lobby of the Seattle Building in the Koger Office Park Center. The office park, constructed when available land was cheap, lies in the direct flight path of Miami international Airport. Every eight to ten minutes a rumbling jetliner flies overhead making nearly every outside conversation cease. I was happy to step into the non-descript lobby and take the elevator to the second floor. Stepping off the elevator I ran into Matias Marroquín. He was holding a white Styrofoam coffee cup in his hand. The coffee inside looked horrid.

"Coming to the big reveal?" he asked me.

"Is it a boy or a girl?"

"Ha. It's Russian, that's all I know," he said.

I followed him into a commercially standard conference room.

Standard.

Already seated were Agent Vince Walker, ASAC Mandeville, and Hammy Garzon. Both Marroquín and I took open available seats. Although we'd all spoken at length many times previously, the room was uncharacteristically quiet. We waited silently for whatever it was we were supposed to be waiting for. Three minutes later in walked SAC John Grayson and two other men. One of the men looked like he might be American; the other was a little bit diminutive, and his suit had definite European tailoring to it. Grayson spoke first.

"Hello everybody. Thank you for getting here on short notice. With me is Inspector John Bazini and Agent Jean Luc Janvier.

Inspector Bazini is with the New York City Police Department, and he is seconded to Interpol. Agent Janvier is with the Belgium National Police, and he is permanently assigned to Interpol. Before you ask, seconded means that the NYPD has loaned Inspector Bazini to Interpol for thirty-six months. Agent Janvier and the Inspector are part of the Odessa Task Force. The Odessa Task Force was established three years ago to infiltrate and combat Russian crime groups. I'll step aside for a minute and let both men talk to you."

Bazini and Janvier looked at each other and with a small comical gesture Janvier nudged Bazini to speak.

"Uh…good afternoon, I'm John Bazini from the NYPD. Originally assigned to Midtown South in Manhattan when I got seconded as an NYPD representative to Interpol. Like Special Agent in Charge Grayson said, me and Jean Luc are part of a task force working Russian crime syndicates. We often hop over the southeastern states and spend our time in North Beach here in Miami and Brighton Beach in New York. We're here today because of the recent information that's come to light about Viktor Moshienko."

Hammy looked at me, a little agape, eyes narrowed with a confused look. It was Jean Luc who spoke next.

"*Allo,* my name is Jean Luc Janvier," he said with a slight French accent. "I would like to dispel the confusion you may have. Interpol has determined that Yury Rudakov is an alias used by a known Russian criminal named Viktor Moshienko. Moshienko entered the United States eight months ago on a forged passport using the alias, Yury Rudakov. Moshienko was being sought by Interpol under a green notice. We have elevated his wanted status to a red notice. After the shooting of your DEA agent I would classify it as a deep red notice, if we had such a thing," he said.

"What's a green notice?" asked Walker.

Jean Luc studied Walker for a second and then spoke. "An Interpol green notice means he was on a list to be monitored. From our headquarters in Lyon, France we track transnational crime groups and individuals. Our personnel became aware of Viktor

Moshienko through investigative channels. We have determined that he's a strong suspect in the murder of an Albanian diplomatic courier in Budapest. We also think he had a hand in the murder of a businessman in Paris. The courier was carrying two and half million dollars of Panamanian Bearer Share Bonds intended for a water treatment project in Tirana, Albania. For those who are unaware, a Bearer Share Bond from Panama has no ownership name on them. Whoever possesses them is considered the rightful legal owner. When he killed the courier, he essentially stole two and half million dollars from the Albanian government."

"And he was only a green notice?" blurted Mandeville, wide-eyed.

Jean Luc gave a slight smile.

"We are a worldwide support law enforcement organization. Adjudication, although highly desirable, is what we try to assist with. It is the investigative support that we excel at. We are here to help you. So please let me and John tell you what we can," he said as Mandeville nodded in agreement.

Jean Luc continued: "We believe last summer the businessman in Paris was going to purchase the Bearer Share Bonds for seventy cents on the dollar in smelted gold from multiple refineries. Moshienko determined the gold's purity was far less than 99.9%, and Moshienko killed him for trying to defraud him."

Inspector Bazini added, "We've been holding some strong evidence linking Moshienko to the murders in Budapest and Paris. When Miss Garzon submitted the fingerprints she extracted from the gun magazine, those prints in conjunction with the prints the DEA gathered from the glass tabletop were slam dunks to us that Moshienko was now in Miami. The prints also matched the scanned fingerprints that INS took of him when he entered the U.S."

"So this guy Moshienko comes into the U.S, under an alias of Yury Rudakov, and now he's loose somewhere after shooting Scott. So how did he end up in a twenty-kilogram deal in Hialeah?" asked Marroquín.

"That's what we'd like to know," said Bazini with one eyebrow raised.

"So where do we start?" asked Marroquín.

Agent Janvier said, "His point of entry was on a Lan Chile flight from Panama into Miami International Airport. We should see if we can pull surveillance video from the airport and see if anybody met him at the airport. That would be a good start. John and I will continue to work our contacts in North Beach and Normandy Beach here in Miami. He's got to be frequenting one of the Russian café's or markets there. Any contacts the DEA have in the field that would be a big help too."

I sat quietly thinking to myself what McBride had said.

"Interpol is going to jump all over this. SAC Grayson and the rest of the Boy Scouts at DEA will be jumping through hoops for Interpol. That will more than likely lead to nothing."

I felt it was time for me to ask a few questions.

"Have the Panama Bearer Share Bonds shown up anywhere yet? Have they been deposited or been converted at any European banks?"

Agent Janvier answered, "The serial numbers of the bonds were recorded by the Albanians but in many banks, especially banks in Panama, that won't matter. Whoever has the bonds has the value of the bonds."

"You said the individual killed last summer in Paris was trying to rip off Moshienko with less than pure gold in an exchange for the bonds. What do you know about him and what exactly is smelted gold from multiple refineries?" I asked him.

Agent Janvier looked down at his shoes contemplating the best way to answer my question. He addressed the room more so than me. "Many companies that refine a lot of gold from Europe usually acquire it in estate jewelry, gilded frames, dental crowns from cadavers, family heirlooms, pre-century war medals, buttons, uniform ornamentations, pre-World War I coins, things like that. I don't know the background of the victim other than that he was in the refining business. What we do know is that Moshienko is a former KGB cleaner,"

"A cleaner?" asked Mandeville.

"A professional killer. A cleaner. " Janvier said with a shake of his head, annoyance written in his raised eyebrows. "The KGB is the absolute heart of the Russian mafia. Russian organized crime poses a major threat to legitimate business development in Russia. That includes any of the former Soviet republics, too. Organized groups are splintering and multiplying as gangs in Russia, they control forty percent of all private businesses, sixty percent of state-owned companies, and easily half of the commercial banks in Russia. This is why the Odessa Task Force is so vital. Its why we are here in front of you today. Interpol believes that more than half of Russia's largest banks are linked to organized crime. The sudden presence of huge amounts of American currency in Russia is alarming to us at Interpol."

"Guys you have to look at it like this," Inspector Bazini piped up. "The Soviet Central Bank has been printing rubles at such a rate that the ruble's been devalued. Now there's a colossal flood of American dollars into the Russian economy. The American dollars were released by the KGB from its war chest of drug-trafficking money obtained over the last fifteen years of drug sales in the United States. If the KGB is the state within the state that we think it is, this will create big problems. Bazini paused to look at us all. "Big problems that we cannot turn away from. The Russian crime groups are making international networks grow, they infiltrate and infect all legitimate business and government agencies and they operate with near impunity around the world. Moshienko is one of many, but *he's* the one who shot your agent, and we think killed two others…and he is here in Miami. Is that bad enough for you?" Inspector Bazini finished.

McBride had said last night that the Russians intended to ally themselves with the South American drug cartel bosses to maximize the distribution of cocaine in Europe. "*Those dollars circulating outside the U.S. can't end up in Russian hands.*" His worry had been that a strong, Russian-controlled drug trade in Europe would infringe upon the McWhatstheirnames' missions over there.

After an odd, sobering pause, SAC Grayson spoke next.

"I think it's important for all of us to try and beat the bushes with any Russian or Baltic State informants or people we know. We need to find this guy, Moshienko. So either as solo artists or in groups, let's get on this. We'll be making it a Priority One for all the field agents in the Miami office. On the desk by the door are business cards for Inspector Bazini and Agent Janvier. Take them with you and notify the Interpol agents if you discover anything. I said it days ago and I'm saying it again: We *need* to find him. He shot one of our own. Now we have a name. We hope to have a picture in an hour or so from his forged passport."

I clearly remember what he looked like. It's hard to forget what the person looks like who fired a gun at you, trying to kill you.

Each of us filed out of the drab, institutional conference room with handshakes from the Interpol duo and their business cards in our hands. Then we congregated in the hallway. It was the meeting after the meeting. None of us had any connections with Russians or any eastern Europeans. Mandeville suggested that Hammy be on standby for evidence collecting that might be needed. She told Marroquín and Walker to start in the Normandy Isles section of Miami Beach and see what they could drum up. She recognized that I wasn't under her command and asked that I go back to Coral Gables and look into if any waiters or waitresses in the hotels and restaurants were Russian. Again, I could hear McBride's voice.

"*Interpol is going to jump all over this. SAC Grayson and the rest of the Boy Scouts at DEA will be jumping through hoops for Interpol. That will more than likely lead to nothing.*"

I said my goodbyes and left. I cursed the day as Miami traffic appeared to be conspiring against me on every road I tried to use. Santiago would be a good person to talk to about Russian influences. Today was a self-inflicted shot-in-the-foot moment for me. I didn't think I could call on him. At least not yet. If Scott Lew's informant

Guillermo "Guille" Fonseca was indeed Santiago's nephew, it would help to talk with him, but there was no guarantee he could tell me anything of value.

How did I get sucked into this quagmire of a case?

Major Brunson was very pleased. We recovered nearly all of the $400,000 and the kilograms that Curbelo was going to sell us were off the streets of Miami. Dario Curbelo, a known drug trafficker, was dead. Convicted criminal Eberardo Rincon-Giraldez "*El Loco Curo*" was also dead. From a Coral Gables perspective this was a done deal. Put a bow on it and send it off.

Unfortunately, Coral Gables the city was different than Cade Taylor, the Coral Gables employee.

Moshienko shot Scott Lew, he killed two men in Europe, he killed *El Loco Curo,* and he tried to kill me. Repeatedly.

They said Moshienko was a cleaner.

A professional killer.

The stop and go slog of traffic gave me time to think about Viktor Moshienko. *This isn't child's play. If he is still in Miami, then he is a threat to not just me but to anybody who stands in his way.* A person like Moshienko could navigate cities like Budapest, Paris, and Miami with ease. He could travel easily in and out of Panama. According to McBride, he'd been in the TBA—the tri-border area of Paraguay, Argentina, and Brazil. I put it all together as quickly as I could, my brain connecting the dots to narrow in on him.

This isn't the kind of guy who will check into a flea bag hotel with a neon vacancy sign flashing outside through his grimy venetian blinds.

He isn't flashy and doesn't want to attract attention to himself.

He prefers five-star hotels but will avoid them as they routinely test and check their guest's credit cards every eight to twelve hours. He doesn't want to risk an overzealous or glitchy fraud protection unit in a credit card company tripping him up.

He more than likely doesn't care about views or amenities.

He wants a hotel room closer to the stairs than to the elevator.

He was pale when I saw him in Hialeah. If he'd been in Miami for a few months then swimming pools, beaches, golf courses, and tennis courts were not part of his routine. Golf courses and tennis courts would necessitate the need to interact with others. He's an isolated coffee shop or back-area bookstore kind of guy.

He'll want to be near an egress point where he can make his way out of Miami if he has to. A nice hotel near the airport that has access to vital roads and drive thru fast-food windows where he won't have to talk to anyone who would remember him. If his credit card gets denied he can just drive quickly away.

The Blue Lagoon area of Miami would be ideal for him.

There was a Hilton Hotel there, the French Hotel Sofitel was there, as well as three or four other notable chains like Hampton and Holiday Inn. It would be a fishing expedition, but I decided to drive to the Hotel Sofitel, find a comfortable chair in their lobby and see what happens.

The drive from the Seattle Building in the Koger Center to Blue Lagoon should have only taken fifteen minutes. Today it was nearly ninety minutes as traffic was backed for miles because a Home Depot truck overturned spilling its contents of faucets, plumbing fixtures, and pre-assembled vanities all across the Palmetto Expressway, stopping traffic in both directions. One direction because of the truck and the other direction because everyone felt a compelling need to slow down and look at the FHP troopers and tow truck drivers standing near the truck. When I got to the Hotel Sofitel, I eschewed the valet telling him it was a company car and I had to park it myself. I gave him five bucks anyway. No reason for him to be penalized because I want to park near the entrance and have quick access to my car.

He'll want to be near an egress point where he can make his way out…

The similarities that both Moshienko and I shared were not unnoticed by me. To be in this ongoing VIN world I must be in this constant VIN mode. All the time. Always. It sure wreaks havoc on the old central nervous system living like this. Even if I walked away from the VIN world, I would forever be changed by my experiences in it. I have come to understand that I am not the same person because of it. Moving forward with my life, I realize the long hours have shorn me of ever being a morning person. I've struck up too strong a relationship with the moon and the characters that cast their shadows in its light. I've learned distant actions tell me more than any words ever whispered up close in my ear. My life became a morass of lies and mistrust until either the lies become truths, or the trust breaks through the deceit.

Real eyes realize real lies.

Maybe that was why Gina and I were no longer together. I became darkness and she remained light. I became lost at sea, and she stayed on shore. My changing world was incomprehensible in her universe. How could I expect her to keep up with my changes when I wasn't in control of them myself? Occupational therapy needs a new title because no therapy could have prepared me for this occupation, being paid to be someone else, living in a world with no boundaries or rules. We as humans see finality in everything. We see finish lines and endings. Our movies have endings. Our automobile races have finish lines. We see death from a distance in a funeral home. We talk amongst ourselves as the body lies in state as though it were some sort of room addition. We experience death in the next to last row. As a minister talks of the deceased, we sneak looks at our cell phones. For most of us death doesn't look us in the eye and say, "*We have started our relationship in a manner unbecoming of the men we are.*"

I walked into the grand lobby of the Hotel Sofitel. I found a comfortable chair and sat down. From my vantage point I could see the elevators and the large sweeping staircase. Near my chair was a pristine *Condé Nast Traveler* magazine. I opened it and put it across my lap. Within ten minutes a vibrant young woman came over to me carrying a circular round tray.

"Can I get you anything?" she asked.

"What kind of beer do you have?"

"We have quite a few but the manager's special is Kronenbourg on draft," she said.

"That sounds excellent. I'll have a Kronenbourg. Thank you."

The magazine was a necessary prop. The beer was just necessary.

She returned minutes later with a frosted Pilsner glass filled to the brim with the French beer. I thanked her and she set it on a thick coaster on the end table next to me. Sipping on the beer, I nonchalantly surveilled the lobby. Within forty minutes she brought me a second beer and I was beginning to think the idea of surveillance was not so bad after all.

I had not heard from anyone since the meeting today. I assumed Marroquín and Walker were trying to figure a way to integrate themselves into the tightly-knit Russian community of North Beach. I sure hoped they weren't trying to work the Russian bath houses. They'd stick out like a tall tree on a Kansas prairie. Here, I felt I blended in very nicely. I had my magazine, a nice rapport with a waitress, a steady flow of French beer and no one was the wiser.

Except I needed to keep reminding myself that although to all the guests and visitors of the hotel I was inconspicuous, Moshienko had seen me.

I needed to stay hypervigilant. If Viktor Moshienko was staying in this hotel, he was very familiar with it, and he'd seen me. He knew what I looked like just like I knew what he looked like.

My cellphone rang. I recognized the number.

"Well?"

"Okay Cade, come on by. We need to talk." Then the phone went dead.

It was Santiago.

Chapter Twenty-Three

It took me another hour to get to Scotty's Landing. The sun had already started to arc over the green and white tent. The crowd had changed from families and businessmen having lunch to businessmen and sunburned water sport enthusiasts having drinks at the bar, their numbers so large they'd spilled over to the first rows of chairs and tables. The mood was festive and the crowd a bit loud as they vied for the bartender's and each other's attention. I saw the Venezuelan waitress, Alondra. She looked weary but was still in the midst of doing her job. She saw me and I motioned that I'd be seating myself back towards the water away from the infectious raucousness of the bar. She immediately understood my sign language. I confidently sat down knowing that she'd tell Santiago I was here. As was my forte, I lost myself in the view of the choppy bay water. This time I didn't see Santiago until he was nearly abreast of me. He had an iced bucket of Kalik beer in his hands. A sullen young man stood behind him. Santiago put down the bucket of Bahamian beer in the center of the table.

"A Cuban peace offering," he said.

"Is that how you do it in Cuba? Use your island tradition to give me something from another island?" I said jokingly.

Santiago quickly sat down and motioned to the young man to sit down at a vacant chair at the table. The young man had a shaved head and a thick mustache. A singular small gold hoop earring glinted in his left ear. His stocky build was starting to evade him and move more towards the chubby side of young adulthood. I figured him to be about twenty years old.

"Cade, this is my nephew, Guillermo," said Santiago as he popped the beer caps off of three beers. He put one of the nicely chilled beers in front of me and one in front of Guillermo.

"Guillermo. I'll bet they call you Guille," I said.

"Yes, sir," he replied.

"Thank you, but you don't need to call me sir. Call me Cade. Which do you prefer, Guillermo or Guille?"

"Guille."

"You prefer Guille because all your life your mother called Guille. Everyone called you Guille but one day you will meet a woman who will steal your heart and she will call you Guillermo. She'll be the only person in your life who does call you Guillermo, and you'll love hearing her voice in every vowel and rolling 'r,'" I said. Then looking at his uncle I said, "Isn't that right Santy?"

"Fuck you. It's Santiago. Just because you got that simplfied first gringo name doesn't mean we have to be shortened like you," he said, laughing.

I turned my attention to Guille.

"Guille, I am sure your uncle told you what I do. I'm going to tell you up front be very careful what you say or tell me. It's not my intention to get you in trouble. I just need to see if you can help me with a little dilemma I have. If I say something or ask you something and you're unsure, you don't have to answer me. You can ask your uncle here if it's okay to respond. Understand?" I said to him as gently as I could.

"We might have our own dilemma here. That is why we asked you to come by," said Santiago.

I wasn't expecting that. I was taken aback by Santiago's comment. I decided to try and at least resolve my own dilemma before I assisted them with whatever it was they had going on. Just like in the airplane in-flight demonstration, you have to put your own mask on before assisting others. I needed to put my mask on first.

"Let me start," I said as I took a long pull off the beer bottle. "Guille, I believe you know the DEA agent who was shot in Hialeah a few days ago. I believe you *both* know him because the DEA agent told me to my face that his source 'is reputable and comes from a family of reliable information.' He also said your name. He said Guillermo Fonseca. Your uncle and I have an arrangement. I don't ask him anything he doesn't want to tell me and vice versa. Guille, if you turned this DEA agent onto some information, I want to know what you know so that I can find the man who shot him. The DEA agent obviously documented you as a confidential informant. You were hoping to be paid for this information. You know the equation. You know how this works. You weren't selling or buying anything, so I don't see any criminality here. I just want to know what you know," I told him.

Guille also took a sip of beer and looked across the table at Santiago.

"Tio?" he said to his uncle.

Santiago leaned forward on the table, resting both elbows on it. He clasped his hands in front of himself.

"Cade, Guille is my sister's only son. She has a daughter, too. Lisandra. Guille and Lisandra are only a year apart in age. He is twenty and she just turned nineteen. They both have been working here for a few months. It's been a good way for me to keep them employed until they decide what they both want to do when they graduate from Florida International University."

"FIU, huh?" I said to Guille, and he flashed a quick evaporating smile.

"Lisandra has gone missing. We haven't seen her for two days. No one has seen her. We tried to ping her cell phone. Nothing. We think it's related to Guille and the situation in Hialeah. When you came in today asking about Guille the lightbulb went off and I asked him, and he told me about Hialeah. I'm going to tell you that I told him to keep his mouth shut, but *I* can tell you. If I tell you, then on the surface it is hearsay and not fully admissible and exonerates Guille from self-incrimination, yada yada yada, you know the bullshit," Santiago said.

I decided to switch gears. A young girl missing was more important than me hearing redundant or already-known information.

"Okay, we can get to what I want later. Tell me about Lisandra. Why do you think she is missing, and do you think someone has her?"

"She's a typical teenage girl. She's never without her cell phone. She has missed two days of shifts and she has not been home to my sister's house in two days."

"Have you called the police?" I asked him.

They looked at each other quizzically.

"I mean the real police. Not me. I'm the police, but you know, the actual police. The ones who handle this stuff," I said.

"Cade, the same bus the police would roll out to find her would roll over both of us, too. We need to keep this in *la familia*. We need to keep this in our circle. Whoever has her, if they want money or anything, I can try and put it together. I can't trust the police to do it correctly, you know what I mean? This is a delicate situation."

"Has anyone reached out to you?" I asked him.

He looked at Guille and nodded. Guille pulled out his phone and scrolled through the keypad before placing the phone on the table. He pushed a button and a voice message played on the telephone's speaker. A man's voice. It was a language I didn't understand.

"U nas yest' ona. Prinesite moi dokumenty."

[Y нас есть она. Принесите мои документы.]

I didn't know what to say. I had no idea what I just heard. I didn't know if they were trying to prank me or make up a story to try and protect Guille.

Santiago said, "One of the guys who we buy octopus from speaks Russian. He said it means 'We have the girl, bring me my papers.'"

“We? As in more than one. You’re sure?” I asked him.

“Yes. He said we.”

Viktor Moshienko by himself was a force. If he was with allies, we had a much more serious problem.

“Papers? What papers?” I asked him.

“We don’t know. He called a second time after we talked to our octopus supplier. Guille was able to shout into the phone ‘proof’ twice before the man hung up.

“Santiago, tell me what you can about Hialeah,” I said trying to shield Guille from incriminating himself.

“Guille wants to live like a man. He thinks what his uncle Santiago does is cool and lucrative. He’s young, he has no idea that the times change and so does the business. What *tio Santiago* used to do is not replicable in today’s new world of technology and the people in the business are not like the early days of my youth. Still, he sees Scotty’s Landing and other things and thinks one big score can tilt the world in his direction. Guille got involved with a guy he thought was reputable and the guy asked him to act as go-between on a twenty kilo deal in Hialeah. He had no idea the guy was setting up the seller to get killed. Actually, it looks like everyone was going to get killed. The guy owed a debt to some Russian, so he set the deal up. Big surprise was that the guy who was supposed to get killed brought some muscle and the muscle got hit first. The buyer had a gun and upended the whole thing. Turns out the buyer was a cop, and the Russian shot the DEA agent as he ran out. Whatever the guy owed the Russian, he told the Russian that Guille has it. We think the Russian kidnapped Lisandra and is holding her hostage. Sound familiar?”

My eyes must have been as big as saucers. I stared at them both in silence. I chugged the remnants of my beer and put the empty bottle on the table. I reached into the ice bucket and pulled out another. I took a healthy swig from that beer. I then sat back in my chair in stunned silence, trying to take in everything I had just heard. It was nearly incomprehensible what Santiago had just said. Unsolicited and without any prodding, Guille spoke.

"I swear, I had no idea it was a set-up, I never thought he would lie to me like that," The boy blurted out with watery eyes.

"Who was this guy who set up the whole deal and the hit? What makes him so reputable and trustworthy?" I asked.

"We've been looking for him, but he's gone. His office is shut down and there is just a note on the door," said Santiago.

"Who is he?" I said again.

"He's a dentist. He's been Guille and Lisandra's dentist for ten years."

I closed my eyes. My elbow was bent on the table. I ran my hands through my hair, keeping my eyes closed. I cradled my forehead in my hand.

"Aroldo Cordozo. His office is in Bay Harbor Islands," I said softly.

"You know him? You know him?" Santiago was nearly shouting with excitement.

I stood up quickly. I was reluctant to leave the casual tropical vibe of the place and the great beer but this whole situation had suddenly taken on a warp-speed pace. If Viktor Moshienko did in fact have Lisandra time was going to be precious. A guy like him would kill her without blinking an eye then come for Guille himself. Santiago might be buying not one, but two caskets in a few days if we didn't act fast

No time for "nice to meet you" or handshakes goodbye. I was racing against the clock. "You need to call the cops. If you choose not to call them then at least keep me informed each step along the way. Guille, don't go anywhere, and you stay in constant contact with your uncle. Santiago, don't let him alone. Anywhere! If they got Lisandra, they'll come for him too. If they call again, keep recording the calls," I said, before briskly walking away.

"Where are you going?" yelled Santiago.

I didn't answer him. I was already dialing my phone as I cut across the marina parking lot. My first call was to DEA Agent Walker.

"What's up?"

"Hey Vincent, when you took the dentist, Aroldo Cordozo to the Miami Detention Center how did that go down?"

"Um, let me see. He begged to make a call to his attorney. I waited until you and Mathias were in place on the house. I held off on having him call his attorney as long as I could. Our legal team said the charges of not reporting a gunshot victim to the authorities, practicing trauma medicine without a medical license, and administering a known opioid to a non-dental, in-need patient would stick but a decent attorney would say the money he received from Curbelo could be argued was payment for providing medical care. Since he showed no knowledge of the money or the kilos in the coffee sack, they said to not charge him with money laundering, and conspiracy to traffic in twenty kilograms of cocaine. The charges were actually more state charges, so he went to Dade County Jail instead of MDC. I had to call an Office of Inspector General agent to co-sign the arrest form. It took the OIG agent about an hour to get there. You know what really pissed me off? He was able to bond out before we were even through with the paperwork."

"Wait! What?" I shouted into the phone.

"Once he was inside Dade County Jail, they let him make a call. There's a whole bank of numbers posted on the wall for bail bond agents. He must have got a good one because she showed up super quick and bonded him out."

"She?"

"Yeah, a female bail bond agent," he said.

"Let me guess. Tight jeans tucked into boots, reddish-brown, curly-wavy hair that went past her shoulders?"

"Yeah, she was a real looker. How'd you know?"

"I gotta go," I said as I hung up abruptly.

If Auburn McKenna had no issue pretending to be a U.S. Marshal, then obviously pretending to be a bail bondsman would be a walk in the park for her.

When I'd been trying to call McKenna, she wasn't in Tampa assisting the Florida Marine Patrol like I thought. She was bailing out Cordozo from jail.

My next call was to Hammy.

"Hello?"

"Hammy, did you ever get a print from the bloody bills that were in the stack that we got from the dentist's office?"

"Hello to you too. Well for your information I went all the way up to Bay Harbor Islands. The guy was still in the office, Agent Walker hadn't transported him yet. The dentist said it was Curbelo's fingerprints on the money. He thought I was some sort of attorney at first, kept saying he was just holding the money for Curbelo. He called it 'oh shit money.' Like when something goes wrong, and you yell 'Oh shit! I have to leave,'" she said.

"Hammy, did you print the money? Yes, or no?"

"Slow down, what's the rush? Yes, I printed the money. The prints weren't Curbelo's."

"Hammy. Listen closely. The dentist's name is Aroldo Cordozo. He was booked by Walker and an OIG agent into DCJ. Hammy, see if you can get those booking prints and compare them to the money print we thought was Curbelo's," I said to her, using her name over and over again as if it would sink in the severity of my words.

"Aye, aye, Capitano!" she said mockingly.

"No messing around. I need that information sooner than later," I said, hanging up on her.

I was doing a very intense burn over the way I missed the obvious. Miami police officer Denny Byrne said that Dr. Aroldo Cordozo bailed Dario Curbelo out of jail. When Auburn Mckenna posed as a U.S. Marshal, she said that the Marshals' office had given Dario Curbelo a new identity of Ricardo Sanabria. That couldn't be true—she wasn't a U.S. Marshal! She must have somehow gotten together with the detained passport-forging Paraguayan woman in Argentina's Chaco Province. Once they had a new identity for Curbelo they needed to have him disappear. What better way to kill off Curbelo than in a raging inferno? Only problem was they never counted on Arson Investigator Jeff Baggett's report to be filed.

Baggett said the body was 100% burned. He even had to use the measurement of the pelvis to determine the sex. Dental records would be the best way to identify the body.

Hammy Garzon had said, *"According to our records, Dario Curbelo from Ciudad de Estes Paraguay died in a 1996 housefire at 160 Northeast 164th Street in North Miami."*

They wanted the body to be burned beyond recognition, so they intentionally set the fire and put some adversary or a problematic individual to the noble lie in the fire. They achieved what they set out to do but now needed to have a dentist submit dental records of the deceased to allow the medical examiner to identify the body.

Dr. Aroldo Cordozo.

"Since then I became his dentist, but we also started socializing."

Then the Washington sneaky gang used their best "in the sense of national security" reason to have the Dade County Medical Examiner seal the file.

The noble lie continued.

It was also starting to crystalize in my mind. How could I have missed all these obvious clues? Dario Curbelo was definitely looking to sell twenty kilograms of cocaine, but he was just a lackey for Aroldo Cordozo. Guille Fonseca was used as an intermediary to put some distance between Cordozo and Moshienko.

"Guille got involved with a guy he thought was reputable and the guy asked him to act as go between on a twenty-kilo deal in Hialeah. He had no idea the guy was setting up the seller to get whacked."

The deal starts to go down and Viktor Moshienko shot Curbelo, but didn't kill him. Curbelo made a hasty retreat to Dr. Aroldo Cordozo's office not only seeking medical attention but to return the unsold twenty kilograms and the money he thought would be a bonus to his friend and possible boss Cordozo. He probably told Cordozo that a tall pale blonde man shot him. Cordozo then knew that his plan to have Curbelo murdered had gone awry and now Viktor Moshienko would be even more pissed that Cordozo put him in that predicament. Cordozo still owed Moshienko a debt. Moshienko would be looking for Cordozo. That is when our favorite family dentist got creative and told Moshienko that Guille had what he was looking for.

"Whatever the guy owed the Russian, he told the Russian that Guille has it. We think the Russian kidnapped Lisandra and is holding her hostage."

Now Santiago's niece Lisandra was being held hostage and would most likely be killed by Moshienko if something wasn't done very soon. Cordozo thought he was in the clear. There was just something that still gnawed at my brain.

Auburn McKenna.

What if McKenna had gone off script from the other McAssholes? What if McCarron and McBride thought she was all patriotic red, white, and blue, when in fact she was U.S. mint green. This might all be about the money. The vast amount of money that is circulating in Europe and in the Tri-Border Area. McCarron had put the annual estimation at twelve billion dollars.

"They aren't mudholes *you moron, they're full-fledged cities. We're talking about population centers of hundreds of thousands of people. Didn't you hear the man? Twelve billion dollars and Russian and Islamic groups!"*

There was more than enough money in twelve billion dollars for McKenna and Cordozo to have a fruitful, affluent life together. McKenna and Cordozo together? I kept thinking she was involved with Curbelo. Maybe she wasn't fully in with Curbelo. Maybe she was an actual accomplished asset gatherer, but was gathering Curbelo for her own incarnation of a noble lie. A noble lie for her own agenda cloaked in the noble lies that she and her companions were spinning. She seemed upset when Curbelo was killed but I made that assumption based on only what I heard on the telephone.

McKenna was more concerned about herself being notified than her alleged U.S. Marshals' office. She corrected herself but her first reaction was "Why wasn't *I* notified?" Whatever her relationship was with Curbelo, be it professional, past, or recent lovers, it made no difference. I was now believing that her relationship with Cordozo was more vital to this investigation. I remembered Cordozo telling me that although he and Curbelo were both from Cuidad de Este they did not know each other growing up. That could be a lie. He said initially his relationship with Curbelo was forged on a love for soccer. Especially Paraguayan soccer.

"You know just shared interests like futból and food. Not American football. Futból like soccer."

McKenna seemed to have a strong love for soccer too. Especially Paraguayan soccer.

"It is one of FIFA's six continental confederations. You know, the soccer governing body? CONMEBOL is responsible for the organization of South American soccer's major international teams and tournaments. You follow soccer? You know the world's game?"

I'd pressed McKenna about whether her passport stamps would align with the stamps in Curbelo's legitimate passport, or with his forged Ricardo Sanabria passport. She hung the telephone up on me.

It seems that everything happened last summer. The Albanian courier was murdered in Budapest last summer. The businessman in the metal refining business was killed in Paris last summer. Moshienko was in those cities last summer… So was McKenna.

"You mean like Pilon or Bustillo? No way. No how. Last summer a whole contingency of us had to go to Europe for the world cup in France. There was a threat concerning CONMEBOL. I spent a lot of time in Belgium and France."

So had Cordozo.

"Yes, Europe is a pleasure. Last summer it was beautiful."

Agent Jean Luc Janvier said the murders occurred last summer.

This was all coming together too coincidentally. I had already put the car in gear and was tearing down Bayshore Drive towards I-95. The first call I made was to Marroquín.

"Hello?"

"Mathias! It's Cade Taylor. Where are you at?"

"I'm in front of the Normandy Isles municipal swimming pool. We got a tip some Russians play Durak here every day."

"What the hell is Durak?"

"It's a Russian card game."

"Listen up. I'm going to ask you to break off from there. I got a feeling about something. The dentist. Aroldo Cordozo. Remember him? I got some intel that he was covering the twenty kilo deal and Curbelo was actually working for him. The dentist owes the Russian, Moshienko, something big and Cordozo was going to have the whole deal whacked and let the Russian take the coke and the money as partial or full repayment. The dentist is out and he's in the wind. I think he might be making a run for the boat."

"Are you serious?" he said, incredulous.

"I'm dead serious. Remember how Curbelo had very few personal items even though it was his house? The boat has always been the way out for all of them. It can make Nassau on one tank of gas. It can also make Cuba. These guys have access to false passports, *plus* they're from Paraguay. Havana would welcome them with open arms. Remember that stack of bloody twenties in his dental office?"

"Yeah, I do," he said.

"Hammy heard him call it 'oh shit money.' Like when something goes wrong, and you yell 'Oh shit! I have to leave." This guy's either gone or about to be GOA."

"What's GOA?"

"Gone On Arrival. I'm getting on I-95 right now. See who you can get on this and meet me there. Oh, and by the way—he might be with a tall American woman. Don't trust her. She is *not* to be taken lightly."

"Who's that?" he asked.

"I'll explain later. Just start working the phones and let's get some people there. In case you forgot, the boat is called *Cassiopeia.* Use your government channels and put a watch order on it with INS and the Coast Guard. I'll see you there."

I drove like a madman. I almost overshot my exit. I pulled a Miami slant and cut across three lanes, darting in a diagonal line for the exit. Whoever and whatever I cut off I may or may not hear about on the evening news. If they were from Miami, surely their driving skills were as treacherously good as mine, and I probably didn't even faze them. I wasn't counting the streets as I drove down Biscayne Boulevard. I kept looking for the home of the Whopper. When I saw the Burger King, I turned sharply and bumped and bounced into the franchise parking lot, then drove right through to the backside where I exited and turned east on 90th Street. I eased my car up to the side of Curbelo's house. A realtor sign was already fastened to the side gates that he busted out of on his fateful night. Two-by-fours were across the broken gates to shore the damage up.

I parked and quietly stepped out of my car. I walked down the street towards the basin in Belmar Lake. There were no signs of anyone around, including Marroquín. I was beginning to have second thoughts about my hypothesis. I looked north. In the same dead-end section of the street that I'd parked in when Marroquín and I first set up on the house, I saw McKenna's Chevy Blazer. I called Marroquín.

"I'm ten out," he said as a way of answering.

"The American woman, the one I told you about? Her car is here in the dead end under some sea grape trees. I'm telling you, don't take her lightly. She's NSA but I think she's freelancing and turned off her own porch light."

"Got it. I'm working on getting more people."

"Call Marine Patrol and see if they can block the channel out to the bay," I said as I hung up.

I kept a watchful eye on the boat. Two minutes later I saw the cabin door open.

McKenna came up from below deck and emptied a bucket of water over the side of the *The Cassiopeia.*

Chapter Twenty-Four

My heart was beating at least three times faster. I wanted to call Marroquín again, but I couldn't risk her overhearing me on the phone. The day was completely quiet, and the air was very still. I pulled my phone from my pocket and deftly switched it to silent mode. She had emptied the bucket and was just standing at the aft of the boat, looking around.

I slowly eased back behind a flowering hibiscus bush. Within a minute Cordozo came up from the lower deck of the boat and joined McKenna. They shared a passionate kiss.

That definitely edged my theory to the reality side of the board.

I decided to keep a watchful eye on them. The bow lines were still tied to the pilings and the engine wasn't on. The bilge pump silently trickled water into the channel in a soft cadence stream. The electrical hook-up was still in the socket on the dock. They weren't going anywhere for a few minutes at least.

McKenna was giddy with happiness, laughing and smiling. It was as though she didn't have a care in the world. She stepped off the boat, which caused me to step back even more into the hibiscus bush, and she walked a few feet from the boat towards a garbage can by the sea wall. She removed the lid from the can then walked back and boarded the boat. She said something in Cordozo's ear as she seductively ran her hand across his back. Next she went down below and came back up with a large bag of garbage which she slung over her shoulder as she walked to the garbage can. She swung the bag off her shoulder and placed it in the can. It looked like she was pushing the garbage down into the can.

I was as far back in the hibiscus as I could be. I momentarily lost sight of her. When I did regain sight of her I saw her rise up from her bent position like an uncoiled spring. She was lightning fast. Unbeknownst to me, in the bag she had concealed a Beneli M4 collapsible stock tactical shotgun that she quickly pulled out of the bag. The Beneli M4 was factory-new. She had the stock collapsed making it practically a sawed-off version of itself. It has an "auto-regulating gas-operated" (ARGO) system. The short-stroke design uses two pistons located just ahead of the chamber to function opposite a rotating bolt, thereby making it incredibly easy to operate.

And she was running straight at me with the shotgun aimed right at me. She was smart enough not to yell or draw any attention to herself and she was on me before I could get out of the bush or draw my Glock.

She shoved the muzzle of the shotgun right under my chin and tilted it up, forcing me to raise my head and stand on my toes. I had my hands up in a surrender position. She had fire in her eyes, anger was spilling out of every one of her pores. She was determined to have the upper hand and if she needed to kill me, I had no doubt she would. She yanked my Glock from my hip and pressed the magazine release, and the drop free magazine fell from my Glock onto the ground. She rubbed the slide of the Glock against her thigh hard and the force of her torquing the weapon ejected its lone remaining bullet. She tucked my Glock behind her back in the waistband of her jeans. There was no doubt that Auburn McKenna was versed in weaponry and counter-surveillance. She'd seen me minutes earlier and must have whispered into Cordozo's ear her intentions. She spoke to me softly, but harshly.

"Drop your cell phone. Keep your mouth shut and do not do anything stupid or as God is my witness, I will blow your head off right here! Clasp your arms across your chest. Stick your hands under your armpits. Now walk!"

I slowly removed my cell phone. I dropped it by my foot, and I side kicked it into the street. She had already started pushing me towards the street. She was very adept. She walked on my left side her right arm around my back and waist with the gun pointing at the back of my knee. Anybody looking out their window would be hard pressed to see the shotgun in her hand. One pull of the trigger and she'd blow out my knee from the back. There isn't an orthopedic surgeon on earth who could repair that. There was also a strong chance of her obliterating one of my main arteries. Death would be painful and slow; surviving it would be a brutal existence.

"Get on the boat and stand in the doorway of the cabin. Do it now!"

I stepped on the boat, where Cordozo looked at me and smiled.

"Looks like the shoe is on the other foot. I give you credit for finding us. I apologize, though, because aside from being shark chum I don't see a very glorious future for you. Oh I know! Maybe I'll have her just *shoot you in both hands.* How do you feel about that? Sound familiar?"

"You're not going to get away with this. The DEA is on their way and the Florida Marine Patrol, and the Coast Guard have been notified."

"Well, I guess we better get shoving off then," he said, laughing.

He turned the key in the boat's ignition causing the blower to start dissipating built-up fumes in the engines. I knew that if they hustled, they could be under way in four minutes. It would take the Florida Marine Patrol and the U.S. Coast Guard at least forty minutes to decipher what was being asked of them. After going through their command approvals, dispatch, and then finally getting a vessel moving even more time probably. Time was not an ally for me here. I could try and stall, but both of them—especially her—seemed to be way too professional to fall for any stall tactics. I decided to use a different tactic.

"You know we have Moshienko, and he says you both killed the Albanian in Budapest."

She briefly looked at him then at me. They both laughed.

"What was it you said to me? Oh yes, now I remember. 'Say your prayers Doc. It's finished for you.' Well, let me assure you my police friend, it is not finished for me. It's actually just starting. Now it may be finished for *you*. You're talking nonsense," he said.

"I'm talking nonsense? Are you aware that Lois Lane here was sleeping with Curbelo *and* you at the same time?" I said.

"Maybe you're not following what I'm saying. Necessary things need to be done to get what you necessarily want. What awaits us is far more desirable than what is behind us," Cordozo said.

I was wondering just how long ten minutes could be. I was learning it can be excruciatingly long when you're waiting on the cavalry. In this case the calvary was Marroquín.

"Did you hear me? Moshienko's in custody, and he says you both killed the Albanian in Budapest."

"Moshienko killed the Albanian, you twit," snarled McKenna.

I took a gamble.

"Then if he did, why does he want to kill you both for the Panama Bearer Shares?"

"Cade, you are good at what you do. Unfortunately, you're too good at what you do," said McKenna.

"Good enough to know you both killed the Albanian," I said to her.

"Hey, you repeating moron. No. No, we didn't kill the Albanian. Moshienko killed the Albanian. We told you that. Moshienko was too dumb to move what he took from the Albanian—"

"The Panama bearer shares," I said.

Cordozo was getting frustrated.

"*Yes*, the Panama shares. So he asked me to find a good mover for him. I knew refiners in Europe that I send all the gold fillings, crowns, and flakes to for refining. Moshienko doesn't know anything about what constitutes precious metals. The problem was that the precious metal term covers all types of alloys. Some are composed of maybe sixty percent high noble metal like gold, platinum, or palladium. The Nazis plundered a lot of gold in Europe during World War II. What's circulating is a blend and amalgamation of metals and gold. It's a sifting and liquifying process. That Russian dickhead had no idea what it takes to get that much gold. Moshienko wanted 99% pure gold. When you blend that much precious metal, you're not going to get a 99% purity! That's just the way it is. We were with him in Paris. He didn't like the purity levels. He got impatient. He killed the refiner. It was horrific. In the confusion we ended up with the bearer shares," he said.

"You ended up with the shares? A trained killer like Moshienko got confused because he killed the refiner? Bullshit. You both killed the refiner and took the shares."

"Does it matter, Cade?" McKenna huffed at me. "It's just more information you'll have in your head when you die."

"And Curbelo? You set him up to be killed."

"He was getting too expensive. We cut him out. Moshienko knew he was supposed to kill Curbelo. Had the cocaine deal gone has planned, Moshienko would have had 400k and twenty kilos to sell in Europe for nearly a million. We would've been pretty much even. He blew his own chance. Not our problem. When Curbelo survived the cocaine bloodbath, what better way to eliminate him than to tell you and those DEA cowboys where he was?" He looked at McKenna. "Right honey? Let the government do what you can't do. Works every time!"

The boat engine was primed, and the blowers had rendered it safe to turn the engine on. Cordozo turned on the engines.

"*Mi amore*, take him downstairs. I'll cast off the lines and we'll toss him overboard once we're out beyond the three-mile line," Cordozo said nonchalantly.

"Move," McKenna hissed at me, leveling the shotgun right at my head.

"What about the kid?" I said as I raised my arms and took a step down into the lower part of the boat.

"What kid?" she snapped.

"Oh! He didn't tell you. He brought in a new kid to broker the deal and thought the kid would never figure it out. How do you think I got here? The kid can identify you, Cordozo," I said, smirking at him.

"What?" McKenna shrieked. "You fucking dumbass! You brought someone into the deal? What are you, crazy or something?" she shouted at him.

I needed to keep the confusion and doubt going.

"Your noble lie fuck buddies neglected to tell you that they had Curbelo arrested in 1994. His fingerprints didn't match the cadaver they pulled out of that North Miami house fire," I embellished to her. "You know, the same crispy critter your dentist boyfriend here submitted Curbelo's dental records as being from the burn victim. Since we booked John Wilkes Tooth here a few days ago, we have his prints on file. So does Interpol. If *a fucking ignorant local yokel* like me can find you, then what do you think Interpol is going to do? You said it yourself. I'm just a *low-life, ignorant cop.* Happy sailing, you two losers," I said to her.

"Get down below. NOW!" she yelled at me, her hands shaking.

"Go with him!" raged Cordozo at McKenna.

"You go with him! *I'll* get us underway. I have to do everything anyway. You're as useless as he is!" she screamed back at him.

I was still on the steps that led down to the galley and sitting area, crouching down more out of instinct than any protective value. I had my hands partially up. Every chance I got I searched the boat for a weapon or anything I could improvise as a weapon. I was secretly wondering if Marroquín was in the drive-thru line at Burger King or somewhere.

"*Hijueputa! Puta de Meirda*!" [Son of a bitch! You piece of shit whore!]

I realized that they were either going to shoot each other or take perversive delight in taking turns shooting me. I could no longer wait for Marroquín to arrive.

I needed to make a move.

She turned her attention away from me. It was now or never. I used the stair to launch myself at her like some sort of ballistic missile. I hit her with all my might, making sure to grab the shotgun as I barreled into her. I think they were both shocked. I landed on top of her and held fast to the shotgun. It was like an iron brace between us, wedged crosswise. I knew as long as I stayed away from the barrel end of the shotgun, I had a slim chance.

Cordozo jumped on my back making the Beneli M4 shotgun sandwich complete. He rained punches down on the back of my head. I tucked my chin into my chest to avoid a lucky glancing blow potentially knocking me out. I held fast and hard onto the shotgun. His weight on top of me made it nearly impossible for McKenna to move. She had both hands on the shotgun. With our combined weight on top of her she was unable to throw any punches herself.

Every fighter falls into a rhythm until exhaustion throws that rhythm off. Cordozo was mostly throwing right hand punches. He kept his left arm across my back alternating between trying to hold me down or pull me off of her. I could almost sense when Cordozo was going to throw a punch and I'd move my head to the left, making his punches even less effective.

When fighting two people upright at the same time, the best advantage is to turn them from two into one. Ideally, you want to maneuver them both into a corner so that they become more like a wide two-armed adversary rather than separated by space and having the ability to use all four arms. The same principle applied here. The weight on McKenna rendered her incapable of doing very much. As long as I controlled the shotgun and stayed away from the barrel, I had a chance. When I could, I tried to head butt her but only succeeded in catching her twice in the cheek. Her face was flushed, and she was having a hard time breathing from the compression on her ribs and chest. At first, she cursed a bloody storm but now she was just trying to breathe.

Cordozo was getting tired too. He couldn't understand that with McKenna pulling the shotgun close to her, and me latching onto it, the shotgun was acting like a horizontal anchor bar for me to hold onto.

He was getting very fatigued. I could feel his body shifting on me. He was moving towards the port side of the boat, sliding to my right side. McKenna was breathing hard and gulping shuddering open mouthfuls of air. I opened my legs quickly, then scissored them together very swiftly. I slid diagonally across McKenna. Cordozo slid further off to my right.

McKenna sensed my body shift, felt that she had a chance to get the upper hand and she pulled the trigger on the shotgun.

The 18.5-inch barrel had a very tight choke on it. The shotgun forcefully released all of its 3.5 shell pellets right into Cordozo. It shredded him like rocks through a wet paper towel. Large droplets of blood and entrails sprayed back across both me and McKenna. We were covered. The blast partially lifted Cordozo off of the boat deck and slid him into the portside. He died instantly. His body slumped against the side of the boat and his blood coated nearly every surface of the deck. The spray that erupted from the initial shot was horrific. What didn't erupt from his body was now oozing out in a thick, viscous pool that was roiling across the deck right towards us.

My ears were ringing from the gunshot. Cordite and gunpowder filled my nostrils. I faintly started to recover my hearing only to hear the shrill pitch of a car alarm somewhere in the neighborhood. It must have been triggered by the shotgun's discharge. I'm sure every neighbor heard the loud shot too, but with McKenna and I both on the floor of the boat's deck none of them knew where the gunfire had come from—unless they'd been able to pinpoint the ear-splitting screams. McKenna was shrieking in my ear. She was angry, confused, shocked, and grief stricken. She vowed to kill me, and I thoroughly believed her, if I ended up on the wrong side of this tussle. Cordozo's blood was now seeping against us, coating her hair and getting in her mouth and eyes. This enraged her even more. I was losing traction because of Cordozo's slippery, yet sticky blood. The more we fought over the gun the more blood seemed to cover the both of us. I thought of trying to break away, but I was scared of slipping on the blood, making it even easier for her to kill me. The blood was oozing under her, surrounding us on both sides.

I pushed with my legs. The copious amount of blood acted like a lubricant under her. I was able to move us closer to Cordozo's lifeless body. She struggled against me. We created swirls and loops of blood on the deck from our movements. She tried to knee me but that only weakened her posture more, allowing me to nudge her even closer to Cordozo. He wore a death stare on his face, with both his eyes open and blood flowing not only from his body but from his mouth as well. We were right up against his fresh corpse. I yanked the shotgun hard and wedged the barrel under Cordozo's body. She still had a firm, albeit messy grip on the shotgun. I did too. With the barrel under Cordozo, I made a split-second decision. I figured she'd have to pull the weapon back and then up to shoot me. In her harried state and with all the obscuring blood I decided to abort the fight. I pushed the shotgun down on her and put my left knee momentarily on the Beneli, pushing it against her. With my right foot I straightened upright quickly and used the momentum to hurl myself, just barely, over the edge of the boat.

I hit the water awkwardly. Before impacting, I took a big, deep breath. I immediately tried to orient myself in the cold greenish water. The saltwater stinging my eyes, I saw light and shadow. I swam to the shadow, knowing it was under the boat. I could hear the soft murmur of the idling engines and the very slow rotation of the props. The shadow was oblong at first but as I swam further under, it came more into view. I needed to get to the bow before I either ran out of air or I surfaced where I might be exposed to her aim. I could faintly hear shouting. The water muffled nearly all above the surface noises.

I popped up right at the apex of where the bottom of the bow touched the water and sucked in a big gulp of air before submerging again straight down from where I came up. I did this two times. Each time I came up for air I could hear McKenna onboard above, frantically searching the channel for me. She was shrieking. Neighbors had to be witnessing this frenzied woman covered in blood waving a shotgun by now.

I came up a third time and it was quieter. I tried to find a way to cling to the bottom of the boat at the water break line. I was in the water up to my top lip just breathing through my nose, worried if she cast off the lines and tore away from the dock at full throttle that I'd be mangled by the propellers. I waited and listened until finally, I heard sirens approaching. The next discernible nearby sound I could hear was Marroquín's voice.

"Cade. In custody. In custody. Cade!"

I was still reluctant to be visible in case she had him at gunpoint. I incrementally moved more to the starboard side closest to the seawall. I saw Marroquín leaning over the side looking for me. He caught a glimpse of me.

"We got her."

"Turn off the engines," I yelled up at him.

The propellers ceased spinning a few seconds later. I took another huge lung-filling inhale and then swam under the boat to the stern. I cautiously raised my head enough to break the surface of the water. Marroquín and a uniformed Miami Shores police officer were there. They helped pull me up and onto the boat.

McKenna was still covered in blood. Her hands were cuffed behind her back, and she was lying in a fetal position. She had her face turned away from Cordozo, but it didn't stifle how loudly she was weeping.

I was chilled to the bone and almost incapacitated, weak with relief. I started to shake from the cold and the adrenaline coursing through me. Another Miami Shores police officer retrieved his winter jacket from the trunk of his cruiser and gave it to me to wear.

Another bloody crime scene, and once again I was wearing a jacket from an agency I didn't work for. It took me a few minutes to compose myself. I just sat there in silence, watching the water and blood mix together on the deck. Finally I looked at Marroquín.

"What took you so long?"

"Bro, you should have seen the line at the drive-thru."

Chapter Twenty-Five

Hours after McKenna had been removed by the DEA, I was still on the scene. The Miami Shores Police Department had set up a small command post and were keeping neighbors and bystanders back. It's amazing how many residents say they *must* walk their dogs through the crime scene when the tape is up and fluttering in the breeze. Miami Shores Assistant Police Chief Nancy Ward was on the scene. Canasta would be cancelled today. She placated many of the residents and showed great acumen for a political future in Miami Shores when her police career ever ends.

Marroquín and I pushed through the boards securing Curbelo's side gate. I stripped down and used the garden hose to wash the salt water and remnants of Cordozo's blood off me. I was creeped out about any of his blood getting in my ears or eyes. I used a towel from my go bag and dried off, then changed into my spare clothes from my go bag. I continued wearing the Miami Shores police jacket to ward off chills, and donned my Hartford Whalers hat with my hair tucked behind my ears. Everything I'd been wearing was "donated" to the crime scene technicians. I knew I'd never see those clothes again, at least not in the same condition. After they process the clothes, take samples and whatever else they do, it isn't worth even having them back.

A search warrant had been obtained for the boat. It was

executed by a cadre of investigators and crime scene technicians. Using magnets and handheld stud finders they located a hidden compartment in the bulkhead above the master suite. Inside they found a messenger bag stuffed with neatly-bound Panama bearer shares in folders. They brought the secreted cache topside and put them on the dock. Practically no one had any idea what they were. Marroquín and I knew immediately what they were. Distinctive red circular stamps were on their folders. I looked at the stamps.

"*Banka E Shiqipêrise.*"

"The Bank of Albania, I'm willing to bet," I said softly to Marroquín.

Hammy was in a full Tyvek suit and sweating heavily. She walked up to us, a Polaroid camera in her hand. I asked her to snap a picture of the folders. She did and then handed me the instant picture that slid out of the camera. I held onto the picture, occasionally shaking it to help activate the processing chemicals. When it was complete, I put it in my back pocket.

Marroquín locked the folders in the trunk of his car. He gave me the car keys.

"Hold onto these until we get a proper chain of custody going here." As an added measure of protection, he sat on the car trunk.

According to Agent Janvier the Panama bearer shares were worth 2.5 million. I had the car keys. Marroquín sat on the trunk. It was an informal unsaid system of checks and balances between us. Marroquín had a lot of phone calls to make and his perch on his car trunk became his ad hoc office. Hammy saw that Marroquín wouldn't be leaving the car and she motioned for me to walk with her.

"There was a ton of blood. You don't need me to tell you that. I processed the shotgun, including the trigger guard and the trigger. They have gold mine fever in there. Since they found the hidden compartment, they're ready to take saws and hammers to anything they think is hinky," she said, gesturing with her head back towards the boat.

My gun had been in McKenna's possession, so it was now part of the crime scene. For good measure the crime scene technicians collected the ejected magazine and the lone discarded unspent round. Because I involuntarily disposed of my cellphone, the crime scene gods didn't think it was necessary for me to have it taken in for evidence. Hammy documented the incoming and outgoing calls in the hour leading up to my *encounter* with McKenna and Cordozo.

Lieutenant Maddalone had already made his requisite appearance. This time there was no gun switch. He provided me with the spare Glock. He told me that he thinks the department should just issue me two guns and save the gas and overtime of having him come see me. Major Brunson had relayed to Lieutenant Maddalone that he wanted to see me but that if it got too late, he'd catch up with me on the scene since he lives only a few blocks away. I was in no hurry to go back to the Coral Gables Police Station.

I saw two missed calls from Santiago on my phone. The wild, crazy turn of events would be hard for him to understand. How could I tell him that the very same items Viktor Moshienko is demanding from Guille for Lisandra's safe return are in the trunk of a car that I have the keys to, but there's a DEA agent currently sitting on the car's trunk? With trepidation and an almost physical wince, I dialed his number.

"Cade! I'm so glad you called back. Shit's getting real here," he said with anxiety in his voice.

"What's happened since we last spoke?" I said, watching a Tyvek-clad technician carrying a large laser level onto the boat.

"The last time he called, Guille yelled 'proof' into the phone. This time the Russian called, and he put Lisandra on the phone. I think the Russian has her drugged. She was making no sense, she's out of it. I swear I'm going to kill this fucker if he's hurt her!" he said, his voice breaking.

"What was she saying?"

"Stupid shit. It makes no sense. All this stuff about her and me going to see a movie and her shoes. Like she was reminiscing about crap that never happened," he said.

"What?"

"Crazy talking stuff! That movie with Dolly Parton and how she missed our times watching it and her shoes are ruined… She said they were ruined."

"Did Guille record the call like I told you to?"

"Yes."

"Did you call the cops?"

"No."

"No? Why not, Santiago? I thought we had agreed—"

"We didn't agree to shit. Cops can't do jack shit. When they finally do, it will be Winnebago's and hostage negotiators drinking stale coffee in paper cups. No way. This Russian and his commie comrades have my niece. I swear if they hurt her, I'll flip every rock over until I find them."

"Call me back. I won't answer. Hold your phone to Guille's phone. Leave me a voice message playing back Guille's message. I'll listen to it. I'll call you back."

Three minutes later I saw the message light blink on my cell phone. Before I got a chance to answer it, Agent Jean Luc Janvier and NYPD Inspector John Bazini pulled up in a marron car. I thought to myself, *that has to be a rental car*. No one under the age of sixty-five chooses a marron-colored car from the dealership. They were both wide-eyed but smiling broadly. They approached Marroquín. He slid down from the trunk but stayed next to the car to shake their hands. All three of them were talking animatedly.

Marroquín called me over and Bazini asked me to open the trunk with the keys. After my experiences with McBride and McKenna I was more than leery about dealing with people I don't know.

"Do you have a warrant, international warrant, a custody letter from a court, anything?" I asked them.

Jean Luc's facial expression spoke volumes. I'm sure he was used to saying "Interpol" with a French Belgium accent and getting doors opened and cocktail waitresses wet. Too bad. I was done with the whole "do you know who we are" attitude of the cozy feds and the phony state department characters.

"Cade, I came down here from New York. Open the trunk. Be a brother," said Bazini.

"Get your papers, gentlemen. Until then, it stays secure in the trunk."

"We just want to look at them," said Agent Janvier.

"So said every kid at his junior prom in the backseat of his dad's car. No way."

"Cade, we are Interpol—"

"No. You're NYPD on a field trip. I just swam in that channel," I hissed, pointing at the water, "with some guy's blood wedged all up in my nostrils. Do it right. Get the paperwork and you can get the papers. All of them. Anything less and both of you can kiss the Interpol between my butt cheeks," I said as I stomped away so I could listen to Santiago's message.

To avoid the noise and commotion of people moving about I needed to move further down the street towards where the channel meets the bay. It was quiet there. The sun was setting soon, and the day was peaceful. Not like it was hours ago when I saw a man die and was nearly shot myself. Again. I sat down on the well-manicured lawn of a palatial house and put the phone to my ear. I played back Santiago's voice message.

I was not expecting the raw emotion that came across in the voice message. A young woman with terror and fear in her voice spoke through choked-back tears.

"*Aye,* Tio, it's me. I miss you all so much. I'm scared. I miss us all watching our favorite movie "*Nine o Five*." Dolly Parton is my favorite. My shoes are falling apart. My Nikes are ruined. I can't even get these Nikes anymore. *Tio*, do what they say. You are the key, or they will cut me from the top into long pieces. *Por favor*, *Tio*. I love you all—"

The message went dead.

The message made my heart fall right into my shoes.

The anguish and fear Lisandra was going through was in my face, vividly real. I listened to the message three times. Each time was just as gut-wrenching as the first time I heard it. I was at the bottom of my emotional well. Ever since Hialeah I had been on a roller coaster of adrenaline, alcohol, sporadic sleep, lies, betrayals, and blood. Lots of blood. It was all catching up to me. I felt queasy. My legs started to shake, and a wave of nausea crested over me. I fell back on the grass, my knees bent, and my feet planted on the ground to quell the unsettled feelings. I put both hands over my forehead. I tried to look up at the darkening sky. I wanted to puke. It was all compiling on me. A lump stuck in my throat. It felt like everyone, and everything was standing on my chest. I kept telling myself I'd be okay. I kept telling myself that I was not going to vomit. I kept silently saying it to myself, thinking it would pacify the urge.

It was of no use. I quickly rose up onto my hands and knees and dry heaved for about forty seconds. Nothing came out but I was making the most guttural of noises. Thankfully no one from the crime scene heard or saw me. Lightheaded and depleted, I sat there staring at the grass for a few minutes until I felt well enough to get up. I slowly walked back to the crime scene. Hammy was now out of her Tyvek suit, her undershirt was soaked in sweat. She met me halfway as I walked back.

"You okay?" she asked me.

"Yeah, I'm cool. I'm good," I said unconvincingly.

"Well, I never thought of you as cool, but you look really pale, maybe you should sit down somewhere and get some air conditioning or something on you. Have you drank anything besides Biscayne Bay today?"

"No," I muttered.

"Come on. Come with me to our van. We have some Gatorades there."

I followed her over to the Hialeah Crime Scene van and sat on the bumper while she retrieved a lime green Gatorade from an iced cooler. Before giving it to me, she held it to the side of my neck. I initially pulled away from the coldness, but she admonished me.

"Let's chill the carotid artery a little. Get some cool flowing blood to your brain. It will make you feel better," she said.

After a minute of holding the cold bottle to my neck, I unscrewed the cap and took a gulp of the cool thirst quencher. The bottle against my neck and the ingestion of the fluid began to make me feel a little better. I thanked her. I looked over and saw both John Bazini and Jean Luc Janvier. They were both pacing and on their cellphones. Marroquín was calmly sitting on his car. He didn't have the keys and he wasn't the one who told the only international police agency on earth to go pound sand. I was. I was sure I'd hear from Major Brunson about this.

Unfortunately for me it would be sooner than later. I could see Brunson near the curve of the channel. He was talking to Nancy Ward. I'm sure it was all niceties. Undoubtedly, soon Assistant Chief Ward would switch the conversation to 'why was your detective in our city with another homicide.' I felt my stomach starting to waver again. Major Brunson saw me and came towards me. He looked like a man who was happy to be home only to find out dinner was burned, and he'd have to go back out again. Hammy saw him coming our way.

"I'll leave you two to discuss how you wrecked another jurisdiction's homicide statistics again," she said as she began walking back to the boat.

"Cade, we've been through a lot together, and most of it has been your fault," Brunson said by way of greeting

"I don't think you give me enough credit for consistency," I said after another swig from the Gatorade.

"Cade, let me put this as nicely as I can. You're either going to ruin my career, ruin my marriage, or ruin yourself. Don't be offended if I tell you I prefer the latter, although the second one was a close call."

"I've already had a hand in ruining a marriage. It isn't that easy. It isn't that fun, and it sure isn't what you want."

"The President of the Miami Dade County Association of Chiefs of Police called me—"

"Don't those guys get switched out every year until at least every one of you serves as the president?"

"Yes, but that's not the point."

"Who is it this year?"

"Chief Cerulo-Robiana from Sweetwater."

"Sweetwater? Does he speak English?"

"Cade, shut the fuck up. It's all shits and giggles until someone giggles and shits and right now Interpol isn't laughing, and they are shitting. You're like a funnel cloud of fuckery. Just give the guys from Interpol what they want. They've been looking for those papers long before this all went down. Why do you have to be so fucking bullheaded all the time? It's like you have an ongoing colossal problem with authority."

"I don't have an issue with your authority."

"You'd better not—"

"But if you think a phone call from some hyphenated revolving door police chief from Sweetwater is going to scare me you might want to try another tact," I said, interrupting him. "I know you're late to the party, but my ribs hurt from laying on a shotgun someone was trying to kill me with, and the taste of a dead guy's blood is still in the back of my throat. I haven't had exactly the greatest of days here. Right now, my ability to cohesively believe anyone is pretty low on the acceptance meter. They want the bearer shares. They can get a warrant or some sort of *duces tecum.* Need I remind you that if I hadn't stuck to my guns from the start there'd be no boat here, no bearer shares, and no save-your-ass $400,000."

Major Brunson stuck his hands in his pockets. He jutted one foot forward. His pants leg rode up a little exposing his brown and burgundy cowboy boats. He looked across the way at Nancy Ward.

"She's the assistant chief here. She plays cards with my wife. They haven't had a murder in this town—town? Hell, it's a village. They actually call it the Miami Shores Village. Now she has *two* murders, both involving one of my VIN detectives. So while she and my wife nibble candied almonds and play canasta, I'll have to hear about what a reckless detective I have. Cade, your actions aren't only affecting my professional life, but my personal life. So I don't give a whopping damn about your days or your nights. I could give a shit what the president of the Miami Dade County Association of chiefs of police says. I don't care how many PBA fucking envelopes he licks, how many fucking rubber chicken dinners he hosts, or a rat's fucking ass about his fucking annual golf tournament. What I care about is results. Today resulted in the recovery of bearer shares that Interpol wants. That's a result. If you don't want to give them the fucking car keys, you can give them to me, and I'll give them the keys. But I don't care if I have to use your own face as a jaws of life, we are opening that trunk and handing those papers over. Now!" he said, his voice rising to an uncomfortable pitch.

I looked over at both Interpol agents. They were still hot and heavy on their cell phones. The sun was nearly setting, and the crime scene technicians were setting up portable lights.

"Major, with all due respect, what's the hurry? They seem to be getting the courts or someone on the phone to get the proper paperwork. Do we really want to cut corners with two guys we really don't know?"

He briefly pondered the idea.

"Okay, Cade. Twenty minutes."

He kept his hands in his pockets. I pretended to be interested in what the technicians were doing on the boat. Finally I tried to break the ice.

"So you have lived here your whole life?" I asked him.

"My father was a World War II first lieutenant. He was in Reims, France when the Germans surrendered. He spent the majority of the war at the Richmond Airfield Blimp base in the south part of the county. My mother was from Miami. My grandparents owned a five and dime store in Downtown Miami. My parents settled in Lemon City before moving here to Miami Shores. I was in my teens then. I went to Morningside Elementary and Miami Senior High School," he said.

"What was Miami like back in the early 1960s?"

"Ah! It was wide open. No big buildings to block the breezes, lots of palm trees and pine trees. Miami Beach was the place you went for entertainment. It was easy living except for that brief period of the Cuban Missile Crisis. Kennedy had intel the Russians had missiles in Cuba. We spent our school mornings practicing duck and cover drills."

"What were those?"

He started laughing.

"It was so stupid. They had us practice pulling our jackets and shirts over our heads and ducking under our school desks in case we ever saw a mushroom cloud. Like that would stop nuclear radiation? I mean we have fucking shadows on walls in Hiroshima where people were vaporized, and they were trying to sell us on this bullshit that my STP cotton windbreaker would protect me from a nuclear blast." He shook his head and laughed even more. "The funny thing is we had missiles of our own from Norland all the way down to Key West. We had our own missiles. My father told me. We had Atlas missiles, Titan missiles, Nike missiles, Ajax missiles… I think we had more missile sites than the Russians did in Cuba, but nobody said anything about that." The irony seemed to hit us both. "It seems we have the capability to blow this whole planet up ten times over. I don't know where we all went wrong," he said ruefully.

At that moment Jean Luc Janvier saw me talking to Major Brunson and came over.

"You must be Major Brunson," he said, extending his hand.

Jean Luc continued to ignore me and deftly evaded looking at me as he spoke to Brunson.

"We have been in constant touch with the American consulate,

Steve Carstensen in Lyon. It is midnight where he is. He is nearing the completion of working with our legal counsel and having a *duces tecum* warrant faxed to the French consulate here in Miami. I must say Monsieur Carstensen is none too pleased. He is very committed to the idea of proper sleep, and he thinks Detective Taylor's obstinance is keeping him and our Lyon associates from getting very necessary sleep," he said, still avoiding looking at me.

I made a big production of feigning a yawn and stretching. This caused Brunson to glance at me out of the corner of his eye.

"It's like you have an ongoing colossal problem with authority."

Inspector Bazini came ambling over. "How far is Brickell Avenue from here?"

"John, this is Major Brunson. Detective Taylor's *superviseur*," said Jean Luc.

"Major. It's a pleasure to meet you," he said, shaking Brunson's hand "I wish I could say the same about your detective here. He doesn't seem to understand the code of the thin blue line."

I was fatigued of being labeled, I didn't feel like fighting, and I knew that in the very near future I'd never see any of these two guys again. I just stayed quiet. The sun had set, and it was getting darker by the minute.

"Brickell? It's about a forty minute drive this time of night," said Brunson.

Bazini said, "We have a courier on his way here now with the warrant and an already completed Interpol release of custody letter. This will put the bearer shares in our care and custody."

"Gentlemen, please excuse me for one minute," said Brunson as he put his arm on my shoulder, steering me away out of ear shot of the Interpol agents.

"Cade, I want you to listen to me and listen to me good. Go home. Go home and stay home. Stay home through Thanksgiving. Go get on a flight and see relatives or friends. Don't spend the holiday alone. Give me the car keys. I'm sure Marroquín wants to go home too. *I* want to go home. We have tons to do here still. This McKenna woman still needs to be interviewed, they're still collecting evidence, Lieutenant Maddalone gave you a replacement gun… Go stick it under your pillow and don't touch it until you come back to work. All of this needs to be wrapped up and wrapped up soon. Nancy Ward doesn't need these residents clamoring after her. We got it from here. I won't hand over the papers until I get the Interpol warrant. Go home, Cade. Go *home*. It's time to put this all behind you."

"What about the Russian that shot Agent Lew?" I asked him.

"That's a them problem. That's a problem for Interpol and the DEA to concern themselves with. We…you…have done your part here. It's over. Put it to rest. Take a week off and just take care of yourself. I'm serious."

He must have been serious because he didn't curse once.

I fished the keys out of my pocket and put them in Brunson's hand. I waved at Marroquín as I left. I motioned to him that Brunson had the keys. He nodded his head and gave me a thumbs up. I saw Hammy in the distance by the boat. She looked at me. I just waved and kept walking to my car.

Chapter Twenty-Six

I breathed a shuddering sigh of relief to be sitting in my own car. The interior had cooled from the heat of the day. The ignition turned over and it seemed to symbolize freedom and the leaving of my problems behind me. It was over. It was done. My part in all of this was done. There was nothing left for me to do. Major Brunson's advice was very point-on, and I couldn't argue with him. Moshienko was an Interpol and DEA problem. Brunson was right. Moshienko did shoot Agent Lew.

But he tried to kill me, too.

I drove away. As I neared Biscayne Boulevard, I called Santiago.

"Cade! Thank God. Did you get the message? What do you think? Tell me what you think? What should we do? Let me—"

I had to interrupt him.

"Santiago. Santiago. Santiago! Slow down, man. Just hold your horses. Slow down. One at a time."

I could feel a massive headache coming on.

"Did you get the message?" he asked expectantly.

"I heard it. I listened to it three times."

"What do you think?"

"Santiago, I think we should do what I've been advocating all along. Call the cops. They have people and units that are trained in this kind of thing."

"No way. No way, man! The cops will be all over us like a blue rash. Guille will take the fall and then they'll be all in my business."

"What do you care more about? Getting Lisandra back or your business?" I asked him.

"That ain't it. They don't know what the fuck they're doing. Did you see LAPD on national TV get the crap kicked out of them during the Rodney King riots? Do the words Ruby Ridge and ATF in Waco mean anything to you? These *comemierdas* can't do anything right. The motherfuckers left over 1200 of our brothers in the Bay of Pigs. No offense, but your cop buddies and this ass-backward government we have can't be trusted. They will tell you whatever you want to hear while they fuck you."

"The noble lie depends on manipulation, subterfuge, sleight of hand, if you will. We know what's is best for the United States and we are always five steps ahead."

Thinking what McBride said to me and what Santiago just said, I stayed quiet on the line. It was as though I was driving on autopilot. I was exhausted and I truly just wanted to take Brunson's advice to heart.

"You still there? Cade? You still there?" Santiago pushed.

"I'm here. Okay, if you don't want cops then I need you to listen to me. We do it my way or I'm out. I don't want any pushback on this. Understand?"

"Yes, yes. You got it!" he said.

"First things first. Cut Guille out. He's young and he has a lifetime to tell stories. I can't have him telling stories. I want you to write down Lisandra's message *exactly* on a piece of paper. In the office at Scotty's print ten copies. You hear me? I want *ten* copies of the message."

"Yes, yes. Ten copies, but why?"

"Santiago, I said no pushback. Answering questions especially after the day I've had sounds like pushback. Just do it!" I snapped at him.

"Okay. Okay. Okay." he said in a surrendering tone.

"Put the ten copies in an envelope. Seal the envelope. Unplug the copier for ten minutes and then plug it back in. Do *not* turn it off—unplug it. I want the memory to erase itself. Guille has one job: Tell him to turn off his cell phone and give it to you. That's it. That's his job. To give you his phone. I need him completely out. No information, no sharing tidbits of stuff. Nothing. You hear me?"

"What? The phone? That's our only way to communicate with these Russian bastards."

"You and I will control the phone. Not Guille. What they think he has is very valuable to them. It's nighttime. They aren't going to do anything at night. At least not kill her. They want what they *think* Guille has. They will wait."

"How can you be sure?" he asked with a questioning lilt to his voice.

"I'm not sure." That response was met with silence. "Now, I'm going to bed as soon as I get home. Tomorrow, be at Scotty's at 9am . Get us a table near the water in the shade. Bring the phone, the envelope, and some pencils. If you got anybody competent enough to make a great colada of Cuban coffee, have some ready. Good night." I hung up. I turned off my phone and literally threw it over my shoulder into the backseat of my car.

It was only 8:30pm when I arrived home. Upstairs I turned on the shower. I tucked my head into my arms with my knees pulled up to my chest as I sat on the floor of the shower for forty-five minutes. The dual showerheads relentlessly poured down on me. I felt like I was on the backside of upside down. Science says our body composition is 60% water. If that truly is a fact then I'd had nearly 60% too much of me. The water in all its forms from a slurry ice bucket, an overflowing bathtub, a stinging shower, a child's raft in the swimming pool, a lunch table with a waterside view, or a briny submersion in Biscayne Bay had intermixed to become a nine foot offshore pipeline curl that either I needed to surf on top of or get my saturated self-tossed off and onto the jagged reef of my life. Underneath the dual shower heads there wasn't enough water to clean me of my emotions. I was feeling depleted and defeated. *"Give me the car keys"* Brunson said. That is a kind way of saying you are done, or you can't be entrusted to go on. Too much had happened in such a short time. Everyone thought it was over. With the exception of finding Moshienko, most of the agencies and people involved would slowly start drifting into their caseloads, their workloads, their flowcharts, spreadsheets, and other rudimentary aspects of their jobs. The DEA would want Moshienko but even they will eventually taper the hunt down to a small task force. There would be a consensus among all of them that Moshienko would emerge somewhere. *Don't worry guys, we'll get him sooner or later.* Maybe he'd be picked up by a traffic-obsessed Alabama State Trooper, and alert Customs inspector in Rotterdam, or end up killed in an East London flat.

Except none of them knew he was now holding a young nineteen-year-old college student hostage. A young woman who probably loved kittens, denim, and chocolate ganache.

I toweled off and went straight to bed. I slept deeply. I didn't have any bad dreams. I can't be certain it was a restful sleep, but I do know the frozen horror on Cordozo's dead face was the very first thing I thought about when I woke up. The sun was streaming through my blinds. I gave heavy consideration to taking another shower. I also gave equally heavy consideration to downing a bottle of mind-numbing Jameson over the next few hours as I marinated in the swimming pool. I needed to put all of the recent events figuratively in a little box and carry them out to a trash compacter. Crush them. Compress them. Flatten them. Do it until they were an unrecognizable coalesced square. Santiago was a grown man who had danced on the edge of blade plenty of times. He may not have foreseen the world he lives in come sweeping into his sister's house and spiriting away his niece, but he knew the risks within the world he always said he long ago retired from. Guille was just a small man looking to live in a big man's world. Unfortunately, natural maturation, the progression of age, and size manufactured in the gym are not the complete qualifiers for that world. To be even considered to qualify in that world there needs to be cagy street smarts, unending patience, flashpoint aggressiveness, impenetrable intestinal resolve, cunning insight, and in many instances, an unbending killer instinct. The drug dealing and money laundering world is not for the faint of heart. Even if you have a badge, you better be prepared to do what's necessary—even if entails choosing a casket at the end of the day.

I dressed quickly. I made sure to bring the Polaroid of the folders with the Albanian stamps on them with me. I slipped into the morass of traffic clogging Old Cutler Road. I gritted my teeth and just came to the realization that I wasn't simply in traffic but to every other driver, I *was* traffic. As I neared Scotty's Landing it was just a few minutes past 9am. Santiago must be on the frantic emotional side of the problem as he called my phone three minutes past nine.

"Hello."

"Cade, you on the way?"

"I'll be there in about five minutes. How does the marina look? Can I get in and park near the door?"

"Yes, yes. It's wide open. Chart House doesn't open for a few hours, and we got our deliveries all in. Just park by the tikis and the ropes near the bathrooms."

"Hey, I know it's not on your menu but is there anybody there who can makes some eggs and toast?"

"Yes, yes. I'll get the cook on it. The colada will be here too."

"The bigger and hotter the better. Thanks," I said as I hung up.

I walked in under the decorative arbor and into the waterside restaurant. Santiago was seated at one of the furthest tables from the bar. It was in the shade of the large green and white tent and had a magnificent view of the bay. I sat down at the table. On it was a cup of pencils, a sealed manila envelope, and Guille's cell phone.

"*Coño,* you look like shit."

I became painfully aware that all the showers, and even a night of sleep was not going to slough off the emotional upheaval of my life.

"Yesterday was one for the record books," I said.

"What the hell happened?" he asked me.

"The vending machine at the station ran out of Snickers bars."

He just looked at me. After a silent beat or two he turned in his chair and waved his arm to catch the attention of the waitress, Alondra. She saw him and simply nodded her head. She went into the kitchen. He turned back towards me. Behind him I could see her coming out of the kitchen carrying a large tray. She placed two plates in front of me and Santiago. The plates were piled high with mounds of trembling scrambled eggs. She put down two baskets of warm buttery Cuban toast, little cups of milk, a bowl of sugar, two small empty coffee cups with saucers, and the *coup de grâce* was a stove-top coffee maker called a Moka Pot. In Spanish it's called a *cafetera*. In the language I was currently feeling and speaking, it was called sustaining. I was hoping it would all help me to elevate myself and raise the mast of my soul again. I was empty in more ways than one. We both thanked her as she walked away. Wordlessly, I started to eat slowly and then grew more ravenous as I gobbled down the eggs and toast. I felt like the color was coming back to my face. Santiago ate slower and with a steady pace. He poured the thick Cuban coffee from the *cafetera* into the coffee cups. I doctored my own with the milk and the sugar. It tasted heavenly. He kept looking at me expectantly, wanting me to say something. I was too famished and in need of the caffeine boost at first to say anything. Finally I spoke in between bites.

"Santiago. I know there's a lot of emotion here. You have to separate the emotion out of the equation. You've done it a hundred times before. Now you're feeling vulnerable. I get it. I understand, but we need to be in the business of business, not the business of emotions. I don't know who's with him or how many there are but the Russian from the deal in Hialeah is a guy named Viktor Moshienko."

Santiago stopped eating and listened attentively.

"Moshienko is ex-KGB, and he's a stone cold killer. I don't say that to worry you, but you need to know. He's also a huge greedy capitalist at heart. He thinks that Guille is holding onto these," I said as I put the Polaroid on the table.

Santiago picked up the picture and studied it.

"What is this?" he asked me.

"That? That is a Polaroid of Panama bearer shares still in their Bank of Albania folders. The red circular stamp is from the Bank of Albania. An Albanian government courier was killed in Budapest trying to deliver those. They're worth about two and a half million."

"So tell me how he thinks Guille has these?"

"He thinks Guille has them because Guille and Lisandra's dentist has been brokering coke deals, and the dentist tried to steal the bearer shares in Paris. Moshienko knew he had them. The dentist was lying and stalling him. Like you said yesterday, he set everyone up to be killed and Moshienko could recoup the loss, but not everyone died. The dentist pinned it all on Guille. So the Russian now has Lisandra and wants the shares."

"Can't we just give him the shares for Lisandra?"

"No. Interpol has them. If my guess is correct there will be some sort of a press conference in the next twenty-four hours saying the shares were recovered here in Miami. If Moshienko sees that press conference on TV, Lisandra is a goner. I'm sorry, but that's just facts. We have to move fast. We need to find him. We need to get her back."

I had wolfed down the meal and pushed the plate aside. I kept the coffee near me. I had already begun making my second cup.

"Open the envelope and grab a pencil. We need to go over every word of her message. It's the only shot we got right now. Turn Guille's phone on. If Moshienko calls again, describe the folders in the picture. Make him think you have the bearer shares. We have to stall him and get an idea of where he is. Until we get another call we have to just listen to her message and see if we can hear traffic, an airplane, a train, anything in the background that will help us know where she is. What number did he call from?"

"When the call came in it said, 'out of area.'"

For the next ninety minutes we worked in silence using the pencils and making notes across the sheets of the translated message. There was a lot of pencil erasing being done too. I tried to read the message backward. I tried to read the message in parts. I quizzed Santiago extensively about the Dolly Parton reference. He said he had no idea. It was a completely jumbled mystery to him. He said he rarely ever spent a lot of time at family gatherings. To him Lisandra had always just been his sister's daughter. His niece, but he didn't ever remember watching movies with her. He swore up and down she was being drugged. He couldn't understand why she cared about her shoes so much. I could see Guille sneaking peeks at us from his manned position at the restaurant bar. Santiago instructed Alondra to put dirty dishes and glasses on the three tables around us. He told her to not bus those tables so we could work uninterrupted. We played and replayed the message over and over again, listening to her anguished voice. It was killing Santiago, but I needed to have any and all tools available. Like I told him, he was going to need to carve the emotion out of it if we were to successfully get Lisandra back. I kept reading the translated version and comparing it to the cell phone's message:

"*Aye Tio* it's me. I miss you all so much. I'm scared. I miss us all watching our favorite movie "Nine o Five." Dolly Parton is my favorite. My shoes are falling apart. My Nikes are ruined. I can't even get these Nikes anymore. *Tio* do what they say. You are the key, or they will cut me from the top into long pieces. *Por favor Tio*. I love you all—"

I scanned the words and matched them verbatim to her message. It was exhausting and we were still at it as the clock struck twelve. The restaurant was packed to the gills with patrons. Alondra was getting nasty looks and comments from waiting customers about the tables around us. To her credit she just kept at her job and tried to turn tables as quickly as she could. The pressure was mounting on her and I told Santiago that with the cacophony of noise the diners were making our arrangement here was useless anyway. He motioned for Alondra to clear the tables and seat patrons near us.

"*Tu dijiste eso—*" she replied.

"I know what I said, but it's okay. Open it up," Santiago said, his voice showing his frustration

I heard her Venezuelan accent when she spoke to Santiago. The way she pronounced her words. The word "*tu*" and "*eso*" sounded like an "oh."

I looked at the words on the paper. "nine to five." "*Nine to five.*" The phone was lying flat on the table. I played the message again and put my ear to the phone. It sounded more like "nine o five" than "nine to five."

"Did you translate this exactly?" I asked him.

"Yes, yes. Why?"

"Listen. Listen to this again. It sounds like she is saying "nine o five," not "nine to five."

He leaned over and put his ear to the phone on the table. He listened once. He listened twice. He listened a third time with his eyes closed. He lifted his head and looked at me.

"The movie is called *Nine to Five*," he said, furrowing his brow in concentration.

"I don't give a damn if it's called nine to nine, she isn't saying nine to five she is saying nine *o* five…905!"

I grabbed my phone and called the VIN office.

"*Veen.*"

"Ileana, put Gary on the phone please."

"*Coño ju ax* like *ju* are the *Rey de Narcoticos—*"

I brusquely cut her off.

"Ileana, its important. Put Gary on the line."

Wordlessly the phone transferred, and I heard Gary's voice as he picked up.

"Dude, I have to work in here with her, man."

"I get it. Big G, you're pretty good with the internet. Can you look up what area code 905 is?"

I heard some keys being tapped.

"Hamilton, Canada and Niagara Falls, New York," he said.

"Is that it?" I asked hoping there would be more.

"Dude, that's it. What's up?"

"I'm looking at a document that has a three-digit code and I can't figure out what it might be."

"You know I have a master's in finance, right?" he said.

"Yeah, I know," I said, secretly wondering if this was going to lead to anything other than the life story of Gary Fowler.

"Well, three-digit codes are used in all sorts of finance. There are 720 possibilities with three-digit codes, each unique combination of three digits can be represented six times. Government always follows the sciences. It's easier that way."

"Okay. What are you saying?"

"I'm reading here currently there are 234 area codes in the United States. Because of cell phones, Manhattan will add another area code to their traditional long established 212 area code. The FCC and states use three-digit codes in all they do. That's why states use three-digit codes for the designation of major roads. As those roads cross state lines the adjacent state doesn't have to replicate the number. That's one combination out of their possible 720 combinations the neighboring state can adopt, or if they choose to use up one of their own three-digit numbers they will renumber the road when it crosses the state line. None of those yahoos in government can do anything on their own, so they follow simple mathematical practices always. Credit cards do the same thing. A three-digit authorization code on the back of the credit card in conjunction with the card number account makes it an infinity of number combinations. Same thing with combination locks on cheap suitcases."

"Wait. Wait. Hold on," I said, snapping my fingers at Santiago to get his attention. I motioned for him to hand me a pencil. "You mean to tell me that 905 is an area code but can also be a state road?"

"You drive on the 836, you drive on the 826, don't you? Whether you call it the Dolphin Expressway or the Palmetto Expressway it still has a three-digit designation," he casually said.

"You still have the internet open?" Before he could answer I asked him to see if there was a State Road 905 in Florida.

"905? Sure is. Actually there's a 905, an Old 905, and 905A."

"Where?"

"They're all in North Key Largo."

"Thanks, Big G, I'll call you back, thanks buddy," I said as I hurriedly hung up.

"905. State Road 905 is in Key Largo," I said to Santiago.

He looked back at the translated message.

"You are the key, or they will cut me from the top into long pieces."

Santiago started crossing out random words.

"...key...long..."

He looked at me astonished. "Key Long" in Spanish is "Key Largo."

"It's all we got. Keep working it. How'd you do that?"

"I started by eliminating the pronouns," he said.

We had already gone through multiple copies of the message already. I took my pencil and I started eliminating as many pronouns as I could from the translated message.

"Aye it's. miss all so much. scared. miss all watching favorite movie "Nine o Five." is favorite. shoes are falling apart. Nikes are ruined. can't even get these Nikes anymore. do what say. are the key, or will cut from the top into long pieces. Por favor. love all..."

I slid the paper over to Santiago.

"Read it to me out loud. Keep reading it to me slowly until I say stop. I need to hear the accent."

I sat with my eyes closed, trying to drown out any ambient noise around me. Santiago began reading the redacted message out loud. At one point I balled my fists up on the table. I laid my forehead on my hands and just listened. I just kept listening. It was something in the accent. Both Santiago's and Lisandra's. I could hear it. I could hear it differently than from the English pronunciation.

"miss all."

"miss all."

When it hit me it was like a tidal wave of relief and euphoria that surged inside me, from my bones out through my skin. It was Major Brunson. It clicked. What he'd told me about growing up in Miami.

"The funny thing is we had missiles of our own from Norland all the way down to Key West. We had our own missiles. My father told me. We had Atlas missiles, Titan missiles, Nike missiles, Ajax missiles..."

"miss all."

Missile.

Nike missiles.

"*Nikes are ruined. can't even get these Nikes anymore.*"

"Santiago, that's it! Nike missiles! Not Nike shoes. Nike *missiles*! The Nike missiles are obsolete. They don't make them anymore. They're ruined...old missile site. Moshienko was KGB, he would know where our old missile sites are located. If there's a decommissioned Nike missile site in Key Largo near State Road 905, that's where she is! She was talking to you in code!"

Santiago jumped up from his seat.

"Stay here!" he said to me.

"*Alondra! Cervezas, ahora, por favor. Hazlos Kalik's de las Bahamas, están debajo del pargo en el refrigerador.*"

["Alondra! Beers, now, please. Make them Kalik's from the Bahamas, they are under the snapper in the cooler."]

"I'll be right back, I have to get my old maps and charts," he said stumbling over a chair as he dashed off.

Alondra dutifully brought an iced bucket of Kalik beer. With a smile she placed the bucket in the center of the table. Santiago returned with some musty maps that had some dust and a lot of fraying on the edges. He had a yellow highlighter held lengthwise between his teeth. He sat down and laid the maps and nautical charts on the table.

"Maybe you actually did retire," I said.

He pulled the cap off of the highlighter with his teeth and spit it out. It bounced on the table.

"Maybe," he said with a sly smile.

The first map we pulled out of the pile was an old American Automobile Association map of the Florida Keys. He squinted at first and then focused in on Key Largo. He quickly located State Road 905 and Old State Road 905. Both roads ran along the northeastern shoreline of north Key Largo. There was also 905A, which was also called Card Sound Road. The notorious watering hole "Alabama Jack's" was on Card Sound Road. It had been the only road into the Florida Keys from the mainland until U.S. 1 was extended into what's known as the "Eighteen Mile Stretch." Tracing the map with my finger I could see where Old state Road 905 intersected with the current State Road 905.

Someone in the AAA office had stamped the map. It had stamps denoting that Old State Road 905 was impassable in certain sections. The roads formed a triangle around a large swatch of barren scrub pine and small bodies of water. Santiago eyed the map with a keen knowing eye.

"I know this place," he said. "I've heard of it. I've never seen it, but I've heard of it. It was a good offshore temporary stash location in the 70s and 80s. Do you remember the Stump?"

"The Stump? No," I said.

"The Stump was an old gringo smuggler. He used to bring stuff in on the backside off of Ocean Reef by Pumpkin Key. He knew his shit. I mean, he was like Poseidon or something. He taught me some good routes. He had drop points if the Coast Guard was onto him and one of those he called the 'High Mighty 40.' One night we were in Homestead's Bayfront Marina on his boat. It was about four in the morning, he was getting real old by then, and we were drinking this vintage Brugal rum. He told me the High Mighty 40 was his nickname for a place called 'HM 40.' He said it was an old missile launch site in Key Largo that was deep in the trees. From the bay side he said the best way in was through Steamboat Creek. From the ocean side there were rocks piled just offshore, just south of Dynamite Docks that were in a direct line with it."

"Dynamite Docks? What are those?" I asked him.

"You heard about the U.S. ship *The Maine* blowing up in Havana Harbor in 1898?"

"Yes," I said.

"When *The Maine* sank, it stopped maritime traffic and commerce for nearly a year. Almost crippled Cuba. So when South Florida was being developed nobody wanted a repeat of that. It took large amounts of explosives to bust out the coral and oolite ridges so the developers could build roads and canals. Ships back then were always running aground, sinking, or blocking the Port of Miami. All it took was one dynamite-loaded ship to create the same thing as what happened in Havana. So back then they built a pier for explosive cargo. It was south of where Ocean Reef is now. They off-loaded the explosives from ships and trucked it up to Miami. They called the pier the 'Dynamite Docks.' In my day we used the rocks where the pier was as a marker for drug and alien-smuggling operations. Between my own methods and what I learned from guys like Stump, I know this whole area really well."

I'd always said, Santiago was a sea ninja. Every dark passage in Biscayne Bay was his.

"Let's face facts, Santiago. The phone hasn't rung. At least not yet. We have time. We can put together a good plan," I said.

"We don't have time and we don't have much more to go on. I mean, it makes a lot of sense. Listen, I know enough about the place that I can go get her. There ain't a Goddamn person on this earth that's going to stop me," he said, forcefully pounding his fist on the table for emphasis.

Santiago. I can see how this is beyond the level of personal, but we have to—"

"Cade. Are you in or out?" he interrupted me.

I could feel the ire in his voice. I looked out at the glistening, lapping waves on Biscayne Bay. He well-intended to go, with or without me. I thought about the two and half million ways this could all go wrong.

"Are you in or out?" he said again.

I looked back at him. It took me at least a minute to answer him.

"I'm in," I said.

Santiago jumped out of his seat and gave me a big hug, beaming with a wide smile.

I set up the situation. "Keep the Kalik's on ice until we get back. Let's play to our strengths. There's a lot that can go wrong with driving down to Key Largo. Car issues, we get pulled over by a state trooper, a toll collector remembers us, all kinds of things can go wrong. You're the sea dweller. Stupid question: Can you get a boat for tonight?"

"Yes, yes. Absolutely," he said, nodding like crazy.

"Second stupid question, Can you get us in by those rocks south of the Dynamite Docks and we can hike in from there?"

"Yes, yes. Absolutely," he said, as if it was the only way he knew how to answer a question.

"I'll bring the guns and ammo. I cannot risk something going wrong and you being intercepted with firearms. Leave all the gear and the guns to me. I'll get a bullet-proof vest for you. Understood?" I said, looking him in the eyes.

He nodded his head. I nodded back.

"Why am I not surprised at any of this from you?" I said, trying to make light of what was shaping up to be a very dangerous night. "I live in Paradise Point. I want to be sure to have my car on camera coming in. I don't want to be on camera leaving. Pick me up at the end of the point at 7pm."

Santiago confirmed, "That's the Cutler Channel. Easy run. Paradise Point? You're moving up in the world."

"I'm *moving* in the world; I just don't know if it's up. Seven sharp!" I said as I shook his hand and gazed at him steadily. I then walked out of the bar for conceivably, the very last time.

Chapter Twenty-Seven

I COULD HEAR THE low rumble of the twin inboard engines.

It was two minutes until seven.

I was waiting for him at the very tip of the Paradise Point. Santiago, like all good dope runners, knew assuredly that being on time meant rendezvous went as planned. He came in through the Cutler Channel, idling very slowly. His profile in the setting sun was nearly imperceptible. I stood on the edge of the dock in the cut-through to the small Paradise Point Marina. His shape and form got larger and more identifiable as he drew closer as he stood in the open cockpit of a 1998 Donzi 33ZX Daytona go-fast boat. The entire fiberglass upper deck was painted green to help it to blend in with the sea. He nosed the tip of the boat right to my feet. When the boat was less than a foot away from me he shifted into reverse. As I stepped onto the boat we were already backing slowly out of the channel. I walked across the deck, stepping over the low slung windshield, and quickly set my bag of weapons and gear behind him on the deck before sitting beside him. I was in the cockpit of this monstrous animal of a boat, sitting so low it felt as though I was just above the water line.

Santiago never said a word. We both knew sound travels across water, and we didn't want any greetings or comments to be heard by the other residents of Paradise Point. Santiago expertly cut the wheel. This epitome of nautical engineering of a vessel just glided from reverse to forward with a switch of the throttle. I had only been on the boat about thirty seconds, and we were now slowly motoring out through the Cutler Channel, the wide open yawning expansiveness of southern Biscayne Bay before us. Santiago had on latex gloves. He was dressed in black from head to toe and he was wearing what I could best describe as large ski goggles. There was a bungee cord attached to the "oh shit handle" in front of my seat. Looped in the chord was a pair of thick latex gloves and an identical pair of the goggles he was wearing. Wordlessly, he pointed at the goggles indicating to me to don the eyewear. I slipped on the gloves then put on the goggles.

The sun was nearly gone. Darkness was falling on us rapidly. I could see the twinkle of the night's first stars over Elliot Key in the distance.

He stayed in the channel as we approached Chicken Key. Many an inexperienced boater would have cut south out of the channel thinking they could navigate between the shoreline and Chicken Key. That would be a huge mistake to make—especially in the dark. The shoals are only about one to two feet deep there. Running aground is an absolute certainty. I had described Santiago as a sea ninja, and he was every bit of that description. As we approached the eastern tip of Chicken Key he steered the boat diagonally out of the channel. He confidently knew the water was at least eight feet deep. It was then that he threw the throttle into full go mode. The tip of the Donzi raised up and the twin inboard 470 horsepower Mercury engines roared to life. The abrupt transformation from slow-moving boat to replicating a speeding bullet streaking across the inky black water under darkening skies was awe-inspiring and exhilarating. He kept the nose pointed straight towards the feather banks. It was over the roar of the beastly engines that he finally spoke to me.

"Eyes, twelve o' clock. Look for the waves. That's Black Ledge. I need to cut south between Black Ledge and the reef. You'll see the waves when we get near. If you see them before I do, let me know!" he shouted over the roaring engines.

By the time I saw the beginning of the rippling waves near

Black Ledge, Santiago had already seen them, and was turning the boat southeast. Santiago knew that Sands Key was out in front of us, waiting dark and silent for us to run aground against its rugged shallow banks. He steered the boat right for the northern tip of the Key and at the last second cut the wheel hard right, steering us away from danger and into a narrow stretch of water between the unseen sandbars on either side of us. He was a maestro, the way he maneuvered us through all the unforgiving and dangerous shallow obstacles. He kept the throttle wide open, and it was as if he was counting paces in his head and knew when and where to turn by timing, just as importantly as by knowledge. Rock ledges, reefs, sandbars, went by us unseen by me but definitely known by Santiago.

The lights of southern Miami Dade County were congested near the Homestead Marina Basin, but after we zoomed past them the shoreline was very dark, with the exception of some sporadic lights. It was invigorating to feel the thrust and the power of the engines, but it was also scary knowing that one mistake and we could be killed by hitting something.

"I got the bay. You help keep your eyes out for anything running dark," he screamed at me so as to be heard over the engines.

I had a brief moment of concern.

"Why would they be running dark?" I yelled back.

He must have thought of me as a momentary idiot.

"Aren't we?" he yelled back.

The lightbulb in my head went off. I might be in a go-fast boat with a prolific retired smuggler but there could be other not-so-experienced smugglers out there right now, and they could definitely ruin the night for all of us if we collided. I became even more hyper-vigilant.

He kept the boat on a direct path to the northern tip of Totten Key. It was apparent that Santiago wanted to stay on "the inside." If the Coast Guard or Florida Marine Patrol should encounter us he wanted to make a run for the mainland near Turkey Point or the mangroves, improving our chances of escape. It was safer on "the outside" off of Elliot Key and Boca Chita Key. Very few mariners, including those in law enforcement, would venture the route we were taking at the speed we were going. Santiago was precision, experience, and guts coming together in one person.

In about fifteen minutes Totten Key became visible dead ahead. The safe route would have been to take Cesar's Creek between the southern tip of Elliot Key and the northern tip of Totten Key. That is a clearly defined and heavily traveled passage from the inside to the outside. There is also a campground on Elliot Key. Santiago couldn't risk an angry boater complaining about our wake or flagging us down to see if we have any butane for their greasy charcoal grill. It was our intention to avoid as many prying eyes as possible. Santiago showed his moxie by powering south just off the mangrove shoreline of Totten Key. He went past Old Rhoades Key. In doing so he bypassed another ideal passageway—the Broad Channel. He slowed the boat and began taking a very circuitous route through a maze of unnamed islands. He kept the boat at the slowest possible speed to thwart any engine noise. We still stayed silent. He maneuvered the boat through the darkened narrow passages like a wizened old curator who knows exactly what he's looking for in the cobwebbed basement of the museum.

I lost track of the turns and switchbacks. The next thing I knew we were coming out of the Linderman Creek Channel, and we were now on the outside of Northern Key Largo. By avoiding Angelfish Creek we slipped past the exclusive Ocean Reef Club unseen in the darkness. From there he opened the throttle all the way again. The boat roared back to life, and we were once again an aquatic meteor streaking across the surface of the bay. As we neared Dynamite Docks, Santiago slowed the boat, letting us bob in the water, barely moving. North Key Largo was off of our starboard side.

The entire island was blanketed in silent darkness. Looking to my north, even from this distance, the lights of Miami cast a glow of soft, almost vanishing light into the sky. Santiago's hands tightly clutching the wheel of the drifting boat as he squinted at the shoreline. The half-moon was still in the lower hemisphere. This time of the year the moon is closest to the sun and when the sun sets in the western sky, the moon doesn't rise much higher. Illumination was sparse and we both strained our eyes to see the eastern shoreline of North Key Largo. The moon was barely rising above the treelined edge of the island. Santiago was looking for some sort of marker or deviation from the brushy tree line, but the shoreline was flat. In the low light of the moon ripples could be seen where the water was breaking over the salty flats and raised coral rocks. The depth finder on the boat said we were in two feet of water. The sea grass on the bottom of the ocean brushed against the hull. I peered hard at the jagged and dark shoreline, not fully knowing what I was supposed to see, but knowing that whatever it was it must be out there.

I heard Santiago whisper, "There. There on the starboard side at three o'clock. Dynamite Docks."

I could barely see the long ago dismantled dock pilings. Santiago kept the boat in a steady position by alternating between forward and reverse gears.

"You going to suit up?" he asked me.

"I will when we finally get there," I said.

He nudged the throttle a little more and we started steadily to the next group of rocks just south of Dynamite Docks. Those rocks were aligned with the HM 40 compound. He cut the engines completely and we drifted up alongside the rocks. On closer inspection it was more of a sandy growth with a lone mangrove tree growing out of it. Boaters over the years had stacked rocks around the edges making it more like an art project than a small island twenty yards offshore. In total it couldn't have been any bigger than maybe twenty yards wide and thirty yards deep. Santiago slipped over the side of the boat. He was in calf deep water. I threw him the bow line. He used an angler's slip knot and tied the line to the mangrove tree. He came back to the boat, I leaned down and we talked quietly to each other. Our faces were right next to each other.

"Santiago, this is not a vigilante mission. Moshienko is wanted by

Interpol. If we can take him alive, I'll make the arrest and we bring him back. No exceptions."

He just looked at me with steely resolve.

"The HM 40 should be straight in front of us. We just have to not get thrown off course," he said.

"You might not see it in the dark, but we have about 700 yards of mud, muck, and mangrove to walk through. I'll carry the gear bag. We can suit up when we get closer."

Slowly we walked in a straight line. I led the way. It was not easy walking. The bag was cumbersome. The mud was difficult to traverse because it was dark. The wetness and the thought of what kind of critters might be in there played with my mind. We trudged steadily. I could hear the water lapping the shoreline behind me.

"I think you're overthinking this," he said to me through gritted teeth as he fought to keep his balance in the muck.

It took us nearly thirty minutes to silently hike through the mangroves and mud, but eventually we could make out the edge of what used to be Old State Road 905. We were sweating. The inland breezes were keeping a majority of the insects away. The inhospitable bramble and mangrove brush started giving way to small oolite rocks and patches of weedy grass. There were large overgrown clumpy bushes on either side of us. In between the brush we could slip unseen as we donned our gear. As a precautionary measure I turned back to face Santiago and silently gestured to him to stay quiet and to get down low. Crouching, I softly placed the gear bag on the salty ground in front of me and quietly unzipped it. I motioned for him to come up beside me. Still crouching, he came up to squat beside me. I then aggressively grabbed him by the back of his shirt and shoved him down onto the bag. I laid on top of him. The clumps of vegetation on either side of us sprung up immediately.

There were four of them.

It was scary and shocking to Santiago. At first he was so stunned by the earth coming to life he couldn't process what was happening.

"Shhhhh, stay quiet. They're with us. They're with us. Stay quiet."

Within seconds the bushes descended upon us, now holding both me and Santiago down on the ground.

"FBI HRT!" one of the bushes harshly whispered in our ears.

"The bushes" were four members of the FBI Hostage Rescue Team. They were head to toe camouflaged in ghillie suits. This type of camouflage was designed to resemble the background environment. These agents were clad in olive and brown netting. Their ghillie suits were a hodge podge of glued loose strips of burlap, dyed cloth, twine, leaves and twigs, with mangrove leaves and sea grape leaves interwoven amongst their patterned BDUs. Their faces were completely covered with wavy striped paint all in the common color palate of the shoreline. The ghillie suits enabled the agents to blend in with the sparse Key Largo topography perfectly. Even now after identifying themselves, they were practically impossible to detect visually.

Once Santiago realized what was going on, he became argumentative and slightly combative. Two of the agents pressed harder on top of him. I harshly reminded him to stay quiet and stop squirming.

"Shut up. Shut the fuck up. You want to get Lisandra killed? Shut up and listen!" I hissed in his ear. "Listen up. We were *not* going to be able do this by ourselves. If they'd seen us approaching and put her in a car and drove off, we'd have been screwed. Too much could go wrong. I know. I know. You don't have any faith in the agencies and the government. I heard you. But this Russian shot and killed a man in Budapest, another one in Paris and he shot a DEA agent. The asshole also tried to kill me. I said we do it my way with no push back. This is my way."

"Would you have done it like this if it was your niece?" he angrily said back to me.

"Without a doubt. You think these are the only four people here from the HRT? We have every road blocked in and out by the Monroe County Sheriff's Office. We have an external ring of Monroe SWAT and a shitload of DEA here too. Once you settle down we can go get Lisandra. Isn't that what you wanted? I told you no vigilantism. You don't have any weapons on you, you just drove me here in the boat.

That's it. You're' a concerned family member. That's all they see you as. No one's in trouble. Guille is a working C.I. for the DEA, and oh, by the way we pulled his files. He's done two other smaller deals with Agent Scott Lew. You might want to have a stronger conversation about steering him from the business since he hasn't been exactly up front with you about his work with the DEA," I said in his ear.

"Detective, will he stay quiet so we can finish this?" asked one of the ghillie-suited HRT members.

Santiago heard him and nodded in silent resignation. The two agents holding Santiago down loosened their grip but kept a firm hold on him. The other two agents stood up and adjusted their gear. They removed their camouflage head covering and each of them put on a tactical helmet that they had stashed nearby. One of them then spoke into a voice-activated microphone pressed against his throat.

"Aqua man is secure. We can go when you say."

There was some radio chatter and then both agents started walking towards the HM 40 site. It was surreal to see other clumps of vegetation rise up between us and the abandoned Nike missile compound and join in a line behind the two agents. They were soon out of our sight, lost in the darkness. It couldn't have been more than four minutes later when me, Santiago and the two HRT agents started feeling a reverberation in our chests. It rapidly increased and it felt as though the ground was trembling. The ground went from trembling to actually shaking. The wind from the east seemed to change.

Two Blackhawk HRT helicopters came in flying low and fast from across the bay. They were totally blacked out and without any lights on at all. What took me and Santiago about thirty minutes to traverse they flew over in three seconds. They were only about forty feet above us and dipping even closer to the ground as they passed overhead. The doors were open on either side of the helicopters. Fast ropes were deployed out the sides of each helicopter and throngs of HRT agents descended on the fast ropes. It only took a minute and the helicopters had deposited all of the agents on the ground. The helicopter pilots immediately lifted up and flew quickly away into the western sky.

Loud explosions could be heard from the flash bangs being thrown by the HRT agents on the ground. A volley of gunfire came from the site. It was loud and sounded like a multitude of weapons firing. I couldn't pinpoint exactly but it was obvious that more than one automatic weapon was being fired. The other two agents hit the ground next to us the second they heard gunfire. We did too. Tension was in every breath as we waited. When the gunfire ceased, we all rose to our feet. Santiago kept looking at the agents for some sort of positive reaction. He was to be disappointed by their stoic demeanor. The agents with us were now watching the distance between us and the site for any reaction or movement. Santiago had tears in his eyes, overcome with fear and concern for Lisandra, I assumed. He dropped to his knees, made the sign of the cross and began praying. The radio traffic on the agent's radios was quiet.

A Monroe County Sheriff's helicopter came swooping in right over us. The Bell and Howell manufactured helicopter was brightly lit and momentarily illuminated us with their high wattage front searchlight. The Sheriff's helicopter veered briefly from the Nike missile site. The operator inside kept the searchlight steadily on the site as the helicopter circled overhead. We waited, the minutes dragging on, agonizingly, stiflingly slow. An HRT agent with us raised his finger as he turned his head away to hear his earpiece. Someone was modulating into his radio.

The agent looked at us and said into his throat mike, "Copy that. Can you repeat please for my partners here?" The agent unplugged his earpiece. We then overheard the transmission on his radio.

"Tangos down. Package secure."

Chapter Twenty Eight

The FBI HRT members stayed on the scene for about ninety minutes. They have their own after-action reports and reviews that they conduct in their Quantico Virginia headquarters. None of the members talked or interacted with any of the local or federal agents on the scene. There was just a *standard*, one paragraph report provided to the Monroe County Sheriff's office.

Standard.

While conducting a hostage rescue mission, members of the FBI's Hostage Rescue Team were confronted with violent resistance from the hostage takers. In that confrontation the two hostage takers were killed. The hostage was rescued and was released to local authorities for medical evaluation.

It was 11pm. A bus from the Monroe County School System pulled up on State Road 905 where it intersects with Old State Road 905. The HRT members quickly boarded the bus. With two marked Monroe County Sheriff's cars in the front and two in the back, the caravan drove off for the very short drive to the Ocean Reef Club. The FBI's HRT airplane was waiting for them. The Ocean Reef Club Board of Governors would definitely get an earful from the community in the morning about an airplane taking off so late at night.

So be it. I'd now been standing around the scene for hours and I was tired.

The scene was crawling with DEA, FBI field agents, and Monroe County investigators. ASAC Mandeville was on the scene. I was able to gather from her that she'd been told that Viktor Moshienko was dead. There was another Russian national dead. He was currently unidentified. She said Moshienko was killed trying to run to the central control room of the missile battery launch site. Lisandra was inside, chained at the ankle to a metal console. Moshienko was armed. When he saw he wasn't going to make it he started shooting at the control room, they assume hoping to hit Lisandra.

"Fortunately he didn't hit her, and they made him road pizza right then and there," she said "The whole place is a huge rats' nest of a mess. It's been abandoned and neglected for decades. It's covered in rust, overgrown vegetation, thick vines crawling on everything, graffiti from kids, rat shit, and bird poop. I have no idea why he'd even choose this place to hole up in," she said, grimacing.

"It might be all he knew from his KGB indoctrinations. Who knows? I'm sure he was in a hotel somewhere and he just kept Lisandra here," I said.

"Monroe County Fire and Rescue took her to Homestead Hospital. She's going to be okay. She's dehydrated, she's got lots of mosquito bites, but all in all she's okay physically."

"Where is her uncle?" I asked.

"He called her mother and he spent time with her before they transported her. Marroquín rode with her to the hospital and Walker followed the rescue truck. We needed to debrief her as soon as we could."

"That phone call must have been—emotional," I said, thinking of how Lisandra's mother must be overwhelmed.

She let out a long breath. "Yeah, that was something to hear. Lisandra's family is on the way to the hospital now." ASAC Mandeville stopped, looking me up and down with barely masked concern. "Moshienko tried to kill Scott, and he tried to kill you. Cade, I know you had the opportunity to do this alone and you did the right thing notifying all of us. We moved Heaven and earth to get everyone and everything in place. Her uncle may not see it that way, but he will in time. In fact, I wouldn't be surprised if he already does," she said.

I heard what she said, and I just nodded. "I'm not going to ask you for your raid jacket this time."

"It's announcement apparel. Get it? Right?" she said as she walked away and into a large gathering of investigators.

I saw Santiago talking with a Monroe County detective. He looked at me approaching him and stopped his conversation in mid-sentence to give me a very tight, long hug.

Through his tears of gratitude he chokingly said, "Thank you, Brother. Thank you."

When we broke from the embrace the detective was waiting.

"I'm Detective Maureen Murphy of the Monroe County Sheriff's Office. I'd like to ask you a few questions," she said to me.

"There isn't much to say. Her uncle and I followed a hunch that brought us down here. I thought the hunch had enough merit that I notified DEA Miami. Neither of us got within seventy-five yards of the scene. It was dark, we couldn't see anything. We heard gunshots and we hit the ground. When we got up, it was over. Anything else and the DEA agent in the announcement apparel jacket can answer it for you," I said pointing at Mandeville.

"You mean the DEA agent in the raid jacket?" she said, looking at Mandeville.

"Yeah. That's what I meant."

Detective Murphy left me to walk towards Mandeville.

It was now after midnight.

"Did anyone say you had to stay?" I asked Santiago.

"No."

"Let's get to the boat, shove off and get home. This time with the running lights on."

"Yes, yes. Absolutely," he said, weariness showing in his eyes and posture.

I SPENT THE next four days lounging in the pool at Paradise Point. I structured my days around food deliveries and different levels of inebriation. Security was called twice to check on me due to the Jameson bottle being so close to the pool edge. I got wise and learned to transfer the Irish whiskey to an insulated thermos. It actually worked in my favor as I could chill the thermos before I went down to the pool. On the fifth day I was just getting ready to start my swimming pool drinking routine when my cell phone rang. It was the VIN office.

"Cade...eh *buenos dias…* Major *Broonsone* says to me to say to *ju* that he know he say to stay *en tu casa,* but he now say be here at *once* today."

"Be there at eleven?"

"*Si. Once.* Eleven."

"Okay, Ileana, I'll see you at eleven."

"Don't see me. See *Broonsone*," she corrected me.

"Okay. I got it."

"Okay then *ju* have been told," she said, and she hung up on me.

At eleven o'clock Charlene notified Major Brunson that I was in the outer office. He told her to send me in.

The *whoosh* of his door rubbing against the carpet announced my arrival in his office. Brunson had on reading glasses and was sitting behind his desk, reviewing, and signing a stack of papers. There was also a bottle of hot sauce off to the side of his desk. "*Burnin' and Churnin*."

"Sit down, Cade," he said.

I plopped into the chair across from his desk. It was a strange feeling. I knew I still worked here, and I still had a job, but being told to stay away for a few days made me feel like I could just get up whenever I wanted to. I felt slightly empowered, but in my core knew that was a false feeling.

"I called my wife today. I needed her to tell me this painter's name," he said, holding a small piece of paper in his hand. "Mostly because that's the kind of shit she remembers and the kind of shit I don't."

My eyes tracked the paper as he held it aloft. He adjusted his reading glasses. "The guy's name is Friedrich Moritz August Retzsch. Ever hear of him?" he asked me.

"No. I don't know who he is," I answered.

He took off the reading glasses and put them on his desk.

"Two years ago we took a trip to France with some other couples. Paris to be exact. So on this trip we went to the Louvre museum. The wives were all fucking happy and shit and I just was wondering why I didn't bring more comfortable shoes. Because it's a big fucking place. You know? So anyway, this Friedrich guy, he painted this painting that really caught my eye."

I listened attentively but was internally yearning to be drinking in the pool.

"The painting is called *'Checkmate.'* Really evocative piece. It depicts a man playing a game of chess with the Devil. In this painting Satan appears super confident and happy, just *oozes* arrogance. The man playing him just looks defeated. It's implied that they're playing the game for the man's soul. There are captured pieces along the edges of the game board. The chess player probably was holding his own for a while until at last, the Devil bested him."

I saw a metaphor coming on.

"The painting hung for centuries in the Louvre. Now here's where it gets interesting," he said, shifting in his seat. "At some point a chess grand master saw this painting in the Louvre. He studied it intently. He just kept looking at it. The grand master chess champion noticed something. The interpretation of the painting was incorrect. To the untrained eye, and by looking at the *players* in the painting and not at the chessboard, it was always thought that the Devil seemed to be on the verge of winning. The Devil actually is *not* winning. The man, who everyone thought was losing his soul, had one more move. He wasn't in checkmate. He had one more move! The chess master told the curator the painting was wrong. The man's king had one more move. That move would make the man the winner."

I blinked a couple of times at him.

"Cade, we always have one more move. No matter how dire it might be, we still have one more move. People will fight to their last breath to stay alive. We have …One. More. Move. It's not over."

I mulled over what he was saying. Pretty heavy conversation for a guy who should be drinking in the pool and didn't feel like he even had to be at work.

"This whole cocaine deal with DEA Group 4 in Hialeah and all that happened after it… It's very obvious to me that you understand the concept of one more move."

He clasped his hands on his desk and then leaned in closer to me.

"The woman. Lydia Vasilyevich. She's saying that what happened on the boat didn't go down as you said it did."

"What? Wait. Who the heck is Lydia Vasilyevich?"

"The woman from the boat."

"No. Her name is Auburn McKenna!"

"Not according to her passport. Her passport says she's from Estonia. She only speaks Russian. Through an interpreter she says she was on the boat. She saw you having some sort of PTSD moment in front of Curbelo's house. She went to see if you were okay. She says you threw your phone in the street. You started waving your gun around, dropping the magazine and ejecting the round. She tried to calm you down and brought you to her boat to get you a glass of water and let you sit, to give you a chance to compose yourself. You grabbed the shotgun they had on the boat. There was a struggle, and you shot the dentist, Cordozo."

"WHAT?" I yelled, rising right out of the chair. "She's NSA and she's *with* that asshole McBride, they're doing all kinds of unlawful shit!"

"Cade, sit down. Sit down. Let me finish," he said calmly.

I was visibly shaking with incredulous anger. I was seeing spots; I was so floored by his words.

"Hammy Garzon was able to match her print on the trigger of the shotgun. She also matched her fingerprints to the bloody bill on the stack of money the dentist had in his office. Thankfully, she knew to print the bloody fingerprints on the money. Those two matches contradict everything she said. *She* pulled the trigger and she had access to our $400,000 on the day of the deal. We got her, dead to rights."

"I told Hammy to make those print comparisons," I said.

"Like I said. One more move. Ships are safe in harbors, Cade. But that's not what ships are built for. We don't want you in the safe space. You're not built to *be* in the safe space. That's why you're in VIN and that's why I back you on nearly everything you do, even when I know it's going to shave months off my life. You always have one more move."

"I'm glad you're sitting for what I'm about to tell you," he said, leaning back in his chair again. "You remember those Interpol guys, Jean Luc Janvier and John Bazini? They got their Interpol custody letter and after you left, they took possession of the bearer shares. You know those guys are more show than go, right? Well they don't really handle arrests, they just assist with investigations."

I remembered what Jean Luc Janvier had said to Mandeville.

"We are a worldwide support law enforcement organization. Adjudication, although highly desirable, is what we try to assist with. It is the investigative support that we excel at. We are here to help you."

I shook my head, knowing the news wasn't going to get any better.

"They signed the Panama bearer shares over to a representative from our government. They handed them over—"

"Don't tell me. McBride!" I shouted, clenching my fists.

"No, someone we haven't seen before. A guy from Washington. He went into the downtown office of the U.S. Attorney with the Interpol guys. Interpol transferred custody over to the United States government."

"They did what?" I said, my voice nearly shrieking.

"Just what I told you. They signed it over," he said.

I slumped in my chair, trying to comprehend the absurdity of what I was just told.

Do you want to know his name?" asked Brunson.

"Tell me," I said.

" C.T. McCade."

THE END

Printed in the USA
CPSIA information can be obtained
at www.ICGtesting.com
CBHW061214120224
4283CB00030B/396